Vampire Stories

Vampire Stories

SIR ARTHUR CONAN DOYLE

EDITED BY

Robert Eighteen-Bisang

&

Martin H. Greenberg

Skyhorse Publishing

A HERMAN GRAF BOOK

Skyhorse Publishing books may be purchased in bulk at special discounts for sales promotion, corporate gifts, fund-raising, or educational purposes. Special editions can also be created to specifications. For details, contact the Special Sales Department, Skyhorse Publishing, 555 Eighth Avenue, Suite 903, New York, NY 10018 or info@skyhorsepublishing.com.

www.skyhorsepublishing.com

10 9 8 7 6 5 4 3 2

Library of Congress Cataloging-in-Publication Data

Doyle, Arthur Conan, Sir, 1859-1930.
[Short stories. Selections]
The vampire stories of Sir Arthur Conan Doyle / Sir Arthur Conan Doyle ; edited by Robert Eighteen-Bisang ; introduction by Martin H. Greenberg.
      p. cm.
   Includes bibliographical references.
ISBN 978-1-60239-797-2
1. Vampires—Fiction. 2. Horror tales, English. I. Eighteen-Bisang, Robert. II. Title.
PR4621.E54 2009
823'.8—dc22

                                        2009022239

Printed in the United States of America

Table of Contents

Introduction

By Robert Eighteen-Bisang

Like Mary Shelley or Bram Stoker, Arthur Conan Doyle seems doomed to live in the shadow of his larger than life literary creation. On his 71st birthday (May 22, 1930), Doyle lamented, "I'm rather tired of hearing myself described as the author of Sherlock Holmes. Why not, for a change, the author of *Rodney Stone* or *The White Company* or *The Lost World?* One would think that I had written nothing but detective stories." His complaint is well founded for, in addition to creating the world's most famous detective, he was a master story teller who wrote numerous essays, political commentaries, and books on spiritualism. Doyle claimed that Edgar Allen Poe influenced his work. Hence, it is not surprising that many of his stories mirror his personal life—which straddled reason and an escalating, irrational belief in occult forces. This tension is apparent in Sherlock Holmes's most famous case, *The Hound of the Baskervilles*, which can be read as a rationalized werewolf story.

Doyle referred to the villains in three of his stories ("The Adventure of the Sussex Vampire," "John Barrington Cowles" and "The Winning Shot") as vampires or vampire-like beings. However, most fans and scholars have overlooked his contributions to fantasy literature in favor of the four novels and fifty-six stories that revolve around the adventures of Holmes, Watson, and company. It seems as if too much emphasis has been placed on a memorable episode in the canon. In the "Adventure of the Sussex Vampire," Holmes seems to dismiss otherworldly phenomena with:

> "Rubbish, Watson, rubbish! What have we to do with walking corpses who can only be held in their grave by stakes driven through their hearts? It's pure lunacy."
>
> "But surely," said I, "the vampire was not necessarily a dead man? A living person might have the habit. I have read, for example, of the old sucking the blood of the young in order to retain their youth."
>
> "You are right, Watson. It mentions the legend in one of these references. But are we to give serious attention to such things? This agency stands flat-footed upon the ground, and there it must remain. The world is big enough for us. No ghosts need apply."

But there is more to Doyle's work than this passage implies. Like many of his friends, he published several vampire tales before *Dracula* established the rules of vampirism. Richard Dalby has collected some of these stories in *Dracula's Brood*,[1] which includes Doyle's story "The Parasite," as well as contributions by William S. Gilbert and Eliza Lynn Linton. In addition, Doyle befriended the young Hesketh Pritchard who, with the assistance of his mother, Kate, created the first psychic detective, Flaxman Low. Although Low was preceded by Le Fanu's Dr. Hesselius and Stoker's redoubtable Abraham Van Helsing, he was the first consulting detective who tackled supernatural menaces on a regular basis. Three of his cases involve vampires, and there can be no doubt that they were written with Doyle's consent and approval.

Doyle congratulated Bram Stoker in a letter dated 20 August, 1897, shortly after the publication of *Dracula*:

---

1 Richard Dalby, ed. *Dracula's Brood: Rare Vampire Stories by Friends and Contemporaries of Bram Stoker*. Crucible: London, 1987.

"I am sure you will not think it impertinent of me if I write to tell you how much I enjoyed reading *Dracula*. I think it is the very best story of diablerie which I have read in many years. It is really wonderful how with so much exciting interest over so long a book there is never an anticlimax. It holds you from the very start and grows more engrossing until it is quite painfully vivid. The old professor is most excellent and so are the two girls. I congratulate you with all my heart for having written so fine a book."[2]

Arthur Conan Doyle and Bram Stoker created two of the most remarkable characters in fantasy fiction. They were friends who not only admired each other's work but each of them wrote a chapter of the episodic novel, *The Fate of Fenella*, which was published in 1892. Sixteen years later, Doyle told Stoker how he had decided on his detective's name: "Finally in 1887," he said, "I wrote *A Study in Scarlet*, the first book which featured Sherlock Holmes. I don't know where I got the name from. I was looking the other day at a piece of paper on which I had scribbled 'Sherrington Holmes's and 'Sherrington Hope' and all sorts of other combinations. Finally at the bottom of the paper I had written 'Sherlock Holmes.'"[3]

It has been claimed that "The Adventure of the Sussex Vampire" is a tribute to or a parody of *Dracula*. This may be true but, as we will see, Bram Stoker influenced Doyle's work in more profound ways.

However, even if Arthur Conan Doyle had never created Sherlock Holmes, this collection attests to the fact that he would be remembered today as the author of many memorable supernatural stories, including the following nine vampire tales.

2 This letter is housed in The Harry Ransom Humanities Research Center, at the University of Texas at Austin.
3 *New York World* (28 July 1907). p. E1

Vampire Stories

The American's Tale

"It air strange, it air," he was saying as I opened the door of the room where our social little semiliterary society met; "but I could tell you queerer things than that 'ere-almighty queer things. You can't learn everything out of books, sirs, nohow. You see it ain't the men as can string English together and as has had good eddications as finds themselves in the queer places I've been in. They're mostly rough men, sirs, as can scarce speak aright, far less tell with pen and ink the things they've seen; but if they could they'd make some of your European's har riz with astonishment. They would, sirs, you bet!"

His name was Jefferson Adams, I believe; I know his initials were J. A., for you may see them yet deeply whittled on the right-hand upper panel of our smoking-room door. He left us this legacy, and also some artistic patterns done in tobacco juice upon our Turkey carpet; but beyond these reminiscences our American storyteller has vanished from our ken. He gleamed across our ordinary quiet conviviality like some brilliant meteor, and then was lost in the outer darkness. That night, however, our Nevada friend was in full swing; and I quietly lit my pipe and dropped into the nearest chair, anxious not to interrupt his story.

London Society (Christmas 1880) pp. 44-48.

"Mind you," he continued, "I hain't got no grudge against your men of science. I likes and respects a chap as can match every beast and plant, from a huckleberry to a grizzly with a jaw-breakin' name; but if you wants real interestin' facts, something a bit juicy, you go to your whalers and your frontiersmen, and your scouts and Hudson Bay men, chaps who mostly can scarce sign their names."

There was a pause here, as Mr. Jefferson Adams produced a long cheroot and lit it. We preserved a strict silence in the room, for we had already learned that on the slightest interruption our Yankee drew himself into his shell again. He glanced round with a self-satisfied smile as he remarked our expectant looks, and continued through a halo of smoke.

"Now which of you gentlemen has ever been in Arizona? None, I'll warrant. And of all English or Americans as can put pen to paper, how many has been in Arizona? Precious few, I calc'late. I've been there, sirs, lived there for years; and when I think of what I've seen there, why, I can scarce get myself to believe it now.

"Ah, there's a country! I was one of Walker's filibusters, as they chose to call us; and after we'd busted up, and the chief was shot, some of us made tracks and located down there. A reg'lar English and American colony, we was, with our wives and children, and all complete. I reckon there's some of the old folk there yet, and that they hain't forgotten what I'm agoing to tell you. No, I warrant they hain't, never on this side of the grave, sirs.

"I was talking about the country, though; and I guess I could astonish you considerable if I spoke of nothing else. To think of such a land being built for a few 'Greasers' and half-breeds! It's a misusing of the gifts of Providence, that's what I calls it. Grass as hung over a chap's head as he rode through it, and trees so thick that you couldn't catch a glimpse of blue sky for leagues and leagues, and orchids like umbrellas! Maybe some of you has seen a plant as they calls the 'fly-catcher,' in some parts of the States?"

"*Dionaea muscipula*," murmured Dawson, our scientific man par excellence.

"Ah, 'Die near a municipal,' that's him! You'll see a fly stand on that 'ere plant, and then you'll see the two sides of a leaf snap up together and catch it between them, and grind it up and mash it to bits, for all the world like some great sea squid with its beak; and hours after, if you open the leaf, you'll see the body lying half-digested, and in bits. Well, I've seen those flytraps in Arizona with leaves eight and ten feet long, and thorns or teeth a foot or more; why, they could—But darn it, I'm going too fast!

"It's about the death of Joe Hawkins I was going to tell you; 'bout as queer a thing, I reckon, as ever you heard tell on. There wasn't nobody in Montana as didn't know of Joe Hawkins— 'Alabama' Joe, as he was called there. A reg'lar out and outer, he was, 'bout the darndest skunk as ever man clapt eyes on. He was a good chap enough, mind ye, as long as you stroked him the right way; but rile him anyhow, and he were worse nor a wildcat. I've seen him empty his six-shooter into a crowd as chanced to jostle him agoing into Simpson's bar when there was a dance on; and he bowied Tom Hooper 'cause he spilt his liquor over his weskit by mistake. No, he didn't stick at murder, Joe didn't; and he weren't a man to be trusted further nor you could see him.

"Now at the time I tell on, when Joe Hawkins was swaggerin' about the town and layin' down the law with his shootin'-irons, there was an Englishman there of the name of Scott—Tom Scott, if I rec'lects aright. This chap Scott was a thorough Britisher (beggin' the present company's pardon), and yet he didn't freeze much to the British set there, or they didn't freeze much to him. He was a quiet simple man, Scott was rather too quiet for a rough set like that; sneakin' they called him, but he weren't that. He kept hisself mostly apart, an' didn't interfere with nobody so long as he were left alone. Some said as how he'd been kinder ill-treated at home—been a Chartist, or something of that sort, and had to up stick and run; but he never spoke of it hisself, an' never complained. Bad luck or good, that chap kept a stiff lip on him.

"This chap Scott was a sort o' butt among the men about Montana, for he was so quiet an' simple-like. There was no party either to take up his grievances; for, as I've been saying, the Britishers hardly counted him one of them, and many a rough joke they played on him. He never cut up rough, but was polite to all hisself. I think the boys got to think he hadn't much grit in him till he showed 'em their mistake.

"It was in Simpson's bar as the row got up, an' that led to the queer thing I was going to tell you of. Alabama Joe and one or two other rowdies were dead on the Britishers in those days, and they spoke their opinions pretty free, though I warned them as there'd be an almighty muss. That partic'lar night Joe was nigh half drunk, an' he swaggered about the town with his six-shooter, lookin' out for a quarrel. Then he turned into the bar where he know'd he'd find some o' the English as ready for one as he was hisself. Sure enough, there was half a dozen lounging about, an' Tom Scott standin' alone before the stove. Joe sat down by the table, and put his revolver and bowie down in front of him. 'Them's my arguments, Jeff,' he says to me, 'if any white-livered Britisher dares give me the lie.' I tried to stop him, sirs; but he weren't a man as you could easily turn, an' he began to speak in a way as no chap could stand. Why, even a 'Greaser' would flare up if you said as much of Grea-serland! There was a commotion at the bar, an' every man laid his hands on his wepin's; but afore they could draw we heard a quiet voice from the stove: 'Say your prayers, Joe Hawkins; for, by Heaven, you're a dead man!' Joe turned round and looked like grabbin' at his iron; but it weren't no manner of use. Tom Scott was standing up, covering him with his Derringer; a smile on his white face, but the very devil shining in his eye. 'It ain't that the old country has used me overwell,' he says, 'but no man shall speak agin it afore me, and live.' For a second or two I could see his finger tighten round the trigger, an' then he gave a laugh, an' threw the pistol on the floor. 'No,' he says,

'I can't shoot a half-drunk man. Take your dirty life, Joe, an' use it better nor you have done. You've been nearer the grave this night than you will be agin until your time comes. You'd best make tracks now, I guess. Nay, never look back at me, man; I'm not afeard at your shootin'-iron. A bully's nigh always a coward.' And he swung contemptuously round, and relit his half-smoked pipe from the stove; while Alabama slunk out o' the bar, with the laughs of the Britishers ringing in his ears. I saw his face as he passed me, and on it I saw murder, sirs—murder, as plain as ever I seed anything in my life.

"I stayed in the bar after the row, and watched Tom Scott as he shook hands with the men about. It seemed kinder queer to me to see him smilin' and cheerful-like; for I knew Joe's bloodthirsty mind, and that the Englishman had small chance of ever seeing the morning. He lived in an out-of-the-way sort of place, you see, clean off the trail, and had to pass through the Flytrap Gulch to get to it. This here gulch was a marshy gloomy place, lonely enough during the day even; for it were always a creepy sort o' thing to see the great eight- and ten-foot leaves snapping up if aught touched them; but at night there were never a soul near. Some parts of the marsh, too, were soft and deep, and a body thrown in would be gone by the morning. I could see Alabama Joe crouchin' under the leaves of the great Flytrap in the darkest part of the gulch, with a scowl on his face and a revolver in his hand; I could see it, sirs, as plain as with my two eyes.

"'Bout midnight Simpson shuts up his bar, so out we had to go. Tom Scott started off for his three-mile walk at a slashing pace. I just dropped him a hint as he passed me, for I kinder liked the chap. 'Keep your Derringer loose in your belt, sir,' I says, 'for you might chance to need it.' He looked round at me with his quiet smile, and then I lost sight of him in the gloom. I never thought to see him again. He'd hardly gone afore Simpson comes up to me and says, 'There'll be a nice job in the Flytrap Gulch tonight, Jeff; the boys say that Hawkins started half an hour ago to wait for Scott and shoot him on sight. I calc'late the coroner'll be wanted tomorrow.'

"What passed in the gulch that night? It were a question as were asked pretty free next morning. A half-breed was in Ferguson's store after daybreak, and he said as he'd chanced to be near the gulch 'bout one in the morning. It warn't easy to get at his story, he seemed so uncommon scared; but he told us, at last, as he'd heard the fearfulest screams in the stillness of the night. There weren't no shots, he said, but scream after scream, kinder muffled, like a man with a serape over his head, an' in mortal pain. Abner Brandon and me, and a few more, was in the store at the time; so we mounted and rode out to Scott's house, passing through the gulch on the way. There weren't nothing partic'lar to be seen there—no blood nor marks of a fight, nor nothing; and when we gets up to Scott's house, out he comes to meet us as fresh as a lark. 'Hullo, Jeff!' says he, 'no need for the pistols after all. Come in an' have a cocktail, boys.' 'Did ye see or hear nothing as ye came home last night?' says I. 'No,' says he; 'all was quiet enough. An owl kinder moaning in the Flytrap Gulch—that was all. Come, jump off and have a glass.' 'Thank ye,' said Abner. So off we gets, and Tom Scott rode into the settlement with us when we went back.

"An all-fired commotion was on in Main Street as we rode into it. The 'Merican party seemed to have gone clean crazed. Alabama Joe was gone, not a darned particle of him left. Since he went out to the gulch nary eye had seen him. As we got off our horses there was a considerable crowd in front of Simpson's, and some ugly looks at Tom Scott, I can tell you. There was a clickin' of pistols, and I saw as Scott had his hand in his bosom too. There weren't a single English face about. 'Stand aside, Jeff Adams,' says Zebb Humphrey, as great a scoundrel as ever lived, 'you hain't got no hand in this game. Say, boys, are we, free Americans, to be murdered by any darned Britisher?' It was the quickest thing as ever I seed. There was a rush an' a crack; Zebb was down, with Scott's ball in his thigh, and Scott hisself was on the ground with a dozen men holding him. It weren't no use struggling, so he lay quiet. They seemed a bit uncertain what to do with him at first, but then one of Alabama's special chums put them up to it. 'Joe's gone,' he said; 'nothing ain't surer nor that, an' there lies the man as killed him. Some on you knows as Joe went on business to the gulch last night; he never came back. That 'ere Britisher passed through after he'd gone; they'd had a row, screams is heard 'mong the great flytraps. I say agin he has played poor Joe some o' his sneakin' tricks, an' thrown him into the swamps. It ain't no wonder as the body is gone. But air we to stan by and see English murderin' our own chums? I guess not. Let Judge Lynch try him, that's what I say. 'Lynch him!' shouted a hundred angry voices—for all the rag-tag an' bobtail o' the settlement was round us by this time. 'Here, boys, fetch a rope, and swing him up. Up with him over Simpson's door!' 'See here though,' says another, coming forrards, 'let's hang him by the great flytrap in the gulch. Let Joe see as he's revenged, if so be as he's buried 'bout theer.' There was a shout for this, an' away they went, with Scott tied on his mustang in the middle, and a mounted guard, with cocked revolvers, round him; for we knew as there was a score or so Britishers about, as didn't seem to recognise Judge Lynch, and was dead on a free fight.

"I went out with them, my heart bleedin' for Scott, though he didn't seem a cent put out, he didn't. He were game to the backbone. Seems kinder queer, sirs, hangin' a man to a flytrap; but our'n were a reg'lar tree, and the leaves like a brace of boats with a hinge between 'em and thorns at the bottom.

"We passed down the gulch to the place where the great one grows, and there we seed it with the leaves, some open, some shut. But we seed something worse nor that. Standin' round the tree was some thirty men, Britishers all, an' armed to the teeth. They was waitin' for us evidently, an' had a business-like look about 'em, as if they'd come for something and meant to have it. There was the raw material there for about as warm a scrimmidge as ever I seed. As we rode up, a great red-bearded Scotch-man—Cameron were his name—stood out afore the rest, his revolver cocked in his hand. 'See here, boys,' he says, 'you've got no call to hurt a hair of that man's head. You hain't proved as Joe is dead yet; and if you had, you hain't proved as Scott killed him. Anyhow, it were in self-defence; for you all know as he was lying in wait for Scott, to shoot him on sight; so I say agin, you hain't got no call to hurt that man; and what's more, I've got thirty six-barrelled arguments against your doin' it.' 'It's an interestin' pint, and worth arguin' out,' said the man as was Alabama Joe's special chum. There was a clickin' of pistols, and a loosenin' of knives, and the two parties began to draw up to one another, an' it looked like a rise in the mortality of Montana. Scott was standing behind with a pistol at his ear if he stirred, lookin' quiet and composd as having no money on the table, when sudden he gives a start an a shout as rang in our ears like a trumpet. 'Joe!' he cried, 'Joe! Look at him! In the flytrap!' We all turned an' looked where he was pointin'. Jerusalem! I think we won't get that picter out of our minds agin. One of the great leaves of the flytrap, that had been shut and touchin' the ground as it lay, was slowly rolling back upon its hinges. There, lying like a child in its cradle, was Alabama Joe in the hollow of the leaf. The great thorns had been slowly driven through his heart as it shut upon him. We could see as he'd tried to cut his way out, for there was a slit in the thick fleshy leaf, an' his bowie was in his hand; but it had smothered him first. He'd lain down on it likely to keep the damp off while he were awaitin' for Scott, and it had closed on him as you've seen your little hothouse ones do on a fly; an' there he were as we found him, torn and crushed into pulp by the great jagged teeth of the man-eatin' plant. There, sirs, I think you'll own as that's a curious story."

"And what became of Scott?" asked Jack Sinclair.

"Why, we carried him back on our shoulders, we did, to Simpson's bar, and he stood us liquors round. Made a speech too—a darned fine speech—from the counter. Somethin' about the British lion an' the 'Merican eagle walkin' arm in arm for ever an' a day. And now, sirs, that yarn was long, and my cheroot's out, so I reckon I'll make tracks afore it's later"; and with a "Good-night!" he left the room.

"A most extraordinary narrative!" said Dawson. "Who would have thought a *Dionaea* had such power!"

"Deuced rum yarn!" said young Sinclair.

"Evidently a matter–of–fact truthful man," said the doctor.

"Or the most original liar that ever lived," said I. I wonder which he was.

† † † † †

Doyle's first published story was a fantasy about diamonds; "The American's Tale" was his second sale. Stories about blood-drinking plants were common a hundred years ago when many parts of the world had not been explored. Phil Robinson's "The Man-Eating Tree" appeared the year after Doyle's tale, while H. G. Wells' story about a blood-drinking orchid, "The Flowering of the Strange Orchid" debuted in the Pall Mall Budget *on August 2, 1894, three years before his blood-drinking Martians threatened to conquer Earth. Another story about a botanical vampire, Fred M. White's "The Purple Terror," appeared in the* Strand Magazine *in September of 1899. In a similar vein, Barry Pain's "The Tree of Death" tells of an oriental vampire that lives in trees.*

The year after "The American's Tale" was published Doyle abandoned his medical practice to become a professional writer.

The Captain
of the Pole-Star

[Being an extract from the singular journal of
John m'alister ray, student of medicine.]

September 11—Lat. 81 degrees 40' N.; long. 2 degrees E. Still
lying-to amid enormous ice fields. The one which stretches
away to the north of us, and to which our ice-anchor is attached,
cannot be smaller than an English county. To the right and left
unbroken sheets extend to the horizon. This morning the mate
reported that there were signs of pack ice to the southward.
Should this form of sufficient thickness to bar our return, we
shall be in a position of danger, as the food, I hear, is already
running somewhat short. It is late in the season, and the nights
are beginning to reappear.

This morning I saw a star twinkling just over the fore-yard,
the first since the beginning of May. There is considerable
discontent among the crew, many of whom are anxious to get
back home to be in time for the herring season, when labour
always commands a high price upon the Scotch coast. As yet
their displeasure is only signified by sullen countenances and
black looks, but I heard from the second mate this afternoon

that they contemplated sending a deputation to the Captain to explain their grievance. I much doubt how he will receive it, as he is a man of fierce temper, and very sensitive about anything approaching to an infringement of his rights. I shall venture after dinner to say a few words to him upon the subject. I have always found that he will tolerate from me what he would resent from any other member of the crew. Amsterdam Island, at the north-west corner of Spitzbergen, is visible upon our starboard quarter—a rugged line of volcanic rocks, intersected by white seams, which represent glaciers. It is curious to think that at the present moment there is probably no human being nearer to us than the Danish settlements in the south of Greenland—a good nine hundred miles as the crow flies. A captain takes a great responsibility upon himself when he risks his vessel under such circumstances. No whaler has ever remained in these latitudes till so advanced a period of the year.

9 P.M.—I have spoken to Captain Craigie, and though the result has been hardly satisfactory, I am bound to say that he listened to what I had to say very quietly and even deferentially. When I had finished he put on that air of iron determination which I have frequently observed upon his face, and paced rapidly backwards and forwards across the narrow cabin for some minutes. At first I feared that I had seriously offended him, but he dispelled the idea by sitting down again, and putting his hand upon my arm with a gesture which almost amounted to a caress. There was a depth of tenderness too in his wild dark eyes which surprised me considerably. "Look here, Doctor," he said, "I'm sorry I ever took you—I am indeed—and I would give fifty pounds this minute to see you standing safe upon the Dundee quay. It's hit or miss with me this time. There are fish to the north of us. How dare you shake your head, sir, when I tell you I saw them blowing from the masthead?"—this in a sudden burst of fury, though I was not conscious of having shown any signs of doubt. "Two-and-twenty fish in as many minutes as I am a living man, and not one under ten

foot.[4] Now, Doctor, do you think I can leave the country when there is only one infernal strip of ice between me and my fortune? If it came on to blow from the north tomorrow we could fill the ship and be away before the frost could catch us. If it came on to blow from the south—well, I suppose the men are paid for risking their lives, and as for myself it matters but little to me, for I have more to bind me to the other world than to this one. I confess that I am sorry for you, though. I wish I had old Angus Tait who was with me last voyage, for he was a man that would never be missed, and you—you said once that you were engaged, did you not?"

"Yes," I answered, snapping the spring of the locket which hung from my watch-chain, and holding up the little vignette of Flora.

"Curse you!" he yelled, springing out of his seat, with his very beard bristling with passion. "What is your happiness to me? What have I to do with her that you must dangle her photograph before my eyes?" I almost thought that he was about to strike me in the frenzy of his rage, but with another imprecation he dashed open the door of the cabin and rushed out upon deck, leaving me considerably astonished at his extraordinary violence. It is the first time that he has ever shown me anything but courtesy and kindness. I can hear him pacing excitedly up and down overhead as I write these lines.

I should like to give a sketch of the character of this man, but it seems presumptuous to attempt such a thing upon paper, when the idea in my own mind is at best a vague and uncertain one. Several times I have thought that I grasped the clue which might explain it, but only to be disappointed by his presenting himself in some new light which would upset all my conclusions. It may be that no human eye but my own shall ever rest upon these lines, yet as a psychological study I shall attempt to leave some record of Captain Nicholas Craigie.

4 A whale is measured among whalers not by the length of its body, but by the length of its whalebone.

A man's outer case generally gives some indication of the soul within. The Captain is tall and well-formed, with dark, handsome face, and a curious way of twitching his limbs, which may arise from nervousness, or be simply an outcome of his excessive energy. His jaw and whole cast of countenance is manly and resolute, but the eyes are the distinctive feature of his face. They are of the very darkest hazel, bright and eager, with a singular mixture of recklessness in their expression, and of something else which I have sometimes thought was more allied with horror than any other emotion. Generally the former predominated, but on occasions, and more particularly when he was thoughtfully inclined, the look of fear would spread and deepen until it imparted a new character to his whole countenance. It is at these times that he is most subject to tempestuous fits of anger, and he seems to be aware of it, for I have known him lock himself up so that no one might approach him until his dark hour was passed. He sleeps badly, and I have heard him shouting during the night, but his cabin is some little distance from mine, and I could never distinguish the words which he said.

This is one phase of his character, and the most disagreeable one. It is only through my close association with him, thrown together as we are day after day, that I have observed it. Otherwise he is an agreeable companion, well-read and entertaining, and as gallant a seaman as ever trod a deck. I shall not easily forget the way in which he handled the ship when we were caught by a gale among the loose ice at the beginning of April. I have never seen him so cheerful, and even hilarious, as he was that night, as he paced backwards and forwards upon the bridge amid the flashing of the lightning and the howling of the wind. He has told me several times that the thought of death was a pleasant one to him, which is a sad thing for a young man to say; he cannot be much more than thirty, though his hair and moustache are already slightly grizzled. Some great sorrow must have overtaken him and blighted his whole life. Perhaps I should be the same if I lost my Flora—God knows! I think if it were not for her that I should care very little whether the wind blew from the north or the south tomorrow.

There, I hear him come down the companion, and he has locked himself up in his room, which shows that he is still in an unamiable mood. And so to bed, as old Pepys would say, for the candle is burning down (we have to use them now since the nights are closing in), and the steward has turned in, so there are no hopes of another one.

SEPTEMBER 12—Calm, clear day, and still lying in the same position. What wind there is comes from the south-east, but it is very slight. Captain is in a better humour, and apologised to me at breakfast for his rudeness. He still looks somewhat distrait, however, and retains that wild look in his eyes which in a Highlander would mean that he was "fey"—at least so our chief engineer remarked to me, and he has some reputation among the Celtic portion of our crew as a seer and expounder of omens.

It is strange that superstition should have obtained such mastery over this hard-headed and practical race. I could not have believed to what an extent it is carried had I not observed it for myself. We have had a perfect epidemic of it this voyage, until I have felt inclined to serve out rations of sedatives and nervetonics with the Saturday allowance of grog. The first symptom of it was that shortly after leaving Shetland the men at the wheel used to complain that they heard plaintive cries and screams in the wake of the ship, as if something were following it and were unable to overtake it. This fiction has been kept up during the whole voyage, and on dark nights at the beginning of the seal-fishing it was only with great difficulty that men could be induced to do their spell. No doubt what they heard was either the creaking of the rudder-chains, or the cry of some passing sea-bird. I have been fetched out of bed several times to listen to it, but I need hardly say that I was never able to distinguish anything unnatural.

The men, however, are so absurdly positive upon the subject that it is hopeless to argue with them. I mentioned the matter to the Captain once, but to my surprise he took it very gravely, and indeed appeared to be considerably disturbed by what I told him. I should have thought that he at least would have been above such vulgar delusions.

All this disquisition upon superstition leads me up to the fact that Mr. Manson, our second mate, saw a ghost last night—or, at least, says that he did, which of course is the same thing. It is quite refreshing to have some new topic of conversation after the eternal routine of bears and whales which has served us for so many months. Manson swears the ship is haunted, and that he would not stay in her a day if he had any other place to go to. Indeed the fellow is honestly frightened, and I had to give him some chloral and bromide of potassium this morning to steady him down. He seemed quite indignant when I suggested that he had been having an extra glass the night before, and I was obliged to pacify him by keeping as grave a countenance as possible during his story, which he certainly narrated in a very straight-forward and matter-of-fact way.

"I was on the bridge," he said, "about four bells in the middle watch, just when the night was at its darkest. There was a bit of a moon, but the clouds were blowing across it so that you couldn't see far from the ship. John M'Leod, the harpooner, came aft from the foc'sle-head and reported a strange noise on the starboard bow.

"I went forrard and we both heard it, sometimes like a bairn crying and sometimes like a wench in pain. I've been seventeen years to the country and I never heard seal, old or young, make a sound like that. As we were standing there on the foc'sle-head the moon came out from behind a cloud, and we both saw a sort of white figure moving across the ice field in the same direction that we had heard the cries. We lost sight of it for a while, but it came back on the port bow, and we could just make it out like a shadow on the ice. I sent a hand aft for the rifles, and M'Leod and I went down on to the pack, thinking that maybe it might be a bear. When we got on the ice I lost sight of M'Leod, but I pushed on in the direction where I could still hear the cries. I followed them for a mile or maybe more, and then running round a hummock I came right on to the top of it standing and waiting for me seemingly. I don't know what it was. It wasn't a bear any way. It was tall and white and straight, and if it wasn't a man nor a woman, I'll stake my davy it was something worse. I made for the ship as hard as I could run, and precious glad I was to find myself aboard. I signed articles to do my duty by the ship, and on the ship I'll stay, but you don't catch me on the ice again after sundown."

That is his story, given as far as I can in his own words. I fancy what he saw must, in spite of his denial, have been a young bear erect upon its hind legs, an attitude which they often assume when alarmed. In the uncertain light this would bear a resemblance to a human figure, especially to a man whose nerves were already somewhat shaken. Whatever it may have been, the occurrence is unfortunate, for it has produced a most unpleasant effect upon the crew. Their looks are more sullen than before, and their discontent more open. The double grievance of being debarred from the herring fishing and of being detained in what they choose to call a haunted vessel, may lead them to do something rash. Even the harpooners, who are the oldest and steadiest among them, are joining in the general agitation.

Apart from this absurd outbreak of superstition, things are looking rather more cheerful. The pack which was forming to the south of us has partly cleared away, and the water is so warm as to lead me to believe that we are lying in one of those branches of the gulfstream which run up between Greenland and Spitzbergen. There are numerous small Medusse and sealemons about the ship, with abundance of shrimps, so that there is every possibility of "fish" being sighted. Indeed one was seen blowing about dinner-time, but in such a position that it was impossible for the boats to follow it.

SEPTEMBER 13—Had an interesting conversation with the chief mate, Mr. Milne, upon the bridge. It seems that our Captain is as great an enigma to the seamen, and even to the owners of the vessel, as he has been to me. Mr. Milne tells me that when the ship is paid off, upon returning from a voyage, Captain Craigie disappears, and is not seen again until the approach of another season, when he walks quietly into the office of the company, and asks whether his services will be required. He has no friend in Dundee, nor does anyone pretend to be acquainted with his early history. His position depends entirely upon his skill as a seaman, and the name for courage and coolness which he had earned in the capacity of mate, before being entrusted with a separate command. The unanimous opinion seems to be that he is not a Scotchman, and that his name is an assumed one. Mr. Milne thinks that he has devoted himself to whaling simply for the reason that it is the most dangerous occupation which he could select, and that he courts death in every possible manner. He mentioned several instances of this, one of which is rather curious, if true. It seems that on one occasion he did not put in an appearance at the office, and a substitute had to be selected in his place. That was at the time of the last Russian and Turkish war. When he turned up again next spring he had a puckered wound in the side of his neck which he used to endeavour to conceal with his cravat. Whether the mate's inference that he had been engaged in the war is true or not I cannot say. It was certainly a strange coincidence.

The wind is veering round in an easterly direction, but is still very slight. I think the ice is lying closer than it did yesterday. As far as the eye can reach on every side there is one wide expanse of spotless white, only broken by an occasional rift or the dark shadow of a hummock. To the south there is the narrow lane of blue water which is our sole means of escape, and which is closing up every day. The Captain is taking a heavy responsibility upon himself. I hear that the tank of potatoes has been finished, and even the biscuits are running short, but he preserves the same impassible countenance, and spends the greater part of the day at the crow's nest, sweeping the horizon with his glass. His manner is very variable, and he seems to avoid my society, but there has been no repetition of the violence which he showed the other night.

7.30 P.M.—My deliberate opinion is that we are commanded by a madman. Nothing else can account for the extraordinary vagaries of Captain Craigie. It is fortunate that I have kept this journal of our voyage, as it will serve to justify us in case we have to put him under any sort of restraint, a step which I should only consent to as a last resource. Curiously enough it was he himself who suggested lunacy and not mere eccentricity as the secret of his strange conduct. He was standing upon the bridge about an hour ago, peering as usual through his glass, while I was walking up and down the quarterdeck. The majority of the men were below at their tea, for the watches have not been regularly kept of late. Tired of walking, I leaned against the bulwarks, and admired the mellow glow cast by the sinking sun upon the great ice fields which surround us. I was suddenly aroused from the reverie into which I had fallen by a hoarse voice at my elbow, and starting round I found that the Captain had descended and was standing by my side. He was staring out over the ice with an expression in which horror, surprise, and something approaching to joy were contending for the mastery. In spite of the cold, great drops of perspiration were coursing down his forehead, and he was evidently fearfully excited. His limbs twitched like those of a man upon the verge of an epileptic fit, and the lines about his mouth were drawn and hard.

"Look!" he gasped, seizing me by the wrist, but still keeping his eyes upon the distant ice, and moving his head slowly in a horizontal direction, as if following some object which was moving across the field of vision. "Look! There, man, there! Between the hummocks! Now coming out from behind the far one! You see her—you MUST see her! There still! Flying from me, by God, flying from me—and gone!"

He uttered the last two words in a whisper of concentrated agony which shall never fade from my remembrance. Clinging to the ratlines he endeavoured to climb up upon the top of the bulwarks as if in the hope of obtaining a last glance at the departing object. His strength was not equal to the attempt, however, and he staggered back against the saloon skylights, where he leaned panting and exhausted. His face was so livid that I expected him to become unconscious, so lost no time in leading him down the companion, and stretching him upon one of the sofas in the cabin. I then poured him out some brandy, which I held to his lips, and which had a wonderful effect upon him, bringing the blood back into his white face and steadying his poor shaking limbs. He raised himself up upon his elbow, and looking round to see that we were alone, he beckoned to me to come and sit beside him.

"You saw it, didn't you?" he asked, still in the same subdued awesome tone so foreign to the nature of the man.

"No, I saw nothing."

His head sank back again upon the cushions. "No, he wouldn't without the glass," he murmured. "He couldn't. It was the glass that showed her to me, and then the eyes of love—the eyes of love.

"I say, Doc, don't let the steward in! He'll think I'm mad. Just bolt the door, will you!"

I rose and did what he had commanded.

He lay quiet for a while, lost in thought apparently, and then raised himself up upon his elbow again, and asked for some more brandy.

"You don't think I am, do you, Doc?" he asked, as I was putting the bottle back into the after-locker. "Tell me now, as man to man, do you think that I am mad?"

"I think you have something on your mind," I answered, "which is exciting you and doing you a good deal of harm."

"Right there, lad!" he cried, his eyes sparkling from the effects of the brandy. "Plenty on my mind—plenty! But I can work out the latitude and the longitude, and I can handle my sextant and manage my logarithms. You couldn't prove me mad in a court of law, could you, now?" It was curious to hear the man lying back and coolly arguing out the question of his own sanity.

"Perhaps not," I said, "but still I think you would be wise to get home as soon as you can, and settle down to a quiet life for a while."

"Get home, eh?" he muttered, with a sneer upon his face. "One word for me and two for yourself, lad. Settle down with Flora—pretty little Flora. Are bad dreams signs of madness?"

"Sometimes," I answered.

"What else? What would be the first symptoms?"

"Pains in the head, noises in the ears flashes before the eyes, delusions—"

"Ah! what about them?" he interrupted. "What would you call a delusion?"

"Seeing a thing which is not there is a delusion."

"But she WAS there!" he groaned to himself. "She WAS there!" and rising, he unbolted the door and walked with slow and uncertain steps to his own cabin, where I have no doubt that he will remain until tomorrow morning. His system seems to have received a terrible shock, whatever it may have been that he imagined himself to have seen. The man becomes a greater mystery every day, though I fear that the solution which he has himself suggested is the correct one, and that his reason is affected. I do not think that a guilty conscience has anything to do with his behaviour. The idea is a popular one among the officers, and, I believe, the crew; but I have seen nothing to support it. He has not the air of a guilty man, but of one who has had terrible usage at the hands of fortune, and who should be regarded as a martyr rather than a criminal.

The wind is veering round to the south tonight. God help us if it blocks that narrow pass which is our only road to safety! Situated as we are on the edge of the main Arctic pack, or the "barrier" as it is called by the whalers, any wind from the north has the effect of shredding out the ice around us and allowing our escape, while a wind from the south blows up all the loose ice behind us and hems us in between two packs. God help us, I say again!

SEPTEMBER 14—Sunday, and a day of rest. My fears have been confirmed, and the thin strip of blue water has disappeared from the southward. Nothing but the great motionless ice fields around us, with their weird hummocks and fantastic pinnacles. There is a deathly silence over their wide expanse which is horrible. No lapping of the waves now, no cries of seagulls or straining of sails, but one deep universal silence in which the murmurs of the seamen, and the creak of their boots upon the white shining deck, seem discordant and out of place. Our only visitor was an Arctic fox, a rare animal upon the pack, though common enough upon the land. He did not come near the ship, however, but after surveying us from a distance fled rapidly across the ice. This was curious conduct, as they generally know nothing of man, and being of an inquisitive nature, become so familiar that they are easily captured. Incredible as it may seem, even this little incident produced a bad effect upon the crew. "Yon puir beastie kens mair, ay, an' sees mair nor you nor me!" was the comment of one of the leading harpooners, and the others nodded their acquiescence. It is vain to attempt to argue against such puerile superstition. They have made up their minds that there is a curse upon the ship, and nothing will ever persuade them to the contrary.

The Captain remained in seclusion all day except for about half an hour in the afternoon, when he came out upon the quarterdeck. I observed that he kept his eye fixed upon the spot where the vision of yesterday had appeared, and was quite prepared for another outburst, but none such came. He did not seem to see me although I was standing close beside him. Divine service was read as usual by the chief engineer. It is a curious thing that in whaling vessels the Church of England Prayer-book is always employed, although there is never a member of that Church among either officers or crew. Our men are all Roman Catholics or Presbyterians, the former predominating. Since a ritual is used which is foreign to both, neither can complain that the other is preferred to them, and they listen with all attention and devotion, so that the system has something to recommend it.

A glorious sunset, which made the great fields of ice look like a lake of blood. I have never seen a finer and at the same time more weird effect. Wind is veering round. If it will blow twenty-four hours from the north all will yet be well.

SEPTEMBER 15—Today is Flora's birthday. Dear lass! it is well that she cannot see her boy, as she used to call me, shut up among the ice fields with a crazy captain and a few weeks' provisions. No doubt she scans the shipping list in the Scotsman every morning to see if we are reported from Shetland. I have to set an example to the men and look cheery and unconcerned; but God knows, my heart is very heavy at times.

The thermometer is at nineteen Fahrenheit today. There is but little wind, and what there is comes from an unfavourable quarter. Captain is in an excellent humour; I think he imagines he has seen some other omen or vision, poor fellow, during the night, for he came into my room early in the morning, and stooping down over my bunk, whispered, "It wasn't a delusion, Doc; it's all right!" After breakfast he asked me to find out how much food was left, which the second mate and I proceeded to do. It is even less than we had expected. Forward they have half a tank full of biscuits, three barrels of salt meat, and a very limited supply of coffee beans and sugar. In the after-hold and lockers there are a good many luxuries, such as tinned salmon, soups, haricot mutton, &c., but they will go a very short way among a crew of fifty men. There are two barrels of flour in the store-room, and an unlimited supply of tobacco. Altogether there is about enough to keep the men on half rations for eighteen or twenty days—certainly not more. When we reported the state of things to the Captain, he ordered all hands to be piped, and addressed them from the quarterdeck. I never saw him to better advantage. With his tall, well-knit figure, and dark animated face, he seemed a man born to command, and he discussed the situation in a cool sailor-like way which showed that while appreciating the danger he had an eye for every loophole of escape.

"My lads," he said, "no doubt you think I brought you into this fix, if it is a fix, and maybe some of you feel bitter against me on account of it. But you must remember that for many a season no ship that comes to the country has brought in as much oil-money as the old Pole-Star, and everyone of you has had his share of it. You can leave your wives behind you in comfort while other poor fellows come back to find their lasses on the parish. If you have to thank me for the one you have to thank me for the other, and we may call it quits. We've tried a bold venture before this and succeeded, so now that we've tried one and failed we've no cause to cry out about it. If the worst comes to the worst, we can make the land across the ice, and lay in a stock of seals which will keep us alive until the spring. It won't come to that, though, for you'll see the Scotch coast again before three weeks are out. At present every man must go on half rations, share and share alike, and no favour to any. Keep up your hearts and you'll pull through this as you've pulled through many a danger before." These few simple words of his had a wonderful effect upon the crew. His former unpopularity was forgotten, and the old harpooner whom I have already mentioned for his superstition, led off three cheers, which were heartily joined in by all hands.

SEPTEMBER 16—The wind has veered round to the north during the night, and the ice shows some symptoms of opening out. The men are in a good humour in spite of the short allowance upon which they have been placed. Steam is kept up in the engine-room, that there may be no delay should an opportunity for escape present itself. The Captain is in exuberant spirits, though he still retains that wild "fey" expression which I have already remarked upon. This burst of cheerfulness puzzles me

more than his former gloom. I cannot understand it. I think I
mentioned in an early part of this journal that one of his oddi-
ties is that he never permits any person to enter his cabin, but
insists upon making his own bed, such as it is, and performing
every other office for himself. To my surprise he handed me the
key today and requested me to go down there and take the time
by his chronometer while he measured the altitude of the sun
at noon. It is a bare little room, containing a washing-stand and
a few books, but little else in the way of luxury, except some
pictures upon the walls. The majority of these are small cheap
oleographs, but there was one watercolour sketch of the head
of a young lady which arrested my attention. It was evidently
a portrait, and not one of those fancy types of female beauty
which sailors particularly affect. No artist could have evolved
from his own mind such a curious mixture of character and
weakness. The languid, dreamy eyes, with their drooping lashes,
and the broad, low brow, unruffled by thought or care, were in
strong contrast with the clean-cut, prominent jaw, and the resolute set of the lower lip. Underneath it in one of the corners
was written, "M. B., aet. 19." That anyone in the short space
of nineteen years of existence could develop such strength of
will as was stamped upon her face seemed to me at the time to
be well-nigh incredible. She must have been an extraordinary
woman. Her features have thrown such a glamour over me that,
though I had but a fleeting glance at them, I could, were I a
draughtsman, reproduce them line for line upon this page of the
journal. I wonder what part she has played in our Captain's life.
He has hung her picture at the end of his berth, so that his eyes
continually rest upon it. Were he a less reserved man I should
make some remark upon the subject. Of the other things in his
cabin there was nothing worthy of mention—uniform coats,
a campstool, small looking-glass, tobacco-box, and numerous
pipes, including an oriental hookah—which, by-the-bye, gives
some colour to Mr. Milne's story about his participation in the
war, though the connection may seem rather a distant one.

11.20 P.M.—Captain just gone to bed after a long and interesting conversation on general topics. When he chooses he can be a most fascinating companion, being remarkably well-read, and having the power of expressing his opinion forcibly without appearing to be dogmatic. I hate to have my intellectual toes trod upon. He spoke about the nature of the soul, and sketched out the views of Aristotle and Plato upon the subject in a masterly manner. He seems to have a leaning for metempsychosis and the doctrines of Pythagoras. In discussing them we touched upon modern spiritualism, and I made some joking allusion to the impostures of Slade, upon which, to my surprise, he warned me most impressively against confusing the innocent with the guilty, and argued that it would be as logical to brand Christianity as an error because Judas, who professed that religion, was a villain. He shortly afterwards bade me good-night and retired to his room.

The wind is freshening up, and blows steadily from the north. The nights are as dark now as they are in England. I hope tomorrow may set us free from our frozen fetters.

SEPTEMBER 17—The Bogie again. Thank Heaven that I have strong nerves! The superstition of these poor fellows, and the circumstantial accounts which they give, with the utmost earnestness and self-conviction, would horrify any man not accustomed to their ways. There are many versions of the matter, but the sum-total of them all is that something uncanny has been flitting round the ship all night, and that Sandie M'Donald of Peterhead and "lang" Peter Williamson of Shetland saw it, as also did Mr. Milne on the bridge—so, having three witnesses, they can make a better case of it than the second mate did. I spoke to Milne after breakfast, and told him that he should be above such nonsense, and that as an officer he ought to set the men a better example. He shook his weatherbeaten head ominously, but answered with characteristic caution, "Mebbe aye, mebbe na, Doctor," he said. "I didna ca' it a ghaist. I canna' say I preen my faith in sea-bogles an' the like, though there's a mony as claims to ha' seen a' that and waur. I'm no easy feared, but maybe your ain bluid would run a bit cauld, mun, if instead o' speerin' aboot it in daylicht ye were wi' me last night, an' seed an awfu' like shape, white an' gruesome, whiles here, whiles there, an' it greetin' and ca'ing in the darkness like a bit lambie that hae lost its mither. Ye would na' be sae ready to put it a' doon to auld wives' clavers then, I'm thinkin'." I saw it was hopeless to reason with him, so contented myself with begging him as a personal favour to call me up the next time the spectre appeared—a request to which he acceded with many ejaculations expressive of his hopes that such an opportunity might never arise.

As I had hoped, the white desert behind us has become broken by many thin streaks of water which intersect it in all directions. Our latitude today was 80 degrees 52' N, which shows that there is a strong southerly drift upon the pack. Should the wind continue favourable it will break up as rapidly as it formed. At present we can do nothing but smoke and wait and hope for the best. I am rapidly becoming a fatalist. When dealing with such uncertain factors as wind and ice a man can be nothing else. Perhaps it was the wind and sand of the Arabian deserts which gave the minds of the original followers of Mahomet their tendency to bow to kismet.

These spectral alarms have a very bad effect upon the Captain. I feared that it might excite his sensitive mind, and endeavoured to conceal the absurd story from him, but unfortunately he overheard one of the men making an allusion to it, and insisted upon being informed about it. As I had expected, it brought out all his latent lunacy in an exaggerated form. I can hardly believe that this is the same man who discoursed philosophy last night with the most critical acumen and coolest judgment. He is pacing backwards and forwards upon the quarterdeck like a caged tiger, stopping now and again to throw out his hands with a yearning gesture, and stare impatiently out over the ice. He keeps up a continual mutter to himself, and

once he called out, "But a little time, love—but a little time!"
Poor fellow, it is sad to see a gallant seaman and accomplished
gentleman reduced to such a pass, and to think that imagination and delusion can cow a mind to which real danger was but
the salt of life. Was ever a man in such a position as I, between
a demented captain and a ghost-seeing mate? I sometimes
think I am the only really sane man aboard the vessel—except
perhaps the second engineer, who is a kind of ruminant, and
would care nothing for all the fiends in the Red Sea so long as
they would leave him alone and not disarrange his tools.

The ice is still opening rapidly, and there is every probability
of our being able to make a start tomorrow morning. They will
think I am inventing when I tell them at home all the strange
things that have befallen me.

12 P.M.—I have been a good deal startled, though I feel steadier
now, thanks to a stiff glass of brandy. I am hardly myself yet,
however, as this handwriting will testify. The fact is, that I have
gone through a very strange experience, and am beginning to
doubt whether I was justified in branding everyone on board as
madmen because they professed to have seen things which did
not seem reasonable to my understanding. *Pshaw*! I am a fool
to let such a trifle unnerve me; and yet, coming as it does after
all these alarms, it has an additional significance, for I cannot
doubt either Mr. Manson's story or that of the mate, now that I
have experienced that which I used formerly to scoff at.

After all it was nothing very alarming—a mere sound, and
that was all. I cannot expect that anyone reading this, if anyone
ever should read it, will sympathise with my feelings, or realise
the effect which it produced upon me at the time. Supper was
over, and I had gone on deck to have a quiet pipe before turning
in. The night was very dark—so dark that, standing under the
quarter-boat, I was unable to see the officer upon the bridge. I
think I have already mentioned the extraordinary silence which
prevails in these frozen seas. In other parts of the world, be they
ever so barren, there is some slight vibration of the air—some

faint hum, be it from the distant haunts of men, or from the leaves of the trees, or the wings of the birds, or even the faint rustle of the grass that covers the ground. One may not actively perceive the sound, and yet if it were withdrawn it would be missed. It is only here in these Arctic seas that stark, unfathomable stillness obtrudes itself upon you in all its gruesome reality. You find your tympanum straining to catch some little murmur, and dwelling eagerly upon every accidental sound within the vessel. In this state I was leaning against the bulwarks when there arose from the ice almost directly underneath me a cry, sharp and shrill, upon the silent air of the night, beginning, as it seemed to me, at a note such as prima donna never reached, and mounting from that ever higher and higher until it culminated in a long wail of agony, which might have been the last cry of a lost soul. The ghastly scream is still ringing in my ears. Grief, unutterable grief, seemed to be expressed in it, and a great longing, and yet through it all there was an occasional wild note of exultation. It shrilled out from close beside me, and yet as I glared into the darkness I could discern nothing. I waited some little time, but without hearing any repetition of the sound, so I came below, more shaken than I have ever been in my life before. As I came down the companion I met Mr. Milne coming up to relieve the watch. "Weel, Doctor," he said, "maybe that's auld wives' clavers tae? Did ye no hear it skirling? Maybe that's a supersteetion? What d'ye think o't noo?" I was obliged to apologise to the honest fellow, and acknowledge that I was as puzzled by it as he was. Perhaps tomorrow things may look different. At present I dare hardly write all that I think. Reading it again in days to come, when I have shaken off all these associations, I should despise myself for having been so weak.

SEPTEMBER 18—Passed a restless and uneasy night, still haunted by that strange sound. The Captain does not look as if he had had much repose either, for his face is haggard and his eyes bloodshot. I have not told him of my adventure of last night, nor shall I. He is already restless and excited, standing up, sitting down, and apparently utterly unable to keep still.

A fine lead appeared in the pack this morning, as I had expected, and we were able to cast off our ice-anchor, and steam about twelve miles in a west-sou'-westerly direction. We were then brought to a halt by a great floe as massive as any which we have left behind us. It bars our progress completely, so we can do nothing but anchor again and wait until it breaks up, which it will probably do within twenty-four hours, if the wind holds. Several bladder-nosed seals were seen swimming in the water, and one was shot, an immense creature more than eleven feet long. They are fierce, pugnacious animals, and are said to be more than a match for a bear. Fortunately they are slow and clumsy in their movements, so that there is little danger in attacking them upon the ice.

The Captain evidently does not think we have seen the last of our troubles, though why he should take a gloomy view of the situation is more than I can fathom, since everyone else on board considers that we have had a miraculous escape, and are sure now to reach the open sea.

"I suppose you think it's all right now, Doctor?" he said, as we sat together after dinner.

"I hope so," I answered.

"We mustn't be too sure—and yet no doubt you are right. We'll all be in the arms of our own true loves before long, lad, won't we? But we mustn't be too sure—we mustn't be too sure."

He sat silent a little, swinging his leg thoughtfully backwards and forwards. "Look here," he continued, "it's a dangerous place this, even at its best—a treacherous, dangerous place. I have known men cut off very suddenly in a land like this. A slip would do it sometimes—a single slip, and down you go through a crack, and only a bubble on the green water to show where it was that you sank. It's a queer thing," he continued with a nervous laugh, "but all the years I've been in this country I never once thought of making a will—not that I have anything to leave in particular, but still when a man is exposed to danger he should have everything arranged and ready—don't you think so?"

"Certainly," I answered, wondering what on earth he was driving at.

"He feels better for knowing it's all settled," he went on. "Now if anything should ever befall me, I hope that you will look after things for me. There is very little in the cabin, but such as it is I should like it to be sold, and the money divided in the same proportion as the oil-money among the crew. The chronometer I wish you to keep yourself as some slight remembrance of our voyage. Of course all this is a mere precaution, but I thought I would take the opportunity of speaking to you about it. I suppose I might rely upon you if there were any necessity?"

"Most assuredly," I answered, "and since you are taking this step, I may as well—"

"You! you!" he interrupted. "YOU'RE all right. What the devil is the matter with YOU? There, I didn't mean to be peppery, but I don't like to hear a young fellow, that has hardly began life, speculating about death. Go up on deck and get some fresh air into your lungs instead of talking nonsense in the cabin, and encouraging me to do the same."

The more I think of this conversation of ours the less do I like it. Why should the man be settling his affairs at the very time when we seem to be emerging from all danger? There must be some method in his madness. Can it be that he contemplates suicide? I remember that upon one occasion he spoke in a deeply reverent manner of the heinousness of the crime of self-destruction. I shall keep my eye upon him, however, and though I cannot obtrude upon the privacy of his cabin, I shall at least make a point of remaining on deck as long as he stays up.

Mr. Milne pooh-poohs my fears, and says it is only the "skipper's little way." He himself takes a very rosy view of the situation. According to him we shall be out of the ice by the day after tomorrow, pass Jan Meyen two days after that, and sight Shetland in little more than a week. I hope he may not be too sanguine. His opinion may be fairly balanced against the gloomy precautions of the Captain, for he is an old and experienced seaman, and weighs his words well before uttering them.

† † † † † †

The long-impending catastrophe has come at last. I hardly know what to write about it.

The Captain is gone. He may come back to us again alive, but I fear me—I fear me. It is now seven o'clock of the morning of the 19th of September. I have spent the whole night traversing the great ice-floe in front of us with a party of seamen in the hope of coming upon some trace of him, but in vain. I shall try to give some account of the circumstances which attended upon his disappearance. Should anyone ever chance to read the words which I put down, I trust they will remember that I do not write from conjecture or from hearsay, but that I, a sane and educated man, am describing accurately what actually occurred before my very eyes. My inferences are my own, but I shall be answerable for the facts.

The Captain remained in excellent spirits after the conversation which I have recorded. He appeared to be nervous and impatient, however, frequently changing his position, and moving his limbs in an aimless choreic way which is characteristic of him at times. In a quarter of an hour he went upon deck seven times, only to descend after a few hurried paces. I followed him each time, for there was something about his face which confirmed my resolution of not letting him out of my sight. He seemed to observe the effect which his movements had produced, for he endeavoured by an over-done hilarity, laughing boisterously at the very smallest of jokes, to quiet my apprehensions.

After supper he went on to the poop once more, and I with him. The night was dark and very still, save for the melancholy soughing of the wind among the spars. A thick cloud was coming up from the northwest, and the ragged tentacles which it threw out in front of it were drifting across the face of the moon, which only shone now and again through a rift in the wrack. The Captain paced rapidly backwards and forwards, and then seeing me still dogging him, he came across and hinted that he thought I should be better below—which, I need hardly say, had the effect of strengthening my resolution to remain on deck.

I think he forgot about my presence after this, for he stood silently leaning over the taffrail, and peering out across the great desert of snow, part of which lay in shadow, while part glittered mistily in the moonlight. Several times I could see by his movements that he was referring to his watch, and once he muttered a short sentence, of which I could only catch the one word "ready." I confess to having felt an eerie feeling creeping over me as I watched the loom of his tall figure through the darkness, and noted how completely he fulfilled the idea of a man who is keeping a tryst. A tryst with whom? Some vague perception began to dawn upon me as I pieced one fact with another, but I was utterly unprepared for the sequel.

By the sudden intensity of his attitude I felt that he saw something. I crept up behind him. He was staring with an eager questioning gaze at what seemed to be a wreath of mist, blown swiftly in a line with the ship. It was a dim, nebulous body, devoid of shape, sometimes more, sometimes less apparent, as the light fell on it. The moon was dimmed in its brilliancy at the moment by a canopy of thinnest cloud, like the coating of an anemone.

"Coming, lass, coming," cried the skipper, in a voice of unfathomable tenderness and compassion, like one who soothes a beloved one by some favour long looked for, and as pleasant to bestow as to receive.

What followed happened in an instant. I had no power to interfere.

He gave one spring to the top of the bulwarks, and another which took him on to the ice, almost to the feet of the pale misty figure. He held out his hands as if to clasp it, and so ran into the darkness with outstretched arms and loving words. I still stood rigid and motionless, straining my eyes after his retreating form, until his voice died away in the distance. I never thought to see him again, but at that moment the moon shone out brilliantly through a chink in the cloudy heaven, and illuminated the great field of ice. Then I saw his dark figure already a very long way off, running with prodigious speed across the frozen plain. That was the last glimpse which we caught of him—perhaps the last we ever shall. A party was organised to follow him, and I accompanied them, but the men's hearts were not in the work, and nothing was found. Another will be formed within a few hours. I can hardly believe I have not been dreaming, or suffering from some hideous nightmare, as I write these things down.

7.30 P.M.—Just returned dead beat and utterly tired out from a second unsuccessful search for the Captain. The floe is of enormous extent, for though we have traversed at least twenty miles of its surface, there has been no sign of its coming to an end. The frost has been so severe of late that the overlying snow is frozen as hard as granite, otherwise we might have had the footsteps to guide us. The crew are anxious that we should cast off and steam round the floe and so to the southward, for the ice has opened up during the night, and the sea is visible upon the horizon. They argue that Captain Craigie is certainly dead, and that we are all risking our lives to no purpose by remaining when we have an opportunity of escape. Mr. Milne and I have had the greatest difficulty in persuading them to wait until tomorrow night, and have been compelled to promise that we will not under any circumstances delay our departure longer than that. We propose therefore to take a few hours' sleep, and then to start upon a final search.

SEPTEMBER 20, EVENING—I crossed the ice this morning with a party of men exploring the southern part of the floe, while Mr. Milne went off in a northerly direction. We pushed on for ten or twelve miles without seeing a trace of any living thing except a single bird, which fluttered a great way over our heads, and which by its flight I should judge to have been a falcon. The southern extremity of the ice field tapered away into a long narrow spit which projected out into the sea. When we came to the base of this promontory, the men halted, but I begged them to continue to the extreme end of it, that we might have the satisfaction of knowing that no possible chance had been neglected.

We had hardly gone a hundred yards before M'Donald of Peterhead cried out that he saw something in front of us, and began to run. We all got a glimpse of it and ran too. At first it was only a vague darkness against the white ice, but as we raced along together it took the shape of a man, and eventually of the man of whom we were in search. He was lying face downwards upon a frozen bank. Many little crystals of ice and feathers of snow had drifted on to him as he lay, and sparkled upon his dark seaman's jacket. As we came up some wandering puff of wind caught these tiny flakes in its vortex, and they whirled up into the air, partially descended again, and then, caught once more in the current, sped rapidly away in the direction of the sea. To my eyes it seemed but a snowdrift, but many of my companions averred that it started up in the shape of a woman, stooped over the corpse and kissed it, and then hurried away across the floe. I have learned never to ridicule any man's opinion, however strange it may seem. Sure it is that Captain Nicholas Craigie had met with no painful end, for there was a bright smile upon his blue pinched features, and his hands were still outstretched as though grasping at the strange visitor which had summoned him away into the dim world that lies beyond the grave.

We buried him the same afternoon with the ship's ensign around him, and a thirty-two-pound shot at his feet. I read the burial service, while the rough sailors wept like children, for there were many who owed much to his kind heart, and who showed now the affection which his strange ways had repelled during his lifetime. He went off the grating with a dull, sullen splash, and as I looked into the green water I saw him go down, down, down until he was but a little flickering patch of white hanging upon the outskirts of eternal darkness. Then even that faded away, and he was gone. There he shall lie, with his secret and his sorrows and his mystery all still buried in his breast, until that great day when the sea shall give up its dead, and Nicholas Craigie come out from among the ice with the smile upon his face, and his stiffened arms outstretched in greeting. I pray that his lot may be a happier one in that life than it has been in this.

I shall not continue my journal. Our road to home lies plain and clear before us, and the great ice field will soon be but a remembrance of the past. It will be some time before I get over the shock produced by recent events. When I began this record of our voyage I little thought of how I should be compelled to finish it. I am writing these final words in the lonely cabin, still starting at times and fancying I hear the quick nervous step of the dead man upon the deck above me. I entered his cabin tonight, as was my duty, to make a list of his effects in order that they might be entered in the official log. All was as it had been upon my previous visit, save that the picture which I have described as having hung at the end of his bed had been cut out of its frame, as with a knife, and was gone. With this last link in a strange chain of evidence I close my diary of the voyage of the Pole-Star.

[NOTE by Dr. John M'Alister Ray, senior.—I have read over the strange events connected with the death of the Captain of the Pole-Star, as narrated in the journal of my son. That everything occurred exactly as he describes it I have the fullest confidence, and, indeed, the most positive certainty, for I know him to be a strong-nerved and unimaginative man, with the strictest regard for veracity. Still, the story is, on the face of it, so vague and so improbable, that I was long opposed to its publication. Within the last few days, however, I have had independent testimony upon the subject which throws a new light upon it. I had run down to Edinburgh to attend a meeting of the British Medical Association, when I chanced to come across Dr. P—, an old college chum of mine, now practising at Saltash, in Devonshire. Upon my telling him of this experience of my son's, he declared to me that he was familiar with the man, and proceeded, to my no small surprise, to give me a description of him, which tallied remarkably well with that given in the journal, except that he depicted him as a younger man. According to his account, he had been engaged to a young lady of singular beauty residing upon the Cornish coast. During his absence at sea his betrothed had died under circumstances of peculiar horror.]

† † † † †

Like all authors, Doyle drew on his own experience for his fiction. His first marine adventure was inspired by a stint on the arctic whaler, the Hope, *where he served as the ship's surgeon for several months. After the* Pole-star *becomes trapped in an ice field, a young medical student named John M'Alister Ray records how Captain Craigie is lured away from the ship by a spectral form that resembles his lost love. The men try to rescue their captain, but he freezes to death before they reach him. Not all vampires drink blood. Many of them feed on energy or other substances that are essential to human existence. The elemental spirit that caused Craigie's death may be a ghost, but it could just as easily be an Eskimo vampire which, unlike many of its western counterparts, drains heat from its victims. (In either case, John M'Alister Ray can be seen as an early incarnation of Dr. John H. Watson.)*

Doyle made the "The Captain of the Pole-star" *the title story of his first collection, which was published in 1890.*

John Barrington Cowles

It might seem rash of me to say that I ascribe the death of my poor friend, John Barrington Cowles, to any preternatural agency. I am aware that in the present state of public feeling a chain of evidence would require to be strong indeed before the possibility of such a conclusion could be admitted.

I shall therefore merely state the circumstances which led up to this sad event as concisely and as plainly as I can, and leave every reader to draw his own deductions. Perhaps there may be someone who can throw light upon what is dark to me.

I first met Barrington Cowles when I went up to Edinburgh University to take out medical classes there. My landlady in Northumberland Street had a large house, and, being a widow without children, she gained a livelihood by providing accommodation for several students.

Barrington Cowles happened to have taken a bedroom upon the same floor as mine, and when we came to know each other better we shared a small sitting-room, in which we took our meals. In this manner we originated a friendship which was unmarred by the slightest disagreement up to the day of his death.

Cassel's Saturday Journal, 1886.

Cowles' father was the colonel of a Sikh regiment and had remained in India for many years. He allowed his son a handsome income, but seldom gave any other sign of parental affection—writing irregularly and briefly.

My friend, who had himself been born in India, and whose whole disposition was an ardent tropical one, was much hurt by this neglect. His mother was dead, and he had no other relation in the world to supply the blank.

Thus he came in time to concentrate all his affection upon me, and to confide in me in a manner which is rare among men. Even when a stronger and deeper passion came upon him, it never infringed upon the old tenderness between us. Cowles was a tall, slim young fellow, with an olive, Velasquez-like face, and dark, tender eyes. I have seldom seen a man who was more likely to excite a woman's interest, or to captivate her imagination. His expression was, as a rule, dreamy, and even languid; but if in conversation a subject arose which interested him he would be all animation in a moment. On such occasions his colour would heighten, his eyes gleam, and he could speak with an eloquence which would carry his audience with him.

In spite of these natural advantages he led a solitary life, avoiding female society, and reading with great diligence. He was one of the foremost men of his year, taking the senior medal for anatomy, and the Neil Arnott prize for physics.

How well I can recollect the first time we met her! Often and often I have recalled the circumstances, and tried to remember what the exact impression was which she produced on my mind at the time.

After we came to know her my judgment was warped, so that I am curious to recollect what my unbiassed (sic) instincts were. It is hard, however, to eliminate the feelings which reason or prejudice afterwards raised in me.

It was at the opening of the Royal Scottish Academy in the spring of 1879. My poor friend was passionately attached to art in every form, and a pleasing chord in music or a delicate effect upon canvas would give exquisite pleasure to his highly-strung nature. We had gone together to see the pictures, and were standing in the grand central salon, when I noticed an extremely beautiful woman standing at the other side of the room. In my whole life I have never seen such a classically perfect countenance. It was the real Greek type—the forehead broad, very low, and as white as marble, with a cloudlet of delicate locks wreathing round it, the nose straight and clean cut, the lips inclined to thinness, the chin and lower jaw beautifully rounded off, and yet sufficiently developed to promise unusual strength of character. But those eyes—those wonderful eyes! If I could but give some faint idea of their varying moods, their steely hardness, their feminine softness, their power of command, their penetrating intensity suddenly melting away into an expression of womanly weakness—but I am speaking now of future impressions!

There was a tall, yellow-haired young man with this lady, whom I at once recognised as a law student with whom I had a slight acquaintance.

Archibald Reeves—for that was his name—was a dashing, handsome young fellow, and had at one time been a ringleader in every university escapade; but of late I had seen little of him, and the report was that he was engaged to be married. His companion was, then, I presumed, his fiancee. I seated myself upon the velvet settee in the centre of the room, and furtively watched the couple from behind my catalogue.

The more I looked at her the more her beauty grew upon me. She was somewhat short in stature, it is true; but her figure was perfection, and she bore herself in such a fashion that it was only by actual comparison that one would have known her to be under the medium height. As I kept my eyes upon them, Reeves was called away for some reason, and the young lady was left alone. Turning her back to the pictures, she passed the time until the return of her escort in taking a deliberate survey of the company, without paying the least heed to the fact that a dozen pair of eyes, attracted by her elegance and beauty, were bent curiously upon her. With one of her hands holding the red silk cord which railed off the pictures, she stood languidly moving her eyes from face to face with as little self-consciousness as if she were looking at the canvas creatures behind her. Suddenly, as I watched her, I saw her gaze become fixed, and, as it were, intense. I followed the direction of her looks, wondering what could have attracted her so strongly.

John Barrington Cowles was standing before a picture—one, I think, by Noel Paton—I know that the subject was a noble and ethereal one. His profile was turned toward us, and never have I seen him to such advantage. I have said that he was a strikingly handsome man, but at that moment he looked absolutely magnificent. It was evident that he had momentarily forgotten his surroundings, and that his whole soul was in sympathy with the picture before him. His eyes sparkled, and a dusky pink shone through his clear olive cheeks. She continued to watch him fixedly, with a look of interest upon her face, until he came out of his reverie with a start, and turned abruptly round, so that his gaze met hers. She glanced away at once, but his eyes remained fixed upon her for some moments. The picture was forgotten already, and his soul had come down to earth once more.

We caught sight of her once or twice before we left, and each time I noticed my friend look after her. He made no remark, however, until we got out into the open air, and were walking arm-in-arm along Princes Street.

"Did you notice that beautiful woman, in the dark dress, with the white fur?" he asked.

"Yes, I saw her," I answered.

"Do you know her?" he asked eagerly. "Have you any idea who she is?"

"I don't know her personally," I replied. "But I have no doubt I could find out all about her, for I believe she is engaged to young Archie Reeves, and he and I have a lot of mutual friends."

"Engaged!" ejaculated Cowles.

"Why, my dear boy," I said, laughing, "you don't mean to say you are so susceptible that the fact that a girl to whom you never spoke in your life is engaged is enough to upset you?"

"Well, not exactly to upset me," he answered, forcing a laugh. "But I don't mind telling you, Armitage, that I never was so taken by any one in my life. It wasn't the mere beauty of the face—though that was perfect enough—but it was the character and the intellect upon it. I hope, if she is engaged, that it is to some man who will be worthy of her."

"Why," I remarked, "you speak quite feelingly. It is a clear case of love at first sight, Jack. However, to put your perturbed spirit at rest, I'll make a point of finding out all about her whenever I meet any fellow who is likely to know."

Barrington Cowles thanked me, and the conversation drifted off into other channels. For several days neither of us made any allusion to the subject, though my companion was perhaps a little more dreamy and distraught than usual. The incident had almost vanished from my remembrance, when one day young Brodie, who is a second cousin of mine, came up to me on the university steps with the face of a bearer of tidings.

"I say," he began, "you know Reeves, don't you?"

"Yes. What of him?"

"His engagement is off."

"Off!" I cried. "Why, I only learned the other day that it was on."

"Oh, yes—it's all off. His brother told me so. Deucedly mean of Reeves, you know, if he has backed out of it, for she was an uncommonly nice girl."

"I've seen her," I said, "but I don't know her name."

"She is a Miss Northcott, and lives with an old aunt of hers in Abercrombie Place. Nobody knows anything about her people, or where she comes from. Anyhow, she is about the most unlucky girl in the world, poor soul!"

"Why unlucky?"

"Well, you know, this was her second engagement," said young Brodie, who had a marvellous knack of knowing everything about everybody. "She was engaged to Prescott—William Prescott, who died. That was a very sad affair. The wedding day was fixed, and the whole thing looked as straight as a die when the smash came."

"What smash?" I asked, with some dim recollection of the circumstances.

"Why, Prescott's death. He came to Abercrombie Place one night, and stayed very late. No one knows exactly when he left, but about one in the morning a fellow who knew him met him walking rapidly in the direction of the Queen's Park. He bade him good night, but Prescott hurried on without heeding him, and that was the last time he was ever seen alive. Three days afterwards his body was found floating in St. Margaret's Loch, under St. Anthony's Chapel. No one could ever understand it, but of course the verdict brought it in as temporary insanity."

"It was very strange," I remarked.

"Yes, and deucedly rough on the poor girl," said Brodie. "Now that this other blow has come it will quite crush her. So gentle and ladylike she is too!"

"You know her personally, then!" I asked.

"Oh, yes, I know her. I have met her several times. I could easily manage that you should be introduced to her."

"Well," I answered, "it's not so much for my own sake as for a friend of mine. However, I don't suppose she will go out much for some little time after this. When she does I will take advantage of your offer."

We shook hands on this, and I thought no more of the matter for some time.

† † † † † †

The next incident which I have to relate as bearing at all upon the question of Miss Northcott is an unpleasant one. Yet I must detail it as accurately as possible, since it may throw some light upon the sequel. One cold night, several months after the conversation with my second cousin which I have quoted above, I was walking down one of the lowest streets in the city on my way back from a case which I had been attending. It was very late, and I was picking my way among the dirty loungers who were clustering round the doors of a great gin-palace, when a man staggered out from among them, and held out his hand to me with a drunken leer. The gaslight fell full upon his face, and, to my intense astonishment, I recognised in the degraded creature before me my former acquaintance, young Archibald Reeves, who had once been famous as one of the most dressy and particular men in the whole college. I was so utterly surprised that for a moment I almost doubted the evidence of my own senses; but there was no mistaking those features, which, though bloated with drink, still retained something of their former comeliness. I was determined to rescue him, for one night at least, from the company into which he had fallen.

"Holloa, Reeves!" I said. "Come along with me. I'm going in your direction."

He muttered some incoherent apology for his condition, and took my arm. As I supported him toward his lodgings I could see that he was not only suffering from the effects of a recent debauch, but that a long course of intemperance had affected his nerves and his brain. His hand when I touched it was dry and feverish, and he started from every shadow which fell upon the pavement. He rambled in his speech, too, in a manner which suggested the delirium of disease rather than the talk of a drunkard.

When I got him to his lodgings I partially undressed him and laid him upon his bed. His pulse at this time was very high, and he was evidently extremely feverish. He seemed to have sunk into a doze; and I was about to steal out of the room to warn his landlady of his condition, when he started up and caught me by the sleeve of my coat.

"Don't go!" he cried. "I feel better when you are here. I am safe from her then."

"From her!" I said. "From whom?"

"Her! her!" he answered peevishly. "Ah! you don't know her. She is the devil! Beautiful—beautiful; but the devil!"

"You are feverish and excited," I said. "Try and get a little sleep. You will wake better."

"Sleep!" he groaned. "How am I to sleep when I see her sitting down yonder at the foot of the bed with her great eyes watching and watching hour after hour? I tell you it saps all the strength and manhood out of me. That's what makes me drink. God help me—I'm half drunk now!"

"You are very ill," I said, putting some vinegar to his temples; "and you are delirious. You don't know what you say."

"Yes, I do," he interrupted sharply, looking up at me. "I know very well what I say. I brought it upon myself. It is my own choice. But I couldn't—no, by heaven, I couldn't—accept the alternative. I couldn't keep my faith to her. It was more than man could do."

I sat by the side of the bed, holding one of his burning hands in mine, and wondering over his strange words. He lay still for some time, and then, raising his eyes to me, said in a most plaintive voice—

"Why did she not give me warning sooner? Why did she wait until I had learned to love her so?"

He repeated this question several times, rolling his feverish head from side to side, and then he dropped into a troubled sleep. I crept out of the room, and, having seen that he would be properly cared for, left the house. His words, however, rang in my ears for days afterwards, and assumed a deeper significance when taken with what was to come.

My friend, Barrington Cowles, had been away for his summer holidays, and I had heard nothing of him for several months. When the winter session came on, however, I received a telegram from him, asking me to secure the old rooms in Northumberland Street for him, and telling me the train by which he would arrive. I went down to meet him, and was delighted to find him looking wonderfully hearty and well.

"By the way," he said suddenly, that night, as we sat in our chairs by the fire, talking over the events of the holidays, "you have never congratulated me yet!"

"On what, my boy?" I asked.

"What! Do you mean to say you have not heard of my engagement?"

"Engagement! No!" I answered. "However, I am delighted to hear it, and congratulate you with all my heart."

"I wonder it didn't come to your ears," he said. "It was the queerest thing. You remember that girl whom we both admired so much at the Academy?"

"What!" I cried, with a vague feeling of apprehension at my heart. "You don't mean to say that you are engaged to her?"

"I thought you would be surprised," he answered. "When I was staying with an old aunt of mine in Peterhead, in Aberdeenshire, the Northcotts happened to come there on a visit, and as we had mutual friends we soon met. I found out that it was a false alarm about her being engaged, and then—well, you know what it is when you are thrown into the society of such a girl in a place like Peterhead. Not, mind you," he added, "that I consider I did a foolish or hasty thing. I have never regretted it for a moment. The more I know Kate the more I admire her and love her. However, you must be introduced to her, and then you will form your own opinion."

I expressed my pleasure at the prospect, and endeavoured to speak as lightly as I could to Cowles upon the subject, but I felt depressed and anxious at heart. The words of Reeves and the unhappy fate of young Prescott recurred to my recollection, and though I could assign no tangible reason for it, a vague, dim fear and distrust of the woman took possession of me. It may be that this was foolish prejudice and superstition upon my part, and that I involuntarily contorted her future doings and sayings to fit into some half-formed wild theory of my own. This has been suggested to me by others as an explanation of my narrative. They are welcome to their opinion if they can reconcile it with the facts which I have to tell.

I went round with my friend a few days afterwards to call upon Miss Northcott. I remember that, as we went down Abercrombie Place, our attention was attracted by the shrill yelping of a dog—which noise proved eventually to come from the house to which we were bound. We were shown upstairs, where I was introduced to old Mrs. Merton, Miss Northcott's aunt, and to the young lady herself. She looked as beautiful as ever, and I could not wonder at my friend's infatuation. Her face was a little more flushed than usual, and she held in her hand a heavy dog-whip, with which she had been chastising a small Scotch terrier, whose cries we had heard in the street. The poor brute was cringing up against the wall, whining piteously, and evidently completely cowed.

"So Kate," said my friend, after we had taken our seats, "you have been falling out with Carlo again."

"Only a very little quarrel this time," she said, smiling charmingly. "He is a dear, good old fellow, but he needs correction now and then." Then, turning to me, "We all do that, Mr. Armitage, don't we? What a capital thing if, instead of receiving a collective punishment at the end of our lives, we were to have one at once, as the dogs do, when we did anything wicked. It would make us more careful, wouldn't it?"

I acknowledged that it would.

"Supposing that every time a man misbehaved himself a gigantic hand were to seize him, and he were lashed with a whip until he fainted"—she clenched her white fingers as she spoke, and cut out viciously with the dog-whip—"it would do more to keep him good than any number of high-minded theories of morality."

"Why, Kate," said my friend, "you are quite savage today."

"No, Jack," she laughed. "I'm only propounding a theory for Mr. Armitage's consideration."

The two began to chat together about some Aberdeenshire reminiscence, and I had time to observe Mrs. Merton, who had remained silent during our short conversation. She was a very strange-looking old lady. What attracted attention most in her appearance was the utter want of colour which she exhibited. Her hair was snow-white, and her face extremely pale. Her lips were bloodless, and even her eyes were of such a light tinge of blue that they hardly relieved the general pallor. Her dress was a gray silk, which harmonised with her general appearance. She had a peculiar expression of countenance, which I was unable at the moment to refer to its proper cause.

She was working at some old-fashioned piece of ornamental needlework, and as she moved her arms her dress gave forth a dry, melancholy rustling, like the sound of leaves in the autumn. There was something mournful and depressing in the sight of her. I moved my chair a little nearer, and asked her how she liked Edinburgh, and whether she had been there long. When I spoke to her she started and looked up at me with a scared look on her face. Then I saw in a moment what the expression was which I had observed there. It was one of fear—intense and overpowering fear. It was so marked that I could have staked my life on the woman before me having at some period of her life been subjected to some terrible experience or dreadful misfortune.

"Oh, yes, I like it," she said, in a soft, timid voice, "and we have been here long—that is, not very long. We move about a great deal." She spoke with hesitation, as if afraid of committing herself.

"You are a native of Scotland, I presume?" I said. "No—that is, not entirely. We are not natives of any place. We are cosmopolitan, you know." She glanced round in the direction of Miss Northcott as she spoke, but the two were still chatting together near the window. Then she suddenly bent forward to me, with a look of intense earnestness upon her face, and said—

"Don't talk to me any more, please. She does not like it, and I shall suffer for it afterwards. Please, don't do it."

I was about to ask her the reason for this strange request, but when she saw I was going to address her, she rose and walked slowly out of the room. As she did so I perceived that the lovers had ceased to talk and that Miss Northcott was looking at me with her keen, gray eyes.

"You must excuse my aunt, Mr. Armitage," she said, "she is odd, and easily fatigued. Come over and look at my album."

We spent some time examining the portraits. Miss Northcott's father and mother were apparently ordinary mortals enough, and I could not detect in either of them any traces of the character which showed itself in their daughter's face. There was one old daguerreotype, however, which arrested my attention. It represented a man of about the age of forty, and strikingly handsome. He was clean shaven, and extraordinary power was expressed upon his prominent lower jaw and firm, straight mouth. His eyes were somewhat deeply set in his head, however, and there was a snake-like flattening at the upper part of his forehead, which detracted from his appearance. I almost involuntarily, when I saw the head, pointed to it, and exclaimed—

"There is your prototype in your family, Miss Northcott."

"Do you think so?" she said. "I am afraid you are paying me a very bad compliment. Uncle Anthony was always considered the black sheep of the family."

"Indeed," I answered. "My remark was an unfortunate one, then."

"Oh, don't mind that," she said. "I always thought myself that he was worth all of them put together. He was an officer in the Forty-first Regiment, and he was killed in action during the Persian War—so he died nobly, at any rate."

"That's the sort of death I should like to die," said Cowles, his dark eyes flashing, as they would when he was excited. "I often wish I had taken to my father's profession instead of this vile pill-compounding drudgery."

"Come, Jack, you are not going to die any sort of death yet," she said, tenderly taking his hand in hers.

I could not understand the woman. There was such an extraordinary mixture of masculine decision and womanly tenderness about her, with the consciousness of something all her own in the background, that she fairly puzzled me. I hardly knew, therefore, how to answer Cowles when, as we walked down the street together, he asked the comprehensive question—

"Well, what do you think of her?"

"I think she is wonderfully beautiful," I answered guardedly.

"That, of course," he replied irritably. "You knew that before you came!"

"I think she is very clever too," I remarked.

Barrington Cowles walked on for some time, and then he suddenly turned on me with the strange question—

"Do you think she is cruel? Do you think she is the sort of girl who would take a pleasure in inflicting pain?"

"Well, really," I answered, "I have hardly had time to form an opinion."

We then walked on for some time in silence.

"She is an old fool," at length muttered Cowles. "She is mad."

"Who is?" I asked.

"Why, that old woman—that aunt of Kate's—Mrs. Merton, or whatever her name is."

Then I knew that my poor colourless friend had been speaking to Cowles, but he never said anything more as to the nature of her communication.

My companion went to bed early that night, and I sat up a long time by the fire, thinking over all that I had seen and heard. I felt that there was some mystery about the girl—some dark fatality so strange as to defy conjecture. I thought of Prescott's interview with her before their marriage, and the fatal termination of it. I coupled it with poor drunken Reeves' plaintive cry, "Why did she not tell me sooner?" and with the other words he had spoken. Then my mind ran over Mrs. Merton's warning to me, Cowles' reference to her, and even the episode of the whip and the cringing dog.

The whole effect of my recollections was unpleasant to a degree, and yet there was no tangible charge which I could bring against the woman. It would be worse than useless to attempt to warn my friend until I had definitely made up my mind what I was to warn him against. He would treat any charge against her with scorn. What could I do? How could I get at some tangible conclusion as to her character and antecedents? No one in Edinburgh knew them except as recent acquaintances. She was an orphan, and as far as I knew she had never disclosed where her former home had been. Suddenly an idea struck me. Among my father's friends there was a Colonel Joyce, who had served a long time in India upon the staff, and who would be likely to know most of the officers who had been out there since the Mutiny. I sat down at once, and, having trimmed the lamp, proceeded to write a letter to the Colonel. I told him that I was very curious to gain some particulars about a certain Captain Northcott, who had served in the Forty-first Foot, and who had fallen in the Persian War. I described the man as well as I could from my recollection of the daguerreotype, and then, having directed the letter, posted it that very night, after which, feeling that I had done all that could be done, I retired to bed, with a mind too anxious to allow me to sleep.

PART II

I got an answer from Leicester, where the Colonel resided, within two days. I have it before me as I write, and copy it verbatim.

> "DEAR BOB," [it said] "I remember the man well. I was with him at Calcutta, and afterwards at Hyderabad. He was a curious, solitary sort of mortal; but a gallant soldier enough, for he distinguished himself at Sobraon, and was wounded, if I remember right. He was not popular in his corps—they said he was a pitiless, cold-blooded fellow, with no geniality in him. There was a rumour, too, that he was a devil-worshipper, or something of that sort, and also that he had the evil eye, which, of course, was all nonsense. He had some strange theories, I remember, about the power of the human will and the effects of mind upon matter.
>
> "How are you getting on with your medical studies? Never forget, my boy, that your father's son has every claim upon me,

and that if I can serve you in any way I am always at your
command.—Ever affectionately yours, EDWARD JOYCE.

"P.S.—By the way, Northcott did not fall in action. He was
killed after peace was declared in a crazy attempt to get some
of the eternal fire from the sun-worshippers' temple. There was
considerable mystery about his death."

I read this epistle over several times—at first with a feeling of satisfaction, and then with one of disappointment. I had come on some curious information, and yet hardly what I wanted. He was an eccentric man, a devil-worshipper, and rumoured to have the power of the evil eye. I could believe the young lady's eyes, when endowed with that cold, gray shimmer which I had noticed in them once or twice, to be capable of any evil which human eye ever wrought; but still the superstition was an effete one. Was there not more meaning in that sentence which followed—"He had theories of the power of the human will and of the effect of mind upon matter"? I remember having once read a quaint treatise, which I had imagined to be mere charlatanism at the time, of the power of certain human minds, and of effects produced by them at a distance.

Was Miss Northcott endowed with some exceptional power of the sort?

The idea grew upon me, and very shortly I had evidence which convinced me of the truth of the supposition.

It happened that at the very time when my mind was dwelling upon this subject, I saw a notice in the paper that our town was to be visited by Dr. Messinger, the well-known medium and mesmerist. Messinger was a man whose perform-ance, such as it was, had been again and again pronounced to be genuine by competent judges. He was far above trickery, and had the reputation of being the soundest living authority upon the strange pseudo-sciences of animal magnetism and electro-biology. Determined, therefore, to see what the human will could do, even against all the disadvantages of glaring footlights and a public platform, I took a ticket for the first night of the performance, and went with several student friends.

We had secured one of the side boxes, and did not arrive until after the performance had begun. I had hardly taken my seat before I recognised Barrington Cowles, with his fiancee and old Mrs. Merton, sitting in the third or fourth row of the stalls. They caught sight of me at almost the same moment, and we bowed to each other. The first portion of the lecture was somewhat commonplace, the lecturer giving tricks of pure legerdemain, with one or two manifestations of mesmerism, performed upon a subject whom he had brought with him. He gave us an exhibition of clairvoyance too, throwing his subject into a trance, and then demanding particulars as to the movements of absent friends, and the whereabouts of hidden objects all of which appeared to be answered satisfactorily. I had seen all this before, however. What I wanted to see now was the effect of the lecturer's will when exerted upon some independent member of the audience.

He came round to that as the concluding exhibition in his performance. "I have shown you," he said, "that a mesmerised subject is entirely dominated by the will of the mesmeriser. He loses all power of volition, and his very thoughts are such as are suggested to him by the master-mind. The same end may be attained without any preliminary process. A strong will can, simply by virtue of its strength, take possession of a weaker one, even at a distance, and can regulate the impulses and the actions of the owner of it. If there was one man in the world who had a very much more highly-developed will than any of the rest of the human family, there is no reason why he should not be able to rule over them all, and to reduce his fellow-creatures to the condition of automatons. Happily there is such a dead level of mental power, or rather of mental weakness, among us that such a catastrophe is not likely to occur; but still within our small compass there are variations which produce surprising effects. I shall now single out one of the audience, and endeavour 'by the mere power of will' to compel him to come upon the platform, and do and say what I wish. Let me assure you that there is no collusion, and that the subject whom I may select is at perfect liberty to resent to the uttermost any impulse which I may communicate to him."

With these words the lecturer came to the front of the platform, and glanced over the first few rows of the stalls. No doubt Cowles' dark skin and bright eyes marked him out as a man of a highly nervous temperament, for the mesmerist picked him out in a moment, and fixed his eyes upon him. I saw my friend give a start of surprise, and then settle down in his chair, as if to express his determination not to yield to the influence of the operator. Messinger was not a man whose head denoted any great brain-power, but his gaze was singularly intense and penetrating. Under the influence of it Cowles made one or two spasmodic motions of his hands, as if to grasp the sides of his seat, and then half rose, but only to sink down again, though with an evident effort. I was watching the scene with intense interest, when I happened to catch a glimpse of Miss Northcott's face. She was sitting with her eyes fixed intently upon the mesmerist, and with such an expression of concentrated power upon her features as I have never seen on any other human countenance. Her jaw was firmly set, her lips compressed, and her face as hard as if it were a beautiful sculpture cut out of the whitest marble. Her eyebrows were drawn down, however, and from beneath them her gray eyes seemed to sparkle and gleam with a cold light. I looked at Cowles again, expecting every moment to see him rise and obey the mesmerist's wishes, when there came from the platform a short, gasping cry as of a man utterly worn out and prostrated by a prolonged struggle. Messinger was leaning against the table, his hand to his forehead, and the perspiration pouring down his face. "I won't go on," he cried, addressing the audience. "There is a stronger will than mine acting against me. You must excuse me for tonight." The man was evidently ill, and utterly unable to proceed, so the curtain was lowered, and the audience dispersed, with many comments upon the lecturer's sudden indisposition.

I waited outside the hall until my friend and the ladies came out. Cowles was laughing over his recent experience.

"He didn't succeed with me, Bob," he cried triumphantly, as he shook my hand. "I think he caught a Tartar that time."

"Yes," said Miss Northcott, "I think that Jack ought to be very proud of his strength of mind; don't you! Mr. Armitage?"

"It took me all my time, though," my friend said seriously. "You can't conceive what a strange feeling I had once or twice. All the strength seemed to have gone out of me—especially just before he collapsed himself."

I walked round with Cowles in order to see the ladies home. He walked in front with Mrs. Merton, and I found myself behind with the young lady. For a minute or so I walked beside her without making any remark, and then I suddenly blurted out, in a manner which must have seemed somewhat brusque to her—

"You did that, Miss Northcott."

"Did what?" she asked sharply.

"Why, mesmerised the mesmeriser—I suppose that is the best way of describing the transaction."

"What a strange idea!" she said, laughing. "You give me credit for a strong will then?"

"Yes," I said. "For a dangerously strong one."

"Why dangerous?" she asked, in a tone of surprise.

"I think," I answered, "that any will which can exercise such power is dangerous—for there is always a chance of its being turned to bad uses."

"You would make me out a very dreadful individual, Mr. Armitage," she said; and then looking up suddenly in my face—"You have never liked me. You are suspicious of me and distrust me, though I have never given you cause."

The accusation was so sudden and so true that I was unable to find any reply to it. She paused for a moment, and then said in a voice which was hard and cold—

"Don't let your prejudice lead you to interfere with me, however, or say anything to your friend, Mr. Cowles, which might lead to a difference between us. You would find that to be very bad policy."

There was something in the way she spoke which gave an indescribable air of a threat to these few words.

"I have no power," I said, "to interfere with your plans for the future. I cannot help, however, from what I have seen and heard, having fears for my friend."

"Fears!" she repeated scornfully. "Pray what have you seen and heard. Something from Mr. Reeves, perhaps—I believe he is another of your friends?"

"He never mentioned your name to me," I answered, truthfully enough. "You will be sorry to hear that he is dying." As I said it we passed by a lighted window, and I glanced down to see what effect my words had upon her. She was laughing—there was no doubt of it; she was laughing quietly to herself. I could see merriment in every feature of her face. I feared and mistrusted the woman from that moment more than ever.

We said little more that night. When we parted she gave me a quick, warning glance, as if to remind me of what she had said about the danger of interference. Her cautions would have made little difference to me could I have seen my way to benefiting Barrington Cowles by anything which I might say. But what could I say? I might say that her former suitors had been unfortunate. I might say that I believed her to be a cruel-hearted woman. I might say that I considered her to possess wonderful, and almost preternatural powers. What impression would any of these accusations make upon an ardent lover—a man with my friend's enthusiastic temperament? I felt that it would be useless to advance them, so I was silent.

And now I come to the beginning of the end. Hitherto much has been surmise and inference and hearsay. It is my painful task to relate now, as dispassionately and as accurately as I can, what actually occurred under my own notice, and to reduce to writing the events which preceded the death of my friend.

Toward the end of the winter Cowles remarked to me that he intended to marry Miss Northcott as soon as possible— probably some time in the spring. He was, as I have already remarked, fairly well off, and the young lady had some money of her own, so that there was no pecuniary reason for a long engagement. "We are going to take a little house out at Corstorphine," he said, "and we hope to see your face at our table, Bob, as often as you can possibly come." I thanked him, and tried to shake off my apprehensions, and persuade myself that all would yet be well.

It was about three weeks before the time fixed for the marriage, that Cowles remarked to me one evening that he feared he would be late that night. "I have had a note from Kate," he said, "asking me to call about eleven o'clock tonight, which seems rather a late hour, but perhaps she wants to talk over something quietly after old Mrs. Merton retires."

It was not until after my friend's departure that I suddenly recollected the mysterious interview which I had been told of as preceding the suicide of young Prescott. Then I thought of the ravings of poor Reeves, rendered more tragic by the fact that I had heard that very day of his death. What was the meaning of it all? Had this woman some baleful secret to disclose which must be known before her marriage? Was it some reason which forbade her to marry? Or was it some reason which forbade others to marry her? I felt so uneasy that I would have followed Cowles, even at the risk of offending him, and endeavoured to dissuade him from keeping his appointment, but a glance at the clock showed me that I was too late.

I was determined to wait up for his return, so I piled some coals upon the fire and took down a novel from the shelf. My thoughts proved more interesting than the book, however, and I threw it on one side. An indefinable feeling of anxiety and depression weighed upon me. Twelve o'clock came, and then half-past, without any sign of my friend. It was nearly one when I heard a step in the street outside, and then a knocking at the door. I was surprised, as I knew that my friend always carried a key—however, I hurried down and undid the latch. As the door flew open I knew in a moment that my worst apprehensions had been fulfilled. Barrington Cowles was leaning against the railings outside with his face sunk upon his breast, and his whole attitude expressive of the most intense despondency. As he passed in he gave a stagger, and would have fallen had I not thrown my left arm around him. Supporting him with this, and holding the lamp in my other hand, I led him slowly upstairs into our sitting-room. He sank down upon the sofa without a word. Now that I could get a good view of him, I was horrified to see the change which had come over him. His face was deadly pale, and his very lips were bloodless. His cheeks and forehead were clammy, his eyes glazed, and his whole expression altered. He looked like a man who had gone through some terrible ordeal, and was thoroughly unnerved.

"My dear fellow, what is the matter?" I asked, breaking the silence. "Nothing amiss, I trust? Are you unwell?"

"Brandy!" he gasped. "Give me some brandy!"

I took out the decanter, and was about to help him, when he snatched it from me with a trembling hand, and poured out nearly half a tumbler of the spirit. He was usually a most abstemious man, but he took this off at a gulp without adding any water to it.

It seemed to do him good, for the colour began to come back to his face, and he leaned upon his elbow.

"My engagement is off, Bob," he said, trying to speak calmly, but with a tremor in his voice which he could not conceal. "It is all over."

"Cheer up!" I answered, trying to encourage him. Don't get down on your luck. How was it? What was it all about?"

"About?" he groaned, covering his face with his hands. "If I did tell you, Bob, you would not believe it. It is too dreadful—too horrible—unutterably awful and incredible! O Kate, Kate!"

and he rocked himself to and fro in his grief; "I pictured you an angel and I find you a—"

"A what?" I asked, for he had paused.

He looked at me with a vacant stare, and then suddenly burst out, waving his arms: "A fiend!" he cried. "A ghoul from the pit! A vampire soul behind a lovely face! Now, God forgive me!" he went on in a lower tone, turning his face to the wall. "I have said more than I should. I have loved her too much to speak of her as she is. I love her too much now."

He lay still for some time, and I had hoped that the brandy had had the effect of sending him to sleep, when he suddenly turned his face toward me.

"Did you ever read of wehr-wolves?" he asked.

I answered that I had.

"There is a story," he said thoughtfully, "in one of Marryat's books, about a beautiful woman who took the form of a wolf at night and devoured her own children. I wonder what put that idea into Marryat's head?"

He pondered for some minutes, and then he cried out for some more brandy. There was a small bottle of laudanum upon the table, and I managed, by insisting upon helping him myself, to mix about half a drachm with the spirits. He drank it off, and sank his head once more upon the pillow. "Anything better than that," he groaned. "Death is better than that. Crime and cruelty; cruelty and crime. Anything is better than that," and so on, with the monotonous refrain, until at last the words became indistinct, his eyelids closed over his weary eyes, and he sank into a profound slumber. I carried him into his bedroom without arousing him; and making a couch for myself out of the chairs, I remained by his side all night.

In the morning Barrington Cowles was in a high fever. For weeks he lingered between life and death. The highest medical skill of Edinburgh was called in, and his vigorous constitution slowly got the better of his disease. I nursed him during this anxious time; but through all his wild delirium and ravings he never let a word escape him which explained the mystery connected with Miss Northcott. Sometimes he spoke of her in the tenderest words and most loving voice. At others he screamed out that she was a fiend, and stretched out his arms, as if to keep her off. Several times he cried that he would not sell his soul for a beautiful face, and then he would moan in a most piteous voice, "But I love her—I love her for all that; I shall never cease to love her."

When he came to himself he was an altered man. His severe illness had emaciated him greatly, but his dark eyes had lost none of their brightness. They shone out with startling brilliancy from under his dark, overhanging brows. His manner was eccentric and variable—sometimes irritable, sometimes recklessly mirthful, but never natural. He would glance about him in a strange, suspicious manner, like one who feared something, and yet hardly knew what it was he dreaded. He never mentioned Miss Northcott's name—never until that fatal evening of which I have now to speak.

In an endeavour to break the current of his thoughts by frequent change of scene, I travelled with him through the highlands of Scotland, and afterwards down the east coast. In one of these peregrinations of ours we visited the Isle of May, an island near the mouth of the Firth of Forth, which, except in the tourist season, is singularly barren and desolate. Beyond the keeper of the lighthouse there are only one or two families of poor fisherfolk, who sustain a precarious existence by their nets, and by the capture of cormorants and solan geese. This grim spot seemed to have such a fascination for Cowles that we engaged a room in one of the fishermen's huts, with the intention of passing a week or two there. I found it very dull, but the loneliness appeared to be a relief to my friend's mind. He lost the look of apprehension which had become habitual to him, and became something like his old self.

He would wander round the island all day, looking down from the summit of the great cliffs which gird it round, and watching the long green waves as they came booming in and burst in a shower of spray over the rocks beneath.

One night—I think it was our third or fourth on the island—Barrington Cowles and I went outside the cottage before retiring to rest, to enjoy a little fresh air, for our room was small, and the rough lamp caused an unpleasant odour. How well I remember every little circumstance in connection with that night! It promised to be tempestuous, for the clouds were piling up in the north-west, and the dark wrack was drifting across the face of the moon, throwing alternate belts of light and shade upon the rugged surface of the island and the restless sea beyond.

We were standing talking close by the door of the cottage, and I was thinking to myself that my friend was more cheerful than he had been since his illness, when he gave a sudden, sharp cry, and looking round at him I saw, by the light of the moon, an expression of unutterable horror come over his features. His eyes became fixed and staring, as if riveted upon some approaching object, and he extended his long thin forefinger, which quivered as he pointed.

"Look there!" he cried. "It is she! It is she! You see her there coming down the side of the brae." He gripped me convulsively by the wrist as he spoke. "There she is, coming toward us!"

"Who?" I cried, straining my eyes into the darkness.

"She—Kate—Kate Northcott!" he screamed. "She has come for me. Hold me fast, old friend. Don't let me go!"

"Hold up, old man," I said, clapping him on the shoulder. "Pull yourself together; you are dreaming; there is nothing to fear."

"She is gone!" he cried, with a gasp of relief. "No, by heaven! there she is again, and nearer—coming nearer. She told me she would come for me, and she keeps her word."

"Come into the house," I said. His hand, as I grasped it, was as cold as ice.

"Ah, I knew it!" he shouted. "There she is, waving her arms. She is beckoning to me. It is the signal. I must go. I am coming, Kate; I am coming!"

I threw my arms around him, but he burst from me with superhuman strength, and dashed into the darkness of the night. I followed him, calling to him to stop, but he ran the more swiftly. When the moon shone out between the clouds I could catch a glimpse of his dark figure, running rapidly in a straight line, as if to reach some definite goal. It may have been imagination, but it seemed to me that in the flickering light I could distinguish a vague something in front of him—a shimmering form which eluded his grasp and led him onwards. I saw his outlines stand out hard against the sky behind him as he surmounted the brow of a little hill, then he disappeared, and that was the last ever seen by mortal eye of Barrington Cowles.

The fishermen and I walked round the island all that night with lanterns, and examined every nook and corner without seeing a trace of my poor lost friend. The direction in which he had been running terminated in a rugged line of jagged cliffs overhanging the sea. At one place here the edge was somewhat crumbled, and there appeared marks upon the turf which might have been left by human feet. We lay upon our faces at this spot, and peered with our lanterns over the edge, looking down on the boiling surge two hundred feet below. As we lay there, suddenly, above the beating of the waves and the howling of the wind, there rose a strange wild screech from the abyss below. The fishermen—a naturally superstitious race—averred that it was the sound of a woman's laughter, and I could hardly persuade them to continue the search. For my own part I think it may have been the cry of some sea-fowl startled from its nest by the flash of the lantern. However that may be, I never wish to hear such a sound again.

And now I have come to the end of the painful duty which I have undertaken. I have told as plainly and as accurately as I could the story of the death of John Barrington Cowles, and the train of events which preceded it. I am aware that to others the sad episode seemed commonplace enough. Here is the prosaic account which appeared in the Scotsman a couple of days afterwards:—"Sad Occurrence on the Isle of May.— The Isle of May has been the scene of a sad disaster. Mr. John Barrington Cowles, a gentleman well known in University circles as a most distinguished student, and the present holder of the Neil Arnott prize for physics, has been recruiting his health in this quiet retreat. The night before last he suddenly left his friend, Mr. Robert Armitage, and he has not since been heard of. It is almost certain that he has met his death by falling over the cliffs which surround the island. Mr. Cowles' health has been failing for some time, partly from over study and partly from worry connected with family affairs. By his death the University loses one of her most promising alumni."

I have nothing more to add to my statement. I have unburdened my mind of all that I know. I can well conceive that many, after weighing all that I have said, will see no ground for an accusation against Miss Northcott. They will say that, because a man of a naturally excitable disposition says and does wild things, and even eventually commits self-murder after a sudden and heavy disappointment, there is no reason why vague charges should be advanced against a young lady. To this, I answer that they are welcome to their opinion. For my own part, I ascribe the death of William Prescott, of Archibald Reeves, and of John Barrington Cowles to this woman with as much confidence as if I had seen her drive a dagger into their hearts.

You ask me, no doubt, what my own theory is which will explain all these strange facts. I have none, or, at best, a dim and vague one. That Miss Northcott possessed extraordinary powers over the minds, and through the minds over the bodies, of others, I am convinced, as well as that her instincts were to use this power for base and cruel purposes. That some even more fiendish and terrible phase of character lay behind this—some horrible trait which it was necessary for her to reveal before marriage—is to be inferred from the experience of her three lovers, while the dreadful nature of the mystery thus revealed can only be surmised from the fact that the very mention of it drove from her those who had loved her so passionately. Their subsequent fate was, in my opinion, the result of her vindictive remembrance of their desertion of her, and that they were forewarned of it at the time was shown by the words of both Reeves and Cowles. Above this, I can say nothing. I lay the facts soberly before the public as they came under my notice. I have never seen Miss Northcott since, nor do I wish to do so. If by the words I have written I can save any one human being from the snare of those bright eyes and that beautiful face, then I can lay down my pen with the assurance that my poor friend has not died altogether in vain.

† † † † †

The narrator tells how a beautiful but evil woman taunts her lovers, then destroys them with her psychic powers. "John Barrington Cowles" was published three years before the first Sherlock Holmes story appeared in Beeton's Christmas Annual for 1887.

John Richard Stephens included it in his vampire anthology Vampires, Wine & Roses (Berkley Books: New York, 1997), which also features stories by Doyle's friends: Rudyard Kipling, Robert Louis Stevenson, Bram Stoker, and H. G. Wells.

The Ring of Thoth

Mr. John Vansittart Smith, F. R.S., of 147-A Gower Street, was a man whose energy of purpose and clearness of thought might have placed him in the very first rank of scientific observers. He was the victim, however, of a universal ambition which prompted him to aim at distinction in many subjects rather than preeminence in one.

In his early days he had shown an aptitude for zoology and for botany which caused his friends to look upon him as a second Darwin, but when a professorship was almost within his reach he had suddenly discontinued his studies and turned his whole attention to chemistry. Here his researches upon the spectra of the metals had won him his fellowship in the Royal Society; but again he played the coquette with his subject, and after a year's absence from the laboratory he joined the Oriental Society, and delivered a paper on the Hieroglyphic and Demotic inscriptions of El Kab, thus giving a crowning example both of the versatility and of the inconstancy of his talents.

The most fickle of wooers, however, is apt to be caught at last, and so it was with John Vansittart Smith. The more he burrowed his way into Egyptology the more impressed he became by the vast field which it opened to the inquirer, and by the extreme importance of a subject which promised to throw a light upon the first germs of human civilisation and the origin of the greater part of our arts and sciences. So struck was Mr. Smith that he straightaway married an Egyptological young lady who had written upon the sixth dynasty, and having thus secured a sound base of operations he set himself to collect materials for a work which should unite the research of Lepsius and the ingenuity of Champollion. The preparation of this magnum opus entailed many hurried visits to the magnificent Egyptian collections of the Louvre, upon the last of which, no longer ago than the middle of last October, he became involved in a most strange and noteworthy adventure.

The trains had been slow and the Channel had been rough, so that the student arrived in Paris in a somewhat befogged and feverish condition. On reaching the Hotel de France, in the Rue Laffitte, he had thrown himself upon a sofa for a couple of hours, but finding that he was unable to sleep, he determined, in spite of his fatigue, to make his way to the Louvre, settle the point which he had come to decide, and take the evening train back to Dieppe. Having come to this conclusion, he donned his greatcoat, for it was a raw rainy day, and made his way across the Boulevard des Italiens and down the Avenue de l'Opera. Once in the Louvre he was on familiar ground, and he speedily made his way to the collection of papyri which it was his intention to consult.

The warmest admirers of John Vansittart Smith could hardly claim for him that he was a handsome man. His high-beaked nose and prominent chin had something of the same acute and incisive character which distinguished his intellect. He held his head in a birdlike fashion, and birdlike, too, was the pecking motion with which, in conversation, he threw out his objections and retorts. As he stood, with the high collar of his greatcoat raised to his ears, he might have seen from the reflection in the glass-case before him that his appearance was a singular one. Yet it came upon him as a sudden jar when an English voice behind him exclaimed in very audible tones, "What a queer-looking mortal!"

The student had a large amount of petty vanity in his composition which manifested itself by an ostentatious and overdone disregard of all personal considerations. He straightened his lips and looked rigidly at the roll of papyrus, while his heart filled with bitterness against the whole race of travelling Britons.

"Yes," said another voice, "he really is an extraordinary fellow."

"Do you know," said the first speaker, "one could almost believe that by the continual contemplation of mummies the chap has become half a mummy himself?"

"He has certainly an Egyptian cast of countenance," said the other.

John Vansittart Smith spun round upon his heel with the intention of shaming his countrymen by a corrosive remark or two. To his surprise and relief, the two young fellows who had been conversing had their shoulders turned toward him, and were gazing at one of the Louvre attendants who was polishing some brass-work at the other side of the room.

"Carter will be waiting for us at the Palais Royal," said one tourist to the other, glancing at his watch, and they clattered away, leaving the student to his labours.

"I wonder what these chatterers call an Egyptian cast of countenance," thought John Vansittart Smith, and he moved his position slightly in order to catch a glimpse of the man's face. He started as his eyes fell upon it. It was indeed the very face with which his studies had made him familiar. The regular statuesque features, broad brow, well-rounded chin, and dusky complexion were the exact counterpart of the innumerable statues, mummy-cases, and pictures which adorned the walls of the apartment.

The thing was beyond all coincidence. The man must be an Egyptian.

The national angularity of the shoulders and narrowness of the hips were alone sufficient to identify him.

John Vansittart Smith shuffled toward the attendant with some intention of addressing him. He was not light of touch in conversation, and found it difficult to strike the happy mean between the brusqueness of the superior and the geniality of the equal. As he came nearer, the man presented his side face to him, but kept his gaze still bent upon his work. Vansittart Smith, fixing his eyes upon the fellow's skin, was conscious of a sudden impression that there was something inhuman and preternatural about its appearance. Over the temple and cheek-bone it was as glazed and as shiny as varnished parchment. There was no suggestion of pores. One could not fancy a drop of moisture upon that arid surface. From brow to chin, however, it was crosshatched by a million delicate wrinkles, which shot and interlaced as though Nature in some Maori mood had tried how wild and intricate a pattern she could devise.

"Ou est la collection de Memphis?" asked the student, with the awkward air of a man who is devising a question merely for the purpose of opening a conversation.

"C'est la," replied the man brusquely, nodding his head at the other side of the room.

"Vous etes un Egyptien, n'est-ce pas?" asked the Englishman.

The attendant looked up and turned his strange dark eyes upon his questioner. They were vitreous, with a misty dry shininess, such as Smith had never seen in a human head before. As he gazed into them he saw some strong emotion gather in their depths, which rose and deepened until it broke into a look of something akin both to horror and to hatred.

"Non, monsieur; je suis Fransais." The man turned abruptly and bent low over his polishing. The student gazed at him for a moment in astonishment, and then turning to a chair in a retired corner behind one of the doors he proceeded to make notes of his researches among the papyri. His thoughts, however refused to return into their natural groove. They would run upon the enigmatical attendant with the sphinx-like face and the parchment skin.

"Where have I seen such eyes?" said Vansittart Smith to himself. "There is something saurian about them, something reptilian. There's the membrana nictitans of the snakes," he mused, bethinking himself of his zoological studies. "It gives a shiny effect. But there was something more here. There was a sense of power, of wisdom—so I read them—and of weariness, utter weariness, and ineffable despair. It may be all imagination, but I never had so strong an impression. By Jove, I must have another look at them!" He rose and paced round the Egyptian rooms, but the man who had excited his curiosity had disappeared.

The student sat down again in his quiet corner, and continued to work at his notes. He had gained the information which he required from the papyri, and it only remained to write it down while it was still fresh in his memory. For a time his pencil travelled rapidly over the paper, but soon the lines became less level, the words more blurred, and finally the pencil tinkled down upon the floor, and the head of the student dropped heavily forward upon his chest.

Tired out by his journey, he slept so soundly in his lonely post behind the door that neither the clanking civil guard, nor the footsteps of sightseers, nor even the loud hoarse bell which gives the signal for closing, were sufficient to arouse him.

Twilight deepened into darkness, the bustle from the Rue de Rivoli waxed and then waned, distant Notre Dame clanged out the hour of midnight, and still the dark and lonely figure sat silently in the shadow. It was not until close upon one in the morning that, with a sudden gasp and an intaking of the breath, Vansittart Smith returned to consciousness. For a moment it flashed upon him that he had dropped asleep in his study-chair at home. The moon was shining fitfully through the unshuttered window, however, and, as his eye ran along the lines of mummies and the endless array of polished cases, he remembered clearly where he was and how he came there. The student was not a nervous man. He possessed that love of a novel situation which is peculiar to his race. Stretching out his cramped limbs, he looked at his watch, and burst into a chuckle as he observed the hour. The episode would make an admirable anecdote to be introduced into his next paper as a relief to the graver and heavier speculations. He was a little cold, but wide awake and much refreshed. It was no wonder that the guardians had overlooked him, for the door threw its heavy black shadow right across him.

The complete silence was impressive. Neither outside nor inside was there a creak or a murmur. He was alone with the dead men of a dead civilisation. What though the outer city reeked of the garish nineteenth century! In all this chamber there was scarce an article, from the shrivelled ear of wheat to the pigment-box of the painter, which had not held its own against four thousand years. Here was the flotsam and jetsam washed up by the great ocean of time from that far-off empire. From stately Thebes, from lordly Luxor, from the great temples of Heliopolis, from a hundred rifled tombs, these relics had been brought. The student glanced round at the long silent figures who flickered vaguely up through the gloom, at the busy toilers who were now so restful, and he fell into a reverent and thoughtful mood. An unwonted sense of his own youth and insignificance came over him. Leaning back in his chair, he gazed dreamily down the long vista of rooms, all silvery with the moonshine, which extend through the whole wing of the widespread building. His eyes fell upon the yellow glare of a distant lamp.

John Vansittart Smith sat up on his chair with his nerves all on edge. The light was advancing slowly toward him, pausing from time to time, and then coming jerkily onwards. The bearer moved noiselessly. In the utter silence there was no suspicion of the pat of a footfall. An idea of robbers entered the Englishman's head. He snuggled up further into the corner. The light was two rooms off. Now it was in the next chamber, and still there was no sound. With something approaching to a thrill of fear the student observed a face, floating in the air as it were, behind the flare of the lamp. The figure was wrapped in shadow, but the light fell full upon the strange eager face. There was no mistaking the metallic glistening eyes and the cadaverous skin. It was the attendant with whom he had conversed.

Vansittart Smith's first impulse was to come forward and address him. A few words of explanation would set the matter clear, and lead doubtless to his being conducted to some side door from which he might make his way to his hotel. As the man entered the chamber, however, there was something so stealthy in his movements, and so furtive in his expression, that the Englishman altered his intention. This was clearly no ordinary official walking the rounds. The fellow wore felt-soled slippers, stepped with a rising chest, and glanced quickly from left to right, while his hurried gasping breathing thrilled the flame of his lamp. Vansittart Smith crouched silently back into the corner and watched him keenly, convinced that his errand was one of secret and probably sinister import.

There was no hesitation in the other's movements. He stepped lightly and swiftly across to one of the great cases, and, drawing a key from his pocket, he unlocked it. From the upper shelf he pulled down a mummy, which he bore away with him, and laid it with much care and solicitude upon the ground. By it he placed his lamp, and then squatting down beside it in Eastern fashion he began with long quivering fingers to undo the cerecloths and bandages which girt it round. As the crackling rolls of linen peeled off one after the other, a strong aromatic odour filled the chamber, and fragments of scented wood and of spices pattered down upon the marble floor.

It was clear to John Vansittart Smith that this mummy had never been unswathed before. The operation interested him keenly. He thrilled all over with curiosity, and his birdlike head protruded further and further from behind the door. When, however, the last roll had been removed from the four-thousand-year-old head, it was all that he could do to stifle an outcry of amazement. First, a cascade of long, black, glossy tresses poured over the workman's hands and arms. A second turn of the bandage revealed a low, white forehead, with a pair of delicately arched eyebrows. A third uncovered a pair of bright, deeply fringed eyes, and a straight, well-cut nose, while a fourth and last showed a sweet, full, sensitive mouth, and a beautifully curved chin. The whole face was one of extraordinary loveliness, save for the one blemish that in the centre of the forehead there was a single irregular, coffee-coloured splotch. It was a triumph of the embalmer's art. Vansittart Smith's eyes grew larger and larger as he gazed upon it, and he chirruped in his throat with satisfaction.

Its effect upon the Egyptologist was as nothing, however, compared with that which it produced upon the strange attendant. He threw his hands up into the air, burst into a harsh clatter of words, and then, hurling himself down upon the ground beside the mummy, he threw his arms round her, and kissed her repeatedly upon the lips and brow. "Ma petite!" he groaned in French. "Ma pauvre petite!" His voice broke with emotion, and his innumerable wrinkles quivered and writhed, but the student observed in the lamplight that his shining eyes were still as dry and tearless as two beads of steel. For some minutes he lay, with a twitching face, crooning and moaning over the beautiful head. Then he broke into a sudden smile, said some words in an unknown tongue, and sprang to his feet with the vigorous air of one who has braced himself for an effort.

In the centre of the room there was a large circular case which contained, as the student had frequently remarked, a magnificent collection of early Egyptian rings and precious stones. To this the attendant strode, and, unlocking it, he threw it open. On the ledge at the side he placed his lamp, and beside it a small earthenware jar which he had drawn from his pocket. He then took a handful of rings from the case, and with a most serious and anxious face he proceeded to smear each in turn with some liquid substance from the earthen pot, holding them to the light as he did so. He was clearly disappointed with the first lot, for he threw them petulantly back into the case, and drew out some more. One of these, a massive ring with a large crystal set in it, he seized and eagerly tested with the contents of the jar. Instantly he uttered a cry of joy, and threw out his arms in a wild gesture which upset the pot and sent the liquid streaming across the floor to the very feet of the Englishman. The attendant drew a red handkerchief from his bosom, and, mopping up the mess, he followed it into the corner, where in a moment he found himself face to face with his observer.

"Excuse me," said John Vansittart Smith, with all imaginable politeness. "I have been unfortunate enough to fall asleep behind this door."

"And you have been watching me?" the other asked in English, with a most venomous look on his corpselike face.

The student was a man of veracity. "I confess," said he, "that I have noticed your movements, and that they have aroused my curiosity and interest in the highest degree."

The man drew a long flamboyant-bladed knife from his bosom. "You have had a very narrow escape," he said. "Had I seen you ten minutes ago, I should have driven this through your heart. As it is, if you touch me or interfere with me in any way you are a dead man."

"I have no wish to interfere with you," the student answered. "My presence here is entirely accidental. All I ask is that you will have the extreme kindness to show me out through some side door." He spoke with great suavity, for the man was still pressing the tip of his dagger against the palm of his left hand, as though to assure himself of its sharpness, while his face preserved its malignant expression.

"If I thought——" said he. "But no, perhaps it is as well. What is your name?"

The Englishman gave it.

"Vansittart Smith," the other repeated. "Are you the same Vansittart Smith who gave a paper in London upon El Kab? I saw a report of it. Your knowledge of the subject is contemptible."

"Sir!" cried the Egyptologist.

"Yet it is superior to that of many who make even greater pretensions. The whole keystone of our old life in Egypt was not the inscriptions or monuments of which you make so much, but was our hermetic philosophy and mystic knowledge, of which you say little or nothing."

"Our old life!" repeated the scholar, wide-eyed; and then suddenly, "Good God, look at the mummy's face!"

The strange man turned and flashed his light upon the dead woman, uttering a long doleful cry as he did so. The action of the air had already undone all the art of the embalmer. The skin had fallen away, the eyes had sunk inwards, the discoloured lips had writhed away from the yellow teeth, and the brown mark upon the forehead alone showed that it was indeed the same face which had shown such youth and beauty a few short minutes before.

The man flapped his hands together in grief and horror. Then mastering himself by a strong effort he turned his hard eyes once more upon the Englishman.

"It does not matter," he said, in a shaking voice. "It does not really matter. I came here tonight with the fixed determination to do something. It is now done. All else is as nothing. I have found my quest. The old curse is broken. I can rejoin her. What matter about her inanimate shell so long as her spirit is awaiting me at the other side of the veil!"

"These are wild words," said Vansittart Smith. He was becoming more and more convinced that he had to do with a madman.

"Time presses, and I must go," continued the other. "The moment is at hand for which I have waited this weary time. But I must show you out first. Come with me."

Taking up the lamp, he turned from the disordered chamber, and led the student swiftly through the long series of the Egyptian, Assyrian, and Persian apartments. At the end of the latter he pushed open a small door let into the wall and descended a winding stone stair. The Englishman felt the cold fresh air of the night upon his brow. There was a door opposite him which appeared to communicate with the street. To the right of this another door stood ajar, throwing a spurt of yellow light across the passage. "Come in here!" said the attendant shortly.

Vansittart Smith hesitated. He had hoped that he had come to the end of his adventure. Yet his curiosity was strong within him. He could not leave the matter unsolved, so he followed his strange companion into the lighted chamber.

It was a small room, such as is devoted to a concierge. A wood fire sparkled in the grate. At one side stood a truckle bed, and at the other a coarse wooden chair, with a round table in the centre, which bore the remains of a meal. As the visitor's eye glanced round he could not but remark with an ever-recurring thrill that all the small details of the room were of the most quaint design and antique workmanship. The candlesticks, the vases upon the chimney-piece, the fire-irons, the ornaments upon the walls, were all such as he had been wont to associate with the remote past. The gnarled heavy-eyed man sat himself down upon the edge of the bed, and motioned his guest into the chair.

"There may be design in this," he said, still speaking excellent English. "It may be decreed that I should leave some account behind as a warning to all rash mortals who would set their wits up against workings of Nature. I leave it with you. Make such use as you will of it. I speak to you now with my feet upon the threshold of the other world.

"I am, as you surmised, an Egyptian—not one of the down-trodden race of slaves who now inhabit the Delta of the Nile, but a survivor of that fiercer and harder people who tamed the Hebrew, drove the Ethiopian back into the southern deserts, and built those mighty works which have been the envy and the wonder of all after generations. It was in the reign of Tuthmosis, sixteen hundred years before the birth of Christ, that I first saw the light. You shrink away from me. Wait, and you will see that I am more to be pitied than to be feared.

"My name was Sosra. My father had been the chief priest of Osiris in the great temple of Abaris, which stood in those days upon the Bubastic branch of the Nile. I was brought up in the temple and was trained in all those mystic arts which are spoken of in your own Bible. I was an apt pupil. Before I was sixteen I had learned all which the wisest priest could teach me. From that time on I studied Nature's secrets for myself, and shared my knowledge with no man.

"Of all the questions which attracted me there were none over which I laboured so long as over those which concern themselves with the nature of life. I probed deeply into the vital principle. The aim of medicine had been to drive away disease when it appeared. It seemed to me that a method might be devised which should so fortify the body as to prevent weakness or death from ever taking hold of it. It is useless that I should recount my researches. You would scarce comprehend them if I did. They were carried out partly upon animals, partly upon slaves, and partly on myself. Suffice it that their result was to furnish me with a substance which, when injected into the blood, would endow the body with strength to resist the effects of time, of violence, or of disease. It would not indeed confer immortality, but its potency would endure for many thousands of years. I used it upon a cat, and afterwards drugged the creature with the most deadly poisons. That cat is alive in Lower Egypt at the present moment. There was nothing of mystery or magic in the matter. It was simply a chemical discovery, which may well be made again.

"Love of life runs high in the young. It seemed to me that I had broken away from all human care now that I had abolished pain and driven death to such a distance. With a light heart I poured the accursed stuff into my veins. Then I looked round for some one whom I could benefit. There was a young priest of Thoth, Parmes by name, who had won my goodwill by his earnest nature and his devotion to his studies. To him I whispered my secret, and at his request I injected him with my elixir. I should now, I reflected, never be without a companion of the same age as myself.

"After this grand discovery I relaxed my studies to some extent, but Parmes continued his with redoubled energy. Every day I could see him working with his flasks and his distiller in the Temple of Thoth, but he said little to me as to the result of his labours. For my own part, I used to walk through the city and look around me with exultation as I reflected that all this was destined to pass away, and that only I should remain. The people would bow to me as they passed me, for the fame of my knowledge had gone abroad.

"There was war at this time, and the Great King had sent down his soldiers to the eastern boundary to drive away the Hyksos. A Governor, too, was sent to Abaris, that he might hold it for the King. I had heard much of the beauty of the daughter of this Governor, but one day as I walked out with Parmes we met her, borne upon the shoulders of her slaves. I was struck with love as with lightning. My heart went out from me. I could have thrown myself beneath the feet of her bearers. This was my woman. Life without her was impossible. I swore by the head of Horus that she should be mine. I swore it to the Priest of Thoth. He turned away from me with a brow which was as black as midnight.

"There is no need to tell you of our wooing. She came to love me even as I loved her. I learned that Parmes had seen her before I did, and had shown her that he too loved her, but I could smile at his passion, for I knew that her heart was mine. The white plague had come upon the city and many were stricken, but I laid my hands upon the sick and nursed them without fear or scathe. She marvelled at my daring. Then I told her my secret, and begged her that she would let me use my art upon her.

"'Your flower shall then be unwithered, Atma,' I said. 'Other things may pass away, but you and I, and our great love for each other, shall outlive the tomb of King Chefru.'

"But she was full of timid, maidenly objections. 'Was it right?' she asked, 'was it not a thwarting of the will of the gods? If the great Osiris had wished that our years should be so long, would he not himself have brought it about?'

"With fond and loving words I overcame her doubts, and yet she hesitated. It was a great question, she said. She would think it over for this one night. In the morning I should know her resolution. Surely one night was not too much to ask. She wished to pray to Isis for help in her decision.

"With a sinking heart and a sad foreboding of evil I left her with her tirewomen. In the morning, when the early sacrifice was over, I hurried to her house. A frightened slave met me upon the steps. Her mistress was ill, she said, very ill. In a frenzy I broke my way through the attendants, and rushed through hall and corridor to my Atma's chamber. She lay upon her couch, her head high upon the pillow, with a pallid face and a glazed eye. On her forehead there blazed a single angry purple patch. I knew that hell-mark of old. It was the scar of the white plague, the sign-manual of death.

"Why should I speak of that terrible time? For months I was mad, fevered, delirious, and yet I could not die. Never did an Arab thirst after the sweet wells as I longed after death. Could poison or steel have shortened the thread of my existence, I should soon have rejoined my love in the land with the narrow portal. I tried, but it was of no avail. The accursed influence was too strong upon me. One night as I lay upon my couch, weak and weary, Parmes, the priest of Thoth, came to my chamber. He stood in the circle of the lamplight, and he looked down upon me with eyes which were bright with a mad joy.

"'Why did you let the maiden die?' he asked. 'Why did you not strengthen her as you strengthened me?'

"'I was too late,' I answered. 'But I had forgot. You also loved her. You are my fellow in misfortune. Is it not terrible to think of the centuries which must pass ere we look upon her again? Fools, fools, that we were to take death to be our enemy!'

"'You may say that,' he cried with a wild laugh, 'the words come well from your lips. For me they have no meaning.'

"'What mean you?' I cried, raising myself upon my elbow. 'Surely, friend, this grief has turned your brain.' His face was aflame with joy, and he writhed and shook like one who hath a devil.

"'Do you know whither I go?' he asked.

"'Nay,' I answered, 'I cannot tell.'

"'I go to her,' said he. 'She lies embalmed in the further tomb by the double palm-tree beyond the city wall.'

"'Why do you go there?' I asked.

"'To die!' he shrieked, 'to die! I am not bound by earthen fetters.'

"'But the elixir is in your blood,' I cried.

"'I can defy it,' said he. 'I have found a stronger principle which will destroy it. It is working in my veins at this moment, and in an hour I shall be a dead man. I shall join her, and you shall remain behind.'

"As I looked upon him I could see that he spoke words of truth. The light in his eye told me that he was indeed beyond the power of the elixir.

"'You will teach me!' I cried.

"'Never!' he answered.

"'I implore you, by the wisdom of Thoth, by the majesty of Anubis!'

"'It is useless,' he said coldly.

"'Then I will find it out,' I cried.

"'You cannot,' he answered; 'it came to me by chance. There is one ingredient which you can never get. Save that which is in the ring of Thoth, none will ever more be made.

"'In the ring of Thoth!' I repeated. 'Where then is the ring of Thoth?'

"'That also you shall never know,' he answered. 'You won her love.'

Who has won in the end? I leave you to your sordid earth life. My chains are broken. I must go!' He turned upon his heel and fled from the chamber. In the morning came the news that the Priest of Thoth was dead.

"My days after that were spent in study. I must find this subtle poison which was strong enough to undo the elixir. From early dawn to midnight I bent over the test-tube and the furnace. Above all, I collected the papyri and the chemical flasks of the Priest of Thoth. Alas! they taught me little. Here and there some hint or stray expression would raise hope in my bosom, but no good ever came of it. Still, month after month, I struggled on. When my heart grew faint I would make my way to the tomb by the palm-trees.

"There, standing by the dead casket from which the jewel had been rifled, I would feel her sweet presence, and would whisper to her that I would rejoin her if mortal wit could solve the riddle.

"Parmes had said that his discovery was connected with the ring of Thoth. I had some remembrance of the trinket. It was a large and weighty circlet, made, not of gold, but of a rarer and heavier metal brought from the mines of Mount Harbal. Platinum, you call it. The ring had, I remembered, a hollow crystal set in it, in which some few drops of liquid might be stored. Now, the secret of Parmes could not have to do with the metal alone, for there were many rings of that metal in the Temple. Was it not more likely that he had stored his precious poison within the cavity of the crystal? I had scarce come to this conclusion before, in hunting through his papers, I came upon one which told me that it was indeed so, and that there was still some of the liquid unused.

"But how to find the ring? It was not upon him when he was stripped for the embalmer. Of that I made sure. Neither was it among his private effects. In vain I searched every room that he had entered, every box, and vase, and chattel that he had owned. I sifted the very sand of the desert in the places where he had been wont to walk; but, do what I would, I could come upon no traces of the ring of Thoth. Yet it may be that my labours would have overcome all obstacles had it not been for a new and unlooked for misfortune.

"A great war had been waged against the Hyksos, and the Captains of the Great King had been cut off in the desert, with all their bowmen and horsemen. The shepherd tribes were upon us like the locusts in a dry year. From the wilderness of Shur to the great bitter lake there was blood by day and fire by night. Abaris was the bulwark of Egypt, but we could not keep the savages back. The city fell. The Governor and the soldiers were put to the sword, and I, with many more, was led away into captivity.

"For years and years I tended cattle in the great plains by the Euphrates. My master died, and his son grew old, but I was still as far from death as ever. At last I escaped upon a swift camel, and made my way back to Egypt. The Hyksos had settled in the land which they had conquered, and their own King ruled over the country Abaris had been torn down, the city had been burned, and of the great Temple there was nothing left save an unsightly mound. Everywhere the tombs had been rifled and the monuments destroyed. Of my Atma's grave no sign was left. It was buried in the sands of the desert, and the palm-trees which marked the spot had long disappeared. The papers of Parmes and the remains of the Temple of Thoth were either destroyed or scattered far and wide over the deserts of Syria. All search after them was vain.

"From that time I gave up all hope of ever finding the ring or discovering the subtle drug. I set myself to live as patiently as might be until the effect of the elixir should wear away. How can you understand how terrible a thing time is, you who have experience only of the narrow course which lies between the cradle and the grave! I know it to my cost, I who have floated down the whole stream of history. I was old when Ilium fell. I was very old when Herodotus came to Memphis. I was bowed down with years when the new gospel came upon earth. Yet you see me much as other men are, with the cursed elixir still sweetening my blood, and guarding me against that which I would court. Now at last, at last I have come to the end of it!

"I have travelled in all lands and I have dwelt with all nations. Every tongue is the same to me. I learned them all to help pass the weary time. I need not tell you how slowly they drifted by, the long dawn of modern civilisation, the dreary middle years, the dark times of barbarism. They are all behind me now, I have never looked with the eyes of love upon another woman. Atma knows that I have been constant to her.

"It was my custom to read all that the scholars had to say upon Ancient Egypt. I have been in many positions, sometimes affluent, sometimes poor, but I have always found enough to enable me to buy the journals which deal with such matters. Some nine months ago I was in San Francisco, when I read an account of some discoveries made in the neighbourhood of Abaris. My heart leapt into my mouth as I read it. It said that the excavator had busied himself in exploring some tombs recently unearthed. In one there had been found an unopened mummy with an inscription upon the outer case setting forth that it contained the body of the daughter of the Governor of the city in the days of Tuthmosis. It added that on removing the outer case there had been exposed a large platinum ring set with a crystal, which had been laid upon the breast of the embalmed woman. This, then was where Parmes had hid the ring of Thoth. He might well say that it was safe, for no Egyptian would ever stain his soul by moving even the outer case of a buried friend.

"That very night I set off from San Francisco, and in a few weeks I found myself once more at Abaris, if a few sand-heaps and crumbling walls may retain the name of the great city. I hurried to the Frenchmen who were digging there and asked them for the ring. They replied that both the ring and the mummy had been sent to the Boulak Museum at Cairo. To Boulak I went, but only to be told that Mariette Bey had claimed them and had shipped them to the Louvre. I followed them, and there at last, in the Egyptian chamber, I came, after close upon four thousand years, upon the remains of my Atma, and upon the ring for which I had sought so long.

"But how was I to lay hands upon them? How was I to have them for my very own? It chanced that the office of attendant was vacant. I went to the Director. I convinced him that I knew much about Egypt. In my eagerness I said too much. He remarked that a Professor's chair would suit me better than a seat in the Conciergerie. I knew more, he said, than he did. It was only by blundering, and letting him think that he had over-estimated my knowledge, that I prevailed upon him to let me move the few effects which I have retained into this chamber. It is my first and my last night here.

"Such is my story, Mr. Vansittart Smith. I need not say more to a man of your perception. By a strange chance you have this night looked upon the face of the woman whom I loved in those faroff days. There were many rings with crystals in the case, and I had to test for the platinum to be sure of the one which I wanted. A glance at the crystal has shown me that the liquid is indeed within it, and that I shall at last be able to shake off that accursed health which has been worse to me than the foulest disease. I have nothing more to say to you. I have unburdened myself. You may tell my story or you may withhold it at your pleasure. The choice rests with you. I owe you some amends, for you have had a narrow escape of your life this night. I was a desperate man, and not to be baulked in my purpose. Had I seen you before the thing was done, I might have put it beyond your power to oppose me or to raise an alarm. This is the door. It leads into the Rue de Rivoli. Good night!"

The Englishman glanced back. For a moment the lean figure of Sosra the Egyptian stood framed in the narrow doorway. The next the door had slammed, and the heavy rasping of a bolt broke on the silent night.

It was on the second day after his return to London that Mr. John Vansittart Smith saw the following concise narrative in the Paris correspondence of the *Times*:

"Curious Occurrence in the Louvre.—Yesterday morning a strange discovery was made in the principal Egyptian Chamber. The ouvriers who are employed to clean out the rooms in the morning found one of the attendants lying dead upon the floor with his arms round one of the mummies. So close was his embrace that it was only with the utmost difficulty that they were separated. One of the cases containing valuable rings had been opened and rifled. The authorities are of opinion that the man was bearing away the mummy with some idea of selling it to a private collector, but that he was struck down in the very act by long-standing disease of the heart. It is said that he was a man of uncertain age and eccentric habits, without any living relations to mourn over his dramatic and untimely end."

† † † † †

An ancient Egyptian priest who served Osiris drank an elixir of immortality thousands of years ago and is searching for the antidote that will reunite him with his former lover in the afterlife. He believes that a ring which was buried with her mummy (which is now in the Louvre) is the key to accomplishing his goal.

In addition to being a fine story in its own right, "The Ring of Thoth" may have inspired Bram Stoker's novel, The Jewel of Seven Stars *(1903) in which Queen Thera's mummy is brought back to life temporarily. Modern readers may associate mummies with Boris Karloff (or Brendan Fraser) but when the quest for immortality is combined with resurrection from the dead, these revenants take on a vampiric coloring.*

E. and H. Heron's "The Story of Baelbow" brings a mummy and a vampire together, but C. Bryson Taylor's In the Dwellings of the Wilderness *(Henry Holt and Company: New York, 1904) is the first novel about a vampire mummy. After archeologists open the tomb of an Egyptian Princess, a woman "as beautiful as any creature created by god or the devil" appears to the men each night and entices them to follow her into the desert. Those who do so are never seen again.*

The Winning Shot

"*Caution.—The public are hereby cautioned against a man calling himself Octavius Gaster. He is to be recognised by his great height, his flaxen hair, and deep scar upon his left cheek, extending from the eye to the angle of the mouth. His predilection for bright colours—green neckties, and the like—may help to identify him. A slightly foreign accent is to be detected in his speech. This man is beyond the reach of the law, but is more dangerous than a mad dog. Shun him as you would shun the pestilence that walketh at noonday. Any communications as to his whereabouts will be thankfully acknowledged by A.C.U., Lincoln's Inn, London.*"

This is a copy of an advertisement which may have been noticed by many readers in the columns of the London morning papers during the early part of the present year. It has, I believe, excited considerable curiosity in certain quarters, and many guesses have been hazarded as to the identity of Octavius Gaster and the nature of the charge brought against him. When I state that the "caution" has been inserted by my elder brother, Arthur Cooper Underwood, barrister-at-law, upon my representations,

Bow Bells (11 July 1893) pp. 61-67.

it will be acknowledged that I am the most fitting person to enter upon an authentic explanation.

Hitherto the horror and vagueness of my suspicion, combined with my grief at the loss of my poor darling on the very eve of our wedding, have prevented me from revealing the events of last August to anyone save my brother.

Now, however, looking back, I can fit in many little facts almost unnoticed at the time, which form a chain of evidence that, though worthless in a court of law, may yet have some effect upon the mind of the public.

I shall therefore relate, without exaggeration or prejudice, all that occurred from the day upon which this man, Octavius Gaster entered Toynby Hall up to the great rifle competition. I know that many people will always ridicule the supernatural, or what our poor intellects choose to regard as supernatural, and that the fact of my being a woman will be thought to weaken my evidence. I can only plead that I have never been weak-minded or impressionable, and that other people formed the same opinions of Octavius Gaster that I did.

Now to the story.

It was at Colonel Pillar's place at Roborough, in the pleasant county of Devon, that we spent our autumn holidays. For some months I had been engaged to his eldest son Charley, and it was hoped that the marriage might take place before the termination of the Long Vacation.

Charley was considered "safe" for his degree, and in any case was rich enough to be practically independent, while I was by no means penniless.

The old Colonel was delighted at the prospect of the match, and so was my mother; so that look what way we would, there seemed to be no cloud above our horizon.

It was no wonder, then, that that August was a happy one. Even the most miserable of mankind would have laid his woes aside under the genial influence of the merry household at Toynby Hall.

There was Lieutenant Daseby, "Jack," as he was invariably called, fresh home from Japan in Her Majesty's ship Shark, who was on the same interesting footing with Fanny Pillar, Charley's sister, as Charley was with me, so that we were able to lend each other a certain moral support.

Then there was Harry, Charley's younger brother, and Trevor, his bosom friend at Cambridge.

Finally there was my mother, dearest of old ladies, beaming at us through her gold-rimmed spectacles, anxiously smoothing every little difficulty in the way of the two young couples, and never weary of detailing to them her own doubts and fears and perplexities when that gay young blood, Mr. Nicholas Underwood, came a-wooing into the provinces, and forswore Crockford's and Tattersall's for the sake of the country parson's daughter.

I must not, however, forget the gallant old warrior who was our host; with his time-honoured jokes, and his gout, and his harmless affectation of ferocity.

"I don't know what's come over the governor lately," Charley used to say. "He has never cursed the Liberal Administration since you've been here, Lottie; and my belief is that unless he has a good blow-off, that Irish question will get into his system and finish him."

Perhaps in the privacy of his own apartment the veteran used to make up for his self-abnegation during the day.

He seemed to have taken a special fancy to me, which he showed in a hundred little attentions.

"You're a good lass," he remarked one evening, in a very port-winey whisper. "Charley's a lucky dog, egad! and has more discrimination than I thought. Mark my words, Miss Underwood, you'll find that young gentleman isn't such a fool as he looks!"

With which equivocal compliment the Colonel solemnly covered his face with his handkerchief, and went off into the land of dreams.

How well I remember the day that was the commencement of all our miseries!

Dinner was over, and we were in the drawing-room, with the windows open to admit the balmy southern breeze.

My mother was sitting in the corner, engaged on a piece of fancy-work, and occasionally purring forth some truism which the dear old soul believed to be an entirely original remark, and founded exclusively upon her own individual experiences.

Fanny and the young lieutenant were billing and cooing upon the sofa, while Charley paced restlessly about the room.

I was sitting by the window, gazing out dreamily at the great wilderness of Dartmoor, which stretched away to the horizon, ruddy and glowing in the light of the sinking sun, save where some rugged tor stood out in bold relief against the scarlet background.

"I say," remarked Charley, coming over to join me at the window, "it seems a positive shame to waste an evening like this."

"Confound the evening!" said Jack Daseby.

"You're always victimising yourself to the weather. Fan and I ar'n't going to move off this sofa are we, Fan?"

That young lady announced her intention of remaining by nestling among the cushions, and glancing defiantly at her brother.

"Spooning is a demoralising thing—isn't it, Lottie?" said Charley, appealing laughingly to me.

"Shockingly so," I answered.

"Why, I can remember Daseby here when he was as active a young fellow as any in Devon; and just look at him now! Fanny, Fanny, you've got a lot to answer for!"

"Never mind him, my dear," said my mother, from the corner. "Still, my experience has always shown me that moderation is an excellent thing for young people. Poor dear Nicholas used to think so too. He would never go to bed of a night until he had jumped the length of the hearthrug. I often told him it was dangerous; but he would do it, until one night he fell on the fender and snapped the muscle of his leg, which made him limp till the day of his death, for Doctor Pearson mistook it for a fracture of the bone, and put him in splints, which had the effect of stiffening his knee. They did say that the doctor was almost out of his mind at the time from anxiety, brought on by his younger daughter swallowing a halfpenny, and that that was what caused him to make the mistake."

My mother had a curious way of drifting along in her conversation, and occasionally rushing off at a tangent, which made it rather difficult to remember her original proposition. On this occasion Charley had, however, stowed it away in his mind as likely to admit of immediate application.

"An excellent thing, as you say, Mrs. Underwood," he remarked, "and we have not been out today. Look here, Lottie, we have an hour of daylight yet. Suppose we go down and have a try for a trout, if your mamma does not object."

"Put something round your throat, dear," said my mother, feeling that she had been outmanoeuvred.

"All right, dear," I answered. "I'll just run up and put on my hat."

"And we'll have a walk back in the gloaming," said Charley, as he made for the door.

When I came down, I found my lover waiting impatiently with his fishing basket in the hall.

We crossed the lawn together, and passed the open drawing-groom windows, where three mischievous faces were looking at us.

"Spooning is a terribly demoralising thing," remarked Jack, reflectively staring up at the clouds.

"Shocking," said Fan; and all three laughed until they woke the sleeping Colonel, and we could hear them endeavouring to explain the joke to that ill-used veteran, who apparently obstinately refused to appreciate it.

We passed down the winding lane together, and through the little wooden gate, which opens on to the Tavistock road.

Charley paused for a moment after we had emerged and seemed irresolute which way to turn.

Had we but known it, our fate depended upon that trivial question.

"Shall we go down to the river, dear," he said, "or shall we try one of the brooks upon the moor?"

"Whichever you like?" I answered.

"Well, I vote that we cross the moor. We'll have a longer walk back that way," he added, looking down lovingly at the little white-shawled figure beside him.

The brook in question runs through a most desolate part of the country. By the path it is several miles from Toynby Hall; but we were both young and active, and struck out across the moor, regardless of rocks and furze-bushes.

Not a living creature did we meet upon our solitary walk, save a few scraggy Devonshire sheep, who looked at us wist-fully, and followed us for some distance, as if curious as to what could possibly have induced us to trespass upon their domains.

It was almost dark before we reached the little stream, which comes gurgling down through a precipitous glen, and mean-ders away to help to form the Plymouth "leat."

Above us towered two great columns of rock, between which the water trickled to form a deep, still pool at the bottom. This pool had always been a favourite spot of Charley's, and was a pretty cheerful place by day; but now, with the rising moon reflected upon its glassy waters, and throwing dark shadows from the overhanging rocks, it seemed anything rather than the haunt of a pleasure-seeker.

"I don't think, darling, that I'll fish, after all," said Charley, as we sat down together on a mossy bank. "It's a dismal sort of place, isn't it?"

"Very," said I, shuddering.

We'll just have a rest, and then we will walk back by the pathway. You're shivering. You're not cold, are you?"

"No," said I, trying to keep up my courage, "I'm not cold, but I'm rather frightened, though it's very silly of me."

"By jove!" said my lover. "I can't wonder at it, for I feel a bit depressed myself. The noise that water makes is like the gurgling in the throat of a dying man."

"Don't, Charley; you frighten me!"

"Come, dear, we mustn't get the blues," he said, with a laugh, trying to reassure me. "Let's run away from this charnel-house place, and—Look!—see!—good gracious! what is that?"

Charley had staggered back, and was gazing upwards with a pallid face.

I followed the direction of his eyes, and could scarcely suppress a scream.

I have already mentioned that the pool by which we were standing lay at the foot of a rough mound of rocks. On the top of this mound, about sixty feet above our heads, a tall dark figure was standing, peering down, apparently, into the rugged hollow in which we were.

The moon was just topping the ridge behind, and the gaunt, angular outlines of the stranger stood out hard and clear against its silvery radiance.

There was something ghastly in the sudden and silent appearance of this solitary wanderer, especially when coupled with the weird nature of the scene.

I clung to my lover in speechless terror, and glared up at the dark figure above us.

"Hullo, you sir!" cried Charley, passing from fear into anger, as Englishmen generally do. "Who are you, and what the devil are you doing?"

"Oh! I thought it, I thought it!" said the man who was overlooking us, and disappeared from the top of the hill.

We heard him scrambling about among the loose stones, and in another moment he emerged upon the banks of the brook and stood facing us.

Weird as his appearance had been when we first caught sight of him, the impression was intensified rather than removed by a closer acquaintance.

The moon shining full upon him revealed a long, thin face of ghastly pallor, the effect being increased by its contrast with the flaring green necktie which he wore.

A scar upon his cheek had healed badly and caused a nasty pucker at the side of his mouth, which gave his whole countenance a most distorted expression, more particularly when he smiled.

The knapsack on his back and stout staff in his hand announced him to be a tourist, while the easy grace with which he raised his hat on perceiving the presence of a lady showed that he could lay claim to the *savoir-faire* of a man of the world.

There was something in his angular proportions and the bloodless face which, taken in conjunction with the black cloak which fluttered from his shoulders, irresistibly reminded me of a bloodsucking species of bat which Jack Daseby had brought from Japan upon his previous voyage, and which was the bugbear of the servants' hall at Toynby.

"Excuse my intrusion," he said, with a slightly foreign lisp, which imparted a peculiar beauty to his voice. "I should have had to sleep on the moor had I not had the good fortune to fall in with you."

"Confound it, man!" said Charley. "Why couldn't you shout out, or give some warning? You quite frightened Miss Underwood when you suddenly appeared up there."

The stranger once more raised his hat as he apologised to me for having given me such a start.

"I am a gentleman from Sweden," he continued, in that peculiar intonation of his, "and am viewing this beautiful land of yours. Allow me to introduce myself as Doctor Octavius Gaster. Perhaps you could tell me where I may sleep, and how I can get from this place, which is truly of great size?"

"You're very lucky in falling in with us," said Charley. "It is no easy matter to find your way upon the moor."

"That can I well believe," remarked our new acquaintance.

"Strangers have been found dead on it before now," continued Charley. "They lose themselves, and then wander in a circle until they fall from fatigue."

"Ha, ha!" laughed the Swede. "It is not I, who have drifted in an open boat from Cape Blanco to Canary, that will starve upon an English moor. But how may I turn to seek an inn?"

"Look here!" said Charley, whose interest was excited by the stranger's allusion, and who was at all times the most open-hearted of men. "There's not an inn for many a mile round; and I daresay you have had a long day's walk already. Come home with us, and my father, the Colonel, will be delighted to see you and find you a spare bed."

"For this great kindness how can I thank you?" returned the traveller. "Truly, when I return to Sweden, I shall have strange stories to tell of the English and the hospitality!"

"Nonsense!" said Charley. "Come, we will start at once, for Miss Underwood is cold. Wrap the shawl well round your neck, Lottie, and we will be home in no time."

We stumbled along in silence, keeping as far as we could to the rugged pathway, sometimes losing it as a cloud drifted over the face of the moon, and then regaining it further on with the return of the light.

The stranger seemed buried in thought, but once or twice I had the impression that he was looking hard at me through the darkness as we strode along together.

"So," said Charley at last, breaking the silence, "you drifted about in an open boat, did you?"

"Ah, yes," answered the stranger, "many strange sights have I seen, and many perils undergone, but none worse than that. It is, however, too sad a subject for a lady's ears. She has been frightened once tonight."

"Oh, you needn't be afraid of frightening me now," said I, as leaned on Charley's arm.

"Indeed there is but little to tell, and yet is it sorrowful.

"A friend of mine, Karl Osgood of Upsala, and myself started on a trading venture. Few white men had been among the wandering Moors at Cape Blanco, but nevertheless we went, and for some months lived well, selling this and that, and gathering much ivory and gold.

"'Tis a strange country, where is neither wood nor stone, so that the huts are made from the weeds of the sea.

"At last, just as what we thought was a sufficiency, the Moors conspired to kill us, and came down against us in the night.

"Short was our warning, but we fled to the beach, launched a canoe and put out to sea, leaving everything behind. The Moors chased us, but lost us in the darkness; and when day dawned the land was out of sight.

"There was no country where we could hope for food nearer than Canary, and for that we made.

"I reached it alive, though very weak and mad; but poor Karl died the day before we sighted the islands.

"I gave him warning!

"I cannot blame myself in the matter.

"I said, 'Karl, the strength that you might gain by eating them would be more than made up for by the blood that you would lose!' He laughed at my words, caught the knife from my belt, cut them off and eat them; and he died."

"Eat what?" asked Charley.

"His ears!" said the stranger.

We both looked round at him in horror.

There was no suspicion of a smile or joke upon his ghastly face.

"He was what you call headstrong," he continued, "but he should have known better than to do a thing like that. Had he but used his will he would have lived as I did."

"And you think a man's will can prevent him from feeling hungry?" said Charley.

"What can it not do?" returned Octavius Gaster, and relapsed into a silence which was not broken until our arrival in Toynby Hall.

Considerable alarm had been caused by our nonappearance, and Jack Daseby was just setting off with Charley's friend Trevor in search of us. They were delighted, therefore, when we marched in upon them, and considerably astonished at the appearance of our companion.

"Where the deuce did you pick up that second Indian corpse?" asked Jack, drawing aside into the smoking room.

"Shut up, man; he'll hear you," growled Charley. "He's Swedish doctor on a tour, and a deuced good fellow. He went ill an open boat from What's-it's-name to another place. I've offered him a bed for the night."

"Well, all I can say is," remarked Jack, "that his face will never be his fortune."

"Ha, ha! Very good! very good!" laughed the subject of the remark, walking calmly into the room, to the complete discomfiture of the sailor. "No, it will never, as you say, in this country be my fortune,"—and he grinned until the hideous gash across the angle of his mouth made him look inore like the reflection in a broken mirror than anything else.

"Come upstairs and have a wash; I can lend you a pair of slippers," said Charley; and hurried the visitor out of the room to put an end to a somewhat embarrassing situation.

Colonel Pillar was the soul of hospitality, and welcomed Doctor Gaster as effusively as if he had been an old friend of the family.

"Egad, sir," he said, "the place is your own; and as long as you care to stop you are very welcome. We're pretty quiet down here, and a visitor is an acquisition."

My mother was a little more distant. "A very well informed young man, Lottie," she remarked to me, "but I wish he would wink his eyes more. I don't like to see people who never wink their eyes. Still, my dear, my life has taught me one great lesson, and that is that a man's looks are of very little importance compared with his actions."

With which brand new and eminently original remark, my mother kissed me and left me to my meditations.

Whatever Doctor Octavius Gaster might be physically, he was certainly a social success.

By next day he had so completely installed himself as a member of the household that the Colonel would not hear of his departure.

He astonished everybody by the extent and variety of his knowledge. He could tell the veteran considerably more about the Crimea than he knew himself; he gave the sailor information about the coast of Japan; and even tackled my athletic lover upon the subject of rowing, discoursing about levers of the first order, and fixed points and fulcra, until the unhappy Cantab was fain to drop the subject.

Yet all this was done so modestly and even deferentially, that he one could possibly feel offended at being beaten upon their own ground. There was a quiet power about everything he said and did which was very striking.

I remember one example of this, which impressed us all at the time.

Trevor had a remarkably savage bulldog, which, however fond of its master, fiercely resented any liberties from the rest of us. This animal was, it may be imagined, rather unpopular, but as it was the pride of the student's heart it was agreed not to banish it entirely, but to lock it up in the stable and give it a wide berth.

From the first, it seemed to have taken a decided aversion to our visitor, and showed every fang in its head whenever he approached it.

On the second day of his visit we were passing the stable in a body, when the growls of the creature inside arrested Doctor Gaster's attention.

"Ha!" he said. "There is that dog of yours, Mr. Trevor, is it not?"

"Yes; that's Towzer," assented Trevor.

"He is a bulldog, I think? What they call the national animal of England on the Continent?"

"Pure-bred," said the student, proudly.

"They are ugly animals—very ugly! Would you come into the stable and unchain him, that I may see him to advantage. It is a pity to keep an animal so powerful and full of life in captivity."

"He's rather a nipper," said Trevor, with a mischievous expression in his eye, "but I suppose you are not afraid of a dog."

"Afraid?—no. Why should I be afraid?"

The mischievous look on Trevor's face increased as he opened the stable door. I heard Charley mutter something to him about its being past a joke, but the other's answer was drowned by the hollow growling from inside.

The rest of us retreated to a respectable distance, while Octavius Gaster stood in the open doorway with a look of mild curiosity upon his pallid face.

"And those," he said, "that I see so bright and red in the darkness—are those his eyes?"

"Those are they," said the student, as he stooped down and unbuckled the strap.

"Come here!" said Octavius Gaster.

The growling of the dog suddenly subsided into a long whimper, and instead of making the furious rush that we expected, he rustled among the straw as if trying to huddle into a coiner.

"What the deuce is the matter with him?" exclaimed his perplexed owner.

"Come here!" repeated Gaster, in sharp metallic accents, with an indescribable air of command in them. "Come here!"

To our astonishment, the dog trotted out and stood at his side, but looking as unlike the usually pugnacious Towzer as is possible to conceive. His ears were drooping, his tail limp, and he altogether presented the very picture of canine humiliation.

"A very fine dog, but singularly quiet," remarked the Swede, as he stroked him down.

"Now, sir, go back!"

The brute turned and slunk back into its corner. We heard the rattling of its chain as it was being fastened, and next moment Trevor came out of the stable-door with blood dripping from his finger.

"Confound the beast!" he said. "I don't know what can have come over him. I've had him three years, and he never bit me before."

I fancy—I cannot say it for certain—but I fancy that there was a spasmodic twitching of the cicatrix upon our visitor's face, which betokened an inclination to laugh.

Looking back, I think that it was from that moment that I began to have a strange indefinable fear and dislike of the man.

Week followed week, and the day fixed for my marriage began to draw near.

Octavius Gaster was still a guest at Tovnby Hall, and, indeed, had so ingratiated himself with the proprietor that any hint at departure was laughed to scorn by that worthy soldier.

"Here you've come, sir, and here you'll stay; you shall, by Jove!"

Whereat Octavius would smile and shrug his shoulders and mutter something about the attractions of Devon, which would put the Colonel in a good humour for the whole day afterwards.

My darling and I were too much engrossed with each other to pay very much attention to the traveller's occupations. We used to come upon him sometimes in our rambles through the woods, sitting reading in the most lonely situations.

He always placed the book in his pocket when he saw us approaching. I remember on one occasion, however, that we stumbled upon him so suddenly that the volume was still lying open before him.

"Ah, Gaster," said Charley, "studying, is usual! What an old bookworm you are! What's the book? Ah, a foreign language; Swedish, I suppose."

"No, it is not Swedish," said Gaster, "it is Arabic."

"You don't mean to say you know Arabic? Al-abic-r—"

"Oh, very well—very well indeed!"

"And what's it about?" I asked, turning over the leaves of the musty old volume.

"Nothing that would interest one so young and fair as yourself, Miss Underwood," he answered, looking at me in a way which had become habitual to him of late. "It treats of the days when mind was stronger than what you call matter; when great spirits lived that were able to exist without these coarse bodies of ours, and could mould all things to their so-powerful wills."

"Oh, I see; a kind of ghost story," said Charley. "Well, adieu; we won't keep you from your studies."

We left him sitting in the little glen still absorbed in his mystical treatise. It must have been imagination which induced me, on turning suddenly round half an hour later, to think that I saw his familiar figure glide rapidly behind a tree.

I mentioned it to Charley at the time, but he laughed my idea to scorn.

I alluded just now to a peculiar manner which this man Gaster had of looking at me. His eyes seemed to lose their usual steely expression when he did so, and soften into something which might be almost called caressing. They seemed to influence me strangely, for I could always tell, without looking at him, when his gaze was fixed upon me.

Sometimes I fancied that this idea was simply due to a disordered nervous sytem or morbid imagination; but my mother dispelled that delusion from my mind.

"Do you know," she said, coming into my bedroom one night, and carefully shutting the door behind her, "if the idea was not so utterly preposterous, Lottie, I should say that that Doctor was madly in love with you?"

"Nonsense, ma!" said I, nearly dropping my candle in my consternation at the thought.

"I really think so, Lottie," continued my mother. "He's got a way of looking which is very like that of your poor dear father, Nicholas, before we were married. Something of this sort, you know."

And the old lady cast an utterly heart-broken glance at the bed-post.

"Now, go to bed," said I, "and don't have such funny ideas. Why, poor Doctor Gaster knows that I am engaged as well as you do."

"Time will show," said the old lady, as she left the room; and I went to bed with the words still ringing in my ears.

Certainly, it is a strange thing that on that very night a thrill which I had come to know well ran through me, and awakened me from my slumbers.

I stole softly to the window, and peered out through the bars of the Venetian blinds, and there was the gaunt, vampire-like figure of our Swedish visitor standing upon the gravel-walk, and apparently gazing up at my window.

It may have been that he detected the movement of the blind, for, lighting a cigarette, he began pacing up and down the avenue.

I noticed that at breakfast next morning he went out of his way to explain the fact that he had been restless during the night, and had steadied his nerves by a short stroll and a smoke.

After all, when I came to consider it calmly, the aversion which I had against the man and my distrust of him were founded on very scanty grounds. A man might have a strange face, and be fond of curious literature, and even look approvingly at an engaged young lady, without being a very dangerous member of society.

I say this to show that even up to that point I was perfectly unbiased and free from prejudice in my opinion of Octavius Gaster.

"I say!" remarked Lieutenant Daseby, one morning. "What do you think of having a picnic today?"

"Capital!" ejaculated everybody.

"You see, they are talking of commissioning the old *Shark* soon, and Trevor here will have to go back to the mill. We may as well compress as much fun as we can into the time."

"What is it that you call picnic?" asked Doctor Gaster.

"It's another of our English institutions for you to study," said Charley. "It's our version of *fête champêtre*."

"Ah, I see! That will be very jolly!" acquiesced the Swede.

"There are half a dozen places we might go to," continued the Lieutenant. "There's the Lover's Leap, or Black Tor, or Beer Ferris Abbey."

"That's the best," said Charley. "Nothing like ruins for a picnic."

"Well the Abbey be it. How far is it?"

"Six miles," said Trevor.

"Seven by the road," remarked the Colonel, with military exactness. "Mrs. Underwood and I shall stay at home, and the rest of you can fit into the waggonette. You'll all have to chaperon each other."

I need hardly say that this motion was carried also without a division.

"Well," said Charley, "I'll order the trap to be round in half an hour, so you'd better all make the best of your time. We'll want salmon, and salad, and hard-boiled eggs, and liquor, and any number of things. I'll look after the liquor department. What will you do, Lottie?"

"I'll take charge of the china," I said.

"I'll bring the fish," said Daseby.

"And I the vegetables," added Fan.

"What will you do, Gaster?" asked Charley.

"Truly," said the Swede, in his strange, musical accents, "but little is left for me to do. I can, however, wait upon the ladies, and I can make what you call a salad."

"You'll be more popular in the latter capacity than in the former," said I, laughingly.

"Ah, you say so," he said, turning sharp round upon me, and flushing up to his flaxen hair. "Yes. Ha! ha! Very good!"

And with a discordant laugh, he strode out of the room.

"I say, Lottie," remonstrated my lover, "you've hurt the fellow's feelings."

"I'm sure I didn't mean to," I answered. "If you like I'll go after him and tell him so."

"Oh, leave him alone," said Daseby. "A man with a mug like that has no right to be so touchy. He'll come round right enough."

It was true that I had not had the slightest intention of offending Gaster, still I felt pained at having annoyed him.

After I had stowed away the knives and plates into the hamper, I found that the others were still busy at their various departments. The moment seemed a favourable one for apologising for my thoughtless remark, so without saying anything to anyone, I slipped away and ran down the corridor in the direction of our visitor's room.

I suppose I must have tripped along very lightly, or it may have been the rich thick matting of Toynby Hall—certain it is that Mr. Gaster seemed unconscious of my approach.

His door was open, and as I came up to it and caught sight of him inside, there was something so strange in his appearance that I paused, literally petrified for the moment with astonishment.

He had in his hand a small slip from a newspaper which he was reading, and which seemed to afford him considerable amusement. There was something horrible too in this mirth of his, for though he writhed his body about as if with laughter, no sound was emitted from his lips.

His face, which was half-turned toward me, wore an expression upon it which I had never seen on it before; I can only describe it as one of savage exultation.

Just as I was recovering myself sufficiently to step forward and knock at the door, he suddenly, with a last convulsive spasm of merriment, dashed down the piece of paper upon the table and hurried out by the other door of his room, which led through the billiard-room to the hall.

I heard his steps dying away in the distance, and peeped once more into his room.

What could be the joke that had moved this stern man to mirth? Surely some masterpiece of humour.

Was there ever a woman whose principles were strong enough to overcome her curiosity?

Looking cautiously round to make sure that the passage was empty, I slipped into the room and examined the paper which he had been reading.

It was a cutting from an English journal, and had evidently been long carried about and frequently perused, for it was almost illegible in places. There was, however, as far as I could see, very little to provoke laughter in its contents. It ran, as well as I can remember, in this way:

"SUDDEN DEATH IN THE DOCKS.—The master of the bark-rigged steamer Olga, from Tromsberg, was found lying dead in his cabin on Wednesday afternoon. Deceased was, it seems, of a violent disposition, and had had frequent altercations with the surgeon of the vessel. On this particular day he had been more than usually offensive, declaring that the surgeon was a necromancer and worshipper of the devil. The latter retired on deck to avoid further persecution. Shortly afterwards the steward had occasion to enter the cabin, and found the captain lying across the table quite dead. Death is attributed to heart disease, accelerated by excessive passion. An inquest will be held today."

And this was the paragraph which this strange man had regarded as the height of humour!

I hurried downstairs, astonishment, not unmixed with repugnance, predominating in my mind. So just was I, however, that the dark inference which has so often occurred to me since never for one moment crossed my mind. I looked upon him as a curious and rather repulsive enigma—nothing more.

When I met him at the picnic, all remembrance of my unfortunate speech seemed to have vanished from his mind. He made himself as agreeable as usual, and his salad was pronounced a *chef-d'oeuvre*, while his quaint little Swedish songs and his tales of all climes and countries alternately thrilled and amused us. It was after luncheon, however, that the conversation turned upon a subject which seemed to have special charms for his daring mind.

I forget who it was that broached the question of the supernatural. I think it was Trevor, by some story of a hoax which he had perpetrated at Cambridge. The story seemed to have a strange effect upon Octavius Gaster, who tossed his long arms about in impassioned invective as he ridiculed those who dared to doubt about the existence of the unseen.

"Tell me," he said, standing up in his excitement, "which among you has ever known what you call an instinct to fail. The wild bird has an instinct which tells it of the solitary rock upon the so boundless sea on which it may lay its egg, and is it disappointed? The swallow turns to the south when the winter is coming, and has its instinct ever led it astray? And shall this instinct which tells us of the unknown spirits around us, and which pervades every untaught child and every race so savage, be wrong? I say, never!"

"Go it, Gaster!" cried Charley.

"Take your wind and have another spell," said the sailor.

"No, never," repeated the Swede, disregarding our amusement. "We can see that matter exists apart from mind; then why should not mind exist apart from matter?"

"Give it up," said Daseby.

"Have we not proofs of it?" continued Gaster, his gray eyes gleaming with excitement. "Who that has read Steinberg's book upon spirits, or that by the eminent American, Madame Crowe, can doubt it? Did not Gustav von Spee meet his brother Leopold in the streets of Strasbourg, the same brother having been drowned three months before in the Pacific? Did not Home, the spiritualist, in open daylight, float above the house-tops of Paris? Who has not heard the voices of the dead around him? I myself—"

"Well, what of yourself?" asked half a dozen of us, in a breath.

"Bah! It matters nothing," he said, passing his hand over his forehead, and evidently controlling himself with difficulty. "Truly, our talk is too sad for such an occasion." And, in spite of all our efforts, we were unable to extract from Gaster any relation of his own experiences of the supernatural.

It was a merry day. Our approaching dissolution seemed to cause each one to contribute his utmost to the general amusement.

It was settled that after the coming rifle match Jack was to return to his ship and Trevor to his university. As to Charley and myself, we were to settle down into a staid respectable couple.

The match was one of our principal topics of conversation.

Shooting had always been a hobby of Charley's, and he was the captain of the Roborough company of Devon volunteers, which boasted some of the crack shots of the county. The match was to be against a picked team of regulars from Plymouth, and as they were no despicable opponents, the issue was considered doubtful. Charley had evidently set his heart on winning, and descanted long and loudly on the chances.

"The range is only a mile from Toynby Hall," he said, "and we'll all drive over, and you shall see the fun. You'll bring me luck, Lottie," he whispered, "I know you will."

Oh, my poor lost darling, to think of the luck that I brought you!

There was one dark cloud to mar the brightness of that happy day.

I could not hide from myself any longer the fact that my mother's suspicions were correct, and that Octavius Gaster loved me.

Throughout the whole of the excursion his attentions had been most assiduous, and his eyes hardly ever wandered away from me. There was a manner, too, in all that he said which spoke louder than words.

I was on thorns lest Charley should perceive it, for I knew his fiery temper; but the thought of such treachery never entered the honest heart of my lover.

He did once look up with mild surprise when the Swede insisted on relieving me of a fern which I was carrying; but the expression faded away into a smile at what he regarded as Gaster's effusive good-nature. My own feeling in the matter was pity for the unfortunate foreigner, and sorrow that I should have been the means of rendering him unhappy.

I thought of the torture it must be for a wild, fierce spirit like his to have a passion gnawing at his heart which honour and pride would alike prevent him from ever expressing in words. Alas! I had not counted upon the utter recklessness and want of principle of the man; but it was not long before I was undeceived.

There was a little arbour at the bottom of the garden, overgrown with honeysuckle and ivy, which had long been a favourite haunt of Charley and myself. It was doubly dear to us from the fact that it was here, on the occasion of my former visit, that words of love had first passed between us.

After dinner on the day following the picnic I sauntered down to this little summer-house, as was my custom. Here I used to wait until Charley, having finished his cigar with the other gentlemen, would come down and join me.

On that particular evening he seemed to be longer away than usual. I waited impatiently for his coming, going to the door every now and then to see if there were any signs if his approach.

I had just sat down again after one of those fruitless excursions, when I heard the tread of a male foot upon the gravel, and a figure emerged from among the bushes.

I sprang up with a glad smile, which changed to an expression of bewilderment, and even fear, when I saw the gaunt, pallid face of Octavius Gaster peering in at me.

There was certainly something about his actions which would have inspired distrust in the mind of anyone in my position. Instead of greeting me, he looked up and down the garden, as if to make sure that we were entirely alone. He then stealthily entered the arbour, and seated himself upon a chair, in such a position that he was between me and the doorway.

"Do not be afraid," he said, as he noticed my scared expression. "There is nothing to fear. I do but come that I may have talk with you.

"Have you seen Mr. Pillar?" I asked, trying hard to seem at my ease.

"Ha! Have I seen your Charley?" he answered, with a sneer upon the last words. "Are you then so anxious that he come? Can no one speak to thee but Charley, little one?"

"Mr. Gaster," I said, "you are forgetting yourself."

"It is Charley, Charley, ever Charley!" continued the Swede, disregarding my interruption. "Yes, I have seen Charley. I have told him that you wait upon the bank of the river, and he has gone thither upon the wings of love."

"Why have you told him this lie?" I asked, still trying not to lose my self-control.

"That I might see you; that I might speak to you. Do you, then, love him so? Cannot the thought of glory, and riches, and power, above all that the mind can conceive, win you from this first maiden fancy of yours? Fly with me, Charlotte, and all this, and more, shall be yours! Come!"

And he stretched his long arms out in passionate entreaty.

Even at that moment the thought flashed through my mind of how like they were to the tentacles of some poisonous insect.

"You insult me, sir!" I cried, rising to my feet. "You shall pay heavily for this treatment of an unprotected girl!"

"Ah, you say it," he cried, "but you mean it not. In your heart so tender there is pity left for the most miserable of men. Nay, you shall not pass me—you shall hear me first!"

"Let me go, sir!"

"Nay; you shall not go until you tell me if nothing that I can do may win your love."

"How dare you speak so?" I almost screamed, losing all my fear in my indignation. "You, who are the guest of my future husband! Let me tell you, once and for all, that I had no feeling toward you before save one of repugnance and contempt, which you have now converted into positive hatred!"

"And is it so?" he gasped, tottering backwards toward the doorway, and putting his hand up to his throat as if he found a difficulty in uttering the words. "And has my love won hatred in return? Ha!" he continued, advancing his face within a foot of mine as I cowered away from his glassy eyes. "I know it now. It is this—it is this!" and he struck the horrible cicatrix on his face with his clenched hand. "Maids love not such faces as this!

I am not smooth, and brown, and curly like this Charley—this brainless school-boy; this human brute who cares but for his sport and his—"

"Let me pass!" I cried, rushing at the door.

"No; you shall not go—you shall not!" he hissed, pushing me backwards.

I struggled furiously to escape from his grasp. His long arms seemed to clasp me like bars of steel. I felt my strength going, and was making one last despairing effort to shake myself loose, when some irresistible power from behind tore my persecutor away from me and hurled him backwards on to the gravel walk.

Looking up, I saw Charley's towering figure and square shoulders in the doorway.

"My poor darling!" he said, catching me in his arms. "Sit here in the angle. There is no danger now. I shall be with you in a minute."

"Don't Charley, don't!" I murmured, as he turned to leave me.

But he was deaf to my entreaties, and strode out of the arbour.

I could not see either him or his opponent from the position in which he had placed me, but I heard every word that was spoken.

"You villain!" said a voice that I could hardly recognise as my lover's. "So this is why you put me on a wrong scent?"

"That is why," answered the foreigner, in a tone of easy indifference.

"And this is how you repay our hospitality, you infernal scoundrel!"

"Yes; we amuse ourselves in your so beautiful summer-house."

"We! You are still on my ground and my guest, and I would wish to keep my hands from you; but, by heavens—"

Charley was speaking very low and in gasps now.

"Why do you swear? What is it, then?" asked the languid voice of Octavius Gaster.

"If you dare to couple Miss Underwood's name with this business, and insinuate that—"

"Insinuate? I insinuate nothing. What I say I say plain for all the world to hear. I say that this so chaste maiden did herself ask—"

I heard the sound of a heavy blow, and a great rattling of the gravel.

I was too weak to rise from where I lay, and could only clasp my hands together and utter a faint scream.

"You cur!" said Charley. "Say as much again, and I'll stop your mouth for all eternity!"

There was a silence, and then I heard Gaster speaking in a husky, strange voice.

"You have struck me!" he said. "You have drawn my blood!"

"Yes; I'll strike you again if you show your cursed face within these grounds. Don't look at me so! You don't suppose your hankey-pankey tricks can frighten me?"

An indefinable dread came over me as my lover spoke. I staggered to my feet and looked out at them, leaning against the door-way for support.

Charley was standing erect and defiant, with his young head in the air, like one who glories in the cause for which he battles.

Octavius Gaster was opposite him, surveying him with pinched lips and a baleful look in his cruel eyes. The blood was running freely from a deep gash on his lip, and spotting the front of his green necktie and white waistcoat. He perceived me the instant I emerged from the arbour.

"Ha, ha!" he cried, with a demoniacal burst of laughter. "She comes! The bride! She comes! Room for the bride! Oh, happy pair, happy pair!"

And with another fiendish burst of merriment he turned and disappeared over the crumbling wall of the garden with such rapidity that he was gone before we had realised what it was that he was about to do.

"Oh, Charley," I said, as my lover came back to my side, "you've hurt him!"

"Hurt him! I should hope I have! Come, darling, you are frightened and tired. He did not injure you, did he?"

"No; but I feel rather faint and sick."

"Come, we'll walk slowly to the house together. The rascal! It was cunningly and deliberately planned, too. He told me he had seen you down by the river, and I was going down when I met young Stokes, the keeper's son, coming back from fishing, and he told me that there was nobody there. Somehow, when Stokes said that, a thousand little things flashed into my mind at once, and I became in a moment so convinced of Gaster's villainy that I ran as hard as I could to the arbour."

"Charley," I said, clinging to my lover's arm, "I fear he will injure you in some way. Did you see the look in his eyes before he leaped the wall?"

"Pshaw!" said Charley. "All these foreigners have a way of scowling and glaring when they are angry, but it never comes to much."

"Still, I am afraid of him," said I, mournfully, as we went up the steps together, "and I wish you had not struck him."

"So do I," Charley answered, "for he was our guest, you know, in spite of his rascality. However, it's done now and it can't be helped, as the cook says in 'Pickwick,' and really it was more than flesh and blood could stand."

I must run rapidly over the events of the next few days. For me, at least, it was a period of absolute happiness. With Gaster's departure a cloud seemed to be lifted off my soul, and a depression which had weighed upon the whole household completely disappeared.

Once more I was the light-hearted girl that I had been before the foreigner's arrival. Even the Colonel forgot to mourn over his absence, owing to the all-absorbing interest in the coming competition in which his son was engaged.

It was our main subject of conversation and bets were freely offered by the gentlemen on the success of the Roborough team, though no one was unprincipled enough to seem to support their antagonists by taking them.

Jack Daseby ran down to Plymouth, and made a book on the event with some officers of the Marines, which he did in such an extraordinary way that we reckoned that in case of Roborough winning, he would lose seventeen shillings; while, should the other contingency occur, he would be involved in hopeless liabilities.

Charley and I had tacitly agreed not to mention the name of Gaster, nor to allude in any way to what had passed.

On the morning after our scene in the garden, Charley had sent a servant up to the Swede's room with instructions to pack up any things he might find there, and leave them at the nearest inn.

It was found, however, that all Gaster's effects had been already removed, though how and when was a perfect mystery to the servants.

I know of few more attractive spots than the shooting-range at Roborough. The glen in which it is situated is about half a mile long and perfectly level, so that the targets were able to range from two to seven hundred yards, the further ones simply showing as square white dots against the green of the rising hills behind.

The glen itself is part of the great moor and its sides, sloping gradually up, lose themselves in the vast rugged expanse. Its symmetrical character suggested to the imaginative mind that some giant of old had made an excavation in the moor with a titanic cheese-scoop, but that a single trial had convinced him of the utter worthlessness of the soil.

He might even be imagined to have dropped the despised sample at the mouth of the cutting which he had made, for there was a considerable elevation there, from which the riflemen were to fire, and thither we bent our steps on that eventful afternoon.

Our opponents had arrived there before us, bringing with them a considerable number of naval and military officers, while a long line of nondescript vehicles showed that many of the good citizens of Plymouth had seized the opportunity of giving their wives and families an outing on the moor.

An enclosure for ladies and distinguished guests had been erected on the top of the hill, which, with the marquee and refreshment tents, made the scene a lively one.

The country people had turned out in force, and were excitedly staking their half-crowns upon their local champions, which were as enthusiastically taken up by the admirers of the regulars.

Through all this scene of bustle and confusion we were safely conveyed by Charley, aided by jack and Trevor, who finally deposited us in a sort of rudimentary grandstand, from which we could look round at our ease on all that was going on.

We were soon, however, so absorbed in the glorious view, that we became utterly unconscious of the betting and pushing and chaff of the crowd in front of us.

Away to the south we could see the blue smoke of Plymouth curling up into the calm summer air, while beyond that was the great sea, stretching away to the horizon, dark and vast, save where some petulant wave dashed it with a streak of foam, as if rebelling against the great peacefulness of nature.

From the Eddystone to the Start the long rugged line of the Devonshire coast lay like a map before us.

I was still lost in admiration when Charley's voice broke half reproachfully on my ear.

"Why, Lottie," he said, "you don't seem to take a bit of interest in it!"

"Oh, yes I do, dear," I answered. "But the scenery is so pretty, and the sea is always a weakness of mine. Come and sit here, and tell me all about the match and how we are to know whether you are winning or losing."

"I've just been explaining it," answered Charley. "But I'll go over it again."

"Do, like a darling," said I; and settled myself down to mark, learn, and inwardly digest.

"Well," said Charley, "there are ten men on each side. We shoot alternately; first, one of our fellows, then one of them, and so on—you understand?"

"Yes, I understand that."

"First we fire at the two hundred yards range—those are the targets nearest of all. We fire five shots each at those. Then we fire five shots at the ones at five hundred yards—those middle ones; and then we finish up by firing at the seven hundred yards range—you see the target far over there on the side of the hill. Whoever makes the most points wins. Do you grasp it now?"

"Oh, yes; that's very simple," I said.

"Do you know what a bull's-eye is?" asked my lover.

"Some sort of sweetmeat, isn't it?" I hazarded.

Charley seemed amazed at the extent of my ignorance. "That's the bull's-eye," he said, "that dark spot in the centre of the target. If you hit that, it counts five. There is another ring, which you can't see, drawn round that, and if you get inside of it, it is called a 'centre,' and counts four. Outside that, again, is called an 'outer,' and only gives you three. You can tell where the shot has hit, for the marker puts out a coloured disc, and covers the place."

"Oh, I understand it all now," said I, enthusiastically. "I'll tell you what I'll do Charley; I'll mark the score on a bit of paper every shot that is fired, and then I'll always know how Roborough is getting on!"

"You can't do better," he laughed as he strode off to get his men together, for a warning bell signified that the contest was about to begin.

There was a great waving of flags and shouting before the ground could be got clear, and then I saw a little cluster of red-coats lying upon the greensward, while a similar group, in gray, took up their position to the left of them.

Pang! went a rifle-shot, and the blue smoke came curling up from the grass.

Fanny shrieked, while I gave a cry of delight, for I saw the white disc go up, which proclaimed a "bull," and the shot had been fired by one of the Roborough men. My elation was, however, promptly checked by the answering shot which put down five to the credit of the regulars. The next was also a "bull," which was speedily cancelled by another. At the end of the competition at the short range each side had scored forty-nine out of a possible fifty, and the question of supremacy was as undecided as ever.

"It's getting exciting," said Charley, lounging over the stand. "We begin shooting at the five hundred yards in a few minutes."

"Oh, Charley," cried Fanny in high excitement, "don't you go and miss, whatever you do!"

"I won't if I can help it," responded Charley, cheerfully.

"You made a 'bull' every time just now," I said.

"Yes, but it's not so easy when you've got your sights up. However, we'll do our best, and we can't do more. They've got some terribly good long-range men among them. Come over here, Lottie, for a moment."

"What is it, Charley?" I asked, as he led me away from the others. I could see by the look in his face that something was troubling him.

"It's that fellow," growled my lover. "What the deuce does he want to come here for? I hoped we had seen the last of him!"

"What fellow?" I gasped, with a vague apprehension at my heart.

"Why, that infernal Swedish fellow, Gaster!"

I followed the direction of Charley's glance, and there, sure enough, standing on a little knoll close to the place where the riflemen were lying, was the tall, angular figure of the foreigner.

He seemed utterly unconscious of the sensation which his singular appearance and hideous countenance excited among the burly farmers around him; but was craning his long neck about, this way and that, as if in search of somebody.

As we watched him, his eye suddenly rested upon us, and it seemed to me that, even at that distance, I could see a spasm of hatred and triumph pass over his livid features.

A strange foreboding came over me, and I seized my lover's hand in both my own.

"Oh, Charley," I cried, "don't—don't go back to the shooting! Say you are ill—make some excuse, and come away!"

"Nonsense, lass!" said he, laughing heartily at my terror. "Why, what in the world are you afraid of?"

"Of him!" I answered.

"Don't be so silly, dear. One would think he was a demi-god to hear the way in which you talk of him. But there! that's the bell, and I must be off."

"Well, promise, at least, that you will not go near him?" I cried, following Charley.

"All right—all right!" said he.

And I had to be content with that small concession.

The contest at the five hundred yards range was a close and exciting one. Roborough led by a couple of points for some time, until a series of "bulls" by one of the crack marksmen of their opponents turned the tables upon them.

At the end of it was found that the volunteers were three points to the bad—a result which was hailed by cheers from the Plymouth contingent and by long faces and black looks among the dwellers on the moor.

During the whole of this competition Octavius Gaster had remained perfectly still and motionless upon the top of the knoll on which he had originally taken up his position.

It seemed to me that he knew little of what was going on, for his face was turned away from the marksmen, and he appeared to be gazing into the distance.

Once I caught sight of his profile, and thought that his lips were moving rapidly as if in prayer, or it may have been the shimmer of the hot air of the almost Indian summer which deceived me. It was, however, my impression at the time.

And now came the competition at the longest range of all, which was to decide the match.

The Roborough men settled down steadily to their task of making up the lost ground; while the regulars seemed determined not to throw away a chance by over-confidence.

As shot after shot was fired, the excitement of the spectators became so great that they crowded round the marksmen, cheering enthusiastically at every "bull."

We ourselves were so far affected by the general contagion that we left our harbor of refuge, and submitted meekly to the pushing and rough ways of the mob, in order to obtain a nearer view of the champions and their doings.

The military stood at seventeen when the volunteers were at sixteen, and great was the despondency of the rustics.

Things looked brighter, however, when the two sides tied at twenty-four, and brighter still when the steady shooting of the local team raised their score to thirty-two against thirty of their opponents.

There were still, however, the three points which had been lost at the last range to be made up for.

Slowly the score rose, and desperate were the efforts of both parties to pull off the victory.

Finally, a thrill ran through the crowd when it was known that the last red-coat had fired, while one volunteer was still left, and that the soldiers were leading by four points.

Even *our* unsportsman-like minds were worked into a state of all-absorbing excitement by the nature of the crisis which now presented itself.

If the last representative of our little town could but hit the bull's-eye the match was won.

The silver cup, the glory, the money of our adherents, all depended upon that single shot.

The reader will imagine that my interest was by no means lessened when, by dint of craning my neck and standing on tiptoe, I caught sight of my Charley coolly shoving a cartridge into his rifle, and realised that it was upon his skill that the honour of Roborough depended.

It was this, I think, which lent me strength to push my way so vigorously through the crowd that I found myself almost in the first row and commanding an excellent view of the proceedings.

There were two gigantic farmers on each side of me, and while we were waiting for the decisive shot to be fired, I could not help listening to the conversation, which they carried on in broad Devon, over my head.

"Mun's a rare ugly 'un," said one.

"He is that," cordially assented the other.

"See to mun's een?"

"Eh, Jock; see to mun's moo', rayther!—Blessed if he bean't foamin' like Farmer Watson's dog—t'bull pup whot died mad o' the hydropathics."

I turned round to see the favoured object of these flattering comments, and my eyes fell upon Doctor Octavius Gaster, whose presence I had entirely forgotten in my excitement.

His face was turned toward me; but he evidently did not see me, for his eyes were bent with unswerving persistence upon a point midway apparently between the distant targets and himself.

I have never seen anything to compare with the extraordinary concentration of that stare, which had the effect of making his eyeballs appear gorged and prominent, while the pupils were contracted to the finest possible point.

Perspiration was running freely down his long, cadaverous face, and, as the farmer had remarked, there were some traces of foam at the corners of his mouth. The jaw was locked, as if with some fierce effort of the will which demanded all the energy of his soul.

To my dying day that hideous countenance shall never fade from my remembrance nor cease to haunt me in my dreams. I shuddered, and turned away my head in the vain hope that perhaps the honest farmer might be right, and mental disease be the cause of all the vagaries of this extraordinary man.

A great stillness fell upon the whole crowd as Charley, having loaded his rifle, snapped up the breech cheerily, and proceeded to lie down in his appointed place.

"That's right, Mr. Charles, sir that's right," I heard old McIntosh, the volunteer sergeant, whisper as I passed. "A cool head and a steady hand, that's what does the trick, sir!"

My lover smiled round at the gray-headed soldier as he lay down upon the grass, and then proceeded to look along the sight of his rifle amid a silence in which the faint rustling of the breeze among the blades of grass was distinctly audible.

For more than a minute he hung upon his aim. His finger seemed to press the trigger, and every eye was fixed upon the distant target, when suddenly, instead of firing, the rifleman staggered up to his knees, leaving his weapon upon the ground.

To the surprise of everyone, his face was deadly pale, and perspiration was standing on his brow.

"I say, McIntosh," he said, in a strange, gasping voice, "is there anybody standing between the target and me?"

"Between, sir? No, not a soul, sir," answered the astonished sergeant.

"There, man, there!" cried Charley, with fierce energy, seizing him by the arm, and pointing in the direction of the target, "Don't you see him there, standing right in the line of fire?"

"There's no one there!" shouted half a dozen voices.

"No one there? Well, it must have been my imagination," said Charley, passing his hand slowly over his forehead. "Yet I could have sworn—Here, give me the rifle!"

He lay down again, and having settled himself into position, raised his weapon slowly to his eye. He had hardly looked along the barrel before he sprang up again with a loud cry.

"There!" he cried. "I tell you I see it! A man dressed in volunteer uniform, and very like myself—the image of myself. "Is this a conspiracy?" he continued, turning fiercely on the crowd. "Do you tell me none of you see a man resembling myself walking from that target, and not two hundred yards from me as I speak?"

I should have flown to Charley's side had I not known how he hated feminine interference, and anything approaching to a scene. I could only listen silently to his strange wild words.

"I protest against this!" said an officer coming forward. "This gentleman must really either take his shot, or we shall remove our men off the field and claim the victory."

"But I'll shoot *him*!" gasped poor Charley.

"Humbug!" "Rubbish!" "Shoot him, then!" growled half a score of masculine voices.

"The fact is," lisped one of the military men in front of me to another, "the young fellow's nerves ar'n't quite equal to the occasion, and he feels it, and is trying to back out."

The imbecile young lieutenant little knew at this point how a feminine hand was longing to stretch forth and deal him a sounding box on the ears.

"It's Martell's three-star brandy, that's what it is," whispered the other. "The 'devils,' don't you know. I've had 'em myself, and know a case when I see it."

This remark was too recondite for my understanding, or the speaker would have run the same risk as his predecessor.

"Well, are you going to shoot or not?" cried several voices.

"Yes, I'll shoot," groaned Charley—"I'll shoot *him* through! It's murder—sheer *murder!*"

I shall never forget the haggard look which he cast round at the crowd. "I'm aiming *through* him, McIntosh," he murmured, as he lay down on the grass and raised the gun for the third time to his shoulder.

There was one moment of suspense, a spurt of flame, the crack of a rifle, and a cheer which echoed across the moor, and might have been heard in the distant village.

"Well done, lad—well done!" shouted a hundred honest Devonshire voices, as the little white disc came out from behind the marker's shield and obliterated the dark "bull" for the moment, proclaiming that the match was won.

"Well done, lad! It's Maister Pillar, of Toynby Hall. Here, let's gie mun a lift, carry mun home, for the honour o' Roborough. Come on, lads! There mun is on the grass. Wake up, Sergeant McIntosh. What be the matter with thee? Eh? What?"

A deadly stillness came over the crowd, and then a low incredulous murmur, changing to one of pity, with whispers of "leave her alone, poor lass—leave her to hersel'!" and then there was silence again, save for the moaning of a woman, and her short, quick cries of despair.

For, reader, my Charley, my beautiful, brave Charley, was lying cold and dead upon the ground, with the rifle still clenched in his stiffening fingers.

I heard kind words of sympathy. I heard Lieutenant Daseby's voice, broken with grief, begging me to control my sorrow, and felt his hand, as he gently raised me from my poor boy's body. This I can remember, and nothing more, until my recovery from my illness, when I found myself in the sick-room at Toynby Hall, and learned that three restless, delirious weeks had passed since that terrible day.

Stay!—do I remember nothing else?

Sometimes I think I do. Sometimes I think I can recall a lucid interval in the midst of my wanderings. I seem to have a dim recollection of seeing my good nurse go out of the room—of seeing a gaunt, bloodless face peering in through the half-open window, and of hearing a voice which said, "I have dealt with thy so beautiful lover, and I have yet to deal with thee." The words come back to me with a familiar ring, as if they had sounded in my ears before, and yet it may have been but a dream.

"And this is all!" you say. "It is for this that a hysterical woman hunts down a harmless *savant* in the advertisement columns of the newspapers! On this shallow evidence she hints at crimes of the most monstrous description!"

Well, I cannot expect that these things should strike you as they struck me. I can but say that if I were upon a bridge with Octavius Gaster standing at one end, and the most merciless tiger that ever prowled in an Indian jungle at the other, I should fly to the wild beast for protection.

For me, my life is broken and blasted. I care not how soon it may end, but if my words shall keep this man out of one honest household, I have not written in vain.

Within a fortnight after writing this narrative, my poor daughter disappeared. All search has failed to find her. A porter at the railway station has deposed to having seen a young lady resembling her description get into a first-class carriage with a tall, thin gentleman. It is, however, too ridiculous to suppose that she can have eloped after her recent grief, and without my having had any suspicions. The detectives are, however, working out the clue.—EMILY UNDERWOOD.

† † † † †

Arthur Conan Doyle mentions this story in a letter to Mary Doyle. "Last week," he says, "I sent 'The Winning Shot' to Temple Bar—a very ghastly Animal Magnetism vampirey sort of tale. It came back again but with a very complimentary letter, & Hogg says he should like to see it."[5]

By "vampirey" Doyle means that his story follows a primitive motif in which vampire-like sorcerers obtained immortality through rituals that involved sacrificing victims—usually women and often virgins—to the devil on a periodic basis. Many stories about Bluebeard and Charles Robert Maturin's Melmoth the Wanderer (1820) follow this formula. John William Polidori's "The Vampyre" (1819), in which Lord Ruthven slays a peasant girl in Greece then slakes his thirst on young Aubrey's sister the following year may be the most famous example of this form of vampirism.

5 Reprinted in: Jon Lellenberg, Daniel Stashower, and Charles Foley, ed. *Arthur Conan Doyle: A Life in Letters* (Penguin Books: New York, 2008) p. 171.

The Parasite

Chapter I

March 24. The spring is fairly with us now. Outside my laboratory window the great chestnut-tree is all covered with the big, glutinous, gummy buds, some of which have already begun to break into little green shuttlecocks. As you walk down the lanes you are conscious of the rich, silent forces of nature working all around you. The wet earth smells fruitful and luscious. Green shoots are peeping out everywhere. The twigs are stiff with their sap; and the moist, heavy English air is laden with a faintly resinous perfume. Buds in the hedges, lambs beneath them—everywhere the work of reproduction going forward!

I can see it without, and I can feel it within. We also have our spring when the little arterioles dilate, the lymph flows in a brisker stream, the glands work harder, winnowing and straining. Every year nature readjusts the whole machine. I can feel the ferment in my blood at this very moment, and as the cool sunshine pours through my window I could dance about in it like a gnat. So I should, only that Charles Sadler would rush upstairs to know what was the matter. Besides, I must remember that I am Professor Gilroy. An old professor may

(1894).

afford to be natural, but when fortune has given one of the first chairs in the university to a man of four-and-thirty he must try and act the part consistently.

What a fellow Wilson is! If I could only throw the same enthusiasm into physiology that he does into psychology, I should become a Claude Bernard at the least. His whole life and soul and energy work to one end. He drops to sleep collating his results of the past day, and he wakes to plan his researches for the coming one. And yet, outside the narrow circle who follow his proceedings, he gets so little credit for it. Physiology is a recognized science. If I add even a brick to the edifice, everyone sees and applauds it. But Wilson is trying to dig the foundations for a science of the future. His work is underground and does not show. Yet he goes on uncomplainingly, corresponding with a hundred semi-maniacs in the hope of finding one reliable witness, sifting a hundred lies on the chance of gaining one little speck of truth, collating old books, devouring new ones, experimenting, lecturing, trying to light up in others the fiery interest which is consuming him. I am filled with wonder and admiration when I think of him, and yet, when he asks me to associate myself with his researches, I am compelled to tell him that, in their present state, they offer little attraction to a man who is devoted to exact science. If he could show me something positive and objective, I might then be tempted to approach the question from its physiological side. So long as half his subjects are tainted with charlatanerie and the other half with hysteria we physiologists must content ourselves with the body and leave the mind to our descendants.

No doubt I am a materialist. Agatha says that I am a rank one. I tell her that is an excellent reason for shortening our engagement, since I am in such urgent need of her spirituality. And yet I may claim to be a curious example of the effect of education upon temperament, for by nature I am, unless I deceive myself, a highly psychic man. I was a nervous, sensitive boy, a dreamer, a somnambulist, full of impressions and intuitions. My black hair, my dark eyes, my thin, olive face, my tapering fingers, are all characteristic of my real temperament, and cause experts like Wilson to claim me as their own. But my brain is soaked with exact knowledge. I have trained myself to deal only with fact and with proof. Surmise and fancy have no place in my scheme of thought. Show me what I can see with my microscope, cut with my scalpel, weigh in my balance, and I will devote a lifetime to its investigation. But when you ask me to study feelings, impressions, suggestions, you ask me to do what is distasteful and even demoralizing. A departure from pure reason affects me like an evil smell or a musical discord.

Which is a very sufficient reason why I am a little loath to go to Professor Wilson's tonight. Still I feel that I could hardly get out of the invitation without positive rudeness; and, now that Mrs. Marden and Agatha are going, of course I would not if I could. But I had rather meet them anywhere else. I know that Wilson would draw me into this nebulous semi-science of his if he could. In his enthusiasm he is perfectly impervious to hints or remonstrances. Nothing short of a positive quarrel will make him realize my aversion to the whole business. I have no doubt that he has some new mesmerist or clairvoyant or medium or trickster of some sort whom he is going to exhibit to us, for even his entertainments bear upon his hobby. Well, it will be a treat for Agatha, at any rate. She is interested in it, as woman usually is in whatever is vague and mystical and indefinite.

10.50 P.M. This diary-keeping of mine is, I fancy, the outcome of that scientific habit of mind about which I wrote this morning. I like to register impressions while they are fresh. Once a day at least I endeavor to define my own mental position. It is a useful piece of self-analysis, and has, I fancy, a steadying effect upon the character. Frankly, I must confess that my own needs what stiffening I can give it. I fear that, after all, much of my neurotic temperament survives, and that I am far from that cool, calm precision which characterizes Murdoch or Pratt-Haldane. Otherwise, why should the tomfoolery which I have witnessed this evening have set my nerves thrilling so that even now I am all unstrung? My only comfort is that neither Wilson nor Miss Penclosa nor even Agatha could have possibly known my weakness.

And what in the world was there to excite me? Nothing, or so little that it will seem ludicrous when I set it down.

The Mardens got to Wilson's before me. In fact, I was one of the last to arrive and found the room crowded. I had hardly time to say a word to Mrs. Marden and to Agatha, who was looking charming in white and pink, with glittering wheat-ears in her hair, when Wilson came twitching at my sleeve.

"You want something positive, Gilroy," said he, drawing me apart into a corner. "My dear fellow, I have a phenomenon—a phenomenon!"

I should have been more impressed had I not heard the same before. His sanguine spirit turns every fire-fly into a star.

"No possible question about the bona fides this time," said he, in answer, perhaps, to some little gleam of amusement in my eyes. "My wife has known her for many years. They both come from Trinidad, you know. Miss Penclosa has only been in England a month or two, and knows no one outside the university circle, but I assure you that the things she has told us suffice in themselves to establish clairvoyance upon an absolutely scientific basis. There is nothing like her, amateur or professional. Come and be introduced!"

I like none of these mystery-mongers, but the amateur least of all. With the paid performer you may pounce upon him and expose him the instant that you have seen through his trick. He is there to deceive you, and you are there to find him out. But what are you to do with the friend of your host's wife? Are you to turn on a light suddenly and expose her slapping a surreptitious banjo? Or are you to hurl cochineal over her evening frock when she steals round with her phosphorus bottle and her supernatural platitude? There would be a scene, and you would be looked upon as a brute. So you have your choice of being that or a dupe. I was in no very good humor as I followed Wilson to the lady.

Anyone less like my idea of a West Indian could not be imagined. She was a small, frail creature, well over forty, I should say, with a pale, peaky face, and hair of a very light shade of chestnut. Her presence was insignificant and her manner retiring. In any group of ten women she would have been the last whom one would have picked out. Her eyes were perhaps her most remarkable, and also, I am compelled to say, her least pleasant, feature. They were gray in colour— gray with a shade of green—and their expression struck me as being decidedly furtive. I wonder if furtive is the word, or should I have said fierce? On second thoughts, feline would have expressed it better. A crutch leaning against the wall told me what was painfully evident when she rose: that one of her legs was crippled.

So I was introduced to Miss Penclosa, and it did not escape me that as my name was mentioned she glanced across at Agatha. Wilson had evidently been talking. And presently, no doubt, thought I, she will inform me by occult means that I am engaged to a young lady with wheat-ears in her hair. I wondered how much more Wilson had been telling her about me.

"Professor Gilroy is a terrible sceptic," said he. "I hope, Miss Penclosa, that you will be able to convert him."

She looked keenly up at me.

"Professor Gilroy is quite right to be sceptical if he has not seen anything convincing," said she. "I should have thought," she added, "that you would yourself have been an excellent subject."

"For what, may I ask?" said I.

"Well, for mesmerism, for example."

"My experience has been that mesmerists go for their subjects to those who are mentally unsound. All their results are vitiated, as it seems to me, by the fact that they are dealing with abnormal organisms."

"Which of these ladies would you say possessed a normal organism?" she asked. "I should like you to select the one who seems to you to have the best balanced mind. Should we say the girl in pink and white?—Miss Agatha Marden, I think the name is."

"Yes, I should attach weight to any results from her."

"I have never tried how far she is impressionable. Of course some people respond much more rapidly than others. May I ask how far your scepticism extends? I suppose that you admit the mesmeric sleep and the power of suggestion."

"I admit nothing, Miss Penclosa."

"Dear me, I thought science had got further than that. Of course I know nothing about the scientific side of it. I only know what I can do. You see the girl in red, for example, over near the Japanese jar. I shall will that she come across to us."

She bent forward as she spoke and dropped her fan upon the floor. The girl whisked round and came straight toward us, with an enquiring look upon her face, as if someone had called her.

"What do you think of that, Gilroy?" cried Wilson, in a kind of ecstasy.

I did not dare to tell him what I thought of it. To me it was the most barefaced, shameless piece of imposture that I had ever witnessed. The collusion and the signal had really been too obvious.

"Professor Gilroy is not satisfied," said she, glancing up at me with her strange little eyes. "My poor fan is to get the credit of that experiment. Well, we must try something else. Miss Marden, would you have any objection to my putting you off?"

"Oh, I should love it!" cried Agatha.

By this time all the company had gathered round us in a circle, the shirt-fronted men, and the white-throated women, some awed, some critical, as though it were something between a religious ceremony and a conjurer's entertainment. A red velvet arm-chair had been pushed into the centre, and Agatha lay back in it, a little flushed and trembling slightly from excitement. I could see it from the vibration of the wheat-ears. Miss Penclosa rose from her seat and stood over her, leaning upon her crutch.

And there was a change in the woman. She no longer seemed small or insignificant. Twenty years were gone from her age. Her eyes were shining, a tinge of colour had come into her sallow cheeks, her whole figure had expanded. So I have seen a dull-eyed, listless lad change in an instant into briskness and life when given a task of which he felt himself master. She looked down at Agatha with an expression which I resented from the bottom of my soul—the expression with which a Roman empress might have looked at her kneeling slave. Then with a quick, commanding gesture she tossed up her arms and swept them slowly down in front of her.

I was watching Agatha narrowly. During three passes she seemed to be simply amused. At the fourth I observed a slight glazing of her eyes, accompanied by some dilation of her pupils. At the sixth there was a momentary rigor. At the seventh her lids began to droop. At the tenth her eyes were closed, and her breathing was slower and fuller than usual. I tried as I watched to preserve my scientific calm, but a foolish, causeless agitation convulsed me. I trust that I hid it, but I felt as a child feels in the dark. I could not have believed that I was still open to such weakness.

"She is in the trance," said Miss Penclosa.

"She is sleeping!" I cried.

"Wake her, then!"

I pulled her by the arm and shouted in her ear. She might have been dead for all the impression that I could make. Her body was there on the velvet chair. Her organs were acting— her heart, her lungs. But her soul! It had slipped from beyond our ken. Whither had it gone? What power had dispossessed it? I was puzzled and disconcerted.

"So much for the mesmeric sleep," said Miss Penclosa. "As regards suggestion, whatever I may suggest Miss Marden will infallibly do, whether it be now or after she has awakened from her trance. Do you demand proof of it?"

"Certainly," said I.

"You shall have it." I saw a smile pass over her face, as though an amusing thought had struck her. She stooped and whispered earnestly into her subject's ear. Agatha, who had been so deaf to me, nodded her head as she listened.

"Awake!" cried Miss Penclosa, with a sharp tap of her crutch upon the floor. The eyes opened, the glazing cleared slowly away, and the soul looked out once more after its strange eclipse.

We went away early. Agatha was none the worse for her strange excursion, but I was nervous and unstrung, unable to listen to or answer the stream of comments which Wilson was pouring out for my benefit. As I bade her good-night Miss Penclosa slipped a piece of paper into my hand.

"Pray forgive me," said she, "if I take means to overcome your scepticism. Open this note at ten o'clock tomorrow morning. It is a little private test."

I can't imagine what she means, but there is the note, and it shall be opened as she directs. My head is aching, and I have written enough for tonight. Tomorrow I dare say that what seems so inexplicable will take quite another complexion. I shall not surrender my convictions without a struggle.

MARCH 25. I am amazed, confounded. It is clear that I must reconsider my opinion upon this matter. But first let me place on record what has occurred.

I had finished breakfast, and was looking over some diagrams with which my lecture is to be illustrated, when my housekeeper entered to tell me that Agatha was in my study and wished to see me immediately. I glanced at the clock and saw with sun rise that it was only half-past nine.

When I entered the room, she was standing on the hearth-rug facing me. Something in her pose chilled me and checked the words which were rising to my lips. Her veil was half down, but I could see that she was pale and that her expression was constrained.

"Austin," she said, "I have come to tell you that our engagement is at an end."

I staggered. I believe that I literally did stagger. I know that I found myself leaning against the bookcase for support.

"But—but—" I stammered. "This is very sudden, Agatha."

"Yes, Austin, I have come here to tell you that our engagement is at an end."

"But surely," I cried, "you will give me some reason! This is unlike you, Agatha. Tell me how I have been unfortunate enough to offend you."

"It is all over, Austin."

"But why? You must be under some delusion, Agatha. Perhaps you have been told some falsehood about me. Or you may have misunderstood something that I have said to you. Only let me know what it is, and a word may set it all right."

"We must consider it all at an end."

"But you left me last night without a hint at any disagreement. What could have occurred in the interval to change you so? It must have been something that happened last night. You have been thinking it over and you have disapproved of my conduct. Was it the mesmerism? Did you blame me for letting that woman exercise her power over you? You know that at the least sign I should have interfered."

"It is useless, Austin. All is over."

Her voice was cold and measured; her manner strangely formal and hard. It seemed to me that she was absolutely resolved not to be drawn into any argument or explanation. As for me, I was shaking with agitation, and I turned my face aside, so ashamed was I that she should see my want of control.

"You must know what this means to me!" I cried. "It is the blasting of all my hopes and the ruin of my life! You surely will not inflict such a punishment upon me unheard. You will let me know what is the matter. Consider how impossible it would be for me, under any circumstances, to treat you so. For God's sake, Agatha, let me know what I have done!"

She walked past me without a word and opened the door.

"It is quite useless, Austin," said she. "You must consider our engagement at an end." An instant later she was gone, and, before I could recover myself sufficiently to follow her, I heard the hall-door close behind her.

I rushed into my room to change my coat, with the idea of hurrying round to Mrs. Marden's to learn from her what the cause of my misfortune might be. So shaken was I that I could hardly lace my boots. Never shall I forget those horrible ten minutes. I had just pulled on my overcoat when the clock upon the mantel-piece struck ten.

Ten! I associated the idea with Miss Penclosa's note. It was lying before me on the table, and I tore it open. It was scribbled in pencil in a peculiarly angular handwriting.

"MY DEAR PROFESSOR GILROY [it said]: *Pray excuse the personal nature of the test which I am giving you. Professor Wilson happened to mention the relations between you and my subject of this evening, and it struck me that nothing could be more convincing to you than if I were to suggest to Miss Marden that she should call upon you at half-past nine tomorrow morning and suspend your engagement for half an hour or so. Science is so exacting that it is difficult to give a satisfying test, but I am convinced that this at least will be an action which she would be most unlikely to do of her own free will. Forget anything that she may have said, as she has really nothing whatever to do with it, and will certainly not recollect anything about it. I write this note to shorten your anxiety, and to beg you to forgive me for the momentary unhappiness which my suggestion must have caused you.*

Yours faithfully;
HELEN PENCLOSA."

Really, when I had read the note, I was too relieved to be angry. It was a liberty. Certainly it was a very great liberty indeed on the part of a lady whom I had only met once. But, after all, I had challenged her by my scepticism. It may have been, as she said, a little difficult to devise a test which would satisfy me.

And she had done that. There could be no question at all upon the point. For me hypnotic suggestion was finally established. It took its place from now onward as one of the facts of life. That Agatha, who of all women of my acquaintance has the best balanced mind, had been reduced to a condition of automatism appeared to be certain. A person at a distance had worked her as an engineer on the shore might guide a Brennan torpedo. A second soul had stepped in, as it were, had pushed her own aside, and had seized her nervous mechanism, saying: "I will work this for half an hour." And Agatha must have been unconscious as she came and as she returned. Could she make her way in safety through the streets in such a state? I put on my hat and hurried round to see if all was well with her.

Yes. She was at home. I was shown into the drawing-room and found her sitting with a book upon her lap.

"You are an early visitor, Austin," said she, smiling.

"And you have been an even earlier one," I answered.

She looked puzzled. "What do you mean?" she asked.

"You have not been out today?"

"No, certainly not."

"Agatha," said I seriously, "would you mind telling me exactly what you have done this morning?"

She laughed at my earnestness.

"You've got on your professional look, Austin. See what comes of being engaged to a man of science. However, I will tell you, though I can't imagine what you want to know for. I got up at eight. I breakfasted at half-past. I came into this room at ten minutes past nine and began to read the 'Memoirs of Mme. de Remusat.' In a few minutes I did the French lady the bad compliment of dropping to sleep over her pages, and I did you, sir, the very flattering one of dreaming about you. It is only a few minutes since I woke up."

"And found yourself where you had been before?"

"Why, where else should I find myself?"

"Would you mind telling me, Agatha, what it was that you dreamed about me? It really is not mere curiosity on my part."

"I merely had a vague impression that you came into it. I cannot recall anything definite."

"If you have not been out today, Agatha, how is it that your shoes are dusty?"

A pained look came over her face.

"Really, Austin, I do not know what is the matter with you this morning. One would almost think that you doubted my word. If my boots are dusty, it must be, of course, that I have put on a pair which the maid had not cleaned."

It was perfectly evident that she knew nothing whatever about the matter, and I reflected that, after all, perhaps it was better that I should not enlighten her. It might frighten her, and could serve no good purpose that I could see. I said no more about it, therefore, and left shortly afterward to give my lecture.

But I am immensely impressed. My horizon of scientific possibilities has suddenly been enormously extended. I no longer wonder at Wilson's demonic energy and enthusiasm. Who would not work hard who had a vast virgin field ready to his hand? Why, I have known the novel shape of a nucleolus, or a trifling peculiarity of striped muscular fibre seen under a 300-diameter lens, fill me with exultation. How petty do such researches seem when compared with this one which strikes at the very roots of life and the nature of the soul! I had always looked upon spirit as a product of matter. The brain, I thought, secreted the mind, as the liver does the bile. But how can this be when I see mind working from a distance and playing upon matter as a musician might upon a violin? The body does not give rise to the soul, then, but is rather the rough instrument by which the spirit manifests itself. The windmill does not give rise to the wind, but only indicates it. It was opposed to my whole habit of thought, and yet it was undeniably possible and worthy of investigation.

And why should I not investigate it? I see that under yesterday's date I said: "If I could see something positive and objective, I might be tempted to approach it from the physiological aspect." Well, I have got my test. I shall be as good as my word. The investigation would, I am sure, be of immense interest. Some of my colleagues might look askance at it, for science is full of unreasoning prejudices, but if Wilson has the courage of his convictions, I can afford to have it also. I shall go to him tomorrow morning—to him and to Miss Penclosa. If she can show us so much, it is probable that she can show us more.

CHAPTER II

MARCH 26. Wilson was, as I had anticipated, very exultant over my conversion, and Miss Penclosa was also demurely pleased at the result of her experiment. Strange what a silent, colourless creature she is save only when she exercises her power! Even talking about it gives her colour and life. She seems to take a singular interest in me. I cannot help observing how her eyes follow me about the room.

We had the most interesting conversation about her own powers. It is just as well to put her views on record, though they cannot, of course, claim any scientific weight.

"You are on the very fringe of the subject," said she, when I had expressed wonder at the remarkable instance of suggestion which she had shown me. "I had no direct influence upon Miss Marden when she came round to you. I was not even thinking of her that morning. What I did was to set her mind as I might set the alarum of a clock so that at the hour named it would go off of its own accord. If six months instead of twelve hours had been suggested, it would have been the same."

"And if the suggestion had been to assassinate me?"

"She would most inevitably have done so."

"But this is a terrible power!" I cried.

"It is, as you say, a terrible power," she answered gravely, "and the more you know of it the more terrible will it seem to you."

"May I ask," said I, "what you meant when you said that this matter of suggestion is only at the fringe of it? What do you consider the essential?"

"I had rather not tell you."

I was surprised at the decision of her answer.

"You understand," said I, "that it is not out of curiosity I ask, but in the hope that I may find some scientific explanation for the facts with which you furnish me."

"Frankly, Professor Gilroy," said she, "I am not at all interested in science, nor do I care whether it can or cannot classify these powers."

"But I was hoping——"

"Ah, that is quite another thing. If you make it a personal matter," said she, with the pleasantest of smiles, "I shall be only too happy to tell you anything you wish to know. Let me see; what was it you asked me? Oh, about the further powers. Professor Wilson won't believe in them, but they are quite true all the same. For example, it is possible for an operator to gain complete command over his subject—presuming that the latter is a good one. Without any previous suggestion he may make him do whatever he likes."

"Without the subject's knowledge?"

"That depends. If the force were strongly exerted, he would know no more about it than Miss Marden did when she came round and frightened you so. Or, if the influence was less powerful, he might be conscious of what he was doing, but be quite unable to prevent himself from doing it."

"Would he have lost his own will power, then?"

"It would be over-ridden by another stronger one."

"Have you ever exercised this power yourself?"

"Several times."

"Is your own will so strong, then?"

"Well, it does not entirely depend upon that. Many have strong wills which are not detachable from themselves. The thing is to have the gift of projecting it into another person and superseding his own. I find that the power varies with my own strength and health."

"Practically, you send your soul into another person's body."

"Well, you might put it that way."

"And what does your own body do?"

"It merely feels lethargic."

"Well, but is there no danger to your own health?" I asked.

"There might be a little. You have to be careful never to let your own consciousness absolutely go; otherwise, you might experience some difficulty in finding your way back again. You must always preserve the connection, as it were. I am afraid I express myself very badly, Professor Gilroy, but of course I don't know how to put these things in a scientific way. I am just giving you my own experiences and my own explanations."

Well, I read this over now at my leisure, and I marvel at myself! Is this Austin Gilroy, the man who has won his way to the front by his hard reasoning power and by his devotion to fact? Here I am gravely retailing the gossip of a woman who tells me how her soul may be projected from her body, and how, while she lies in a lethargy, she can control the actions of people at a distance. Do I accept it? Certainly not. She must prove and re-prove before I yield a point. But if I am still a sceptic, I have at least ceased to be a scoffer. We are to have a sitting this evening, and she is to try if she can produce any mesmeric effect upon me. If she can, it will make an excellent starting-point for our investigation. No one can accuse me, at any rate, of complicity. If she cannot, we must try and find some subject who will be like Caesar's wife. Wilson is perfectly impervious.

10 P.M. I believe that I am on the threshold of an epoch-making investigation. To have the power of examining these phenomena from inside—to have an organism which will respond, and at the same time a brain which will appreciate and criticise—that is surely a unique advantage. I am quite sure that Wilson would give five years of his life to be as susceptible as I have proved myself to be.

There was no one present except Wilson and his wife. I was seated with my head leaning back, and Miss Penclosa, standing in front and a little to the left, used the same long, sweeping strokes as with Agatha. At each of them a warm current of air seemed to strike me, and to suffuse a thrill and glow all through me from head to foot. My eyes were fixed upon Miss Penclosa's face, but as I gazed the features seemed to blur and to fade away. I was conscious only of her own eyes looking down at me, gray, deep, inscrutable. Larger they grew and larger, until they changed suddenly into two mountain lakes toward which I seemed to be falling with horrible rapidity. I shuddered, and as I did so some deeper stratum of thought told me that the shudder represented the rigor which I had observed in Agatha. An instant later I struck the surface of the lakes, now joined into one, and down I went beneath the water with a fulness in my head and a buzzing in my ears. Down I went, down, down, and then with a swoop up again until I could see the light streaming brightly through the green water. I was almost at the surface when the word "Awake!" rang through my head, and, with a start, I found myself back in the arm-chair, with Miss Penclosa leaning on her crutch, and Wilson, his note book in his hand, peeping over her shoulder. No heaviness or weariness was left behind. On the contrary, though it is only an hour or so since the experiment, I feel so wakeful that I am more inclined for my study than my bedroom. I see quite a vista of interesting experiments extending before us, and am all impatience to begin upon them.

MARCH 27. A blank day, as Miss Penclosa goes with Wilson and his wife to the Suttons'. Have begun Binet and Ferre's "Animal Magnetism." What strange, deep waters these are! Results, results, results—and the cause an absolute mystery. It is stimulating to the imagination, but I must be on my guard against that. Let us have no inferences nor deductions, and nothing but solid facts. I KNOW that the mesmeric trance is true; I KNOW that mesmeric suggestion is true; I KNOW that I am myself sensitive to this force. That is my present position. I have a large new note-book which shall be devoted entirely to scientific detail.

Long talk with Agatha and Mrs. Marden in the evening about our marriage. We think that the summer vac. (the beginning of it) would be the best time for the wedding. Why should we delay? I grudge even those few months. Still, as Mrs. Marden says, there are a good many things to be arranged.

MARCH 28. Mesmerized again by Miss Penclosa. Experience much the same as before, save that insensibility came on more quickly. See Note-book A for temperature of room, barometric pressure, pulse, and respiration as taken by Professor Wilson.

MARCH 29. Mesmerized again. Details in Note-book A.

MARCH 30. Sunday, and a blank day. I grudge any interruption of our experiments. At present they merely embrace the physical signs which go with slight, with complete, and with extreme insensibility. Afterward we hope to pass on to the phenomena of suggestion and of lucidity. Professors have demonstrated these things upon women at Nancy and at the Salpetriere. It will be more convincing when a woman demonstrates it upon a professor, with a second professor as a witness. And that I should be the subject—I, the sceptic, the materialist! At least, I have shown that my devotion to science is greater than to my own personal consistency. The eating of our own words is the greatest sacrifice which truth ever requires of us.

My neighbor, Charles Sadler, the handsome young demonstrator of anatomy, came in this evening to return a volume of Virchow's "Archives" which I had lent him. I call him young, but, as a matter of fact, he is a year older than I am.

"I understand, Gilroy," said he, "that you are being experimented upon by Miss Penclosa."

"Well," he went on, when I had acknowledged it, "if I were you, I should not let it go any further. You will think me very impertinent, no doubt, but, nonetheless, I feel it to be my duty to advise you to have no more to do with her."

Of course I asked him why.

"I am so placed that I cannot enter into particulars as freely as I could wish," said he. "Miss Penclosa is the friend of my friend, and my position is a delicate one. I can only say this: that I have myself been the subject of some of the woman's experiments, and that they have left a most unpleasant impression upon my mind."

He could hardly expect me to be satisfied with that, and I tried hard to get something more definite out of him, but without success. Is it conceivable that he could be jealous at my having superseded him? Or is he one of those men of science who feel personally injured when facts run counter to their preconceived opinions? He cannot seriously suppose that because he has some vague grievance I am, therefore, to abandon a series of experiments which promise to be so fruitful of results. He appeared to be annoyed at the light way in which I treated his shadowy warnings, and we parted with some little coldness on both sides.

MARCH 31. Mesmerized by Miss P.

APRIL 1. Mesmerized by Miss P. (Note-book A.)

APRIL 2. Mesmerized by Miss P. (Sphygmographic chart taken by Professor Wilson.)

APRIL 3. It is possible that this course of mesmerism may be a little trying to the general constitution. Agatha says that I am thinner and darker under the eyes. I am conscious of a nervous irritability which I had not observed in myself before. The least noise, for example, makes me start, and the stupidity of a student causes me exasperation instead of amusement. Agatha wishes me to stop, but I tell her that every course of study is trying, and that one can never attain a result without paying some price for it. When she sees the sensation which my forthcoming paper on "The Relation between Mind and Matter" may make, she will understand that it is worth a little nervous wear and tear. I should not be surprised if I got my F. R. S. over it.

Mesmerized again in the evening. The effect is produced more rapidly now, and the subjective visions are less marked. I keep full notes of each sitting. Wilson is leaving for town for a week or ten days, but we shall not interrupt the experiments, which depend for their value as much upon my sensations as on his observations.

APRIL 4. I must be carefully on my guard. A complication has crept into our experiments which I had not reckoned upon. In my eagerness for scientific facts I have been foolishly blind to the human relations between Miss Penclosa and myself. I can write here what I would not breathe to a living soul. The unhappy woman appears to have formed an attachment for me.

I should not say such a thing, even in the privacy of my own intimate journal, if it had not come to such a pass that it is impossible to ignore it. For some time—that is, for the last week—there have been signs which I have brushed aside and refused to think of. Her brightness when I come, her dejection when I go, her eagerness that I should come often, the expression of her eyes, the tone of her voice—I tried to think that they meant nothing, and were, perhaps, only her ardent West Indian manner. But last night, as I awoke from the mesmeric sleep, I put out my hand, unconsciously, involuntarily, and clasped hers. When I came fully to myself, we were sitting with them locked, she looking up at me with an expectant smile. And the horrible thing was that I felt impelled to say what she expected me to say. What a false wretch I should have been! How I should have loathed myself today had I yielded to the temptation of that moment! But, thank God, I was strong enough to spring up and hurry from the room. I was rude, I fear, but I could not, no, I COULD not, trust myself another moment. I, a gentleman, a man of honor, engaged to one of the sweetest girls in England— and yet in a moment of reasonless passion I nearly professed love for this woman whom I hardly know. She is far older than myself and a cripple. It is monstrous, odious; and yet the impulse was so strong that, had I stayed another minute in her presence, I should have committed myself. What was it? I have to teach others the workings of our organism, and what do I know of it myself? Was it the sudden upcropping of some lower stratum in my nature—a brutal primitive instinct suddenly asserting itself?

I could almost believe the tales of obsession by evil spirits, so overmastering was the feeling.

Well, the incident places me in a most unfortunate position. On the one hand, I am very loath to abandon a series of experiments which have already gone so far, and which promise such brilliant results. On the other, if this unhappy woman has conceived a passion for me——But surely even now I must have made some hideous mistake. She, with her age and her deformity! It is impossible. And then she knew about Agatha. She understood how I was placed. She only smiled out of amusement, perhaps, when in my dazed state I seized her hand. It was my half-mesmerized brain which gave it a meaning, and sprang with such bestial swiftness to meet it. I wish I could persuade myself that it was indeed so. On the whole, perhaps, my wisest plan would be to postpone our other experiments until Wilson's return. I have written a note to Miss Penclosa, therefore, making no allusion to last night, but saying that a press of work would cause me to interrupt our sittings for a few days. She has answered, formally enough, to say that if I should change my mind I should find her at home at the usual hour.

10 P.M. Well, well, what a thing of straw I am! I am coming to know myself better of late, and the more I know the lower I fall in my own estimation. Surely I was not always so weak as this. At four o'clock I should have smiled had anyone told me that I should go to Miss Penclosa's tonight, and yet, at eight, I was at Wilson's door as usual. I don't know how it occurred. The influence of habit, I suppose. Perhaps there is a mesmeric craze as there is an opium craze, and I am a victim to it. I only know that as I worked in my study I became more and more uneasy. I fidgeted. I worried. I could not concentrate my mind upon the papers in front of me. And then, at last, almost before I knew what I was doing, I seized my hat and hurried round to keep my usual appointment.

We had an interesting evening. Mrs. Wilson was present during most of the time, which prevented the embarrassment which one at least of us must have felt. Miss Penclosa's manner was quite the same as usual, and she expressed no surprise at my having come in spite of my note. There was nothing in her bearing to show that yesterday's incident had made any impression upon her, and so I am inclined to hope that I overrated it.

APRIL 6, EVENING. No, no, no, I did not overrate it. I can no longer attempt to conceal from myself that this woman has conceived a passion for me. It is monstrous, but it is true. Again, tonight, I awoke from the mesmeric trance to find my hand in hers, and to suffer that odious feeling which urges me to throw away my honor, my career, everything, for the sake of this creature who, as I can plainly see when I am away from her influence, possesses no single charm upon earth. But when I am near her, I do not feel this. She rouses something in me, something evil, something I had rather not think of. She paralyzes my better nature, too, at the moment when she stimulates my worse. Decidedly it is not good for me to be near her.

Last night was worse than before. Instead of flying I actually sat for some time with my hand in hers talking over the most intimate subjects with her. We spoke of Agatha, among other things. What could I have been dreaming of? Miss Penclosa said that she was conventional, and I agreed with her. She spoke once or twice in a disparaging way of her, and I did not protest. What a creature I have been!

Weak as I have proved myself to be, I am still strong enough to bring this sort of thing to an end. It shall not happen again. I have sense enough to fly when I cannot fight. From this Sunday night onward I shall never sit with Miss Penclosa again. Never! Let the experiments go, let the research come to an end; anything is better than facing this monstrous temptation which drags me so low. I have said nothing to Miss Penclosa, but I shall simply stay away. She can tell the reason without any words of mine.

APRIL 7. Have stayed away as I said. It is a pity to ruin such an interesting investigation, but it would be a greater pity still to ruin my life, and I KNOW that I cannot trust myself with that woman.

11 P.M. God help me! What is the matter with me? Am I going mad? Let me try and be calm and reason with myself. First of all I shall set down exactly what occurred.

It was nearly eight when I wrote the lines with which this day begins. Feeling strangely restless and uneasy, I left my rooms and walked round to spend the evening with Agatha and her mother. They both remarked that I was pale and haggard. About nine Professor Pratt-Haldane came in, and we played a game of whist. I tried hard to concentrate my attention upon the cards, but the feeling of restlessness grew and grew until I found it impossible to struggle against it. I simply COULD not sit still at the table. At last, in the very middle of a hand, I threw my cards down and, with some sort of an incoherent apology about having an appointment, I rushed from the room. As if in a dream I have a vague recollection of tearing through the hall, snatching my hat from the stand, and slamming the door behind me. As in a dream, too, I have the impression of the double line of gas-lamps, and my bespattered boots tell me that I must have run down the middle of the road. It was all misty and strange and unnatural. I came to Wilson's house; I saw Mrs. Wilson and I saw Miss Penclosa. I hardly recall what we talked about, but I do remember that Miss P. shook the head of her crutch at me in a playful way, and accused me of being late and of losing interest in our experiments. There was no mesmerism, but I stayed some time and have only just returned.

My brain is quite clear again now, and I can think over what has occurred. It is absurd to suppose that it is merely weakness and force of habit. I tried to explain it in that way the other night, but it will no longer suffice. It is something much deeper and more terrible than that. Why, when I was at the Mardens' whist-table, I was dragged away as if the noose of a rope had been cast round me. I can no longer disguise it from myself. The woman has her grip upon me. I am in her clutch. But I must keep my head and reason it out and see what is best to be done.

But what a blind fool I have been! In my enthusiasm over my research I have walked straight into the pit, although it lay gaping before me. Did she not herself warn me? Did she not tell me, as I can read in my own journal, that when she has acquired power over a subject she can make him do her will? And she has acquired that power over me. I am for the moment at the beck and call of this creature with the crutch. I must come when she wills it. I must do as she wills. Worst of all, I must feel as she wills. I loathe her and fear her, yet, while I am under the spell, she can doubtless make me love her.

There is some consolation in the thought, then, that those odious impulses for which I have blamed myself do not really come from me at all. They are all transferred from her, little as I could have guessed it at the time. I feel cleaner and lighter for the thought.

APRIL 8. Yes, now, in broad daylight, writing coolly and with time for reflection, I am compelled to confirm everything which I wrote in my journal last night. I am in a horrible position, but, above all, I must not lose my head. I must pit my intellect against her powers. After all, I am no silly puppet, to dance at the end of a string. I have energy, brains, courage. For all her devil's tricks I may beat her yet. May! I MUST, or what is to become of me?

Let me try to reason it out! This woman, by her own explanation, can dominate my nervous organism. She can project herself into my body and take command of it. She has a parasite soul; yes, she is a parasite, a monstrous parasite. She creeps into my frame as the hermit crab does into the whelk's shell. I am powerless. What can I do? I am dealing with forces of which I know nothing. And I can tell no one of my trouble. They would set me down as a madman. Certainly, if it got noised abroad, the university would say that they had no need of a devil-ridden professor. And Agatha! No, no, I must face it alone.

CHAPTER III

I read over my notes of what the woman said when she spoke about her powers. There is one point which fills me with dismay. She implies that when the influence is slight the subject knows what he is doing, but cannot control himself, whereas when it is strongly exerted he is absolutely unconscious. Now, I have always known what I did, though less so last night than on the previous occasions. That seems to mean that she has never yet exerted her full powers upon me. Was ever a man so placed before?

Yes, perhaps there was, and very near me, too. Charles Sadler must know something of this! His vague words of warning take a meaning now. Oh, if I had only listened to him then, before I helped by these repeated sittings to forge the links of the chain which binds me! But I will see him today. I will apologize to him for having treated his warning so lightly. I will see if he can advise me.

4 P.M. No, he cannot. I have talked with him, and he showed such surprise at the first words in which I tried to express my unspeakable secret that I went no further. As far as I can gather (by hints and inferences rather than by any statement), his own experience was limited to some words or looks such as I have myself endured. His abandonment of Miss Penclosa is in itself a sign that he was never really in her toils. Oh, if he only knew his escape! He has to thank his phlegmatic Saxon temperament for it. I am black and Celtic, and this hag's clutch is deep in my nerves. Shall I ever get it out? Shall I ever be the same man that I was just one short fortnight ago?

Let me consider what I had better do. I cannot leave the university in the middle of the term. If I were free, my course would be obvious. I should start at once and travel in Persia. But would she allow me to start? And could her influence not reach me in Persia, and bring me back to within touch of her crutch? I can only find out the limits of this hellish power by my own bitter experience. I will fight and fight and fight—and what can I do more?

I know very well that about eight o'clock tonight that craving for her society, that irresistible restlessness, will come upon me. How shall I overcome it? What shall I do? I must make it impossible for me to leave the room. I shall lock the door and throw the key out of the window. But, then, what am I to do in the morning? Never mind about the morning. I must at all costs break this chain which holds me.

APRIL 9. Victory! I have done splendidly! At seven o'clock last night I took a hasty dinner, and then locked myself up in my bedroom and dropped the key into the garden. I chose a cheery novel, and lay in bed for three hours trying to read it, but really in a horrible state of trepidation, expecting every instant that I should become conscious of the impulse. Nothing of the sort occurred, however, and I awoke this morning with the feeling that a black nightmare had been lifted off me. Perhaps the creature realized what I had done, and understood that it was useless to try to influence me. At any rate, I have beaten her once, and if I can do it once, I can do it again.

It was most awkward about the key in the morning. Luckily, there was an under-gardener below, and I asked him to throw it up. No doubt he thought I had just dropped it. I will have doors and windows screwed up and six stout men to hold me down in my bed before I will surrender myself to be hag-ridden in this way.

I had a note from Mrs. Marden this afternoon asking me to go round and see her. I intended to do so in any case, but had not excepted to find bad news waiting for me. It seems that the Armstrongs, from whom Agatha has expectations, are due home from Adelaide in the Aurora, and that they have written to Mrs. Marden and her to meet them in town. They will probably be away for a month or six weeks, and, as the Aurora is due on Wednesday, they must go at once—tomorrow, if they are ready in time. My consolation is that when we meet again there will be no more parting between Agatha and me.

"I want you to do one thing, Agatha," said I, when we were alone together. "If you should happen to meet Miss Penclosa, either in town or here, you must promise me never again to allow her to mesmerize you."

Agatha opened her eyes.

"Why, it was only the other day that you were saying how interesting it all was, and how determined you were to finish your experiments."

"I know, but I have changed my mind since then."

"And you won't have it any more?"

"No."

"I am so glad, Austin. You can't think how pale and worn you have been lately. It was really our principal objection to going to London now that we did not wish to leave you when you were so pulled down. And your manner has been so strange occasionally—especially that night when you left poor Professor Pratt-Haldane to play dummy. I am convinced that these experiments are very bad for your nerves."

"I think so, too, dear."

"And for Miss Penclosa's nerves as well. You have heard that she is ill?"

"No."

"Mrs. Wilson told us so last night. She described it as a nervous fever. Professor Wilson is coming back this week, and of course Mrs. Wilson is very anxious that Miss Penclosa should be well again then, for he has quite a programme of experiments which he is anxious to carry out."

I was glad to have Agatha's promise, for it was enough that this woman should have one of us in her clutch. On the other hand, I was disturbed to hear about Miss Penclosa's illness. It rather discounts the victory which I appeared to win last night. I remember that she said that loss of health interfered with her power. That may be why I was able to hold my own so easily. Well, well, I must take the same precautions tonight and see what comes of it. I am childishly frightened when I think of her.

APRIL 10. All went very well last night. I was amused at the gardener's face when I had again to hail him this morning and to ask him to throw up my key. I shall get a name among the servants if this sort of thing goes on. But the great point is that I stayed in my room without the slightest inclination to leave it. I do believe that I am shaking myself clear of this incredible bond—or is it only that the woman's power is in abeyance until she recovers her strength? I can but pray for the best.

The Mardens left this morning, and the brightness seems to have gone out of the spring sunshine. And yet it is very beautiful also as it gleams on the green chestnuts opposite my windows, and gives a touch of gayety to the heavy, lichen-mottled walls of the old colleges. How sweet and gentle and soothing is Nature! Who would think that there lurked in her also such vile forces, such odious possibilities! For of course I understand that this dreadful thing which has sprung out at me is neither super-natural nor even preternatural. No, it is a natural force which this woman can use and society is ignorant of. The mere fact that it ebbs with her strength shows how entirely it is subject to physical laws. If I had time, I might probe it to the bottom and lay my hands upon its antidote. But you cannot tame the tiger when you are beneath his claws. You can but try to writhe away from him. Ah, when I look in the glass and see my own dark eyes and clear-cut Spanish face, I long for a vitriol splash or a bout of the small-pox. One or the other might have saved me from this calamity.

I am inclined to think that I may have trouble tonight. There are two things which make me fear so. One is that I met Mrs. Wilson in the street, and that she tells me that Miss Penclosa is better, though still weak. I find myself wishing in my heart that the illness had been her last. The other is that Professor Wilson comes back in a day or two, and his presence would act as a constraint upon her. I should not fear our interviews if a third person were present. For both these reasons I have a presentiment of trouble tonight, and I shall take the same precautions as before.

APRIL 10. No, thank God, all went well last night. I really could not face the gardener again. I locked my door and thrust the key underneath it, so that I had to ask the maid to let me out in the morning. But the precaution was really not needed, for I never had any inclination to go out at all. Three evenings in succession at home! I am surely near the end of my troubles, for Wilson will be home again either today or tomorrow. Shall I tell him of what I have gone through or not? I am convinced that I should not have the slightest sympathy from him. He would look upon me as an interesting case, and read a paper about me at the next meeting of the Psychical Society, in which he would gravely discuss the possibility of my being a deliberate liar, and weigh it against the chances of my being in an early stage of lunacy. No, I shall get no comfort out of Wilson.

I am feeling wonderfully fit and well. I don't think I ever lectured with greater spirit. Oh, if I could only get this shadow off my life, how happy I should be! Young, fairly wealthy, in the front rank of my profession, engaged to a beautiful and charming girl—have I not everything which a man could ask for? Only one thing to trouble me, but what a thing it is!

Midnight. I shall go mad. Yes, that will be the end of it. I shall go mad. I am not far from it now. My head throbs as I rest it on my hot hand. I am quivering all over like a scared horse. Oh, what a night I have had! And yet I have some cause to be satisfied also.

At the risk of becoming the laughing-stock of my own servant, I again slipped my key under the door, imprisoning myself for the night. Then, finding it too early to go to bed, I lay down with my clothes on and began to read one of Dumas's novels. Suddenly I was gripped—gripped and dragged from the couch. It is only thus that I can describe the overpowering nature of the force which pounced upon me. I clawed at the coverlet. I clung to the wood-work. I believe that I screamed out in my frenzy. It was all useless, hopeless. I MUST go. There was no way out of it. It was only at the outset that I resisted. The force soon became too overmastering for that. I thank goodness that there were no watchers there to interfere with me. I could not have answered for myself if there had been.

And, besides the determination to get out, there came to me, also, the keenest and coolest judgment in choosing my means. I lit a candle and endeavored, kneeling in front of the door, to pull the key through with the feather-end of a quill pen. It was just too short and pushed it further away. Then with quiet persistence I got a paper-knife out of one of the drawers, and with that I managed to draw the key back. I opened the door, stepped into my study, took a photograph of myself from the bureau, wrote something across it, placed it in the inside pocket of my coat, and then started off for Wilson's.

It was all wonderfully clear, and yet disassociated from the rest of my life, as the incidents of even the most vivid dream might be. A peculiar double consciousness possessed me. There was the predominant alien will, which was bent upon drawing me to the side of its owner, and there was the feebler protesting personality, which I recognized as being myself, tugging feebly at the overmastering impulse as a led terrier might at its chain. I can remember recognizing these two conflicting forces, but I recall nothing of my walk, nor of how I was admitted to the house.

Very vivid, however, is my recollection of how I met Miss Penclosa. She was reclining on the sofa in the little boudoir in which our experiments had usually been carried out. Her head was rested on her hand, and a tiger-skin rug had been partly drawn over her. She looked up expectantly as I entered, and, as the lamp-light fell upon her face, I could see that she was very pale and thin, with dark hollows under her eyes. She smiled at me, and pointed to a stool beside her. It was with her left hand that she pointed, and I, running eagerly forward, seized it—I loathe myself as I think of it—and pressed it passionately to my lips. Then, seating myself upon the stool, and still retaining her hand, I gave her the photograph which I had brought with me, and talked and talked and talked—of my love for her, of my grief over her illness, of my joy at her recovery, of the misery it was to me to be absent a single evening from her side. She lay quietly looking down at me with imperious eyes and her

provocative smile. Once I remember that she passed her
over my hair as one caresses a dog; and it gave me pleasure—
caress. I thrilled under it. I was her slave, body and soul, and b
the moment I rejoiced in my slavery.

And then came the blessed change. Never tell me that there
is not a Providence! I was on the brink of perdition. My feet
were on the edge. Was it a coincidence that at that very instant
help should come? No, no, no; there is a Providence, and its
hand has drawn me back. There is something in the universe
stronger than this devil woman with her tricks. Ah, what a
balm to my heart it is to think so!

As I looked up at her I was conscious of a change in her.
Her face, which had been pale before, was now ghastly. Her
eyes were dull, and the lids drooped heavily over them. Above
all, the look of serene confidence had gone from her features.
Her mouth had weakened. Her forehead had puckered. She
was frightened and undecided. And as I watched the change
my own spirit fluttered and struggled, trying hard to tear itself
from the grip which held it—a grip which, from moment to
moment, grew less secure.

"Austin," she whispered, "I have tried to do too much. I was
not strong enough. I have not recovered yet from my illness.
But I could not live longer without seeing you. You won't leave
me, Austin? This is only a passing weakness. If you will only
give me five minutes, I shall be myself again. Give me the small
decanter from the table in the window."

But I had regained my soul. With her waning strength the
influence had cleared away from me and left me free. And I was
aggressive—bitterly, fiercely aggressive. For once at least I could
make this woman understand what my real feelings toward her
were. My soul was filled with a hatred as bestial as the love
against which it was a reaction. It was the savage, murderous
passion of the revolted serf. I could have taken the crutch from
her side and beaten her face in with it. She threw her hands
up, as if to avoid a blow, and cowered away from me into the
corner of the settee.

"The brandy!" she gasped. "The brandy!"

I took the decanter and poured it over the roots of a palm in the window. Then I snatched the photograph from her hand and tore it into a hundred pieces.

"You vile woman," I said, "if I did my duty to society, you would never leave this room alive!"

"I love you, Austin; I love you!" she wailed.

"Yes," I cried, "and Charles Sadler before. And how many others before that?"

"Charles Sadler!" she gasped. "He has spoken to you? So, Charles Sadler, Charles Sadler!" Her voice came through her white lips like a snake's hiss.

"Yes, I know you, and others shall know you, too. You shameless creature! You knew how I stood. And yet you used your vile power to bring me to your side. You may, perhaps, do so again, but at least you will remember that you have heard me say that I love Miss Marden from the bottom of my soul, and that I loathe you, abhor you!

"The very sight of you and the sound of your voice fill me with horror and disgust. The thought of you is repulsive. That is how I feel toward you, and if it pleases you by your tricks to draw me again to your side as you have done tonight, you will at least, I should think, have little satisfaction in trying to make a lover out of a man who has told you his real opinion of you. You may put what words you will into my mouth, but you cannot help remembering—"

I stopped, for the woman's head had fallen back, and she had fainted. She could not bear to hear what I had to say to her! What a glow of satisfaction it gives me to think that, come what may, in the future she can never misunderstand my true feelings toward her. But what will occur in the future? What will she do next? I dare not think of it. Oh, if only I could hope that she will leave me alone! But when I think of what I said to her—Never mind; I have been stronger than she for once.

APRIL 11. I hardly slept last night, and found myself in the morning so unstrung and feverish that I was compelled to ask

Pratt-Haldane to do my lecture for me. It is the first that I have ever missed. I rose at mid-day, but my head is aching, my hands quivering, and my nerves in a pitiable state.

Who should come round this evening but Wilson. He has just come back from London, where he has lectured, read papers, convened meetings, exposed a medium, conducted a series of experiments on thought transference, entertained Professor Richet of Paris, spent hours gazing into a crystal, and obtained some evidence as to the passage of matter through matter. All this he poured into my ears in a single gust.

"But you!" he cried at last. "You are not looking well. And Miss Penclosa is quite prostrated today. How about the experiments?"

"I have abandoned them."

"Tut, tut! Why?"

"The subject seems to me to be a dangerous one."

Out came his big brown note-book.

"This is of great interest," said he. "What are your grounds for saying that it is a dangerous one? Please give your facts in chronological order, with approximate dates and names of reliable witnesses with their permanent addresses."

"First of all," I asked, "would you tell me whether you have collected any cases where the mesmerist has gained a command over the subject and has used it for evil purposes?"

"Dozens!" he cried exultantly. "Crime by suggestion—"

"I don't mean suggestion. I mean where a sudden impulse comes from a person at a distance—an uncontrollable impulse."

"Obsession!" he shrieked, in an ecstasy of delight. "It is the rarest condition. We have eight cases, five well attested. You don't mean to say—" His exultation made him hardly articulate.

"No, I don't," said I. "Good-evening! You will excuse me, but I am not very well tonight." And so at last I got rid of him, still brandishing his pencil and his note-book. My troubles may be bad to hear, but at least it is better to hug them to myself than to have myself exhibited by Wilson, like a freak at a fair.

He has lost sight of human beings. Everything to him is a case and a phenomenon. I will die before I speak to him again upon the matter.

APRIL 12. Yesterday was a blessed day of quiet, and I enjoyed an uneventful night. Wilson's presence is a great consolation. What can the woman do now? Surely, when she has heard me say what I have said, she will conceive the same disgust for me which I have for her. She could not, no, she COULD not, desire to have a lover who had insulted her so. No, I believe I am free from her love—but how about her hate? Might she not use these powers of hers for revenge? Tut! why should I frighten myself over shadows? She will forget about me, and I shall forget about her, and all will be well.

APRIL 13. My nerves have quite recovered their tone. I really believe that I have conquered the creature. But I must confess to living in some suspense. She is well again, for I hear that she was driving with Mrs. Wilson in the High Street in the afternoon.

APRIL 14. I do wish I could get away from the place altogether. I shall fly to Agatha's side the very day that the term closes. I suppose it is pitiably weak of me, but this woman gets upon my nerves most terribly. I have seen her again, and I have spoken with her.

It was just after lunch, and I was smoking a cigarette in my study, when I heard the step of my servant Murray in the passage. I was languidly conscious that a second step was audible behind, and had hardly troubled myself to speculate who it might be, when suddenly a slight noise brought me out of my chair with my skin creeping with apprehension. I had never particularly observed before what sort of sound the tapping of a crutch was, but my quivering nerves told me that I heard it now in the sharp wooden clack which alternated with the muffled thud of the foot fall. Another instant and my servant had shown her in.

I did not attempt the usual conventions of society, nor did she. I simply stood with the smouldering cigarette in my hand,

and gazed at her. She in her turn looked silently at me, and at her look I remembered how in these very pages I had tried to define the expression of her eyes, whether they were furtive or fierce. Today they were fierce—coldly and inexorably so.

"Well," said she at last, "are you still of the same mind as when I saw you last?"

"I have always been of the same mind."

"Let us understand each other, Professor Gilroy," said she slowly. "I am not a very safe person to trifle with, as you should realize by now. It was you who asked me to enter into a series of experiments with you, it was you who won my affections, it was you who professed your love for me, it was you who brought me your own photograph with words of affection upon it, and, finally, it was you who on the very same evening thought fit to insult me most outrageously, addressing me as no man has ever dared to speak to me yet. Tell me that those words came from you in a moment of passion and I am prepared to forget and to forgive them. You did not mean what you said, Austin? You do not really hate me?"

I might have pitied this deformed woman—such a longing for love broke suddenly through the menace of her eyes. But then I thought of what I had gone through, and my heart set like flint.

"If ever you heard me speak of love," said I, "you know very well that it was your voice which spoke, and not mine. The only words of truth which I have ever been able to say to you are those which you heard when last we met."

"I know. Someone has set you against me. It was he!" She tapped with her crutch upon the floor. "Well, you know very well that I could bring you this instant crouching like a spaniel to my feet. You will not find me again in my hour of weakness, when you can insult me with impunity. Have a care what you are doing, Professor Gilroy. You stand in a terrible position. You have not yet realized the hold which I have upon you."

I shrugged my shoulders and turned away.

"Well," said she, after a pause, "if you despise my love, I must see what can be done with fear. You smile, but the day will come when you will come screaming to me for pardon. Yes, you will grovel on the ground before me, proud as you are, and you will curse the day that ever you turned me from your best friend into your most bitter enemy. Have a care, Professor Gilroy!" I saw a white hand shaking in the air, and a face which was scarcely human, so convulsed was it with passion. An instant later she was gone, and I heard the quick hobble and tap receding down the passage.

But she has left a weight upon my heart. Vague presentiments of coming misfortune lie heavy upon me. I try in vain to persuade myself that these are only words of empty anger. I can remember those relentless eyes too clearly to think so. What shall I do—ah, what shall I do? I am no longer master of my own soul. At any moment this loathsome parasite may creep into me, and then——I must tell someone my hideous secret—I must tell it or go mad. If I had someone to sympathize and advise! Wilson is out of the question. Charles Sadler would understand me only so far as his own experience carries him. Pratt-Haldane! He is a well-balanced man, a man of great common-sense and resource. I will go to him. I will tell him everything. God grant that he may be able to advise me!

Chapter IV

6.45 P.M. No, it is useless. There is no human help for me; I must fight this out single-handed. Two courses lie before me. I might become this woman's lover. Or I must endure such persecutions as she can inflict upon me. Even if none come, I shall live in a hell of apprehension. But she may torture me, she may drive me mad, she may kill me: I will never, never, never give in. What can she inflict which would be worse than the loss of Agatha, and the knowledge that I am a perjured liar, and have forfeited the name of gentleman?

Pratt-Haldane was most amiable, and listened with all politeness to my story. But when I looked at his heavy set features, his slow eyes, and the ponderous study furniture which surrounded him, I could hardly tell him what I had come to say. It was all so substantial, so material. And, besides, what would I myself have said a short month ago if one of my colleagues had come to me with a story of demonic possession? Perhaps. I should have been less patient than he was. As it was, he took notes of my statement, asked me how much tea I drank, how many hours I slept, whether I had been overworking much, had I had sudden pains in the head, evil dreams, singing in the ears, flashes before the eyes—all questions which pointed to his belief that brain congestion was at the bottom of my trouble. Finally he dismissed me with a great many platitudes about open-air exercise, and avoidance of nervous excitement. His prescription, which was for chloral and bromide, I rolled up and threw into the gutter.

No, I can look for no help from any human being. If I consult any more, they may put their heads together and I may find myself in an asylum. I can but grip my courage with both hands, and pray that an honest man may not be abandoned.

APRIL 10. It is the sweetest spring within the memory of man. So green, so mild, so beautiful! Ah, what a contrast between nature without and my own soul so torn with doubt and terror! It has been an uneventful day, but I know that I am on the edge of an abyss. I know it, and yet I go on with the routine of my life. The one bright spot is that Agatha is happy and well and out of all danger. If this creature had a hand on each of us, what might she not do?

APRIL 16. The woman is ingenious in her torments. She knows how fond I am of my work, and how highly my lectures are thought of. So it is from that point that she now attacks me. It will end, I can see, in my losing my professorship, but I will fight to the finish. She shall not drive me out of it without a struggle.

I was not conscious of any change during my lecture this morning save that for a minute or two I had a dizziness and swimminess which rapidly passed away. On the contrary, I congratulated myself upon having made my subject (the functions of the red corpuscles) both interesting and clear. I was surprised, therefore, when a student came into my laboratory immediately after the lecture, and complained of being puzzled by the discrepancy between my statements and those in the text books. He showed me his note-book, in which I was reported as having in one portion of the lecture championed the most outrageous and unscientific heresies. Of course I denied it, and declared that he had misunderstood me, but on comparing his notes with those of his companions, it became clear that he was right, and that I really had made some most preposterous statements. Of course I shall explain it away as being the result of a moment of aberration, but I feel only too sure that it will be the first of a series. It is but a month now to the end of the session, and I pray that I may be able to hold out until then.

APRIL 26. Ten days have elapsed since I have had the heart to make any entry in my journal. Why should I record my own humiliation and degradation? I had vowed never to open it again. And yet the force of habit is strong, and here I find myself taking up once more the record of my own dreadful experiences—in much the same spirit in which a suicide has been known to take notes of the effects of the poison which killed him.

Well, the crash which I had foreseen has come—and that no further back than yesterday. The university authorities have taken my lectureship from me. It has been done in the most delicate way, purporting to be a temporary measure to relieve me from the effects of overwork, and to give me the opportunity of recovering my health. Nonetheless, it has been done, and I am no longer Professor Gilroy. The laboratory is still in my charge, but I have little doubt that that also will soon go.

The fact is that my lectures had become the laughing-stock of the university. My class was crowded with students who came to see and hear what the eccentric professor would do or say next. I cannot go into the detail of my humiliation. Oh, that devilish woman! There is no depth of buffoonery and imbecility to which she has not forced me. I would begin my lecture clearly and well, but always with the sense of a coming eclipse. Then as I felt the influence I would struggle against it, striving with clenched hands and beads of sweat upon my brow to get the better of it, while the students, hearing my incoherent words and watching my contortions, would roar with laughter at the antics of their professor. And then, when she had once fairly mastered me, out would come the most outrageous things—silly jokes, sentiments as though I were proposing a toast, snatches of ballads, personal abuse even against some member of my class. And then in a moment my brain would clear again, and my lecture would proceed decorously to the end. No wonder that my conduct has been the talk of the colleges. No wonder that the University Senate has been compelled to take official notice of such a scandal. Oh, that devilish woman!

And the most dreadful part of it all is my own loneliness. Here I sit in a commonplace English bow-window, looking out upon a commonplace English street with its garish buses and its lounging policeman, and behind me there hangs a shadow which is out of all keeping with the age and place. In the home of knowledge I am weighed down and tortured by a power of which science knows nothing. No magistrate would listen to me. No paper would discuss my case. No doctor would believe my symptoms. My own most intimate friends would only look upon it as a sign of brain derangement. I am out of all touch with my kind. Oh, that devilish woman! Let her have a care! She may push me too far. When the law cannot help a man, he may make a law for himself.

She met me in the High Street yesterday evening and spoke to me. It was as well for her, perhaps, that it was not between the hedges of a lonely country road. She asked me with her cold smile whether I had been chastened yet. I did not deign to answer her. "We must try another turn of the screw;" said she. Have a care, my lady, have a care! I had her at my mercy once. Perhaps another chance may come.

APRIL 28. The suspension of my lectureship has had the effect also of taking away her means of annoying me, and so I have enjoyed two blessed days of peace. After all, there is no reason to despair. Sympathy pours in to me from all sides, and everyone agrees that it is my devotion to science and the arduous nature of my researches which have shaken my nervous system. I have had the kindest message from the council advising me to travel abroad, and expressing the confident hope that I may be able to resume all my duties by the beginning of the summer term. Nothing could be more flattering than their allusions to my career and to my services to the university. It is only in misfortune that one can test one's own popularity. This creature may weary of tormenting me, and then all may yet be well. May God grant it!

APRIL 29. Our sleepy little town has had a small sensation. The only knowledge of crime which we ever have is when a rowdy undergraduate breaks a few lamps or comes to blows with a policeman. Last night, however, there was an attempt made to break into the branch of the Bank of England, and we are all in a flutter in consequence.

Parkenson, the manager, is an intimate friend of mine, and I found him very much excited when I walked round there after breakfast. Had the thieves broken into the counting house, they would still have had the safes to reckon with, so that the defence was considerably stronger than the attack. Indeed, the latter does not appear to have ever been very formidable. Two of the lower windows have marks as if a chisel or some such instrument had been pushed under them to force them open. The police should have a good clue, for the wood-work had been done with green paint only the day before, and from the smears it is evident that some of it has found its way on to the criminal's hands or clothes.

4.30 P.M. Ah, that accursed woman! That thrice accursed woman! Never mind! She shall not beat me! No, she shall not! But, oh, the she-devil! She has taken my professorship. Now she would take my honor. Is there nothing I can do against her, nothing save—Ah, but, hard pushed as I am, I cannot bring myself to think of that!

It was about an hour ago that I went into my bedroom, and was brushing my hair before the glass, when suddenly my eyes lit upon something which left me so sick and cold that I sat down upon the edge of the bed and began to cry. It is many a long year since I shed tears, but all my nerve was gone, and I could but sob and sob in impotent grief and anger. There was my house jacket, the coat I usually wear after dinner, hanging on its peg by the wardrobe, with the right sleeve thickly crusted from wrist to elbow with daubs of green paint.

So this was what she meant by another turn of the screw! She had made a public imbecile of me. Now she would brand me as a criminal. This time she has failed. But how about the next? I dare not think of it—and of Agatha and my poor old mother! I wish that I were dead!

Yes, this is the other turn of the screw. And this is also what she meant, no doubt, when she said that I had not realized yet the power she has over me. I look back at my account of my conversation with her, and I see how she declared that with a slight exertion of her will her subject would be conscious, and with a stronger one unconscious. Last night I was unconscious. I could have sworn that I slept soundly in my bed without so much as a dream. And yet those stains tell me that I dressed, made my way out, attempted to open the bank windows, and returned. Was I observed? Is it possible that some one saw me do it and followed me home? Ah, what a hell my life has become! I have no peace, no rest. But my patience is nearing its end.

10 P.M. I have cleaned my coat with turpentine. I do not think that anyone could have seen me. It was with my screw-driver that I made the marks. I found it all crusted with paint, and I have cleaned it. My head aches as if it would burst, and I

have taken five grains of antipyrine. If it were not for Agatha, I should have taken fifty and had an end of it.

MAY 3. Three quiet days. This hell fiend is like a cat with a mouse. She lets me loose only to pounce upon me again. I am never so frightened as when everything is still. My physical state is deplorable—perpetual hiccough and ptosis of the left eyelid.

I have heard from the Mardens that they will be back the day after tomorrow. I do not know whether I am glad or sorry. They were safe in London. Once here they may be drawn into the miserable network in which I am myself struggling. And I must tell them of it. I cannot marry Agatha so long as I know that I am not responsible for my own actions. Yes, I must tell them, even if it brings everything to an end between us.

Tonight is the university ball, and I must go. God knows I never felt less in the humor for festivity, but I must not have it said that I am unfit to appear in public. If I am seen there, and have speech with some of the elders of the university it will go a long way toward showing them that it would be unjust to take my chair away from me.

10 P.M. I have been to the ball. Charles Sadler and I went together, but I have come away before him. I shall wait up for him, however, for, indeed, I fear to go to sleep these nights. He is a cheery, practical fellow, and a chat with him will steady my nerves. On the whole, the evening was a great success. I talked to someone who has influence, and I think that I made them realize that my chair is not vacant quite yet. The creature was at the ball—unable to dance, of course, but sitting with Mrs. Wilson. Again and again her eyes rested upon me. They were almost the last things I saw before I left the room. Once, as I sat sideways to her, I watched her, and saw that her gaze was following someone else. It was Sadler, who was dancing at the time with the second Miss Thurston. To judge by her expression, it is well for him that he is not in her grip as I am. He does not know the escape he has had. I think I hear his step in the street now, and I will go down and let him in. If he will——

MAY 4. Why did I break off in this way last night? I never went down stairs, after all—at least, I have no recollection of doing so. But, on the other hand, I cannot remember going to bed. One of my hands is greatly swollen this morning, and yet I have no remembrance of injuring it yesterday. Otherwise, I am feeling all the better for last night's festivity. But I cannot understand how it is that I did not meet Charles Sadler when I so fully intended to do so. Is it possible——My God, it is only too probable! Has she been leading me some devil's dance again? I will go down to Sadler and ask him.

Mid-day. The thing has come to a crisis. My life is not worth living. But, if I am to die, then she shall come also. I will not leave her behind, to drive some other man mad as she has me. No, I have come to the limit of my endurance. She has made me as desperate and dangerous a man as walks the earth. God knows I have never had the heart to hurt a fly, and yet, if I had my hands now upon that woman, she should never leave this room alive. I shall see her this very day, and she shall learn what she has to expect from me.

I went to Sadler and found him, to my surprise, in bed. As I entered he sat up and turned a face toward me which sickened me as I looked at it.

"Why, Sadler, what has happened?" I cried, but my heart turned cold as I said it.

"Gilroy," he answered, mumbling with his swollen lips, "I have for some weeks been under the impression that you are a madman. Now I know it, and that you are a dangerous one as well. If it were not that I am unwilling to make a scandal in the college, you would now be in the hands of the police."

"Do you mean——" I cried.

"I mean that as I opened the door last night you rushed out upon me, struck me with both your fists in the face, knocked me down, kicked me furiously in the side, and left me lying almost unconscious in the street. Look at your own hand bearing witness against you."

Yes, there it was, puffed up, with sponge-like knuckles, as after some terrific blow. What could I do? Though he put me down as a madman, I must tell him all. I sat by his bed and went over all my troubles from the beginning. I poured them out with quivering hands and burning words which might have carried conviction to the most sceptical. "She hates you and she hates me!" I cried. "She revenged herself last night on both of us at once. She saw me leave the ball, and she must have seen you also. She knew how long it would take you to reach home. Then she had but to use her wicked will. Ah, your bruised face is a small thing beside my bruised soul!"

He was struck by my story. That was evident. "Yes, yes, she watched me out of the room," he muttered. "She is capable of it. But is it possible that she has really reduced you to this? What do you intend to do?"

"To stop it!" I cried. "I am perfectly desperate; I shall give her fair warning today, and the next time will be the last."

"Do nothing rash," said he.

"Rash!" I cried. "The only rash thing is that I should post-pone it another hour." With that I rushed to my room, and here I am on the eve of what may be the great crisis of my life. I shall start at once. I have gained one thing today, for I have made one man, at least, realize the truth of this monstrous experience of mine. And, if the worst should happen, this diary remains as a proof of the goad that has driven me.

Evening. When I came to Wilson's, I was shown up, and found that he was sitting with Miss Penclosa. For half an hour I had to endure his fussy talk about his recent research into the exact nature of the spiritualistic rap, while the creature and I sat in silence looking across the room at each other. I read a sinister amusement in her eyes, and she must have seen hatred and menace in mine. I had almost despaired of having speech with her when he was called from the room, and we were left for a few moments together.

"Well, Professor Gilroy—or is it Mr. Gilroy?" said she, with that bitter smile of hers. "How is your friend Mr. Charles Sadler after the ball?"

"You fiend!" I cried. "You have come to the end of your tricks now. I will have no more of them. Listen to what I say." I strode across and shook her roughly by the shoulder "As sure as there is a God in heaven, I swear that if you try another of your deviltries upon me I will have your life for it. Come what may, I will have your life. I have come to the end of what a man can endure."

"Accounts are not quite settled between us," said she, with a passion that equalled my own. "I can love, and I can hate. You had your choice. You chose to spurn the first; now you must test the other. It will take a little more to break your spirit, I see, but broken it shall be. Miss Marden comes back tomorrow, as I understand."

"What has that to do with you?" I cried. "It is a pollution that you should dare even to think of her. If I thought that you would harm her—"

She was frightened, I could see, though she tried to brazen it out. She read the black thought in my mind, and cowered away from me.

"She is fortunate in having such a champion," said she. "He actually dares to threaten a lonely woman. I must really congratulate Miss Marden upon her protector."

The words were bitter, but the voice and manner were more acid still.

"There is no use talking," said I. "I only came here to tell you—and to tell you most solemnly—that your next outrage upon me will be your last." With that, as I heard Wilson's step upon the stair, I walked from the room. Ay, she may look venomous and deadly, but, for all that, she is beginning to see now that she has as much to fear from me as I can have from her. Murder! It has an ugly sound. But you don't talk of murdering a snake or of murdering a tiger. Let her have a care now.

MAY 5. I met Agatha and her mother at the station at eleven o'clock. She is looking so bright, so happy, so beautiful. And she was so overjoyed to see me. What have I done to deserve such love? I went back home with them, and we lunched together. All the troubles seem in a moment to have been shredded back from my life. She tells me that I am looking pale and worried and ill. The dear child puts it down to my loneliness and the perfunctory attentions of a housekeeper. I pray that she may never know the truth! May the shadow, if shadow there must be, lie ever black across my life and leave hers in the sunshine. I have just come back from them, feeling a new man. With her by my side I think that I could show a bold face to anything which life might send.

5 P.M. Now, let me try to be accurate. Let me try to say exactly how it occurred. It is fresh in my mind, and I can set it down correctly, though it is not likely that the time will ever come when I shall forget the doings of today.

I had returned from the Mardens' after lunch, and was cutting some microscopic sections in my freezing microtome, when in an instant I lost consciousness in the sudden hateful fashion which has become only too familiar to me of late.

When my senses came back to me I was sitting in a small chamber, very different from the one in which I had been working. It was cosey and bright, with chintz-covered settees, coloured hangings, and a thousand pretty little trifles upon the wall. A small ornamental clock ticked in front of me, and the hands pointed to half-past three. It was all quite familiar to me, and yet I stared about for a moment in a half-dazed way until my eyes fell upon a cabinet photograph of myself upon the top of the piano. On the other side stood one of Mrs. Marden. Then, of course, I remembered where I was. It was Agatha's boudoir.

But how came I there, and what did I want? A horrible sinking came to my heart. Had I been sent here on some devilish errand? Had that errand already been done? Surely it must; otherwise, why should I be allowed to come back to consciousness? Oh, the agony of that moment! What had I done? I sprang to my feet in my despair, and as I did so a small glass bottle fell from my knees on to the carpet.

It was unbroken, and I picked it up. Outside was written "Sulphuric Acid. Fort." When I drew the round glass stopper, a thick fume rose slowly up, and a pungent, choking smell pervaded the room. I recognized it as one which I kept for chemical testing in my chambers. But why had I brought a bottle of vitriol into Agatha's chamber? Was it not this thick, reeking liquid with which jealous women had been known to mar the beauty of their rivals? My heart stood still as I held the bottle to the light. Thank God, it was full! No mischief had been done as yet. But had Agatha come in a minute sooner, was it not certain that the hellish parasite within me would have dashed the stuff into her—Ah, it will not bear to be thought of! But it must have been for that. Why else should I have brought it? At the thought of what I might have done my worn nerves broke down, and I sat shivering and twitching, the pitiable wreck of a man.

It was the sound of Agatha's voice and the rustle of her dress which restored me. I looked up, and saw her blue eyes, so full of tenderness and pity, gazing down at me.

"We must take you away to the country, Austin," she said. "You want rest and quiet. You look wretchedly ill."

"Oh, it is nothing!" said I, trying to smile. "It was only a momentary weakness. I am all right again now."

"I am so sorry to keep you waiting. Poor boy, you must have been here quite half an hour! The vicar was in the drawing-room, and, as I knew that you did not care for him, I thought it better that Jane should show you up here. I thought the man would never go!"

"Thank God he stayed! Thank God he stayed!" I cried hysterically.

"Why, what is the matter with you, Austin?" she asked, holding my arm as I staggered up from the chair. "Why are you glad that the vicar stayed? And what is this little bottle in your hand?"

"Nothing," I cried, thrusting it into my pocket. "But I must go. I have something important to do."

"How stern you look, Austin! I have never seen your face like that. You are angry?"

"Yes, I am angry."

"But not with me?"

"No, no, my darling! You would not understand."

"But you have not told me why you came."

"I came to ask you whether you would always love me—no matter what I did, or what shadow might fall on my name. Would you believe in me and trust me however black appearances might be against me?"

"You know that I would, Austin."

"Yes, I know that you would. What I do I shall do for you. I am driven to it. There is no other way out, my darling!" I kissed her and rushed from the room.

The time for indecision was at an end. As long as the creature threatened my own prospects and my honor there might be a question as to what I should do. But now, when Agatha—my innocent Agatha—was endangered, my duty lay before me like a turnpike road. I had no weapon, but I never paused for that. What weapon should I need, when I felt every muscle quivering with the strength of a frenzied man? I ran through the streets, so set upon what I had to do that I was only dimly conscious of the faces of friends whom I met—dimly conscious also that Professor Wilson met me, running with equal precipitance in the opposite direction. Breathless but resolute I reached the house and rang the bell. A white cheeked maid opened the door, and turned whiter yet when she saw the face that looked in at her.

"Show me up at once to Miss Penclosa," I demanded.

"Sir," she gasped, "Miss Penclosa died this afternoon at half-past three!"

† † † † † †

Montague Summers was the first authority to identify "The Parasite" as a vampire story. His survey of the vampire in literature includes a summary of "The Parasite," which opens with the following passage:

"Sir Arthur Conan Doyle in his little story, 'The Parasite,' has depicted a human vampire or psychic sponge in the person of Miss Penclosa, who is described as being a small frail creature, 'with a pale peaky face, an insignificant presence and a retiring manner.' Nevertheless she is able to obsess Professor Gilroy who says: 'She has a parasite soul, yes, she is a parasite; a monster parasite. She creeps into my form as the hermit crab creeps into the whelk's shell.' To his horror he realizes that under her influence his will becomes weaker and weaker and he is bound to seek her presence. He resists for a while, but the force becomes so overmastering that he is compelled to yield, loathing himself as he does so."[6]

Professor Austin Gilroy introduces himself with the claim:

"But my brain is soaked with exact knowledge. I have trained myself to deal only with fact and with proof. Surmise and fancy have no place in my scheme of thought. Show me what I can see with my microscope, cut with my scalpel, weigh in my balance, and I will devote a lifetime to its investigation. But when you ask me to study feelings, impressions, suggestions, you ask me to do what is distasteful and even demoralizing. A departure from pure reason affects me like an evil smell or a musical discord."

His initial skepticism about Miss Penclosa's psychic powers predates Sherlock Holmes's attitude toward supernatural forces in "The Adventure of the Sussex Vampire" by three decades.

---

6 Montague Summers. *The Vampire: His Kith and Kin.* Kegan Paul, Trench & Trubner: London, 1928. p. 323-324.

The Adventure
of the Illustrious Client

"It can't hurt now," was Mr. Sherlock Holmes's comment when, for the tenth time in as many years, I asked his leave to reveal the following narrative. So it was that at last I obtained permission to put on record what was, in some ways, the supreme moment of my friend's career.

Both Holmes and I had a weakness for the Turkish bath. It was over a smoke in the pleasant lassitude of the drying-room that I have found him less reticent and more human than anywhere else. On the upper floor of the Northumberland Avenue establishment there is an isolated corner where two couches lie side by side, and it was on these that we lay upon September 3, 1902, the day when my narrative begins. I had asked him whether anything was stirring, and for answer he had shot his long, thin, nervous arm out of the sheets which enveloped him and had drawn an envelope from the inside pocket of the coat which hung beside him.

Collier's Weekly Magazine: New York (8 November 1924) pp. 5-7, 30, 32, 34. With four illustrations by John Richard Flanagan. Reprinted: *The Strand Magazine* (February-March 1925) pp. 109-118 and 259-266. With five illustrations; four by Howard K. Elcock.

"It may be some fussy, self-important fool; it may be a matter of life or death," said he as he handed me the note. "I know no more than this message tells me."

It was from the Carlton Club and dated the evening before. This is what I read:

Sir James Damery presents his compliments to Mr. Sherlock Holmes and will call upon him at 4.30 tomorrow. Sir James begs to say that the matter upon which he desires to consult Mr. Holmes is very delicate and also very important. He trusts, therefore, that Mr. Holmes will make every effort to grant this interview, and that he will confirm it over the telephone to the Carlton Club.

"I need not say that I have confirmed it, Watson," said Holmes as I returned the paper. "Do you know anything of this man Damery?"

"Only that this name is a household word in society."

"Well, I can tell you a little more than that. He has rather a reputation for arranging delicate matters which are to be kept out of the papers. You may remember his negotiations with Sir George Lewis over the Hammerford Will case. He is a man of the world with a natural turn for diplomacy. I am bound, therefore, to hope that it is not a false scent and that he has some real need for our assistance."

"Our?"

"Well, if you will be so good, Watson."

"I shall be honoured."

"Then you have the hour—4.30. Until then we can put the matter out of our heads."

I was living in my own rooms in Queen Anne Street at the time, but I was round at Baker Street before the time named. Sharp to the half-hour, Colonel Sir James Damery was announced. It is hardly necessary to describe him, for many will remember that large, bluff, honest personality, that broad, cleanshaven face, and, above all, that pleasant, mellow voice. Frankness shone from his gray Irish eyes, and good humour played round his mobile, smiling lips. His lucent top-hat, his dark frock-coat, indeed, every detail, from the pearl pin in the black satin cravat to the lavender spats over the varnished shoes, spoke of the meticulous care in dress for which he was famous. The big, masterful aristocrat dominated the little room.

"Of course, I was prepared to find Dr. Watson," he remarked with a courteous bow. "His collaboration may be very necessary, for we are dealing on this occasion, Mr. Holmes, with a man to whom violence is familiar and who will, literally, stick at nothing. I should say that there is no more dangerous man in Europe."

"I have had several opponents to whom that flattering term has been applied," said Holmes with a smile. "Don't you smoke? Then you will excuse me if I light my pipe. If your man is more dangerous than the late Professor Moriarty, or than the living Colonel Sebastian Moran, then he is indeed worth meeting. May I ask his name?"

"Have you ever heard of Baron Gruner?"

"You mean the Austrian murderer?"

Colonel Damery threw up his kid-gloved hands with a laugh. "There is no getting past you, Mr. Holmes! Wonderful! So you have already sized him up as a murderer?"

"It is my business to follow the details of Continental crime. Who could possibly have read what happened at Prague and have any doubts as to the man's guilt! It was a purely technical legal point and the suspicious death of a witness that saved him! I am as sure that he killed his wife when the so called 'accident' happened in the Splugen Pass as if I had seen him do it. I knew, also, that he had come to England and had a presentiment that sooner or later he would find me some work to do. Well, what has Baron Gruner been up to? I presume it is not this old tragedy which has come up again?"

"No, it is more serious than that. To revenge crime is important, but to prevent it is more so. It is a terrible thing, Mr. Holmes, to see a dreadful event, an atrocious situation, preparing itself before your eyes, to clearly understand whither it will lead and yet to be utterly unable to avert it. Can a human being be placed in a more trying position?"

"Perhaps not."

"Then you will sympathize with the client in whose interests I am acting."

"I did not understand that you were merely an intermediary. Who is the principal?"

"Mr. Holmes, I must beg you not to press that question. It is important that I should be able to assure him that his honoured name has been in no way dragged into the matter. His motives are, to the last degree, honourable and chivalrous, but he prefers to remain unknown. I need not say that your fees will be assured and that you will be given a perfectly free hand. Surely the actual name of your client is immaterial?"

"I am sorry," said Holmes. "I am accustomed to have mystery at one end of my cases, but to have it at both ends is too confusing. I fear, Sir James, that I must decline to act."

Our visitor was greatly disturbed. His large, sensitive face was darkened with emotion and disappointment.

"You hardly realize the effect of your own action, Mr. Holmes," said he. "You place me in a most serious dilemma for I am perfectly certain that you would be proud to take over the case if I could give you the facts, and yet a promise forbids me from revealing them all. May I, at least, lay all that I can before you?"

"By all means, so long as it is understood that I commit myself to nothing."

"That is understood. In the first place, you have no doubt heard of General de Merville?"

"De Merville of Khyber fame? Yes, I have heard of him."

"He has a daughter, Violet de Merville, young, rich, beautiful, accomplished, a wonder-woman in every way. It is this daughter, this lovely, innocent girl, whom we are endeavouring to save from the clutches of a fiend."

"Baron Gruner has some hold over her, then?"

"The strongest of all holds where a woman is concerned—the hold of love. The fellow is, as you may have heard, extraordinarily handsome, with a most fascinating manner, a gentle voice and that air of romance and mystery which means so much to a woman. He is said to have the whole sex at his mercy and to have made ample use of the fact."

"But how came such a man to meet a lady of the standing of Miss Violet de Merville?"

"It was on a Mediterranean yachting voyage. The company, though select, paid their own passages. No doubt the promoters hardly realized the Baron's true character until it was too late. The villain attached himself to the lady, and with such effect that he has completely and absolutely won her heart. To say that she loves him hardly expresses it. She dotes upon him, she is obsessed by him. Outside of him there is nothing on earth. She will not hear one word against him. Everything has been done to cure her of her madness, but in vain. To sum up, she proposes to marry him next month. As she is of age and has a will of iron, it is hard to know how to prevent her."

"Does she know about the Austrian episode?"

"The cunning devil has told her every unsavoury public scandal of his past life, but always in such a way as to make himself out to be an innocent martyr. She absolutely accepts his version and will listen to no other."

"Dear me! But surely you have inadvertently let out the name of your client? It is no doubt General de Merville."

Our visitor fidgeted in his chair.

"I could deceive you by saying so, Mr. Holmes, but it would not be true. De Merville is a broken man. The strong soldier has been utterly demoralized by this incident. He has lost the nerve which never failed him on the battlefield and has become a weak, doddering old man, utterly incapable of contending with a brilliant, forceful rascal like this Austrian. My client however is an old friend, one who has known the General intimately for many years and taken a paternal interest in this young girl since she wore short frocks. He cannot see this tragedy consummated without some attempt to stop it. There is nothing in which ScotlandYard can act. It was his own suggestion that you should be called in, but it was, as I have said, on the express stipulation that he should not be personally involved in the matter. I have no doubt, Mr. Holmes, with your great powers you could easily trace my client back through me, but I must ask you, as a point of honour, to refrain from doing so, and not to break in upon his incognito."

Holmes gave a whimsical smile.

"I think I may safely promise that," said he. "I may add that your problem interests me, and that I shall be prepared to look into it. How shall I keep in touch with you?"

"The Carlton Club will find me. But in case of emergency, there is a private telephone call, 'XX.31.'"

Holmes noted it down and sat, still smiling, with the open memorandum-book upon his knee.

"The Baron's present address, please?"

"Vernon Lodge, near Kingston. It is a large house. He has been fortunate in some rather shady speculations and is a rich man, which naturally makes him a more dangerous antagonist."

"Is he at home at present?"

"Yes."

"Apart from what you have told me, can you give me any further information about the man?"

"He has expensive tastes. He is a horse fancier. For a short time he played polo at Hurlingham, but then this Prague affair got noised about and he had to leave. He collects books and pictures. He is a man with a considerable artistic side to his nature. He is, I believe, a recognized authority upon Chinese pottery and has written a book upon the subject."

"A complex mind," said Holmes. "All great criminals have that. My old friend Charlie Peace was a violin virtuoso. Wainwright was no mean artist. I could quote many more. Well, Sir James, you will inform your client that I am turning my mind upon Baron Gruner. I can say no more. I have some sources of information of my own, and I dare say we may find some means of opening the matter up."

When our visitor had left us Holmes sat so long in deep thought that it seemed to me that he had forgotten my presence. At last, however, he came briskly back to earth.

"Well, Watson, any views?" he asked.

"I should think you had better see the young lady herself."

"My dear Watson, if her poor old broken father cannot move her, how shall I, a stranger, prevail? And yet there is something in the suggestion if all else fails. But I think we must begin from a different angle. I rather fancy that Shinwell Johnson might be a help."

I have not had occasion to mention Shinwell Johnson in these memoirs because I have seldom drawn my cases from the latter phases of my friend's career. During the first years of the century he became a valuable assistant. Johnson, I grieve to say, made his name first as a very dangerous villain and served two terms at Parkhurst. Finally he repented and allied himself to Holmes, acting as his agent in the huge criminal underworld of London and obtaining information which often proved to be of vital importance. Had Johnson been a "nark" of the police he would soon have been exposed, but as he dealt with cases which never came directly into the courts, his activities were never realized by his companions. With the glamour of his two convictions upon him, he had the entree of every night-club, doss house, and gambling-den in the town, and his quick observation and active brain made him an ideal agent for gaining information. It was to him that Sherlock Holmes now proposed to turn.

It was not possible for me to follow the immediate steps taken by my friend, for I had some pressing professional business of my own, but I met him by appointment that evening at Simpson's, where, sitting at a small table in the front window and looking down at the rushing stream of life in the Strand, he told me something of what had passed.

"Johnson is on the prowl," said he. "He may pick up some garbage in the darker recesses of the underworld, for it is down there, amid the black roots of crime that we must hunt for this man's secrets."

"But if the lady will not accept what is already known, why should any fresh discovery of yours turn her from her purpose?"

"Who knows, Watson? Woman's heart and mind are insoluble puzzles to the male. Murder might be condoned or explained, and yet some smaller offence might rankle. Baron Gruner remarked to me—"

"He remarked to you!"

"Oh, to be sure, I had not told you of my plans. Well, Watson, I love to come to close grips with my man. I like to meet him eye to eye and read for myself the stuff that he is made of. When I had given Johnson his instructions I took a cab out to Kingston and found the Baron in a most affable mood."

"Did he recognize you?"

"There was no difficulty about that, for I simply sent in my card. He is an excellent antagonist, cool as ice, silky voiced and soothing as one of your fashionable consultants, and poisonous as a cobra. He has breeding in him—a real aristocrat of crime with a superficial suggestion of afternoon tea and all the cruelty of the grave behind it. Yes, I am glad to have had my attention called to Baron Adelbert Gruner."

"You say he was affable?"

"A purring cat who thinks he sees prospective mice. Some people's affability is more deadly than the violence of coarser souls. His greeting was characteristic. 'I rather thought I should see you sooner or later, Mr. Holmes,' said he. 'You have been engaged, no doubt by General de Merville, to endeavour to stop my marriage with his daughter, Violet. That is so, is it not?'

"I acquiesced.

"'My dear man,' said he, 'you will only ruin your own well-deserved reputation. It is not a case in which you can possibly succeed. You will have barren work, to say nothing of incurring some danger. Let me very strongly advise you to draw off at once.'

"'It is curious,' I answered, 'but that was the very advice which I had intended to give you. I have a respect for your brains, Baron, and the little which I have seen of your personality has not lessened it. Let me put it to you as man to man. No one wants to rake up your past and make you unduly uncomfortable. It is over, and you are now in smooth waters, but if you persist in this marriage you will raise up a swarm of powerful enemies who will never leave you alone until they have made England too hot to hold you. Is the game worth it? Surely you would be wiser if you left the lady alone. It would not be pleasant for you if these facts of your past were brought to her notice.'

"The Baron has little waxed tips of hair under his nose, like the short antennae of an insect. These quivered with amusement as he listened, and he finally broke into a gentle chuckle.

"'Excuse my amusement, Mr. Holmes,' said he, 'but it is really funny to see you trying to play a hand with no cards in it. I don't think anyone could do it better, but it is rather pathetic all the same. Not a colour card there, Mr. Holmes, nothing but the smallest of the small.'

"'So you think.'

"'So I know. Let me make the thing clear to you, for my own hand is so strong that I can afford to show it. I have been fortunate enough to win the entire affection of this lady. This was given to me in spite of the fact that I told her very clearly of all the unhappy incidents in my past life. I also told her that certain wicked and designing persons—I hope you recognize yourself—would come to her and tell her these things, and I warned her how to treat them. You have heard of post-hypnotic suggestion, Mr. Holmes? Well you will see how it works for a man of personality can use hypnotism without any vulgar passes or tomfoolery. So she is ready for you and, I have no doubt, would give you an appointment, for she is quite amenable to her father's will—save only in the one little matter.'

"Well, Watson, there seemed to be no more to say, so I took my leave with as much cold dignity as I could summon, but, as I had my hand on the door-handle, he stopped me.

"'By the way, Mr. Holmes,' said he, 'did you know Le Brun, the French agent?'

"'Yes,' said I.

"'Do you know what befell him?'

"'I heard that he was beaten by some Apaches in the Montmartre district and crippled for life.'

"'Quite true, Mr. Holmes. By a curious coincidence he had been inquiring into my affairs only a week before. Don't do it, Mr. Holmes; it's not a lucky thing to do. Several have found that out. My last word to you is, go your own way and let me go mine. Good-bye!'

"So there you are, Watson. You are up to date now."

"The fellow seems dangerous."

"Mighty dangerous. I disregard the blusterer, but this is the sort of man who says rather less than he means."

"Must you interfere? Does it really matter if he marries the girl?"

"Considering that he undoubtedly murdered his last wife, I should say it mattered very much. Besides, the client! Well, well, we need not discuss that. When you have finished your coffee you had best come home with me, for the blithe Shinwell will be there with his report."

We found him sure enough, a huge, coarse, red-faced, scorbutic man, with a pair of vivid black eyes which were the only external sign of the very cunning mind within. It seems that he had dived down into what was peculiarly his kingdom, and beside him on the settee was a brand which he had brought up in the shape of a slim, flame-like young woman with a pale, intense face, youthful, and yet so worn with sin and sorrow that one read the terrible years which had left their leprous mark upon her.

"This is Miss Kitty Winter," said Shinwell Johnson, waving his fat hand as an introduction. "What she don't know—well, there, she'll speak for herself. Put my hand right on her, Mr. Holmes, within an hour of your message."

"I'm easy to find," said the young woman. "Hell, London, gets me every time. Same address for Porky Shinwell. We're old mates, Porky, you and I. But, by cripes! there is another who ought to be down in a lower hell than we if there was any justice in the world! That is the man you are after, Mr. Holmes."

Holmes smiled. "I gather we have your good wishes, Miss Winter."

"If I can help to put him where he belongs, I'm yours to the rattle," said our visitor with fierce energy. There was an intensity of hatred in her white, set face and her blazing eyes such as woman seldom and man never can attain.

"You needn't go into my past, Mr. Holmes. That's neither here nor there. But what I am Adelbert Gruner made me. If I could pull him down!" She clutched frantically with her hands into the air. "Oh, if I could only pull him into the pit where he has pushed so many!"

"You know how the matter stands?"

"Porky Shinwell has been telling me. He's after some other poor fool and wants to marry her this time. You want to stop it. Well, you surely know enough about this devil to prevent any decent girl in her senses wanting to be in the same parish with him."

"She is not in her senses. She is madly in love. She has been told all about him. She cares nothing."

"Told about the murder?"

"Yes."

"My Lord, she must have a nerve!"

"She puts them all down as slanders."

"Couldn't you lay proofs before her silly eyes?"

"Well, can you help us do so?"

"Ain't I a proof myself? If I stood before her and told her how he used me—"

"Would you do this?"

"Would I? Would I not!"

"Well, it might be worth trying. But he has told her most of his sins and had pardon from her, and I understand she will not reopen the question."

"I'll lay he didn't tell her all," said Miss Winter. "I caught a glimpse of one or two murders besides the one that made such a fuss. He would speak of someone in his velvet way and then look at me with a steady eye and say: 'He died within a month.' It wasn't hot air, either. But I took little notice—you see, I loved him myself at that time. Whatever he did went with me, same as with this poor fool! There was just one thing that shook me. Yes, by cripes! if it had not been for his poisonous, lying tongue that explains and soothes. I'd have left him that very night. It's a book he has—a brown leather book with a lock, and his arms in gold on the outside. I think he was a bit drunk that night, or he would not have shown it to me."

"What was it, then?"

"I tell you, Mr. Holmes, this man collects women, and takes a pride in his collection, as some men collect moths or butterflies. He had it all in that book. Snapshot photographs, names, details, everything about them. It was a beastly book—a book no man, even if he had come from the gutter, could have put together. But it was Adelbert Gruner's book all the same. 'Souls I have ruined.' He could have put that on the outside if he had been so minded. However, that's neither here nor there, for the book would not serve you, and, if it would, you can't get it."

"Where is it?"

"How can I tell you where it is now? It's more than a year since I left him. I know where he kept it then. He's a precise, tidy cat of a man in many of his ways, so maybe it is still in the pigeon-hole of the old bureau in the inner study. Do you know his house?"

"I've been in the study," said Holmes.

"Have you, though? You haven't been slow on the job if you only started this morning. Maybe dear Adelbert has met his match this time. The outer study is the one with the Chinese crockery in it—big glass cupboard between the windows. Then behind his desk is the door that leads to the inner study—a small room where he keeps papers and things."

"Is he not afraid of burglars?"

"Adelbert is no coward. His worst enemy couldn't say that of him. He can look after himself. There's a burglar alarm at night. Besides, what is there for a burglar—unless they got away with all this fancy crockery?"

"No good," said Shinwell Johnson with the decided voice of the expert. "No fence wants stuff of that sort that you can neither melt nor sell."

"Quite so," said Holmes. "Well, now, Miss Winter, if you would call here tomorrow evening at five. I would consider in the meanwhile whether your suggestion of seeing this lady personally may not be arranged. I am exceedingly obliged to you for your cooperation. I need not say that my clients will consider liberally—"

"None of that, Mr. Holmes," cried the young woman. "I am not out for money. Let me see this man in the mud, and I've got all I've worked for—in the mud with my foot on his cursed face. That's my price. I'm with you tomorrow or any other day so long as you are on his track. Porky here can tell you always where to find me."

I did not see Holmes again until the following evening when we dined once more at our Strand restaurant. He shrugged his shoulders when I asked him what luck he had had in his interview. Then he told the story, which I would repeat in this way. His hard, dry statement needs some little editing to soften it into the terms of real life.

"There was no difficulty at all about the appointment," said Holmes, "for the girl glories in showing abject filial obedience in all secondary things in an attempt to atone for her flagrant breach of it in her engagement. The General phoned that all was ready, and the fiery Miss W. turned up according to schedule, so that at half-past five a cab deposited us outside 104 Berkeley Square, where the old soldier resides—one of those awful gray London castles which would make a church seem frivolous. A footman showed us into a great yellow-curtained drawing-room, and there was the lady awaiting us, demure, pale, self-contained, as inflexible and remote as a snow image on a mountain.

"I don't quite know how to make her clear to you, Watson. Perhaps you may meet her before we are through, and you can use your own gift of words. She is beautiful, but with the ethereal other-world beauty of some fanatic whose thoughts are set on high. I have seen such faces in the pictures of the old masters of the Middle Ages. How a beastman could have laid his vile paws upon such a being of the beyond I cannot imagine. You may have noticed how extremes call to each other, the spiritual to the animal, the cave-man to the angel. You never saw a worse case than this.

"She knew what we had come for, of course—that villain had lost no time in poisoning her mind against us. Miss Winter's advent rather amazed her, I think, but she waved us into our respective chairs like a reverend abbess receiving two rather leprous mendicants. If your head is inclined to swell, my dear Watson, take a course of Miss Violet de Merville.

"'Well, sir,' said she in a voice like the wind from an iceberg, 'your name is familiar to me. You have called, as I understand, to malign my fiance, Baron Gruner. It is only by my father's request that I see you at all, and I warn you in advance that anything you can say could not possibly have the slightest effect upon my mind.'

"I was sorry for her, Watson. I thought of her for the moment as I would have thought of a daughter of my own. I am not often eloquent. I use my head, not my heart. But I really did plead with her with all the warmth of words that I could find in my nature. I pictured to her the awful position of the woman who only wakes to a man's character after she is his wife—a woman who has to submit to be caressed by bloody hands and lecherous lips. I spared her nothing—the shame, the fear, the agony, the hopelessness of it all. All my hot words could not bring one tinge of colour to those ivory cheeks or one gleam of emotion to those abstracted eyes. I thought of what the rascal had said about a post-hypnotic influence. One could really believe that she was living above the earth in some ecstatic dream. Yet there was nothing indefinite in her replies.

"'I have listened to you with patience, Mr. Holmes,' said she. 'The effect upon my mind is exactly as predicted. I am aware that Adelbert, that my fiance, has had a stormy life in which he has incurred bitter hatreds and most unjust aspersions. You are only the last of a series who have brought their slanders before me. Possibly you mean well, though I learn that you are a paid agent who would have been equally willing to act for the Baron as against him. But in any case I wish you to understand once for all that I love him and that he loves me, and that the opinion of all the world is no more to me than the twitter of those birds outside the window. If his noble nature has ever for an instant fallen, it may be that I have been specially sent to raise it to its true and lofty level. I am not clear'—here she turned eyes upon my companion—'who this young lady may be.'

"I was about to answer when the girl broke in like a whirlwind. If ever you saw flame and ice face to face, it was those two women.

"'I'll tell you who I am,' she cried, springing out of her chair, her mouth all twisted with passion—'I am his last mistress. I am one of a hundred that he has tempted and used and ruined and thrown into the refuse heap, as he will you also. Your refuse heap is more likely to be a grave, and maybe that's the best. I tell you, you foolish woman, if you marry this man he'll be the death of you. It may be a broken heart or it may be a broken neck, but he'll have you one way or the other. It's not out of love for you I'm speaking. I don't care a tinker's curse whether you live or die. It's out of hate for him and to spite him and to get back on him for what he did to me. But it's all the same, and you needn't look at me like that, my fine lady, for you may be lower than I am before you are through with it.'

"'I should prefer not to discuss such matters,' said Miss de Merville coldly. 'Let me say once for all that I am aware of three passages in my fiance's life in which he became entangled with designing women, and that I am assured of his hearty repentance for any evil that he may have done.'

"'Three passages!' screamed my companion. 'You fool! You unutterable fool!'

"'Mr. Holmes, I beg that you will bring this interview to an end,' said the icy voice. 'I have obeyed my father's wish in seeing you, but I am not compelled to listen to the ravings of this person.'

"With an oath Miss Winter darted forward, and if I had not caught her wrist she would have clutched this maddening woman by the hair. I dragged her toward the door and was lucky to get her back into the cab without a public scene, for she was beside herself with rage. In a cold way I felt pretty furious myself, Watson, for there was something indescribably annoying in the calm aloofness and supreme self-complaisance of the woman whom we were trying to save. So now once again you know exactly how we stand, and it is clear that I must plan some fresh opening move, for this gambit won't work. I'll keep in touch with you, Watson, for it is more than likely that you will have your part to play, though it is just possible that the next move may lie with them rather than with us."

And it did. Their blow fell—or his blow rather, for never could I believe that the lady was privy to it. I think I could show you the very paving-stone upon which I stood when my eyes fell upon the placard, and a pang of horror passed through my very soul. It was between the Grand Hotel and Charing Cross Station, where a one-legged news-vender displayed his evening papers. The date was just two days after the last conversation. There, black upon yellow, was the terrible news-sheet:

MURDEROUS ATTACK UPON SHERLOCK HOLMES

I think I stood stunned for some moments. Then I have a confused recollection of snatching at a paper, of the remonstrance of the man, whom I had not paid, and, finally, of standing in the doorway of a chemist's shop while I turned up the fateful paragraph. This was how it ran:

"We learn with regret that Mr. Sherlock Holmes, the well-known private detective, was the victim this morning of a murderous assault which has left him in a precarious position. There are no exact details to hand, but the event seems to have occurred about twelve o'clock in Regent Street, outside the Cafe Royal. The attack was made by two men armed with sticks, and Mr. Holmes was beaten about the head and body, receiving injuries which the doctors describe as most serious. He was carried to Charing Cross Hospital and afterwards insisted upon being taken to his rooms in Baker Street. The miscreants who attacked him appear to have been respectably dressed men, who escaped from the bystanders by passing through the Cafe Royal and out into Glasshouse Street behind it. No doubt they belonged to that criminal fraternity which has so often had occasion to bewail the activity and ingenuity of the injured man."

I need not say that my eyes had hardly glanced over the paragraph before I had sprung into a hansom and was on my way to Baker Street. I found Sir Leslie Oakshott, the famous surgeon, in the hall and his brougham waiting at the curb.

"No immediate danger," was his report. "Two lacerated scalp wounds and some considerable bruises. Several stitches have been necessary. Morphine has been injected and quiet is essential, but an interview of a few minutes would not be absolutely forbidden."

With this permission I stole into the darkened room. The sufferer was wide awake, and I heard my name in a hoarse whisper. The blind was three-quarters down, but one ray of sunlight slanted through and struck the bandaged head of the injured man. A crimson patch had soaked through the white linen compress. I sat beside him and bent my head.

"All right, Watson. Don't look so scared," he muttered in a very weak voice. "It's not as bad as it seems."

"Thank God for that!"

"I'm a bit of a single-stick expert, as you know. I took most of them on my guard. It was the second man that was too much for me."

"What can I do, Holmes? Of course, it was that damned fellow who set them on. I'll go and thrash the hide off him if you give the word."

"Good old Watson! No, we can do nothing there unless the police lay their hands on the men. But their get-away had been well prepared. We may be sure of that. Wait a little. I have my plans. The first thing is to exaggerate my injuries. They'll come to you for news. Put it on thick, Watson. Lucky if I live the week out concussion delirium—what you like! You can't overdo it."

"But Sir Leslie Oakshott?"

"Oh, he's all right. He shall see the worst side of me. I'll look after that."

"Anything else?"

"Yes. Tell Shinwell Johnson to get that girl out of the way. Those beauties will be after her now. They know, of course, that she was with me in the case. If they dared to do me in it is not likely they will neglect her. That is urgent. Do it tonight."

"I'll go now. Anything more?"

"Put my pipe on the table—and the tobacco-slipper. Right! Come in each morning and we will plan our campaign."

I arranged with Johnson that evening to take Miss Winter to a quiet suburb and see that she lay low until the danger was past.

For six days the public were under the impression that Holmes was at the door of death. The bulletins were very grave and there were sinister paragraphs in the papers. My continual visits assured me that it was not so bad as that. His wiry constitution and his determined will were working wonders. He was recovering fast, and I had suspicions at times that he was really finding himself faster than he pretended even to me. There was a curious secretive streak in the man which led to many dramatic effects, but left even his closest friend guessing as to what his exact plans might be. He pushed to an extreme the axiom that the only safe plotter was he who plotted alone. I was nearer him than anyone else, and yet I was always conscious of the gap between.

On the seventh day the stitches were taken out, in spite of which there was a report of erysipelas in the evening papers. The same evening papers had an announcement which I was bound, sick or well, to carry to my friend. It was simply that among the passengers on the Cunard boat Ruritania, starting from Liverpool on Friday, was the Baron Adelbert Gruner, who had some important financial business to settle in the States before his impending wedding to Miss Violet de Merville, only daughter of, etc., etc. Holmes listened to the news with a cold, concentrated look upon his pale face, which told me that it hit him hard.

"Friday!" he cried. "Only three clear days. I believe the rascal wants to put himself out of danger's way. But he won't, Watson! By the Lord Harry, he won't! Now, Watson, I want you to do something for me."

"I am here to be used, Holmes."

"Well, then, spend the next twenty-four hours in an intensive study of Chinese pottery."

He gave no explanations and I asked for none. By long experience I had learned the wisdom of obedience. But when I had left his room I walked down Baker Street, revolving in my head how on earth I was to carry out so strange an order. Finally I drove to the London Library in St. James's Square, put the matter to my friend Lomax, the sublibrarian, and departed to my rooms with a goodly volume under my arm.

It is said that the barrister who crams up a case with such care that he can examine an expert witness upon the Monday has forgotten all his forced knowledge before the Saturday. Certainly I should not like now to pose as an authority upon ceramics. And yet all that evening, and all that night with a short interval for rest, and all next morning, I was sucking in knowledge and committing names to memory. There I learned of the hall-marks of the great artist-decorators, of the mystery of cyclical dates, the marks of the Hung-wu and the beauties of the Yung-lo, the writings of Tang-ying, and the glories of the primitive period of the Sung and the Yuan. I was charged with all this information when I called upon Holmes next evening. He was out of bed now, though you would not have guessed it from the published reports, and he sat with his much-bandaged head resting upon his hand in the depth of his favourite armchair.

"Why, Holmes," I said, "if one believed the papers, you are dying."

"That," said he, "is the very impression which I intended to convey. And now, Watson, have you learned your lessons?"

"At least I have tried to."

"Good. You could keep up an intelligent conversation on the subject?"

"I believe I could."

"Then hand me that little box from the mantelpiece."

He opened the lid and took out a small object most carefully wrapped in some fine Eastern silk. This he unfolded, and disclosed a delicate little saucer of the most beautiful deep-blue colour.

"It needs careful handling, Watson. This is the real egg-shell pottery of the Ming dynasty. No finer piece ever passed through Christie's. A complete set of this would be worth a king's ransom—in fact, it is doubtful if there is a complete set outside the imperial palace of Peking. The sight of this would drive a real connoisseur wild."

"What am I to do with it?"

Holmes handed me a card upon which was printed: "Dr. Hill Barton, 369 Half Moon Street."

"That is your name for the evening, Watson. You will call upon Baron Gruner. I know something of his habits, and at half-past eight he would probably be disengaged. A note will tell him in advance that you are about to call, and you will say that you are bringing him a specimen of an absolutely unique set of Ming china. You may as well be a medical man, since that is a part which you can play without duplicity. You are a collector, this set has come your way, you have heard of the Baron's interest in the subject, and you are not averse to selling at a price."

"What price?"

"Well asked, Watson. You would certainly fall down badly if you did not know the value of your own wares. This saucer was got for me by Sir James, and comes, I understand, from the collection of his client. You will not exaggerate if you say that it could hardly be matched in the world."

"I could perhaps suggest that the set should be valued by an expert."

"Excellent, Watson! You scintillate today. Suggest Christie or Sotheby. Your delicacy prevents your putting a price for yourself."

"But if he won't see me?"

"Oh, yes, he will see you. He has the collection mania in its most acute form—and especially on this subject, on which he is an acknowledged authority. Sit down, Watson, and I will dictate the letter. No answer needed. You will merely say that you are coming, and why."

It was an admirable document, short, courteous, and stimulating to the curiosity of the connoisseur. A district messenger was duly dispatched with it. On the same evening, with the precious saucer in my hand and the card of Dr. Hill Barton in my pocket, I set off on my own adventure.

The beautiful house and grounds indicated that Baron Gruner was, as Sir James had said, a man of considerable wealth. A long winding drive, with banks of rare shrubs on either side, opened out into a great gravelled square adorned with statues. The place had been built by a South African gold king in the days of the great boom, and the long, low house with the turrets at the corners, though an architectural nightmare, was imposing in its size and solidity. A butler, who would have adorned a bench of bishops, showed me in and handed me over to a plush-clad footman, who ushered me into the Baron's presence.

He was standing at the open front of a great case which stood between the windows and which contained part of his Chinese collection. He turned as I entered with a small brown vase in his hand.

"Pray sit down, Doctor," said he. "I was looking over my own treasures and wondering whether I could really afford to add to them. This little Tang specimen, which dates from the seventh century, would probably interest you. I am sure you never saw finer workmanship or a richer glaze. Have you the Ming saucer with you of which you spoke?"

I carefully unpacked it and handed it to him. He seated himself at his desk, pulled over the lamp, for it was growing dark, and set himself to examine it. As he did so the yellow light beat upon his own features, and I was able to study them at my ease.

He was certainly a remarkably handsome man. His European reputation for beauty was fully deserved. In figure he was not more than of middle size, but was built upon graceful and active lines. His face was swarthy, almost Oriental, with large, dark, languorous eyes which might easily hold an irresistible fascination for women. His hair and moustache were raven black, the latter short, pointed, and carefully waxed. His features were regular and pleasing, save only his straight, thin-lipped mouth. If ever I saw a murderer's mouth it was there—a cruel, hard gash in the face, compressed, inexorable, and terrible. He was ill-advised to train his moustache away from it, for it was Nature's danger-signal, set as a warning to his victims. His voice was engaging and his manners perfect. In age I should have put him at little over thirty, though his record afterwards showed that he was forty-two.

"Very fine—very fine indeed!" he said at last. "And you say you have a set of six to correspond. What puzzles me is that I should not have heard of such magnificent specimens. I only know of one in England to match this, and it is certainly not likely to be in the market. Would it be indiscreet if I were to ask you, Dr. Hill Barton, how you obtained this?"

"Does it really matter?" I asked with as careless an air as I could muster.

"You can see that the piece is genuine, and, as to the value, I am content to take an expert's valuation."

"Very mysterious," said he with a quick, suspicious flash of his dark eyes. "In dealing with objects of such value, one naturally wishes to know all about the transaction. That the piece is genuine is certain. I have no doubts at all about that. But suppose—I am bound to take every possibility into account—that it should prove afterwards that you had no right to sell?"

"I would guarantee you against any claim of the son."

"That, of course, would open up the question as to what your guarantee was worth."

"My bankers would answer that."

"Quite so. And yet the whole transaction strikes me as rather unusual."

"You can do business or not," said I with indifference. "I have given you the first offer as I understood that you were a connoisseur, but I shall have no difficulty in other quaerers."

"Who told you I was a connoisseur?"

"I was aware that you had written a book upon the subject."

"Have you read the book?"

"No."

"Dear me, this becomes more and more difficult for me to understand! You are a connoisseur and collector with a very valuable piece in your collection, and yet you have never troubled to consult the one book which would have told you of the real meaning and value of what you held. How do you explain that?"

"I am a very busy man. I am a doctor in practice."

"That is no answer. If a man has a hobby he follows it up, whatever his other pursuits may be. You said in your note that you were a connoisseur."

"So I am."

"Might I ask you a few questions to test you? I am obliged to tell you, Doctor—if you are indeed a doctor—that the incident becomes more and more suspicious. I would ask you what do you know of the Emperor Shomu and how do you associate him with the Shoso-in near Nara? Dear me, does that puzzle you? Tell me a little about the Nonhern Wei dynasty and its place in the history of ceramics."

I sprang from my chair in simulated anger.

"This is intolerable, sir," said I. "I came here to do you a favour, and not to be examined as if I were a schoolboy. My knowledge on these subjects may be second only to your own, but I certainly shall not answer questions which have been put in so offensive a way."

He looked at me steadily. The languor had gone from his eyes. They suddenly glared. There was a gleam of teeth from between those cruel lips.

"What is the game? You are here as a spy. You are an emissary of Holmes. This is a trick that you are playing upon me. The fellow is dying I hear, so he sends his tools to keep watch upon me. You've made your way in here without leave, and, by God! You may find it harder to get out than to get in."

He had sprung to his feet, and I stepped back, bracing myself for an attack, for the man was beside himself with rage. He may have suspected me from the first; certainly this cross-examination had shown him the truth; but it was clear that I could not hope to deceive him. He dived his hand into a side-drawer and rummaged furiously. Then something struck upon his ear, for he stood listening intently.

"Ah!" he cried. "Ah!" and dashed into the room behind him.

Two steps took me to the open door, and my mind will ever carry a clear picture of the scene within. The window leading out to the garden was wide open. Beside it, looking like some terrible ghost, his head gin with bloody bandages, his face drawn and white, stood Sherlock Holmes. The next instant he was through the gap, and I heard the crash of his body among the laurel bushes outside. With a howl of rage the master of the house rushed after him to the open window.

And then! It was done in an instant, and yet I clearly saw it. An arm—a woman's arm—shot out from among the leaves. At the same instant the Baron uttered a horrible cry—a yell which will always ring in my memory. He clapped his two hands to his face and rushed round the room, beating his head horribly against the walls. Then he fell upon the carpet, rolling and writhing, while scream after scream resounded through the house.

"Water! For God's sake, water!" was his cry.

I seized a carafe from a side-table and rushed to his aid. At the same moment the butler and several footmen ran in from the hall. I remember that one of them fainted as I knelt by the injured man and turned that awful face to the light of the lamp. The vitriol was eating into it everywhere and dripping from the ears and the chin. One eye was already white and glazed. The other was red and inflamed. The features which I had admired a few minutes before were now like some beautiful painting over which the artist has passed a wet and foul sponge. They were blurred, discoloured, inhuman, terrible.

In a few words I explained exactly what had occurred, so far as the vitriol attack was concerned. Some had climbed through the window and others had rushed out on to the lawn, but it was dark and it had begun to rain. Between his screams the victim raged and raved against the avenger. "It was that hell-cat, Kitty Winter!" he cried. "Oh, the she-devil! She shall pay for it! She shall pay! Oh, God in heaven, this pain is more than I can bear!"

I bathed his face in oil, put cotton wadding on the raw surfaces, and administered a hypodermic of morphia. All suspicion of me had passed from his mind in the presence of this shock, and he clung to my hands as if I might have the power even yet to clear those dead-fish eyes which glazed up at me.

I could have wept over the ruin had I not remembered very clearly the vile life which had led up to so hideous a change. It was loathsome to feel the pawing of his burning hands, and I was relieved when his family surgeon, closely followed by a specialist, came to relieve me of my charge. An inspector of police had also arrived, and to him I handed my real card. It would have been useless as well as foolish to do otherwise, for I was nearly as well known by sight at the Yard as Holmes himself. Then I left that house of gloom and terror. Within an hour I was at Baker Street.

Holmes was seated in his familiar chair, looking very pale and exhausted. Apart from his injuries, even his iron nerves had been shocked by the events of the evening, and he listened with horror to my account of the Baron's transformation.

"The wages of sin, Watson—the wages of sin!" said he. "Sooner or later it will always come. God knows, there was sin enough," he added, taking up a brown volume from the table. "Here is the book the woman talked of. If this will not break off the marriage, nothing ever could. But it will, Watson. It must. No self-respecting woman could stand it."

"It is his love diary?"

"Or his lust diary. Call it what you will. The moment the woman told us of it I realized what a tremendous weapon was there if we could but lay our hands on it. I said nothing at the time to indicate my thoughts, for this woman might have given it away. But I brooded over it. Then this assault upon me gave me the chance of letting the Baron think that no precautions need be taken against me. That was all to the good. I would have waited a little longer, but his visit to America forced my hand. He would never have left so compromising a document behind him. Therefore we had to act at once. Burglary at night is impossible. He takes precautions. But there was a chance in the evening if I could only be sure that his attention was engaged. That was where you and your blue saucer came in. But I had to be sure of the position of the book, and I knew I had only a few minutes in which to act, for my time was limited by your knowledge of Chinese pottery. Therefore I gathered the girl up at the last moment. How could I guess what the little packet was that she carried so carefully under her cloak? I thought she had come altogether on my business, but it seems she had some of her own."

"He guessed I came from you."

"I feared he would. But you held him in play just long enough for me to get the book, though not long enough for an unobserved escape. Ah, Sir James, I am very glad you have come!"

Our courtly friend had appeared in answer to a previous summons. He listened with the deepest attention to Holmes's account of what had occurred.

"You have done wonders—wonders!" he cried when he had heard the narrative. "But if these injuries are as terrible as Dr. Watson describes, then surely our purpose of thwarting the marriage is sufficiently gained without the use of this horrible book."

Holmes shook his head.

"Women of the De Merville type do not act like that. She would love him the more as a disfigured martyr. No, no. It is his moral side, not his physical, which we have to destroy. That book will bring her back to earth—and I know nothing else that could. It is in his own writing. She cannot get past it."

Sir James carried away both it and the precious saucer. As I was myself overdue, I went down with him into the street. A brougham was waiting for him. He sprang in, gave a hurried order to the cockaded coachman, and drove swiftly away. He flung his overcoat half out of the window to cover the armorial bearings upon the panel, but I had seen them in the glare of our fanlight nonetheless. I gasped with surprise. Then I turned back and ascended the stair to Holmes's room.

"I have found out who our client is," I cried, bursting with my great news. "Why, Holmes, it is—"

"It is a loyal friend and a chivalrous gentleman," said Holmes, holding up a restraining hand. "Let that now and forever be enough for us."

I do not know how the incriminating book was used. Sir James may have managed it. Or it is more probable that so delicate a task was entrusted to the young lady's father. The effect, at any rate, was all that could be desired.

Three days later appeared a paragraph in the Morning Post to say that the marriage between Baron Adelbert Gruner and Miss Violet de Merville would not take place. The same paper had the first police-court hearing of the proceedings against Miss Kitty Winter on the grave charge of vitriol-throwing. Such extenuating circumstances came out in the trial that the sentence, as will be remembered was the lowest that was possible for such an offence. Sherlock Holmes was threatened with a prosecution for burglary, but when an object is good and a client is sufficiently illustrious, even the rigid British law becomes human and elastic. My friend has not yet stood in the dock.

† † † † †

"The Adventure of the Illustrious Client" repeats elements of "A Scandal in Bohemia." There is no crime or mystery to be solved; an important client asks Holmes to obtain evidence that will permit or prevent a marriage as the case may be. However, just as The Hound of the Baskervilles can be seen as a rationalized werewolf story, this tale is an abridged version of Dracula.

The similarities with Bram Stoker's masterpiece transcend mere coincidence. Their evil protagonists—Count Dracula or Baron Adelbert Gruner—are European noblemen who use hypnotism to "collect women." Both of them can be described as "a real aristocrat of crime with a superficial suggestion of afternoon tea and all the cruelty of the grave behind it." An erotic undercurrent runs throughout both tales, for they have come to London where they have ruined one woman (Lucy/Kitty) and threaten another (Mina/Violet). A group of "vampire hunters" band together to thwart the nobleman's plans. Their quest is aided by a woman who has special knowledge about the fiend (Mina's telepathic link to the Count or Kitty's awareness of the Baron's "lust diary"). A turning point occurs when the villain, who—as Holmes predicted, has encountered "a swarm of powerful enemies"—is forced to (or plans to) leave London by ship. After numerous twists and turns, the heroes prevent Mina's transformation into a vampire and stop Violet's marriage to Gruner. All is well.

The names that Doyle chose for the characters in this story are another broad clue about the source of the story:

- "Adelbert" shares four letters with "Dracula"—D, R, A, and L.
- One of Dracula's pseudonyms is Count "DeVille." Violet's family name, "DeMerville" is almost an anagram of "Mr. Deville."
- The description of Kitty Winter as "the fiery Miss W." suggests Lucy Westenra who, like Kitty, was the "vampire's" first victim in England.

There are too many tongue-in-cheek allusions to be or chalked up to coincidence. It is possible that Doyle shared some of the in-jokes with his friends: both tales can be traced to a "large, bluff" Irishman (Bram Stoker or Sir James Damery); concomitantly, the mention of the Strand suggests Bram Stoker's Lyceum Theatre on Wellington Street; the "Café Royale" does duty for the Hotel Royal, which is mentioned on the first page of the novel; the "three incidents" in Gruner's past are a nod to the three vampire women in Dracula's castle; both tales include a confrontation at and a leap from a window in the second half of the story; and the climax occurs when the villain's body or face dissolves.

This analysis conjures up the image of Dracula playing polo at Hillingham/Hurlingham, which may have given the author a chuckle, while Holmes's appearance as a "terrible ghost, his head gin with bloody bandages, his face drawn and white" takes on new meaning. It may also explain why Watson introduces the case as " . . . the supreme moment of my friend's career."

The Adventure
of the Sussex Vampire

Holmes had read carefully a note which the last post had brought him. Then, with the dry chuckle which was his nearest approach to a laugh, he tossed it over to me.

"For a mixture of the modern and the medieval, of the practical and of the wildly fanciful, I think this is surely the limit," said he. "What do you make of it, Watson?"

I read as follows:

46, OLD JEWRY,
Nov. 19th.
Re Vampires
SIR:
Our client, Mr. Robert Ferguson, of Ferguson and Muirhead, tea brokers, of Mincing Lane, has made some inquiry from us in a communication of even date concerning vampires. As our firm specializes entirely upon the assessment of machinery the matter hardly comes within our purview, and we have therefore recommended Mr. Ferguson to call upon you and lay the matter

The Strand Magazine, (January 1924) with four illustrations by Howard K. Elcock, and reprinted in Hearst's International Magazine, January 1924, with four illustrations by W. T. Benda.

before you. We have not forgotten your successful action in the
case of Matilda Briggs.
We are, sir,
Faithfully yours,
MORRISON, MORRISON, AND DODD.
per E. J. C.

"Matilda Briggs was not the name of a young woman, Watson,"
said Holmes in a reminiscent voice. "It was a ship which is associated with the giant rat of Sumatra, a story for which the world
is not yet prepared. But what do we know about vampires?
Does it come within our purview either? Anything is better
than stagnation, but really we seem to have been switched on
to a Grimms' fairy tale. Make a long arm, Watson, and see what
V has to say."

I leaned back and took down the great index volume to
which he referred. Holmes balanced it on his knee, and his eyes
moved slowly and lovingly over the record of old cases, mixed
with the accumulated information of a lifetime.

"Voyage of the *Gloria Scott*," he read. "That was a bad business.
I have some recollection that you made a record of it, Watson,
though I was unable to congratulate you upon the result. Victor
Lynch, the forger. Venomous lizard or gila. Remarkable case,
that! Vittoria, the circus belle. Vanderbilt and the Yeggman.
Vipers. Vigor, the Hammersmith wonder. Hullo! Hullo! Good
old index. You can't beat it. Listen to this, Watson. Vampirism in
Hungary. And again, Vampires in Transylvania." He turned over
the pages with eagerness, but after a short intent perusal he
threw down the great book with a snarl of disappointment.

"Rubbish, Watson, rubbish! What have we to do with
walking corpses who can only be held in their grave by stakes
driven through their hearts? It's pure lunacy."

"But surely," said I, "the vampire was not necessarily a dead
man? A living person might have the habit. I have read, for
example, of the old sucking the blood of the young in order to
retain their youth."

"You are right, Watson. It mentions the legend in one of these references. But are we to give serious attention to such things? This agency stands flat-footed upon the ground, and there it must remain. The world is big enough for us. No ghosts need apply. I fear that we cannot take Mr. Robert Ferguson very seriously. Possibly this note may be from him and may throw some light upon what is worrying him."

He took up a second letter which had lain unnoticed upon the table while he had been absorbed with the first. This he began to read with a smile of amusement upon his face which gradually faded away into an expression of intense interest and concentration. When he had finished he sat for some little time lost in thought with the letter dangling from his fingers. Finally, with a start, he aroused himself from his reverie.

"Cheeseman's, Lamberley. Where is Lamberley, Watson?"

"It is in Sussex, South of Horsham."

"Not very far, eh? And Cheeseman's?"

"I know that country, Holmes. It is full of old houses which are named after the men who built them centuries ago. You get Odley's and Harvey's and Carriton's—the folk are forgotten but their names live in their houses."

"Precisely," said Holmes coldly. It was one of the peculiarities of his proud, self-contained nature that though he docketed any fresh information very quietly and accurately in his brain, he seldom made any acknowledgment to the giver. "I rather fancy we shall know a good deal more about Cheeseman's, Lamberley, before we are through. The letter is, as I had hoped, from Robert Ferguson. By the way, he claims acquaintance with you."

"With me!"

"You had better read it."

He handed the letter across. It was headed with the address quoted.

DEAR MR HOLMES [it said]:

I have been recommended to you by my lawyers, but indeed the matter is so extraordinarily delicate that it is most difficult to discuss. It concerns a friend for whom I am acting. This gentleman married some five years ago a Peruvian lady the daughter of a Peruvian merchant, whom he had met in connection with the importation of nitrates. The lady was very beautiful, but the fact of her foreign birth and of her alien religion always caused a separation of interests and of feelings between husband and wife, so that after a time his love may have cooled toward her and he may have come to regard their union as a mistake. He felt there were sides of her character which he could never explore or understand. This was the more painful as she was as loving a wife as a man could have—to all appearance absolutely devoted.

Now for the point which I will make more plain when we meet. Indeed, this note is merely to give you a general idea of the situation and to ascertain whether you would care to interest yourself in the matter. The lady began to show some curious traits quite alien to her ordinarily sweet and gentle disposition. The gentleman had been married twice and he had one son by the first wife. This boy was now fifteen, a very charming and affectionate youth, though unhappily injured through an accident in childhood. Twice the wife was caught in the act of assaulting this poor lad in the most unprovoked way. Once she struck him with a stick and left a great weal on his arm.

This was a small matter, however, compared with her conduct to her own child, a dear boy just under one year of age. On one occasion about a month ago this child had been left by its nurse for a few minutes. A loud cry from the baby, as of pain, called the nurse back. As she ran into the room she saw her employer, the lady, leaning over the baby and apparently biting his neck. There was a small wound in the neck from which a stream of blood had escaped. The nurse was so horrified that she wished to call the husband, but the lady implored her not to do so and actually gave her five pounds as a price for her silence. No explanation was ever given, and for the moment the matter was passed over.

It left, however, a terrible impression upon the nurse's mind, and from that time she began to watch her mistress closely and to keep a closer guard upon the baby, whom she tenderly loved. It seemed to her that even as she watched the mother, so the mother watched her, and that every time she was compelled to leave the baby alone the mother was waiting to get at it. Day and night the nurse covered the child, and day and night the silent, watchful mother seemed to be lying in wait as a wolf waits for a lamb. It must read most incredible to you, and yet I beg you to take it seriously, for a child's life and a man's sanity may depend upon it.

At last there came one dreadful day when the facts could no longer be concealed from the husband. The nurse's nerve had given way; she could stand the strain no longer, and she made a clean breast of it all to the man. To him it seemed as wild a tale as it may now seem to you. He knew his wife to be a loving wife, and, save for the assaults upon her stepson, a loving mother. Why, then, should she wound her own dear little baby? He told the nurse that she was dreaming, that her suspicions were those of a lunatic, and that such libels upon her mistress were not to be tolerated. While they were talking a sudden cry of pain was heard. Nurse and master rushed together to the nursery.

Imagine his feelings, Mr. Holmes, as he saw his wife rise from a kneeling position beside the cot and saw blood upon the child's exposed neck and upon the sheet. With a cry of horror, he turned his wife's face to the light and saw blood all round her lips. It was she—she beyond all question—who had drunk the poor baby's blood.

So the matter stands. She is now confined to her room. There has been no explanation. The husband is half demented. He knows, and I know, little of vampirism beyond the name. We had thought it was some wild tale of foreign parts. And yet here in the very heart of the English Sussex—well, all this can be discussed with you in the morning. Will you see me? Will you use your great powers in aiding a distracted man? If so, kindly wire to

*Ferguson, Cheeseman's, Lamberley, and I will be at your rooms
by ten o'clock.
Yours faithfully,*
ROBERT FERGUSON.

*P. S. I believe your friend Watson played Rugby for Blackheath
when I was three-quarter for Richmond. It is the only personal
introduction which I can give.*

"Of course I remembered him," said I as I laid down the letter.
"Big Bob Ferguson, the finest three-quarter Richmond ever
had. He was always a good-natured chap. It's like him to be so
concerned over a friend's case."

Holmes looked at me thoughtfully and shook his head.

"I never get your limits, Watson," said he. "There are unex-
plored possibilities about you. Take a wire down, like a good
fellow. Will examine your case with pleasure."

"Your case!"

"We must not let him think that this agency is a home for
the weak-minded. Of course it is his case. Send him that wire
and let the matter rest till morning."

Promptly at ten o'clock the next morning Ferguson strode
into our room. I had remembered him as a long, slab-sided man
with loose limbs and a fine turn of speed which had carried
him round many an opposing back. There is surely nothing
in life more painful than to meet the wreck of a fine athlete
whom one has known in his prime. His great frame had fallen
in, his flaxen hair was scanty, and his shoulders were bowed. I
fear that I roused corresponding emotions in him.

"Hullo, Watson," said he, and his voice was still deep and
hearty. "You don't look quite the man you did when I threw
you over the ropes into the crowd at the Old Deer Park. I
expect I have changed a bit also. But it's this last day or two that
has aged me. I see by your telegram, Mr. Holmes, that it is no
use my pretending to be anyone's deputy."

"It is simpler to deal direct," said Holmes.

"Of course it is. But you can imagine how difficult it is when you are speaking of the one woman whom you are bound to protect and help. What can I do? How am I to go to the police with such a story? And yet the kiddies have got to be protected. Is it madness, Mr. Holmes? Is it something in the blood? Have you any similar case in your experience? For God's sake, give me some advice, for I am at my wit's end."

"Very naturally, Mr. Ferguson. Now sit here and pull yourself together and give me a few clear answers. I can assure you that I am very far from being at my wit's end, and that I am confident we shall find some solution. First of all, tell me what steps you have taken. Is your wife still near the children?"

"We had a dreadful scene. She is a most loving woman, Mr. Holmes. If ever a woman loved a man with all her heart and soul, she loves me. She was cut to the heart that I should have discovered this horrible, this incredible, secret. She would not even speak. She gave no answer to my reproaches, save to gaze at me with a sort of wild, despairing look in her eyes. Then she rushed to her room and locked herself in. Since then she has refused to see me. She has a maid who was with her before her marriage, Dolores by name—a friend rather than a servant. She takes her food to her."

"Then the child is in no immediate danger?"

"Mrs. Mason, the nurse, has sworn that she will not leave it night or day. I can absolutely trust her. I am more uneasy about poor little Jack, for, as I told you in my note, he has twice been assaulted by her."

"But never wounded?"

"No, she struck him savagely. It is the more terrible as he is a poor little inoffensive cripple." Ferguson's gaunt features softened as he spoke of his boy. "You would think that the dear lad's condition would soften anyone's heart. A fall in childhood and a twisted spine, Mr. Holmes. But the dearest, most loving heart within."

Holmes had picked up the letter of yesterday and was reading it over. "What other inmates are there in your house, Mr. Ferguson?"

"Two servants who have not been long with us. One stable-hand, Michael, who sleeps in the house. My wife, myself, my boy Jack, baby, Dolores, and Mrs. Mason. That is all."

"I gather that you did not know your wife well at the time of your marriage?"

"I had only known her a few weeks."

"How long had this maid Dolores been with her?"

"Some years."

"Then your wife's character would really be better known by Dolores than by you?"

"Yes, you may say so."

Holmes made a note.

"I fancy," said he, "that I may be of more use at Lamberley than here. It is eminently a case for personal investigation. If the lady remains in her room, our presence could not annoy or inconvenience her. Of course, we would stay at the inn."

Ferguson gave a gesture of relief.

"It is what I hoped, Mr. Holmes. There is an excellent train at two from Victoria if you could come."

"Of course we could come. There is a lull at present. I can give you my undivided energies. Watson, of course, comes with us. But there are one or two points upon which I wish to be very sure before I start. This unhappy lady, as I understand it, has appeared to assault both the children, her own baby and your little son?"

"That is so."

"But the assaults take different forms, do they not? She has beaten your son."

"Once with a stick and once very savagely with her hands."

"Did she give no explanation why she struck him?"

"None save that she hated him. Again and again she said so."

"Well, that is not unknown among stepmothers. A posthumous jealousy, we will say. Is the lady jealous by nature?"

"Yes, she is very jealous—jealous with all the strength of her fiery tropical love."

"But the boy—he is fifteen, I understand, and probably very developed in mind, since his body has been circumscribed in action. Did he give you no explanation of these assaults?"

"No, he declared there was no reason."

"Were they good friends at other times?"

"No, there was never any love between them."

"Yet you say he is affectionate?"

"Never in the world could there be so devoted a son. My life is his life. He is absorbed in what I say or do."

Once again Holmes made a note. For some time he sat lost in thought.

"No doubt you and the boy were great comrades before this second marriage. You were thrown very close together, were you not?"

"Very much so."

"And the boy, having so affectionate a nature, was devoted, no doubt, to the memory of his mother?"

"Most devoted."

"He would certainly seem to be a most interesting lad. There is one other point about these assaults. Were the strange attacks upon the baby and the assaults upon your son at the same period?"

"In the first case it was so. It was as if some frenzy had seized her, and she had vented her rage upon both. In the second case it was only Jack who suffered. Mrs. Mason had no complaint to make about the baby."

"That certainly complicates matters."

"I don't quite follow you, Mr. Holmes."

"Possibly not. One forms provisional theories and waits for time or fuller knowledge to explode them. A bad habit, Mr. Ferguson, but human nature is weak. I fear that your old friend here has given an exaggerated view of my scientific methods. However, I will only say at the present stage that your problem does not appear to me to be insoluble, and that you may expect to find us at Victoria at two o'clock."

It was evening of a dull, foggy November day when, having left our bags at the Chequers, Lamberley, we drove through the Sussex clay of a long winding lane and finally reached the isolated and ancient farmhouse in which Ferguson dwelt. It was a large, straggling building, very old in the centre, very new at the wings with towering Tudor chimneys and a lichen-spotted, high-pitched roof of Horsham slabs. The doorsteps were worn into curves, and the ancient tiles which lined the porch were marked with the rebus of a cheese and a man after the original builder. Within, the ceilings were corrugated with heavy oaken beams, and the uneven floors sagged into sharp curves. An odour of age and decay pervaded the whole crumbling building.

There was one very large central room into which Ferguson led us. Here, in a huge old-fashioned fireplace with an iron screen behind it dated 1670, there blazed and spluttered a splendid log fire.

The room, as I gazed round, was a most singular mixture of dates and of places. The half-panelled walls may well have belonged to the original yeoman farmer of the seventeenth century. They were ornamented, however, on the lower part by a line of well-chosen modern watercolours; while above, where yellow plaster took the place of oak, there was hung a fine collection of South American utensils and weapons, which had been brought, no doubt, by the Peruvian lady upstairs. Holmes rose, with that quick curiosity which sprang from his eager mind, and examined them with some care. He returned with his eyes full of thought.

"Hullo!" he cried. "Hullo!"

A spaniel had lain in a basket in the corner. It came slowly forward toward its master, walking with difficulty. Its hind legs moved irregularly and its tail was on the ground. It licked Ferguson's hand.

"What is it, Mr. Holmes?"

"The dog. What's the matter with it?"

"That's what puzzled the vet. A sort of paralysis. Spinal meningitis, he thought. But it is passing. He'll be all right soon—won't you, Carlo?"

A shiver of assent passed through the drooping tail. The dog's mournful eyes passed from one of us to the other. He knew that we were discussing his case.

"Did it come on suddenly?"

"In a single night."

"How long ago?"

"It may have been four months ago."

"Very remarkable. Very suggestive."

"What do you see in it, Mr. Holmes?"

"A confirmation of what I had already thought."

"For God's sake, what do you think, Mr. Holmes? It may be a mere intellectual puzzle to you, but it is life and death to me! My wife a would-be murderer—my child in constant danger! Don't play with me, Mr. Holmes. It is too terribly serious."

The big Rugby three-quarter was trembling all over. Holmes put his hand soothingly upon his arm.

"I fear that there is pain for you, Mr. Ferguson, whatever the solution may be," said he. "I would spare you all I can. I cannot say more for the instant, but before I leave this house I hope I may have something definite."

"Please God you may! If you will excuse me, gentlemen, I will go up to my wife's room and see if there has been any change."

He was away some minutes, during which Holmes resumed his examination of the curiosities upon the wall. When our host returned it was clear from his downcast face that he had made no progress. He brought with him a tall, slim, brown-faced girl.

"The tea is ready, Dolores," said Ferguson. "See that your mistress has everything she can wish."

"She verra ill," cried the girl, looking with indignant eyes at her master. "She no ask for food. She verra ill. She need doctor. I frightened stay alone with her without doctor."

Ferguson looked at me with a question in his eyes.

"I should be so glad if I could be of use."

"Would your mistress see Dr. Watson?"

"I take him. I no ask leave. She needs doctor."

"Then I'll come with you at once."

I followed the girl, who was quivering with strong emotion, up the staircase and down an ancient corridor. At the end was an iron-clamped and massive door. It struck me as I looked at it that if Ferguson tried to force his way to his wife he would find it no easy matter. The girl drew a key from her pocket, and the heavy oaken planks creaked upon their old hinges. I passed in and she swiftly followed, fastening the door behind her.

On the bed a woman was lying who was clearly in a high fever. She was only half conscious, but as I entered she raised a pair of frightened but beautiful eyes and glared at me in apprehension. Seeing a stranger, she appeared to be relieved and sank back with a sigh upon the pillow. I stepped up to her with a few reassuring words, and she lay still while I took her pulse and temperature. Both were high, and yet my impression was that the condition was rather that of mental and nervous excitement than of any actual seizure.

"She lie like that one day, two day. I 'fraid she die," said the girl.

The woman turned her flushed and handsome face toward me.

"Where is my husband?"

"He is below and would wish to see you."

"I will not see him. I will not see him." Then she seemed to wander off into delirium. "A fiend! A fiend! Oh, what shall I do with this devil?"

"Can I help you in any way?"

"No. No one can help. It is finished. All is destroyed. Do what I will, all is destroyed."

The woman must have some strange delusion. I could not see honest Bob Ferguson in the character of fiend or devil.

"Madame," I said, "your husband loves you dearly. He is deeply grieved at this happening."

Again she turned on me those glorious eyes.

"He loves me. Yes. But do I not love him? Do I not love him even to sacrifice myself rather than break his dear heart? That is how I love him. And yet he could think of me—he could speak of me so."

"He is full of grief, but he cannot understand."

"No, he cannot understand. But he should trust."

"Will you not see him?" I suggested.

"No, no, I cannot forget those terrible words nor the look upon his face. I will not see him. Go now. You can do nothing for me. Tell him only one thing. I want my child. I have a right to my child. That is the only message I can send him." She turned her face to the wall and would say no more.

I returned to the room downstairs, where Ferguson and Holmes still sat by the fire. Ferguson listened moodily to my account of the interview.

"How can I send her the child?" he said. "How do I know what strange impulse might come upon her? How can I ever forget how she rose from beside it with its blood upon her lips?" He shuddered at the recollection. "The child is safe with Mrs. Mason, and there he must remain."

A smart maid, the only modern thing which we had seen in the house, had brought in some tea. As she was serving it the door opened and a youth entered the room. He was a remarkable lad, pale-faced and fair-haired, with excitable light blue eyes which blazed into a sudden flame of emotion and joy as they rested upon his father. He rushed forward and threw his arms round his neck with the abandon of a loving girl.

"Oh, daddy," he cried, "I did not know that you were due yet. I should have been here to meet you. Oh, I am so glad to see you!"

Ferguson gently disengaged himself from the embrace with some little show of embarrassment.

"Dear old chap," said he, patting the flaxen head with a very tender hand. "I came early because my friends, Mr. Holmes and Dr. Watson, have been persuaded to come down and spend an evening with us."

"Is that Mr. Holmes, the detective?"

"Yes."

The youth looked at us with a very penetrating and, as it seemed to me, unfriendly gaze.

"What about your other child, Mr. Ferguson?" asked Holmes. "Might we make the acquaintance of the baby?"

"Ask Mrs. Mason to bring baby down," said Ferguson. The boy went off with a curious, shambling gait which told my surgical eyes that he was suffering from a weak spine. Presently he returned, and behind him came a tall, gaunt woman bearing in her arms a very beautiful child, dark-eyed, golden-haired, a wonderful mixture of the Saxon and the Latin. Ferguson was evidently devoted to it, for he took it into his arms and fondled it most tenderly.

"Fancy anyone having the heart to hurt him," he muttered as he glanced down at the small, angry red pucker upon the cherub throat.

It was at this moment that I chanced to glance at Holmes and saw a most singular intentness in his expression. His face was as set as if it had been carved out of old ivory, and his eyes, which had glanced for a moment at father and child, were now fixed with eager curiosity upon something at the other side of the room. Following his gaze I could only guess that he was looking out through the window at the melancholy, dripping garden. It is true that a shutter had half closed outside and obstructed the view, but nonetheless it was certainly at the window that Holmes was fixing his concentrated attention. Then he smiled, and his eyes came back to the baby. On its chubby neck there was this small puckered mark. Without speaking, Holmes examined it with care. Finally he shook one of the dimpled fists which waved in front of him.

"Good-bye, little man. You have made a strange start in life. Nurse, I should wish to have a word with you in private."

He took her aside and spoke earnestly for a few minutes. I only heard the last words, which were: "Your anxiety will soon, I hope, be set at rest." The woman, who seemed to be a sour, silent kind of creature, withdrew with the child.

"What is Mrs. Mason like?" asked Holmes.

"Not very prepossessing externally, as you can see, but a heart of gold, and devoted to the child."

"Do you like her, Jack?" Holmes turned suddenly upon the boy. His expressive mobile face shadowed over, and he shook his head.

"Jacky has very strong likes and dislikes," said Ferguson, putting his arm round the boy. "Luckily I am one of his likes."

The boy cooed and nestled his head upon his father's breast. Ferguson gently disengaged him.

"Run away, little Jacky," said he, and he watched his son with loving eyes until he disappeared. "Now, Mr. Holmes," he continued when the boy was gone, "I really feel that I have brought you on a fool's errand, for what can you possibly do save give me your sympathy? It must be an exceedingly delicate and complex affair from your point of view."

"It is certainly delicate," said my friend with an amused smile, "but I have not been struck up to now with its complexity. It has been a case for intellectual deduction, but when this original intellectual deduction is confirmed point by point by quite a number of independent incidents, then the subjective becomes objective and we can say confidently that we have reached our goal. I had, in fact, reached it before we left Baker Street, and the rest has merely been observation and confirmation."

Ferguson put his big hand to his furrowed forehead.

"For heaven's sake, Holmes," he said hoarsely, "if you can see the truth in this matter, do not keep me in suspense. How do I stand? What shall I do? I care nothing as to how you have found your facts so long as you have really got them."

"Certainly I owe you an explanation, and you shall have it. But you will permit me to handle the matter in my own way? Is the lady capable of seeing us, Watson?"

"She is ill, but she is quite rational."

"Very good. It is only in her presence that we can clear the matter up. Let us go up to her."

"She will not see me," cried Ferguson.

"Oh, yes, she will," said Holmes. He scribbled a few lines upon a sheet of paper. "You at least have the entree, Watson. Will you have the goodness to give the lady this note?"

I ascended again and handed the note to Dolores, who cautiously opened the door. A minute later I heard a cry from within, a cry in which joy and surprise seemed to be blended. Dolores looked out.

"She will see them. She will leesten," said she.

At my summons Ferguson and Holmes came up. As we entered the room Ferguson took a step or two toward his wife, who had raised herself in the bed, but she held out her hand to repulse him. He sank into an armchair, while Holmes seated himself beside him, after bowing to the lady, who looked at him with wide-eyed amazement.

"I think we can dispense with Dolores," said Holmes. "Oh, very well, madame, if you would rather she stayed I can see no objection. Now, Mr. Ferguson, I am a busy man with many calls, and my methods have to be short and direct. The swiftest surgery is the least painful. Let me first say what will ease your mind. Your wife is a very good, a very loving, and a very ill-used woman."

Ferguson sat up with a cry of joy.

"Prove that, Mr. Holmes, and I am your debtor forever."

"I will do so, but in doing so I must wound you deeply in another direction."

"I care nothing so long as you clear my wife. Everything on earth is insignificant compared to that."

"Let me tell you, then, the train of reasoning which passed through my mind in Baker Street. The idea of a vampire was to me absurd. Such things do not happen in criminal practice in England. And yet your observation was precise. You had seen the lady rise from beside the child's cot with the blood upon her lips."

"I did."

"Did it not occur to you that a bleeding wound may be sucked for some other purpose than to draw the blood from it? Was there not a queen in English history who sucked such a wound to draw poison from it?"

"Poison!"

"A South American household. My instinct felt the presence of those weapons upon the wall before my eyes ever saw them. It might have been other poison, but that was what occurred to me. When I saw that little empty quiver beside the small bird-bow, it was just what I expected to see. If the child were pricked with one of those arrows dipped in curare or some other devilish drug, it would mean death if the venom were not sucked out.

"And the dog! If one were to use such a poison, would one not try it first in order to see that it had not lost its power? I did not foresee the dog, but at least I understand him and he fitted into my reconstruction.

"Now do you understand? Your wife feared such an attack. She saw it made and saved the child's life, and yet she shrank from telling you all the truth, for she knew how you loved the boy and feared lest it break your heart."

"Jacky!"

"I watched him as you fondled the child just now. His face was clearly reflected in the glass of the window where the shutter formed a background. I saw such jealousy, such cruel hatred, as I have seldom seen in a human face."

"My Jacky!"

"You have to face it, Mr. Ferguson. It is the more painful because it is a distorted love, a maniacal exaggerated love for you, and possibly for his dead mother, which has prompted his action. His very soul is consumed with hatred for this splendid child, whose health and beauty are a contrast to his own weakness."

"Good God! It is incredible!"

"Have I spoken the truth, madame?"

The lady was sobbing, with her face buried in the pillows. Now she turned to her husband.

"How could I tell you, Bob? I felt the blow it would be to you. It was better that I should wait and that it should come from some other lips than mine. When this gentleman, who seems to have powers of magic, wrote that he knew all, I was glad."

"I think a year at sea would be my prescription for Master Jacky," said Holmes, rising from his chair. "Only one thing is still clouded, madame. We can quite understand your attacks upon Master Jacky. There is a limit to a mother's patience. But how did you dare to leave the child these last two days?"

"I had told Mrs. Mason. She knew."

"Exactly. So I imagined."

Ferguson was standing by the bed, choking, his hands outstretched and quivering.

"This, I fancy, is the time for our exit, Watson," said Holmes in a whisper. "If you will take one elbow of the too faithful Dolores, I will take the other. There, now," he added as he closed the door behind him. "I think we may leave them to settle the rest among themselves."

I have only one further note of this case. It is the letter which Holmes wrote in final answer to that with which the narrative begins. It ran thus:

BAKER STREET,
Nov. 21st.
Re Vampires
SIR:
Referring to your letter of the 19th, I beg to state that I have looked into the inquiry of your client, Mr. Robert Ferguson, of

Ferguson and Muirhead, tea brokers, of Mincing Lane, and that
the matter has been brought to a satisfactory conclusion.
With thanks for your recommendation, I am, sir,
Faithfully yours,
SHERLOCK HOLMES.

† † † † †

Fans and scholars alike have taken the passing reference to
"Transylvania" in "The Adventure of the Sussex Vampire" as
an homage to Dracula. However, Doyle's work includes other
allusions to the king of the vampires. He must have had his
friend's work in mind when he named Lady Frances Carfax for,
as he knew, "Carfax" is the name of the house Count Dracula
purchased in Purfleet. In one of the earliest biographies of ACD,
Hesketh Pearson observed that his fantasy about Atlantis, The
Maracot Deep *of 1929, concludes when "Maracot . . . exor-*
cises the demon, who is destroyed somewhat in the manner of the
vampire in Dracula."[7]

---

7 Hesketh Pearson. *Conan Doyle.* MacDonald and Jane's: London, 1943. p. 82.

The Adventure
of the Three Gables

I don't think that any of my adventures with Mr. Sherlock Holmes opened quite so abruptly, or so dramatically, as that which I associate with the Three Gables. I had not seen Holmes for some days and had no idea of the new channel into which his activities had been directed. He was in a chatty mood that morning, however, and had just settled me into the well-worn low armchair on one side of the fire, while he had curled down with his pipe in his mouth upon the opposite chair, when our visitor arrived. If I had said that a mad bull had arrived it would give a clearer impression of what occurred.

The door had flown open and a huge negro had burst into the room. He would have been a comic figure if he had not been terrific, for he was dressed in a very loud gray check suit with a flowing salmon-coloured tie. His broad face and flattened nose were thrust forward, as his sullen dark eyes, with a smouldering gleam of malice in them, turned from one of us to the other.

"Which of you gen'l'men is Masser Holmes?" he asked.

The Strand Magazine (October 1926) p. 319-328. With four illustrations by Howard K. Elcock. Reprinted in *The Case Book of Sherlock Holmes*, 1927.

Holmes raised his pipe with a languid smile.

"Oh! it's you, is it?" said our visitor, coming with an unpleasant, stealthy step round the angle of the table. "See here, Masser Holmes, you keep your hands out of other folks' business. Leave folks to manage their own affairs. Got that, Masser Holmes?"

"Keep on talking," said Holmes. "It's fine."

"Oh! it's fine, is it?" growled the savage. "It won't be so damn fine if I have to trim you up a bit. I've handled your kind before now, and they didn't look fine when I was through with them. Look at that, Masser Holmes!"

He swung a huge knotted lump of a fist under my friend's nose. Holmes examined it closely with an air of great interest.

"Were you born so?" he asked. "Or did it come by degrees?"

It may have been the icy coolness of my friend, or it may have been the slight clatter which I made as I picked up the poker. In any case, our visitor's manner became less flamboyant.

"Well, I've given you fair warnin'," said he. "I've a friend that's interested out Harrow way—you know what I'm meaning—and he don't intend to have no buttin' in by you. Got that? You ain't the law, and I ain't the law either, and if you come in I'll be on hand also. Don't you forget it."

"I've wanted to meet you for some time," said Holmes. "I won't ask you to sit down, for I don't like the smell of you, but aren't you Steve Dixie, the bruiser?"

"That's my name, Masser Holmes, and you'll get put through it for sure if you give me any lip."

"It is certainly the last thing you need," said Holmes, staring at our visitor's hideous mouth. "But it was the killing of young Perkins outside the Holborn—Bar What! You're not going?"

The negro had sprung back, and his face was leaden. "I won't listen to no such talk," said he. "What have I to do with this 'ere Perkins, Masser Holmes? I was trainin' at the Bull Ring in Birmingham when this boy done gone get into trouble."

"Yes, you'll tell the magistrate about it, Steve," said Holmes. "I've been watching you and Barney Stockdale—"

"So help me the Lord! Masser Holmes—"

"That's enough. Get out of it. I'll pick you up when I want you."

"Good-mornin', Masser Holmes. I hope there ain't no hard feelin's about this 'ere visit?"

"There will be unless you tell me who sent you."

"Why, there ain't no secret about that, Masser Holmes. It was that same gen'l'man that you have just done gone mention."

"And who set him on to it?"

"S'elp me. I don't know, Masser Holmes. He just say, 'Steve, you go see Mr. Holmes, and tell him his life ain't safe if he go down Harrow way.' That's the whole truth." Without waiting for any further questioning, our visitor bolted out of the room almost as precipitately as he had entered. Holmes knocked out the ashes of his pipe with a quiet chuckle.

"I am glad you were not forced to break his woolly head, Watson. I observed your manoeuvres with the poker. But he is really rather a harmless fellow, a great muscular, foolish, blustering baby, and easily cowed, as you have seen. He is one of the Spencer John gang and has taken part in some dirty work of late which I may clear up when I have time. His immediate principal, Barney, is a more astute person. They specialize in assaults, intimidation, and the like. What I want to know is, who is at the back of them on this particular occasion?"

"But why do they want to intimidate you?"

"It is this Harrow Weald case. It decides me to look into the matter, for if it is worth anyone's while to take so much trouble, there must be something in it."

"But what is it?"

"I was going to tell you when we had this comic interlude. Here is Mrs. Maberley's note. If you care to come with me we will wire her and go out at once."

DEAR MR. SHERLOCK HOLMES [I read]:

I have had a succession of strange incidents occur to me in connection with this house, and I should much value your advice. You would find me at home any time tomorrow. The house is within a short walk of the Weald Station. I believe that my late husband, Mortimer Maberley, was one of your early clients.

Yours faithfully,

MARY MABERLEY.

The address was "the Three Gables, Harrow Weald."

"So that's that!" said Holmes. "And now, if you can spare the time, Watson, we will get upon our way."

A short railway journey, and a shorter drive, brought us to the house, a brick and timber villa, standing in its own acre of undeveloped grassland. Three small projections above the upper windows made a feeble attempt to justify its name. Behind was a grove of melancholy, half-grown pines, and the whole aspect of the place was poor and depressing. Nonetheless, we found the house to be well furnished, and the lady who received us was a most engaging elderly person, who bore every mark of refinement and culture.

"I remember your husband well, madam," said Holmes, "though it is some years since he used my services in some trifling matter."

"Probably you would be more familiar with the name of my son Douglas."

Holmes looked at her with great interest.

"Dear me! Are you the mother of Douglas Maberley? I knew him slightly. But of course all London knew him. What a magnificent creature he was! Where is he now?"

"Dead, Mr. Holmes, dead! He was attaché at Rome, and he died there of pneumonia last month."

"I am sorry. One could not connect death with such a man. I have never known anyone so vitally alive. He lived intensely— every fibre of him!"

"Too intensely, Mr. Holmes. That was the ruin of him. You remember him as he was—debonair and splendid. You did not see the moody, morose, brooding creature into which he developed. His heart was broken. In a single month I seemed to see my gallant boy turn into a worn-out cynical man."

"A love affair—a woman?"

"Or a fiend. Well, it was not to talk of my poor lad that I asked you to come, Mr. Holmes."

"Dr. Watson and I are at your service."

"There have been some very strange happenings. I have been in this house more than a year now, and as I wished to lead a retired life I have seen little of my neighbours. Three days ago I had a call from a man who said that he was a house agent. He said that this house would exactly suit a client of his, and that if I would part with it money would be no object. It seemed to me very strange as there are several empty houses on the market which appear to be equally eligible, but naturally I was interested in what he said. I therefore named a price which was five hundred pounds more than I gave. He at once closed with the offer, but added that his client desired to buy the furniture as well and would I put a price upon it. Some of this furniture is from my old home, and it is, as you see, very good, so that I named a good round sum. To this also he at once agreed. I had always wanted to travel, and the bargain was so good a one that it really seemed that I should be my own mistress for the rest of my life.

"Yesterday the man arrived with the agreement all drawn out. Luckily I showed it to Mr. Sutro, my lawyer, who lives in Harrow. He said to me, 'This is a very strange document. Are you aware that if you sign it you could not legally take anything out of the house—not even your own private possessions?' When the man came again in the evening I pointed this out, and I said that I meant only to sell the furniture.

"'No, no, everything,' said he.

"'But my clothes? My jewels?'

"'Well, well, some concession might be made for your personal effects. But nothing shall go out of the house unchecked. My client is a very liberal man, but he has his fads and his own way of doing things. It is everything or nothing with him.'

"'Then it must be nothing,' said I. And there the matter was left, but the whole thing seemed to me to be so unusual that I thought—"

Here we had a very extraordinary interruption.

Holmes raised his hand for silence. Then he strode across the room, flung open the door, and dragged in a great gaunt woman whom he had seized by the shoulder. She entered with ungainly struggle like some huge awkward chicken, torn, squawking, out of its coop.

"Leave me alone! What are you a–doin' of?" she screeched.

"Why, Susan, what is this?"

"Well, ma'am, I was comin' in to ask if the visitors was stayin' for lunch when this man jumped out at me."

"I have been listening to her for the last five minutes, but did not wish to interrupt your most interesting narrative. Just a little wheezy, Susan, are you not? You breathe too heavily for that kind of work."

Susan turned a sulky but amazed face upon her captor. "Who be you, anyhow, and what right have you a–pullin' me about like this?"

"It was merely that I wished to ask a question in your presence. Did you, Mrs. Maberley, mention to anyone that you were going to write to me and consult me?"

"No, Mr. Holmes, I did not."

"Who posted your letter?"

"Susan did."

"Exactly. Now, Susan, to whom was it that you wrote or sent a message to say that your mistress was asking advice from me?"

"It's a lie. I sent no message."

"Now, Susan, wheezy people may not live long, you know. It's a wicked thing to tell fibs. Whom did you tell?"

"Susan!" cried her mistress, "I believe you are a bad, treacherous woman. I remember now that I saw you speaking to someone over the hedge."

"That was my own business," said the woman sullenly.

"Suppose I tell you that it was Barney Stockdale to whom you spoke?" said Holmes.

"Well, if you know, what do you want to ask for?"

"I was not sure, but I know now. Well now, Susan, it will be worth ten pounds to you if you will tell me who is at the back of Barney."

"Someone that could lay down a thousand pounds for every ten you have in the world."

"So, a rich man? No; you smiled—a rich woman. Now we have got so far, you may as well give the name and earn the tenner."

"I'll see you in hell first."

"Oh, Susan! Language!"

"I am clearing out of here. I've had enough of you all. I'll send for my box tomorrow." She flounced for the door.

"Good-bye, Susan. Paregoric is the stuff. . . . Now," he continued, turning suddenly from lively to severe when the door had closed behind the flushed and angry woman, "this gang means business. Look how close they play the game. Your letter to me had the 10 P.M. postmark. And yet Susan passes the word to Barney. Barney has time to go to his employer and get instructions; he or she—I incline to the latter from Susan's grin when she thought I had blundered—forms a plan. Black Steve is called in, and I am warned off by eleven o'clock next morning. That's quick work, you know."

"But what do they want?"

"Yes, that's the question. Who had the house before you?"

"A retired sea captain called Ferguson."

"Anything remarkable about him?"

"Not that ever I heard of."

"I was wondering whether he could have buried something. Of course, when people bury treasure nowadays they do it in the Post-Office bank. But there are always some lunatics about. It would be a dull world without them. At first I thought of some buried valuable. But why, in that case, should they want your furniture? You don't happen to have a Raphael or a first folio Shakespeare without knowing it?"

"No, I don't think I have anything rarer than a Crown Derby tea-set."

"That would hardly justify all this mystery. Besides, why should they not openly state what they want? If they covet your tea-set, they can surely offer a price for it without buying you out, lock, stock, and barrel. No, as I read it, there is something which you do not know that you have, and which you would not give up if you did know."

"That is how I read it," said I.

"Dr. Watson agrees, so that settles it."

"Well, Mr. Holmes, what can it be?"

"Let us see whether by this purely mental analysis we can get it to a finer point. You have been in this house a year."

"Nearly two."

"All the better. During this long period no one wants anything from you. Now suddenly within three or four days you have urgent demands. What would you gather from that?"

"It can only mean," said I, "that the object, whatever it may be, has only just come into the house."

"Settled once again," said Holmes. "Now, Mrs. Maberley has any object just arrived?"

"No, I have bought nothing new this year."

"Indeed! That is very remarkable. Well, I think we had best let matters develop a little further until we have clearer data. Is that lawyer of yours a capable man?"

"Mr. Sutro is most capable."

"Have you another maid, or was the fair Susan, who has just banged your front door alone?"

"I have a young girl."

"Try and get Sutro to spend a night or two in the house. You might possibly want protection."

"Against whom?"

"Who knows? The matter is certainly obscure. If I can't find what they are after, I must approach the matter from the other end and try to get at the principal. Did this house-agent man give any address?"

"Simply his card and occupation. Haines-Johnson, Auctioneer and Valuer."

"I don't think we shall find him in the directory. Honest business men don't conceal their place of business. Well, you will let me know any fresh development. I have taken up your case, and you may rely upon it that I shall see it through."

As we passed through the hall, Holmes's eyes, which missed nothing, lighted upon several trunks and cases which were piled in a corner. The labels shone out upon them.

"'Milano.' 'Lucerne.' These are from Italy."

"They are poor Douglas's things."

"You have not unpacked them? How long have you had them?"

"They arrived last week."

"But you said—why, surely this might be the missing link. How do we know that there is not something of value there?"

"There could not possibly be, Mr. Holmes. Poor Douglas had only his pay and a small annuity. What could he have of value?"

Holmes was lost in thought.

"Delay no longer, Mrs. Maberley," he said at last. "Have these things taken upstairs to your bedroom. Examine them as soon as possible and see what they contain. I will come tomorrow and hear your report."

It was quite evident that the Three Gables was under very close surveillance, for as we came round the high hedge at the end of the lane there was the negro prize-fighter standing in the shadow. We came on him quite suddenly, and a grim and menacing figure he looked in that lonely place. Holmes clapped his hand to his pocket.

"Lookin' for your gun, Masser Holmes?"

"No, for my scent-bottle, Steve."

"You are funny, Masser Holmes, ain't you?"

"It won't be funny for you, Steve, if I get after you. I gave you fair warning this morning."

"Well, Masser Holmes, I done gone think over what you said, and I don't want no more talk about that affair of Masser Perkins. S'pose I can help you, Masser Holmes, I will."

"Well, then, tell me who is behind you on this job."

"So help me the Lord! Masser Holmes, I told you the truth before. I don't know. My boss Barney gives me orders and that's all."

"Well, just bear in mind, Steve, that the lady in that house, and everything under that roof, is under my protection. Don't forget it."

"All right, Masser Holmes. I'll remember."

"I've got him thoroughly frightened for his own skin, Watson," Holmes remarked as we walked on. "I think he would double-cross his employer if he knew who he was. It was lucky I had some knowledge of the Spencer John crowd, and that Steve was one of them. Now, Watson, this is a case for Langdale Pike, and I am going to see him now. When I get back I may be clearer in the matter."

I saw no more of Holmes during the day, but I could well imagine how he spent it, for Langdale Pike was his human book of reference upon all matters of social scandal. This strange, languid creature spent his waking hours in the bow window of a St. James's Street club and was the receiving-station as well as the transmitter for all the gossip of the metropolis. He made, it was said, a four-figure income by the paragraphs which he contributed every week to the garbage papers which cater to an inquisitive public. If ever, far down in the turbid depths of London life, there was some strange swirl or eddy, it was marked with automatic exactness by this human dial upon the surface. Holmes discreetly helped Langdale to knowledge, and on occasion was helped in turn.

When I met my friend in his room early next morning, I was conscious from his bearing that all was well, but nonetheless a most unpleasant surprise was awaiting us. It took the shape of the following telegram.

> *Please come out at once. Client's house burgled in the night.*
> *Police in possession.*
> SUTRO.

Holmes whistled. "The drama has come to a crisis, and quicker than I had expected. There is a great driving-power at the back of this business, Watson, which does not surprise me after what I have heard. This Sutro, of course, is her lawyer. I made a mistake, I fear, in not asking you to spend the night on guard. This fellow has clearly proved a broken reed. Well, there is nothing for it but another journey to Harrow Weald."

We found the Three Gables a very different establishment to the orderly household of the previous day. A small group of idlers had assembled at the garden gate, while a couple of constables were examining the windows and the geranium beds. Within we met a gray old gentleman, who introduced himself as the lawyer together with a bustling, rubicund inspector, who greeted Hoimes as an old friend.

"Well, Mr. Holmes, no chance for you in this case, I'm afraid. Just a common, ordinary burglary, and well within the capacity of the poor old police. No experts need apply."

"I am sure the case is in very good hands," said Holmes. "Merely a common burglary, you say?"

"Quite so. We know pretty well who the men are and where to find them. It is that gang of Barney Stockdale, with the big nigger in it—they've been seen about here."

"Excellent! What did they get?"

"Well, they don't seem to have got much. Mrs. Maberley was chloroformed and the house was—Ah! here is the lady herself."

Our friend of yesterday, looking very pale and ill, had entered the room, leaning upon a little maidservant.

"You gave me good advice, Mr. Holmes," said she, smiling ruefully. "Alas, I did not take it! I did not wish to trouble Mr. Sutro, and so I was unprotected."

"I only heard of it this morning," the lawyer explained.

"Mr. Holmes advised me to have some friend in the house. I neglected his advice, and I have paid for it."

"You look wretchedly ill," said Holmes. "Perhaps you are hardly equal to telling me what occurred."

"It is all here," said the inspector, tapping a bulky notebook.

"Still, if the lady is not too exhausted——"

"There is really so little to tell. I have no doubt that wicked Susan had planned an entrance for them. They must have known the house to an inch. I was conscious for a moment of the chloroform rag which was thrust over my mouth, but I have no notion how long I may have been senseless. When I woke, one man was at the bedside and another was rising with a bundle in his hand from among my son's baggage, which was partially opened and littered over the floor. Before he could get away I sprang up and seized him."

"You took a big risk," said the inspector.

"I clung to him, but he shook me off, and the other may have struck me, for I can remember no more. Mary the maid heard the noise and began screaming out of the window. That brought the police, but the rascals had got away."

"What did they take?"

"Well, I don't think there is anything of value missing. I am sure there was nothing in my son's trunks."

"Did the men leave no clue?"

"There was one sheet of paper which I may have torn from the man that I grasped. It was lying all crumpled on the floor. It is in my son's handwriting."

"Which means that it is not of much use," said the inspector. "Now if it had been in the burglar's—"

"Exactly," said Holmes. "What rugged common sense! Nonetheless, I should be curious to see it."

The inspector drew a folded sheet of foolscap from his pocketbook.

"I never pass anything, however trifling," said he with some pomposity. "That is my advice to you, Mr. Holmes. In twenty-five years' experience I have learned my lesson. There is always the chance of finger-marks or something."

Holmes inspected the sheet of paper.

"What do you make of it, Inspector?"

"Seems to be the end of some queer novel, so far as I can see."

"It may certainly prove to be the end of a queer tale," said Holmes. "You have noticed the number on the top of the page. It is two hundred and forty-five. Where are the odd two hundred and forty-four pages?"

"Well, I suppose the burglars got those. Much good may it do them!"

"It seems a queer thing to break into a house in order to steal such papers as that. Does it suggest anything to you, Inspector?"

"Yes, sir, it suggests that in their hurry the rascals just grabbed at what came first to hand. I wish them joy of what they got."

"Why should they go to my son's things?" asked Mrs. Maberley.

"Well, they found nothing valuable downstairs, so they tried their luck upstairs. That is how I read it. What do you make of it, Mr. Holmes?"

"I must think it over, Inspector. Come to the window, Watson." Then, as we stood together, he read over the fragment of paper. It began in the middle of a sentence and ran like this:

"*. . . face bled considerably from the cuts and blows, but it was nothing to the bleeding of his heart as he saw that lovely face,* *the face for which he had been prepared to sacrifice his very life, looking out at his agony and humiliation. She smiled—yes, by Heaven! she smiled, like the heartless fiend she was, as he looked up at her. It was at that moment that love died and hate was born. Man must live for something. If it is not for your embrace, my lady, then it shall surely be for your undoing and my complete revenge."*

"Queer grammar!" said Holmes with a smile as he handed the paper back to the inspector. "Did you notice how the 'he' suddenly changed to 'my'? The writer was so carried away by his own story that he imagined himself at the supreme moment to be the hero."

"It seemed mighty poor stuff," said the inspector as he replaced it in his book. "What! Are you off, Mr. Holmes?"

"I don't think there is anything more for me to do now that the case is in such capable hands. By the way, Mrs. Maberley, did you say you wished to travel?"

"It has always been my dream, Mr. Holmes."

"Where would you like to go—Cairo, Madeira, the Riviera?"

"Oh if I had the money I would go round the world."

"Quite so. Round the world. Well, good-morning. I may drop you a line in the evening." As we passed the window I caught a glimpse of the inspector's smile and shake of the head. "These clever fellows have always a touch of madness." That was what I read in the inspector's smile.

"Now, Watson, we are at the last lap of our little journey," said Holmes when we were back in the roar of central London once more. "I think we had best clear the matter up at once, and it would be well that you should come with me, for it is safer to have a witness when you are dealing with such a lady as Isadora Klein."

We had taken a cab and were speeding to some address in Grosvenor Square. Holmes had been sunk in thought, but he roused himself suddenly.

"By the way, Watson, I suppose you see it all clearly?"

"No, I can't say that I do. I only gather that we are going to see the lady who is behind all this mischief."

"Exactly! But does the name Isadora Klein convey nothing to you? She was, of course, the celebrated beauty. There was never a woman to touch her. She is pure Spanish, the real blood of the masterful Conquistadors, and her people have been leaders in Pernambuco for generations. She married the aged German sugar king, Klein, and presently found herself the richest as well as the most lovely widow upon earth. Then there was an interval of adventure when she pleased her own tastes. She had several lovers, and Douglas Maberley, one of the most striking men in London, was one of them. It was by all accounts more than an adventure with him. He was not a society butterfly but a strong, proud man who gave and expected all. But she is the 'belle dame sans merci' of fiction. When her caprice is satisfied the matter is ended, and if the other party in the matter can't take her word for it she knows how to bring it home to him."

"Then that was his own story—"

"Ah! you are piecing it together now. I hear that she is about to marry the young Duke of Lomond, who might almost be her son. His Grace's ma might overlook the age, but a big scandal would be a different matter, so it is imperative— Ah! here we are."

It was one of the finest corner-houses of the West End. A machine-like footman took up our cards and returned with word that the lady was not at home. "Then we shall wait until she is," said Holmes cheerfully.

The machine broke down.

"Not at home means not at home to you," said the footman.

"Good," Holmes answered. "That means that we shall not have to wait. Kindly give this note to your mistress."

He scribbled three or four words upon a sheet of his notebook, folded it, and handed it to the man.

"What did you say, Holmes?" I asked.

"I simply wrote: 'Shall it be the police, then?' I think that should pass us in."

It did—with amazing celerity. A minute later we were in an Arabian Nights drawing-room, vast and wonderful, in a half gloom, picked out with an occasional pink electric light. The lady had come, I felt, to that time of life when even the proudest beauty finds the half light more welcome. She rose from a settee as we entered: tall, queenly, a perfect figure, a lovely mask-like face, with two wonderful Spanish eyes which looked murder at us both.

"What is this intrusion—and this insulting message?" she asked, holding up the slip of paper.

"I need not explain, madame. I have too much respect for your intelligence to do so—though I confess that intelligence has been surprisingly at fault of late."

"How so, sir?"

"By supposing that your hired bullies could frighten me from my work. Surely no man would take up my profession if it were not that danger attracts him. It was you, then, who forced me to examine the case of young Maberley."

"I have no idea what you are talking about. What have I to do with hired bullies?"

Holmes turned away wearily.

"Yes, I have underrated your intelligence. Well, good-afternoon!"

"Stop! Where are you going?"

"To Scotland Yard."

We had not got halfway to the door before she had overtaken us and was holding his arm. She had turned in a moment from steel to velvet.

"Come and sit down, gentlemen. Let us talk this matter over. I feel that I may be frank with you, Mr. Holmes. You have the feelings of a gentleman. How quick a woman's instinct is to find it out. I will treat you as a friend."

"I cannot promise to reciprocate, madame. I am not the law, but I represent justice so far as my feeble powers go. I am ready to listen, and then I will tell you how I will act."

"No doubt it was foolish of me to threaten a brave man like yourself."

"What was really foolish, madame, is that you have placed yourself in the power of a band of rascals who may blackmail or give you away."

"No, no! I am not so simple. Since I have promised to be frank, I may say that no one, save Barney Stockdale and Susan, his wife, have the least idea who their employer is. As to them, well, it is not the first—" She smiled and nodded with a charming coquettish intimacy.

"I see. You've tested them before."

"They are good hounds who run silent."

"Such hounds have a way sooner or later of biting the hand that feeds them. They will be arrested for this burglary. The police are already after them."

"They will take what comes to them. That is what they are paid for. I shall not appear in the matter."

"Unless I bring you into it."

"No, no, you would not. You are a gentleman. It is a woman's secret."

"In the first place, you must give back this manuscript."

She broke into a ripple of laughter and walked to the fireplace. There was a calcined mass which she broke up with the poker. "Shall I give this back?" she asked. So roguish and exquisite did she look as she stood before us with a challenging smile that I felt of all Holmes's criminals this was the one whom he would find it hardest to face. However, he was immune from sentiment.

"That seals your fate," he said coldly. "You are very prompt in your actions, madame, but you have overdone it on this occasion."

She threw the poker down with a clatter.

"How hard you are!" she cried. "May I tell you the whole story?"

"I fancy I could tell it to you."

"But you must look at it with my eyes, Mr. Holmes. You must realize it from the point of view of a woman who sees all her life's ambition about to be ruined at the last moment. Is such a woman to be blamed if she protects herself?"

"The original sin was yours."

"Yes, yes! I admit it. He was a dear boy, Douglas, but it so chanced that he could not fit into my plans. He wanted marriage—marriage, Mr. Holmes—with a penniless commoner. Nothing less would serve him. Then he became pertinacious. Because I had given he seemed to think that I still must give, and to him only. It was intolerable. At last I had to make him realize it."

"By hiring ruffians to beat him under your own window."

"You do indeed seem to know everything. Well, it is true. Barney and the boys drove him away, and were, I admit, a little rough in doing so. But what did he do then? Could I have believed that a gentleman would do such an act? He wrote a book in which he described his own story. I, of course, was the wolf; he the lamb. It was all there, under different names, of course; but who in all London would have failed to recognize it? What do you say to that, Mr. Holmes?"

"Well, he was within his rights."

"It was as if the air of Italy had got into his blood and brought with it the old cruel Italian spirit. He wrote to me and sent me a copy of his book that I might have the torture of anticipation. There were two copies, he said—one for me, one for his publisher."

"How did you know the publisher's had not reached him?"

"I knew who his publisher was. It is not his only novel, you know. I found out that he had not heard from Italy. Then came Douglas's sudden death. So long as that other manuscript was in the world there was no safety for me. Of course, it must be among his effects, and these would be returned to his mother. I set the gang at work. One of them got into the house as servant. I wanted to do the thing honestly. I really and truly did. I was ready to buy the house and everything in it. I offered any price she cared to ask. I only tried the other way when everything else had failed. Now, Mr. Holmes, granting that I was too hard on Douglas—and, God knows, I am sorry for it!—what else could I do with my whole future at stake?"

Sherlock Holmes shrugged his shoulders.

"Well, well," said he, "I suppose I shall have to compound a felony as usual. How much does it cost to go round the world in first-class style?"

The lady stared in amazement.

"Could it be done on five thousand pounds?"

"Well, I should think so, indeed!"

"Very good. I think you will sign me a check for that, and I will see that it comes to Mrs. Maberley. You owe her a little change of air. Meantime, lady—" he wagged a cautionary forefinger "—have a care! Have a care! You can't play with edged tools forever without cutting those dainty hands."

† † † † † †

"The Adventure of the Three Gables" incorporates elements from two previous stories: "John Barrington Cowles," which was written in 1884, near the beginning of Doyle's writing career and "The Parasite." Isadora Klein retains her youth and beauty and prospers financially while her lovers sicken and die. This type of vampire was far more common in early fantasy and horror literature than it is today. Both Julien Gordon's "Vampires" (in Vampires [and] Mademoiselle Reseda. *J. B. Lippen-*

cott Company: Philadelphia, 1891) and Lavinia Leitch's "A Vampire" (in A Vampire: And Other Stories. The Christopher Publishing House: Boston, 1927) were published during Doyle's long career as an author. The best-known example of a vampiric femme fatale may be the protagonist of Potter Emerson Browne's play and subsequent novel, A Fool There Was (Grosset & Dunlap: New York, 1909). Browne's work, which was based on Rudyard Kipling's poem "The Vampire," was the basis of the silent film A Fool There Was. Theda Bera, who was one of the first sex symbols of the silent screen, assumed the title role.

THE CASE OF THE
VANISHED VAMPIRE

By Bill Crider

In the spring of the year 1897, Sherlock Holmes was advised by
Dr. Moore Agar, of Harley Street, to take a complete rest from
detective work for the sake of his health. I concurred with this
opinion, and Holmes, being fatigued beyond measure, agreed.
Thus he and I found ourselves in Cornwall, where we were
almost immediately embroiled in the bizarre events which I
have recounted in "The Adventure of the Devil's Foot."

Instead of tiring Holmes, as Dr. Agar and I would have had
it, the activities in Cornwall invigorated him. It was then that
I suspected his fatigue was not physical but more related to his
mental activities. Holmes, as my readers may be aware, is a man
who needs mental activity even more than the physical sort.
When he lacks it, he falls into a dangerous state of ennui. That
was exactly the case upon our return to London. The boredom
did not return immediately, but as the days passed with no sign of
an interesting client whose problems were greater than Holmes's
own, my friend began to evince signs that he might fall back into
his dependence on other means of stimulation. Though I had
long ago helped him reduce his dependence on the needle, I knew
well enough that the fiend had not been conquered so much
as rendered temporarily dormant, as certain references in the
tale referred to above will have shown to the attentive reader.

So it was that I found myself both worried and saddened by the prospect before us one evening after our supper. Holmes wore a mouse-coloured dressing gown and lay in lethargy on the couch. I tried to cheer him up by reading to him from one of the agony columns, which he of late had not even had the energy to clip and file. The plaintive whining contained in the advertisements, which would at one time have roused his enthusiasm, did not stir him, however, and I was on the point of giving up when I heard someone ascending the stairs.

Had Holmes been in his usual state of keen awareness, he would have heard the footsteps long before I, but as it was, he hardly glanced up when I rose from my chair to see who our visitor might be.

"There is no hurry, Watson," Holmes said, and then he proved that he was not so deficient in alertness as I had thought. "There are two of them, and judging by the slow sluff of their tread, I would say they are not eager to see us."

Indeed, they were not, for the footsteps ceased at the head of the stairs, and I heard muffled whispers through the door. I hesitated for a moment, but then the footfalls resumed and someone knocked on the door, which I opened at once.

Two men, as Holmes had informed me there would be, stood there, hats in their hands. One man was well-formed and athletic, with a well-trimmed beard and hair combed close to his head. His clean-shaven companion had a square chin and wide forehead. He too had the look of an athlete, with a powerful build and wide chest. Both men wore black suits and waistcoats under their topcoats.

"Do I have the honor of addressing Mr. Sherlock Holmes?" asked the man with the beard.

"No," I responded. "I am Dr. Watson."

I turned to indicate Holmes, but he was no longer on the couch behind me.

"Holmes will be here momentarily," I said, hoping that I was correct. "Please come in."

I ushered our visitors into the room, and Holmes emerged from his bedroom almost at once, the mouse-coloured gown now removed to reveal him fully dressed and alert, his eyes alight in his thin hawk-like face as if he had never been drowsing at all.

"Good evening, gentlemen," he said with an enthusiasm I had not heard in quite some time. He clearly anticipated something of interest. "I am Sherlock Holmes."

"And I am Bram Stoker," said the bearded man. "My companion is Dr. Abraham Van Helsing. We have come to seek your help and advice."

"Please take their hats, Watson," Holmes said, and when I had done so, he waved the men toward the couch that had somehow been made to look fresh in the seconds when I had not been looking. "Take a seat and tell me more specifically what it is that brings you here."

The men took their places on the couch, both of them sitting on the edge, their backs straight. I returned to my chair, while Holmes leaned on the mantel. Stoker looked at Holmes, but Van Helsing's gaze was fixed on Holmes's old work table with its acid-stained deal top covered with beakers and bottles and tubes containing chemicals whose nature was unknown to me but certainly important to Holmes's studies when he was in better fettle.

"I take it that you have an interest in science, Dr. Van Helsing," said Holmes.

Van Helsing turned to look at Holmes, but it was Stoker who spoke. "Dr. Van Helsing is from Amsterdam, where he is considered one of the most advanced scientists of the present day. But he is much more. He is a medical doctor, a doctor of letters, and a student of . . . let us call them the occult sciences."

Holmes kept a perfectly straight face, which must have been difficult for him, considering his opinion of the occult.

"Indeed," he said. "And what brings you to London, Dr. Van Helsing?"

"A matter of some urgency," Van Helsing said. "Made even more urgent by certain recent events."

"And you are from Amsterdam?"

Van Helsing straightened a bit. "My family has lived there for generations."

"Yet you speak with a German accent."

I had not detected such an accent, but Holmes's ear was much keener than mine.

"German is one of my languages," Van Helsing said. "I use it so often in my travels that it has become almost second nature to me. Perhaps that would explain it."

"Perhaps," said Holmes. "But now you must tell us of the urgent matter that has brought you not only to London but to seek my advice."

"Vampires," said Stoker.

Sherlock Holmes is not an entirely humorless man, and I believe I saw a smile twitch at the corners of his mouth. The movement was so slight that it would have passed unnoticed by anyone less accustomed than I to his feelings about such things as vampires, and I do not believe our guests took notice of it.

"Vampires," Holmes said. "In London."

"Yes," said Stoker, leaning forward, his voice urgent. "We have killed one."

"My word!" I said, almost leaping from my chair.

Holmes did not stir. He said, "Vampires have existed in legend for many years. I had not heard of one in London before now."

While Holmes did not believe in the occult, he was well versed in tales of blood down through the centuries. He had spoken to me before of Vlad Tepes and Countess Bathory, whose depredations had been worked into some of the vampire legends.

"Despite what you have heard or not heard," Stoker said, "the vampires are here now. Soon many people will be dying if they are not stopped."

"You have stopped one of them, however," said Holmes. "Or so you said."

"Therein lies the problem," said Van Helsing. "We killed the creature, but we did not take the proper precautions. The thing has escaped! *Mein Gott!* I fear that it has risen from its gory bed to walk the night and create others of its hellish kind! And the fault is ours!"

Holmes's eyes widened. "Create others?"

"When the vampire feeds on the blood of its victims, they can be transformed," said Stoker. "The victims become hungry for blood themselves."

"We must stop them!" Van Helsing cried, rising from his seat. "Before it is too late!"

I shared the man's agitation, but Holmes, as always, remained calm.

"First," said he, "tell me how you killed this . . . vampire, and of the precautions you failed to take."

"The vampire was killed properly," Van Helsing said, looking at Stoker.

Stoker hung his head and stared at his boots. "The fault is mine. The death itself was gory beyond anything I could imagine. I could not allow Van Helsing to go through with the rest."

"The rest?" said Holmes.

"The creature must be beheaded to make certain that it never rises from its grave again," Van Helsing said. "I was prepared to do the job, but Mr. Stoker was not. And now it is too late." He shook his head. "Too late."

"I refuse to believe that it is too late," said Stoker. He looked at Holmes. "You can see our predicament. We must find the creature before it feeds. We must find it tonight."

"Have you informed the police?" asked Holmes.

"The police?" Stoker gave a bitter laugh. "Do you think they would believe us? Creatures of the night, men who become bats? If they did not put us in a madhouse, they would arrest us and put us in prison as if *we* were the killers."

"And why," said Holmes, "would they do such a thing as that?"

Van Helsing stood up. "Because of the evidence. You must see it. You must help us, we beg of you."

Holmes was no more likely to believe in creatures of the night than were the police, but he was certainly interested in physical evidence. He moved away from the mantel and stood near our visitors.

"It appears, then, that we must look into this matter," he said, with a glance in my direction. "Dr. Watson will, of course assist me in my inquiries."

It was Stoker's turn to rise from where he sat. "That is wonderful news," he said. "For I believe that you are the only man in London who can help us."

Holmes gave a slight smile. "In all modesty, I must say that there are others. Two, possibly three. But that is beside the point. Where is the evidence you spoke of?"

"The St. Marylebone Cemetery," Stoker said. "The creature must sleep in a coffin on his native earth. Where better than in a crypt?"

"Where, indeed?" said Holmes. "I must ask you and Dr. Van Helsing to go there at once. Watson and I will meet you at the gate, as there are certain preparations that we must make."

"The matter is urgent," said Stoker. "You must not delay."

"There will be no delay," said Holmes. "We will be arriving almost as soon as you do."

Stoker did not appear convinced, but at a look from Holmes I gathered up our visitors' hats and handed them to their owners. After a few more protestations about the urgency of the affair, Van Helsing and Stoker departed.

Holmes at once moved to the mantel and selected a briar pipe from among several that lay there. He took tobacco from the toe of a Persian slipper, tamped it into the bowl of the pipe, and lit it. When he had it going to his satisfaction, he turned and addressed me.

"What do you make of our visitors, Watson?" he asked between puffs.

"They seem desperately in earnest," I said, "though I find it difficult to credit their vanished vampire."

Holmes nodded. "So do I, Watson. So do I. I could list for you all the reasons why such a creature as a vampire could not possibly exist, but that is, I am sure, quite unnecessary."

"Yes, it is. As a doctor, I know something about the spread of disease. If vampirism existed in the form Mr. Stoker described, it would be something like a communicable disease. It would be like a plague. Before many years had passed all of Europe would be infected."

"That has not happened, of course," said Holmes.

"No." I watched him as he smoked calmly. "Should we not be making the preparations you mentioned?"

"And what might those be?" Holmes asked.

"A wooden stake?"

Holmes chuckled. "You can be quite droll at times, Watson. I have always said you had hidden depths. But fetch your pistol, for I believe that will be all we might need for this night's work."

The possibility of danger, along with a puzzle, were just the things to bring Holmes back to a semblance of his better self. I got the pistol, and we were ready to go.

It was a warm but misty night, and an oily fog seemed to rise up out of the ground. Clouds obscured the stars and moon, and the street lamps were merely a hazy glow. Holmes wore a close-fitting cloth cap, and I wore a hat against the dampness. Occasionally a cab would rattle past us in the street, but we could hardly glimpse it through the fog.

The walk to the cemetery seemed to take a long time because the fog made the city an unfamiliar territory, but we arrived eventually and found Stoker and Van Helsing waiting at the gate.

The cemetery itself was not associated with a church. It had not been so long that so many people were buried in London churchyards that there was no more room for the dead. Bodies lay atop bodies, and those who came to visit the graves of their departed relatives were sometimes greeted by the gruesome sight of bones that stuck out of the ground as if the dead were seeking to rejoin the living. As a doctor, I knew that such burial practices were a hazard to the health of the city, and I was quite pleased when laws were passed to allow the establishment of private cemeteries, such as the one at whose entrance we now stood.

Stoker and Van Helsing were already present, awaiting our arrival. They greeted us, but Holmes brushed the greeting aside and said, "Take us to the vampire."

"The vampire, as we told you," is gone," said Stoker. "We can, however, take you to the tomb where he lay."

"Then do so," said Holmes, and we followed the two men into the cemetery.

Van Helsing had a dark lantern, and he led us along a winding route through the graveyard. In the darkness and the fog, I was soon disoriented. The fog dampened my face, and I glimpsed dark stones and obelisks that reared up out of the fog on all sides. I hoped that I would not trip over a foot stone and fall.

As we walked, it seemed to me that I heard someone else in the graveyard, the occasional ghostly step that might have been only the echo of our own. I glanced at Holmes, who was close beside me, but if he heard, he gave no sign.

I thought about vampires and their need to sleep in their native earth. I thought about the supposedly empty crypt to which we were making our way. What if the vampire was returning?

I knew, of course, that there were no vampires, but in the fog and darkness, it was only too easy for the logical part of one's mind to allow strange notions to intrude. I mentally brushed them aside and followed along behind Stoker and Van Helsing, but while I kept listening for the sounds, I did not hear them again.

After what seemed quite some time, though it must have been only a few minutes, we reached a stone crypt. The door stood open, and the inside was even darker than the night around us.

Van Helsing did not hesitate but walked right inside, Stoker following. Holmes and I stopped outside.

"Well, Watson," said Holmes, "what do you think? Shall we follow them?"

I did not know what to think, so all I said was, "That is why we came."

Holmes nodded. "You are right, as usual. Come. Let us see what our friends have to show us."

Shadows cast by the lantern danced around the crypt as we entered. Just as I passed through the doorway, I thought I heard the spectral sound once again, but I refused to give in and glance back.

The inside of the crypt was ghastly enough in its own aspect to make me forget the foolish idea that vampire might be lurking outside. On a raised block there sat a wooden coffin, the lid flung back as if someone inside had made a hasty exit. The cerements were flung about and horribly stained with something that must have been blood, though its colour was impossible to discern in the dim light of the lanterns. From my vantage point, it appeared to be almost black.

The smell in the confined space was terrible. In wartime, one becomes all too accustomed to the smell of blood, and in Afghanistan, my nostrils had been clogged with it more than once. The jezail bullet that I had taken at the Battle of Maiwand seemed suddenly to throb within me.

There was, however, something different, although indefinable about the smell inside the crypt. Could it have been the difference between vampire and human?

Van Helsing and Stoker had paused upon entering, but now the doctor strode to the coffin and reached within. From among the bloody winding-sheets, he pulled an object that he then held aloft for Holmes to see. It was a wooden stake, sharpened to a point and covered in gore.

"This is the instrument of the vampire's supposed death," Van Helsing said. "Would that we had done all that was necessary to dispatch it forever."

"I bear the blame for that," Stoker said. "But if Sherlock Holmes can find the creature, I will not fail you again."

Holmes closed the distance between himself and the doctor.

"May I see the stake?" he said, and Van Helsing handed it to him.

Holmes ran his hand over the smooth wood and gave the stake back to Van Helsing, who put it back into the coffin.

From somewhere, Holmes brought out his magnifying lens and examined the cerements, not touching them but moving slowly down the side of the box. At one point, he reached out and plucked something from the sheets and held it under the lens.

"A hair?" said Van Helsing.

"So it appears," Holmes said, tucking it away without further comment.

After a few more moments of examining the coffin and its contents, Holmes bent down to the stone floor of the crypt, which, like the cerements, was stained with blood. A small pool if it had formed in a pocket in the stone, and Holmes touched it with a finger. A droplet clung to his fingertip, and he rubbed the blood between fingertip and thumb. Nodding as if satisfied, he wiped the blood on the cerements.

"Well?" said Van Helsing. "Do you believe you can be of any help in this case?"

"I daresay I can." He paused and turned toward the entrance of the crypt. "But what was that noise?"

I, too, heard the stealthy sound of a footstep, and a chill went through me, such a chill that the throb of the jezail bullet was forgotten.

"Someone is out there," I said. "Someone has been following us since we entered the cemetery."

"Someone?" said Stoker. "Or something?"

I had no answer for that, but Holmes did. He walked to the heavy iron door of the crypt and pushed it shut. It ground across the stone floor, and I leapt to help him. Just as it was about to close someone—or something—fell heavily against it as if trying to push it back upon us, but we were too strong, and the door closed with a satisfying clank. There was, of course, no lock on the inside, but I leant back against it. I would hold it firm, I told myself, no what might be outside striving against me. I felt several hard shoves, but though my feet slipped a bit, I was equal to the task of keeping the door well closed.

"What is out there?" I gasped. "Is it a man or monster?"

"A man," said Holmes with his usual confidence, "and I believe I can tell you easily enough what manner of man it is."

"A half-human one," said Stoker. "One of the undead!"

"Not at all," said Holmes. "More likely the same kind of man that the so-called Dr. Van Helsing is."

"A polymath?" said Stoker. "Hardly likely."

"As likely as that Van Helsing himself is one," said Holmes.

No one pushed back against me now, so I relaxed a bit.

"But Holmes," I said, "we have heard Dr. Van Helsing's credentials."

"Indeed we have. But what else have we heard? Nothing at all, I think. Why not ask him a medical question, Watson. See if he can answer you."

I thought it an odd request, but recalling the jezail bullet, I asked Van Helsing if he could tell me the location of the subclavian artery. Judging from the look on his face, I might as well have asked him if he could fly around the inside of the crypt like a bat.

"It is as I had concluded," said Holmes after a moment of silence. "Van Helsing is no more a doctor than I am a vampire. The masquerade is over, and is now time for the unmasking."

As so often happened when I was in the company of Holmes, I had only a dim idea of what he must be thinking.

"Masquerade?" I said. "Is Stoker, too, playing a part?"

"He is real enough," said Holmes, "but the errand on which they have brought us is all part of a game. I have known from the beginning that it was, but I wanted to see what they had planned."

Stoker was crestfallen, and he did not try to deny anything.

"How did you know?" he said.

"There are too many things for me to list them all," said Holmes.

"Please," said Stoker.

"Very well. First of all, there are no vampires."

Something heaved against the door at my back, and I wondered what it could be.

"Perhaps," Stoker said, "but that is not enough evidence of anything."

"No," said Holmes. "It is not. There is much more. For instance, you did not mention how you came to be in the company of Van Helsing when you are a theater manager, an odd choice for a vampire hunter."

"How did you know about my occupation?"

"I do read the newspapers," said Holmes. "At times I even see the theater section."

"And Van Helsing?"

"Almost too easy. While *van* is a Dutch prefix, I have made a study of the patronyms various countries, and the name Van Helsing does not exist. Then too, there was the man's German accent and his use of a German expression. Clearly he is an actor, most likely recruited for this work at the theater you manage. As was the supposed vampire outside, who is not very strong for a supernatural creature." Holmes turned to me. "Open the door, Watson, and invite him inside."

I recalled something I had once read. "Inviting a vampire inside can cause certain problems, Holmes."

"There is no vampire, Watson, I assure you."

"I know," I said, "but nevertheless. . . ."

"Please, Watson," Holmes said, with a broad gesture, and I opened the door.

Outside it stood a man shrouded in darkness and wrapped in a black cape. When he saw me, he spread the cape and began to speak with a thick accent.

Startled, I stepped back.

"It is no use, Oliver," called Stoker. "They are onto my game. Come inside and meet Sherlock Holmes."

The man called Oliver dropped the ends of his cloak and entered the crypt.

"How did they know?" he asked.

"Sherlock Holmes is not so easy to fool as a member of your audience," said I, and he glared at me.

Van Helsing was not yet willing to give in. "But the stake, the blood. Did that not give you pause?"

Holmes gave him a contemptuous look. "Pig's blood, which is easily obtained at a butcher's shop and which is thinner and more watery than human blood. Even the odor is not exactly the same."

I knew there had been some subtle difference, and felt I should have known what it was.

"Only an expert could tell the difference, I grant you," Holmes continued, and I felt marginally better. "You should not, however, have left a pig's bristle in it."

So he had not discovered a hair, I thought.

"Besides all that," Holmes said, "there is the stake." He reached into the casket and took it out. "Had you pounded it into the heart of a vampire instead of merely staining it with the blood of a pig, the head would have been marked by the hammer, yet it is as smooth as the rest of the stake."

"Why?" I asked. "Why would anyone create such a scheme?"

"I would not be surprised," said Holmes, "if a reporter showed up quite soon, someone to confirm for the press that a vampire had been enclosed in this crypt, escaped, and then returned to attack as we sought him."

Almost as if on cue, another man stood at the doorway of the crypt.

Leaning casually against the frame, he said, "Did someone mention a vampire?"

"It is nothing," Stoker said. "Please leave us."

"You promised me a story," the man said. "A sensation, you said. Something that would make a name for me and sell out ten editions of the newspaper."

I looked at Holmes, who wore a look of grim satisfaction.

"There will be no story," he said. "I think it best that you leave now."

"I know you," said the reporter. "You are Sherlock Holmes. If you are involved in this, there must be a story."

I could see that Holmes was pleased to be recognized. He had a forgivable touch of vanity.

"No story worth the writing," he said, with a glance in my direction as if to warn me not to record the adventure myself. "I believe this was a mere bit of playacting arranged to drum up business for Mr. Stoker's theater."

"Is that true?" the reporter asked.

Stoker shook his head, but did not speak.

The reporter waited for a few moments as the silence gathered in the dank crypt.

"It is rather unpleasant in here," he said at least. "I believe I shall take Mr. Holmes's advice and go on my way."

With that he turned and left us. Holmes waited until he was well away and then said, "Now, Mr. Stoker. Will you not tell us why this was all arranged?"

Stoker sighed. "As you have no doubt guessed, I had hoped to create a sensation for the newspapers, trading on your name and your reputation. For that, I apologize."

Holmes did not appear satisfied.

"And for having us come out to a graveyard on this dank evening?" said I.

"For that, too," said Stoker.

"But this was not to drum up business for a play?" said Holmes.

"No. You see, I have written a novel."

"Ah. A novel. About a vampire, I assume."

"Yes," said Stoker. "I hoped to create a sensation and make my fortune."

"What about this, Watson?" said Holmes. "Have you heard of this book?"

I admitted that I had not. I seldom read the reviewers, though they have been kind to my own modest efforts.

"The book has been praised," said Stoker, "but it has not sold as well as I had hoped."

"So you believed that the publicity you received from tonight's adventure, had it been successful, would have propelled your book into prominence?"

"Yes. It would have benefitted you, too, of course."

"No," said Holmes. "It would not. I have no wish to be associated with such schemes, and I believe it is more becoming for a writer to devote himself to his work rather than to such things as this."

"But Dickens travels the world to boost his sales. While Byron—"

"Is long dead," said I. "This was unworthy, Stoker, both of yourself and your actors."

Van Helsing and Oliver were not shamed by my comments. I suspect that, being actors, they regarded any kind of notice by the newspapers as a good thing.

"Had you not thought that you might throw an entire city into panic?" I asked. "Vampires on the loose, lives threatened?"

"No," said Stoker. "I had not. I believed that with Mr. Holmes on the case, the populace would be calm enough."

"Let us leave this place, Holmes," said I, out of patience with the man. "The dampness begins to affect my temper."

Holmes nodded his agreement, and we departed, leaving Stoker and his friends in the blood-stained crypt with their useless stake.

Later that evening, I asked Holmes if he thought Stoker's plan might have worked had someone other than Holmes been called in to help perpetuate it.

"Certainly the police might have been taken in," said Holmes.

He had no great respect for the police, though occasionally they did their jobs well, I thought.

"At least," I said, "the fiasco has cheered you up remarkably well."

"Ah," Holmes said. "But for how long? I need something to challenge my abilities, not something as simple as tonight's affair."

He sank down upon the couch.

"Something will turn up," I said. "Something always does."

"I hope that you are right, Watson, but no more vampires. I have done with them."

I thought of how I had felt in the cemetery, of how for a fleeting moment I might even have believed there was a vampire nearby.

"Indeed," said I, and I gave him a smile. "No more vampires."

† † † † †

Dr. John H. Watson may be the inspiration for Dr. John Seward, who chronicles the exceptional qualities of his friend and teacher Professor Abraham Van Helsing, while, as we have seen, Dracula *inspired "The Adventure of the Illustrious Client." However, one can only wonder what Doyle and Stoker might have come up with if they had collaborated on a tale in which their most famous creations crossed paths. (This honor went to Loren D. Estleman, whose seminal novel* Sherlock Holmes Versus Dracula; or the Adventure of the Exsanguinary Count *was published by Doubleday & Company in 1978, and has remained in print ever since.)*

Since there is no canonical tale in which Sherlock Holmes meets Dracula, we went with the next best thing—a clever story from longtime Holmes pastiche author Bill Crider, who has the eminent detective meet Bram Stoker and one of his literary creations, the vampire hunter Abraham Van Helsing. But, of course, all is not as it first seems, and the keen mind of the inhabitant of 221B Baker Street deduces why a vampire seems to be prowling the streets of London long before the reader does.

Bill Crider is the author of more than fifty published novels and numerous short stories under his own and other names. His short fiction has been nominated for the Anthony, Derringer, and Edgar awards (winning the first two). His latest novel is Murder in Four Parts *(St. Martin's). You can find his homepage at www.billcrider.com or take a look at his peculiar blog at http://billcrider.blogspot.com*

A Sherlock Holmes Vampire Bibliography

By Robert Eighteen-Bisang

Sherlock Holmes and Count Dracula are two of the best-known, most recognizable figures in popular culture. Most children can tell you that one of them is a brilliant detective; the other, a "vampire" from "Transylvania." Like Frankenstein's Monster, both characters are more famous than their creators. Their stories have never been out of print since they debuted more than a century ago, and have been translated into every major language in the world. Nor is their allure limited to literature. According to Wikipedia: "An estimated 160 films (as of 2004) feature Dracula in a major role, a number second only to Sherlock Holmes. The total number of films that include a reference to Dracula may reach as high as 649 movies . . . "

Count Dracula is the protagonist of an erotic horror novel, while Holmes embodies the rational detective. However, Doyle's sleuth and Stoker's vampire have much in common. Both of them are tall, thin, charismatic gentlemen who are endowed with extraordinary strength and powers that transcend those of most human beings. Like "Jack the Ripper," they also have unique, memorable names. Would we be reading about either of them today had they been called "Count Vampire" or "Sherrington Hope," as they were named in early drafts of their stories?

The fact that Holmes is a cultural icon who represents the "good" while Dracula is our favorite monster all but guarantees that contemporary writers would bring them into conflict with each other. Their encounters follow three general trends: Authors who use Dracula as their starting point are often content to create an identifiable but "loose" version of the Great Detective. A deerstalker cap, a pipe, an "Elementary, my Dear Watson," and they get on with the business of creating a story. They may insert Holmes and Watson into Stoker's novel or devise an original tale in which he or his friends encounter a vampire. Fred Saberhagen's *The Holmes-Dracula File* exemplifies the former type of story. Authors who take Sherlock Holmes's adventures as their point of departure take pains to follow the "rules" Doyle laid down in the canon. David Stuart Davies works the Count into his sequel of *The Hound of the Baskervilles*, while Steven Seitz's novel is marked by Holmes's refusal to believe that the undead exist, even after he has been bitten by them! Mark Frost's *The List of 7* exemplifies the third trend which uses Arthur Conan Doyle and Bram Stoker as characters who embark on an adventure together. Purists may label all of these creations "heresies," but they cannot deny that later authors have made valuable contributions to both myths. Holmes's meerschaum pipe was added by the actor William Gillette, who played the detective on stage and screen. Dracula's billowing cape and formal evening wear were invented by the author and actor Hamilton Deane, when he adapted Stoker's work for the stage. He believed the Count would be more menacing if he were the type of person one would invite to a formal dinner party.

The following lists describe Holmes's most important encounters with Dracula or other vampires in literature and comic books. It does not include numerous tongue-in-cheek articles which go to amazing lengths to prove that Holmes was Van Helsing; Dracula was Moriarty; or Holmes was a "real" character who could never encounter an "imaginary" vampire.

PART 1: LITERATURE

Anderson, Kevin J.

LXG: The League of Extraordinary Gentlemen. Pocket Star Books: New York, 2003. 294 p. pb. • *LXG* is the novelization of the screenplay by James Dale Robinson, which, in turn, was based on the comic book series by Alan Moore. In contrast to the original story Mina Harker [Peta Wilson] has become a vampire while a new cast of characters includes Dorian Gray and Tom Sawyer. See: *The League of Extraordinary Gentlemen,* q.v.

Andrews, Val.

Sherlock Holmes and the Longacre Vampire. Breese Books: London, 2001. 125 p. pb. • Holmes ponders the possibility of a connection between Henry Irving's new adaptation of *Dracula,* which is opening in Brighton and a series of vampire-like murders.

Campbell, J. R. and Charles Prepolec. ed.

Gaslight Grimoire: Fantastic Tales of Sherlock Holmes. Edge Science Fiction and Fantasy Publishing: Calgary, AB, Canada, 2008. 317 p. pb. illus. by Phil Cornell. Contents: Bob Madison, "Red Sunset." Kim Newman, "The Red Planet."

Crider, Bill. b. 1941.

"The Case of the Vampire's Mark" in Martin H. Greenberg, Jon L. Lellenberg and Daniel Stashower, ed. *Murder in Baker Street,* 2001. • Bram Stoker seeks Holmes's assistance when his friend's young son appears to have been bitten by a vampire. This case is assumed to be the inspiration for "The Adventure of the Sussex Vampire" as well as *Dracula.*

Crime Time.

Crime Time. London: Crime Time, No. 26 (2002). The Sherlock Holmes Issue. Contents: Kim Newman, "The Private Files of Mycroft Holmes."

Davies, David Stuart. b. 1946. ed.

ed. *Sherlock Holmes: The Game's Afoot.* Wordsworth Editions: Ware, 2008. 400 p. pb. Tales of Mystery & The Supernatural Ser. Contents: Christopher Sequeira, "The Return of the Sussex Vampire."

---. *The Tangled Skein.* Island Publishing: Channel Islands, Alderney, 1992. [xii], 244 p. hb. frontis. by Kathryn White. illus. by Charles Rees. 500 numbered copies with the owner's name printed on the copyright page. Copies 1–50 are signed by the author and Peter Cushing. "Foreword by Peter Cushing, OBE p. vii–ix. rpt. Penyffordd, Chester, UK, Calabash Press: 1995. [xii], 159 p. hb. dj. by Paul Lowe. frontis. by Kathryn White. illus. by Paul Lowe. Foreword by Peter Cushing OBE p. ix–x. rpt. Ashcroft, BC, Canada, Calabash Press: 1998. 159 p. pb. Foreword by Peter Cushing OBE p. 910. rpt. Ware, Wordsworth Editions: 2006. 174 p. pb. Tales of Mystery & The Supernatural Ser. Foreword by Peter Cushing OBE p. 9–10. • Sherlock Holmes encounters Count Dracula and Professor Van Helsing while investigating a mystery that was subsequently recorded as *The Hound of the Baskervilles.*

Douglas, Carole Nelson. b. 1944.

"Dracula on the Rocks" in Martin H. Greenberg, ed., Celebrity Vampires, 1995. rpt. in: Robert Weinberg; Stefan Dziemianowicz and Martin H. Greenberg. ed. *Rivals of Dracula*, 1996. • Irene Adler, the femme fatale who bested Holmes in "A Scandal in Bohemia," protects "Lucille" from a lecherous, repulsive Count Dracula—and mentions this to her friend, Bram Stoker.

---. *Chapel Noir: A Novel of Suspense Featuring Sherlock Holmes, Irene Adler, and Jack the Ripper.* New York: Forge, 2001. 494 p. hb. dj. by Glenn Harrington. Irene Adler Ser. #5. rpt. pb. • Irene Norton (see Adler) is asked to investigate a gruesome murder that took place in a Bordello in Paris. After she determines that the serial killer known as "Jack the Ripper" is responsible, Sherlock Holmes comes to her assistance. The story is continued in *Castle Rouge.*

---. *Castle Rouge: A Novel of Suspense Featuring Sherlock Holmes, Irene Adler, and Jack the Ripper.* Forge: New York, 2002. 540 p. dj. by Glenn Harrington. Irene Adler Ser. #6. rpt. pb. • The second part of the story that opened with *Chapel Noir* changes location frequently from England to France, Bohemia and Transylvania. While Holmes and Watson look into the murders in Whitechapel, Bram Stoker studies ancient legends about vampires. Finally, a surprising new candidate emerges as the Ripper.

Dziemanowicz, Stefan; Robert Weinberg and Martin H. Greenberg. ed.

Virtuous Vampires. Barnes & Noble Books: New York, 1996. 470 p. hb. dj. Contents: Brian Stableford, "The Hunger and Ecstasy of Vampires."

Elrod, [P. N]. b. 1954. ed.

Dracula in London. Ace Books: New York, 2001. 263 p. tr. pb. Contents: Bradley H. Sinor, "Places for Act Two!" rpt. pb.

Estleman, Loren D. (a.k.a. John H. Watson, M.D.). b. 1952.

Sherlock Holmes vs. Dracula; or The Adventure of the Sanguinary Count. New York Doubleday & Company, Inc. 1978. 214 p. hb. dj. by Fred Marcellino. rpt. London, New English Library: 1978. 207 p. hb. dj. rpt. Harmonsworth, Penguin Books: 1979. 214 p. pb. rpt. in: *Sherlock Holmes vs. Dracula [and] Dr. Jekyll and Mr. Holmes,* 1995. rpt. enlarged: ibooks: New York, 2000. 215p. tr. pb. illus. With: "The Master Sleuth Meets the Master Tooth: A Word After by Loren D. Estleman" p. 211-215. rpt. ibooks: New York, 2003. 215p. pb. "Special Advance Preview" p. 217-224. • The first and, many say, best of the Holmes/Dracula pastiches informs us of the hitherto unacknowledged part Holmes and Watson played in driving Dracula from England. The adventure begins when a journalist from Whitby asks Holmes to investigate the mysterious wreck of the Demeter—the ship that carried Dracula to England—whose crew was missing while the corpse of the captain was lashed to the wheel.

---. *Sherlock Holmes vs. Dracula* [and] Dr. Jekyll and Mr. Holmes. Quality Paperback Book Club: New York, 1995. pb. Contents: Sherlock Holmes Vs. Dracula.

Frost, Mark. b. 1953.

The List of 7: A Novel. William Morrow and Company, Inc.: New York, 1993. 368 p. hb. dj. by Robert Aulicino. rpt. William Morrow and Company, Inc.: New York, 1993. 366 p. tr. pb. Note: The epilogue is sealed under the rear cover flap, to conceal the ending. With "Erratum" slip. rpt. retitled: The List of Seven. Hutchinson: London, 1993. 377 p. hb. dj. rpt. Avon Books: New York, 1994. 401 p. pb. Special Reading Edition. rpt. Avon Books: New York, 1994. 401 p. pb. Cover by Daniel R. Horne. rpt. Arrow: London, 1994. 426 p. pb. Cover by Les Edwards. • Arthur Conan Doyle and Holmes's prototype, the flamboyant Jack Sparks, battle the occult powers of a Satanic cult in London. Bram Stoker has a cameo.

---. *The Six Messiahs*. William Morrow and Company, Inc.: New York, 1995. 404 p. hb. dj. by Daniel Horne. rpt. William Morrow and Company, Inc.: New York, 1995. 404 p. tr. pb. Advance Reading Copy. rpt. retitled: *The 6 Messiahs*. Avon Books: 1996. 423 p. pb. • *Sequel to The List of 7*.

Gaiman, Neil (Richard). b. 1960.

"A Study in Emerald." *Shadows Over Baker Street*, edited by Michael Reaves and John Pelan. Random House: New York, 2003. • All of the stories in *Shadows Over Baker Street* take place in an alternate universe where H. P. Lovecraft's monstrous elder gods rule Victorian England. Gaiman's award-winning tale has Holmes investigate the death of an alien prince who was murdered when it planned to feed on a young girl's fear and madness.

Geare, Michael & Michael Corby.

Dracula's Diary. Buchan and Enright: London, 1992. 153 p. hb. dj. rpt. Beaufort Books: New York, 1992. 153 p. hb. dj. • Young Dracula, who has yet to acquire all of his vampiric powers, is enrolled at Eton. This pastiche is peppered with real and imaginary characters from Victorian times, including Holmes, Stoker, and Van Helsing.

Greenberg, Martin H. ed.

Fantastic Chicago. Chicon V: Chicago, 1991. 136 p. pb. illus. 2,000 copies. Contents: Fred Saberhagen, "From the Tree of Time."

---. *Celebrity Vampires*. DAW Books, Inc.: New York, 1995. 318 p. pb. Contents: Carole Nelson Douglas, "Dracula on the

Rocks." Roman A. Ranieri, "A Singular Event on a Night in 1912."

Greenberg, Martin H.; Jon L. Lellenberg & Daniel Stashower. ed.

Murder in Baker Street: New Tales of Sherlock Holmes. Carroll & Graf: New York, 2001. 277 p. hb. dj. Contents: Bill Crider, "The Case of the Vampire's Mark." rpt. pb.

Hawke, Simon. b. 1951. Legalized name of Nicholas Valentin Yermakov.

The Dracula Caper. Ace Books: New York, 1988. 212 p. pb. Time Wars Ser. #8. rpt. Headline: London, 1990. 212 p. pb. • Arthur Conan Doyle, Dr. Moreau, Bram Stoker and H. G. Wells confront genetically engineered vampires and werewolves from the 27th century.

Interzone: Science Fiction and Fantasy.

Stableford, Brian. "The Hunger and Ecstasy of Vampires." *Interzone*: Science Fiction and Fantasy, January–February, 91–92.

Kaye, Marvin (Nathan). b. 1938.

The Incredible Umbrella. Doubleday & Company, Inc., New York, 1979. 218 p. hb. dj. by Cathy Canzani. rpt. Dell Publishing Company: New York:, 1980. 301 p. pb. illus. by Dan Steffan. Combines: "The Incredible Umbrella," "The Flight of the Umbrella" and "In Pursuit of the Umbrella." • J. Adrian Fillmore purchases a magical umbrella (which was invented by Professor Moriarty) that transports him to alternate realms where Holmes, Dracula, and Frankenstein come to life.

Madison, Bob.

"Red Sunset" in *Gaslight Grimoire*. Edited by J. R. Campbell and Charles Prepolec. Edge Science Fiction and Fantasy Publishing: Calgary, Alberta, Canada. 2008. • Holmes, who was evacuated from London during World War II, is living in an old-age home in Los Angeles. A private investigator asks for his help after a man he had shot twice in the chest and once in the head got up and walked away.

Murdoch, Mordecai. pseud.

The Wroclaw Dracula. Caedmon of Whitby: Whitby, UK, 1985. 130 p. pb. • The introduction, "About the Author," claims that this abridged, narrative adaptation of *Dracula* was brought to the publisher through the auspices of Mycroft Holmes. Note: This book was reprinted anonymously in 2007 as *Bram Stoker's Dracula*, without the introduction.

Newman, Kim. b. 1959.

Anno Dracula. Simon & Schuster: London, 1992. 359 p. hb. dj. by Stephen Player. Anno Dracula Ser. #1. rpt. Carroll & Graf: New York, 1993. 359 p. hb. dj. by Stephen Player. rpt. Pocket Books: New York, 1993. 469 p. pb. rpt. Avon Books: New York, 1994. 409 p. pb. (white cover). Special Reading Edition. rpt. Avon Books: New York, 1994. 409 p. pb. (black cover). • The first book in the Anno-Dracula series features a spectrum of vampires from literature, movies, and television. Van Helsing has failed to kill the Count, and Dracula has become Queen Victoria's consort. Sherlock Holmes is in a concentration camp, but Mycroft is plotting behind the scenes. Note: The novel is an expanded version of the novella, "Red Reign," which first appeared in Stephen Jones, ed. *The Mammoth Book of Vampires* (Robson: London, 1992).

---. *The Bloody Red Baron*. Carroll & Graf: New York, 1995. 358 p. hb. dj. by Tony Greco. Anno Dracula Ser. #2. rpt. Simon & Schuster: London, 1996. 358p. hb. dj by Fred Gambino. rpt. AvoNova: New York, 1997. 370 p. pb. rpt. Pocket Books: New York, 1997. 356 p. pb. Cover by Fred Gambino. • Sequel to *Anno Dracula*. The story takes place during WWI, when Mycroft investigates Germany's attempt to create undead soldiers.

---. "The Private Files of Mycroft Holmes" in Crime Time 26 (2002). • Following Mycroft's death, someone burned the secrets contained in his safe before Prime Minister Ruthven or other vampires could open it. This vignette is an unused chapter from *The Bloody Red Baron*.

---. "The Red Planet" in J. R. Campbell and Charles Prepolec, ed. Gaslight Grimoire, 2008. • This parody of H. G. Wells' *The War of the Worlds* revolves around Professor James Moriarty fiendish use of vampire squid.

Randisi, Robert J(oesph). b. 1951.

Curtains of Blood. Leisure Books: New York, 2002. 351 p. pb. • When Bram Stoker decides to hunt for Jack the Ripper, he turns to Arthur Conan Doyle for advice. As the story unfolds, Stoker becomes the Ripper's unwilling confidant.

Ranieri, Roman A.

"A Singular Event on a Night in 1912" in Martin H. Greenberg, ed. Celebrity Vampires, 1995. • Ranieri manages to bring Doyle, Stoker, and Vlad the Impaler together in this story, which ends with a twist.

Reaves, Michael and John Pelan. ed.

Shadows Over Baker Street. Del Rey: New York, 2003. 446 p. hb. dj. Contents: Neil Gaiman, "A Study in Emerald." rpt. 2005. pb.

Resnick, Laura.

"The Adventure of the Missing Coffin" in Mike Resnick & Martin H. Greenberg, ed. *Sherlock Holmes in Orbit*, 1995. • A vampire asks Holmes to help him find his missing coffin which, he believes, was stolen by a "Transylvanian Count."

Resnick, Mike & Martin H. Greenberg. ed.

"The Adventure of the Missing Coffin" and "The Mouse and the Master." In *Sherlock Holmes in Orbit*, edited by Laura Resnick and Brian M. Thompsen. DAW Books: New York, 1995.

Richards, Kel.

The Vampire Serpent. Beacon Booka: Lane Cove, Australia, 1997. 111 p. pb. Sherlock Holmes's Tales of Terror Ser. 3. • Lestrad is baffled. A vampire-like creature is stalking the streets of London. Only Sherlock Holmes can solve this case, but . . . .

Saberhagen, Fred(erick Thomas). 1930–2007.

"From the Tree of Time" in *Sorcerer's Apprentice* #14 (1982). rpt. in: Martin H. Greenberg, ed. *Fantastic Chicago*, 1991. rpt. in: Fred Saberhagen, ed. Saberhagen: My Best, 1987. • Holmes seeks Dracula's advice on a new case.

Saberhagen, Fred(erick Thomas). *The Holmes-Dracula File*. New York, Ace Books: 1978. 249 p. pb. Cover by Robert Adragna. The Dracula Tape Ser. #2. rpt. Tor: New York, 1989. 249 p. pb. Cover by Glenn Hastings. *The Holmes-Dracula File is* a sequel to *The Dracula Tape* which turns Bram Stoker's opus on its head, retelling the novel from the Count's point of view. Here, criminals are threatening to flood the streets of London with plague-infested rats, while Holmes meets his spitting image—his cousin, Count Dracula.

---. ed. *Saberhagen: My Best.* Baen Books: New York, 1987. 311 p. pb. Contents: "From the Tree of Time."

Séance for a Vampire. Tor: New York, 1994. 285 p. hb. dj. by Jim Theaston. The Dracula Tape Ser. #8. rpt. 1997. pb. • 1903. At a fraudulent séance, the Altamont's daughter Louisa appears to them in the flesh as a vampire. When Holmes goes missing during the séance Watson contacts his cousin, Dracula, for assistance. *Séance for a Vampire* is narrated by both Watson and Dracula.

Seitz, Stephen.

Sherlock Holmes and the Plague of Dracula. Mountainside Press: Shaftsbury, VT, 2006. 208 p. pb. • Holmes and Watson travel to Transylvania after Mina Murray asks them to help her find her missing fiancé, Jonathan Harker.

Sequeira, Christopher. b. 1962.

"The Return of the Sussex Vampire" in *Sherlock Holmes: The Game's Afoot.* Edited by David Stuart Davies. Wordsworth Editions, Ltd: Ware: *2008.* • Holmes, age 72, comes out of retirement when Robert Ferguson's uncle Joshiah claims that his family is being attacked by an ancient curse.

Sinor, Bradley H.

"Places for Act Two!" in *Dracula in London.* Edited by P. N. Elrod. Ace Books: New York, 2004. • In this farce, Dracula's role in Gilbert and Sullivan's comic opera, *The Pirates of Pinzanz*, brings him into contact with Watson and Mycroft.

Sorcerer's Apprentice.

The Sorcerer's Apprentice. Scottsdale, AZ. Flying Buffalo, Inc.: #14 (Spring 1982). Contents: Fred Saberhagen, "From the Tree of Time."

Stableford, Brian (Michael). b. 1948.

"The Hunger and Ecstasy of Vampire" in Interzone (January–February 1995). 2 parts. rpt. revised: *The Hunger and Ecstasy of Vampires: A Novel*. Mark V. Ziesing Books: Shingletown, CA, 1996. 207 p. hb. dj. by Arnie Fenner. rpt. A signed, numbered and slipcased edition of 300 copies. rpt. in: Stefan Dziemanowicz; Robert Weinberg and Martin H. Greenberg, ed. *Virtuous Vampires*, 1996. rpt. in: Stephen Jones, ed. *The Mammoth Book of Best New Horror: Volume Seven*, 1996. rpt. expanded: *Sherlock Holmes and the Vampires of Eternity*. Black Coat Press: Encino, CA. 2009. 348 p. pb. Cover by Daniele Serra. • In 1895, Professor Edward Copplestone tells a group of historical and imaginary figures, including Doyle, Holmes, Stoker, and the mysterious Count Lugard, of his visits to the future where mankind is ruled by vampires.

Thomsen, Brian M(ichael).

"Mouse and the Master" in Mike Resnick & Martin H. Greenberg, ed. *Sherlock Holmes in Orbit*, 1995. • Holmes investigates a séance which both Dracula and Dr. Watson are attending.

Waters, T. A.

The Probability Pad. Pyramid Books: New York, 1970. 144 p. pb. Greenwich Village Ser. • T. A., Mike, and Chester encounter Altamont and Dr. Hudson (Sherlock Holmes and Dr. Watson) who battle Dracula in an alternate version of Transylvania.

Weinberg, Robert; Stefan Dziemianowicz and Martin H. Greenberg. ed.

Rivals of Dracula. Barnes & Noble Books: New York, 1996. 377 p. hb. dj. Contents: Carole Nelson Douglas, "Dracula on the Rocks: An Irene Adler Adventure."

Zelazny, Roger (Joseph Christopher). 1937-1995.

A Night in the Lonesome October. New York: An AvoNova Book, August 1993. [xii], 270 p. tr. pb. Cover by James Warhola. frontis. & illus. by Gahan Wilson. Advanced Reading Gallery. rpt. New York, An AvoNova Book: August 1993. [ix], 280 p. hb. dj. by James Warhola (front cover) & Gahan Wilson (back cover). illus. by Gahan Wilson. rpt. Easton Press: Norwalk, CT, October 1993. Leather-bound, gilt-edged. "Signed First Editions of Science Fiction" Ser. rpt. An AvoNova Book: New York, 1993. [ix], 280 p. pb. rpt. London, Orbit: 1994. 240 p. pb. Cover by Mike Posen. • This light-hearted fantasy is narrated by Jack the Ripper's dog Snuff; it includes Sherlock Holmes, Jack the Ripper, Dracula, the Frankenstein monster, and Larry Talbot.

PART II: COMICS

Ghosts of Dracula.

Ghosts of Dracula. Eternity Comics: Westlake Village, CA. b&w. 2 (Oct. 1991). "The Magician and the Master" by Martin Powell & Seppo Makinen. 27 p. • In the second part of this five-part story, Professor Van Helsing asks his old friend, Sherlock Holmes, to help him find Dracula.

The League of Extraordinary Gentlemen.

"The League of Extraordinary Gentlemen" by Alan Moore & Kevin O'Neal. America's Best Comics: La Jolla, CA. 6 issues from #1 (March 1999) to #6 (September 2000). rpt. 2 volumes: 2002. rpt. 2 volumes: *The Absolute Edition*, 2005. • In 1898, "M." [Moriarty] recruits an all-star cast of characters, including Mina Harker, to combat Professor James Moriarty, who does double duty as the head of MI5 and the villain. See: Kevin J. Anderson, *LXG: The League of Extraordinary Gentlemen*, q.v.

The Rook.

The Rook. Warren: New York. 10 (August 1981). "The Singular Case of the Anemic Hier" by Will Richardson, Kevin Duane, & Anton Carvana. 10 p. • Holmes is forced to believe in the scientifically impossible when Dracula visits Baker Street.

Scarlet in Gaslight.

"Scarlet in Gaslight" by Martin Powell & Seppo Makinen. Eternity Comics: Malibu, CA. 4 issues from #1 (November 1987) to # 4 (June 1988). rpt. graphic novel: Eternity Comics, 1990. rpt. graphic novel: Caliber Comics, 1996. rpt. graphic novel: Starburst Press, 1996. rpt. in: *The Sherlock Holmes Mysteries: Vol. I TPB*, 2003. • On the centennial of "A Study in Scarlet," Sherlock Holmes and Professor Van Helsing join forces to combat Moriarty and Dracula, who have conspired to plunge London into a new dark age.

The Sussex Vampire.

"The Sussex Vampire" by Warren Ellis & Craig Gilmore. Caliber Comics, 1996. 30p. • A graphic adaptation of Arthur Conan Doyle's "The Adventure of the Sussex Vampire."

About the Editors

Robert Eighteen-Bisang is best-known as the owner of the world's most famous collection of rare vampire books. He has written several articles on Dracula and other vampires, and given lectures on these subjects in New York, Los Angeles, London and other cities. His first book, *Bram Stoker's Notes for Dracula* (which he wrote with Elizabeth Miller) was not only nominated "best book of the year" by *Famous Monsters of Filmland* but won The Lord Ruthven Award for the "best vampire book of 2008."

Martin H. Greenberg is the CEP of Tekno Books and its predecessor companies, now the largest book developer of commercial fiction and non-fiction in the world, with over 2,000 published books that have been translated into 33 languages. He is the recipient of an unprecedented four Lifetime Achievement Awards in the Science Fiction, Mystery, and Paranormal Horror genres—the Milford Award and Solstice Award in Science Fiction, the Bram Stoker Award in Horror, the Ellery Queen Award in Mystery—the only person in publishing history to have received all four awards.